The Upside Down of Things

Tara T. Greene

To. Lorette

Thank you so much

for your support!.

Sara

Acknowledgement

First and foremost I would like to thank God for the motivation and ability to create a piece of work that I could share with others. Without spiritual guidance and patience, I would not have been able to complete this book. It was his grace and mercy that allowed me to continue to write and create this impeccable work, at the same time, balancing out my other responsibilities and for that, I give God all the honor, glory and praise.

Secondly, I would like to thank all the family and friends who supported me from the beginning. There were many who contributed physically and there were some who continued to support and motivate me each day. I thank everyone who inspired my story, my characters, and each situation that I faced in making this book successful. There are so many people who influenced me that I couldn't name them all. For those who were there from the beginning, but didn't happen to make it to the end of this journey with me, I thank you from the bottom of my heart. You were not forgotten.

Lastly, I would like to thank my pastor, father, and friend, who has always supported my decisions in whatever I decided to do. This has been a long journey, but he was right there supporting and guiding me to make the right decision for myself. Thank you for remaining the same. Thank you for dividing yourself in those times that I needed a father and not a friend. Thank you for being my pastor; keeping me spiritually filled and connected with God all of my life. For this, I am thankful. I love you and God Bless!

Introduction

The book entails the lives of four young, beautiful successful women, who have strived to achieve the goals that they have worked so hard to obtain. They are all from different realms of the world--morally and mentally. As they try to meet everyday expectations from their jobs to home and family, they find out what life is all about. While coming from various backgrounds, their struggles range from professional, social, to personal. Entering into the real world after college, they learn the bonds that African American women face and deal with everyday. They learn to understand the life lessons that were taught to them early on as children, but they are able to appreciate the hard lessons they received during their adolescent years.

Chapter 1: Dalia Little

"A long day at work, and all I want to do is go home to my man, have a nice dinner and take a long bath...and go to bed"...Dalia opens the door and notices that something isn't right. She puts her pocketbook down and her keys on the counter. She sees the light on in the bathroom and wonders who left the light on. As she enters her bedroom, she pushes the door open to see Terrance with another woman in her bed. Instantly, she reacts as any woman.... "What the Fuck?" I can't believe you did this to me after all that we have been through". Terrance immediately jumped out of the bed trying to explain to Dalia that he did not mean to and it just happened. When Dalia finally looked at the other woman in her bedroom, she realized that it was her co-worker, Carmen, who had been eyeing Terrance for a long time. Frustrated and upset, Dalia put Terrance and the other woman out naked into the street. When Dalia looked Carmen in her eyes and asked her, "Why? She just said, "While you were too busy to take care of home, I was here when he needed me." Little did Dalia know, she never realized what Carmen really meant until it was too late.

When Terrance and Carmen left, Dalia sat in the middle of the floor crying her eyes out. Forgetting all about the date she had already planned with Lauren, Jayden, and Blake; she sat there until the middle of the night. When she finally moved from that one spot, she turned off the house phone and her cell phone. She did not even make it to work the next day. Her friends didn't think anything of it because sometimes Dalia would get so consumed with work and Terrance that she wouldn't have any time for them, but this time, she needed her friends more than ever. She did not know what to do without Terrance because even though she did not put faith in marriage or men, he was the next best constant man in her life after her father died. After several years together and trials experienced together, for the first time, she could not believe that it was over. From the beginning of their relationship, the one thing that Terrance knew that Dalia hated the most was infidelity. He had betrayed her very much. So Dalia, the one who would never take a drink, began drinking for the first time. She had reached her lowest point; thinking that nothing could be worse and that every man in her life had failed her.

After several days in her condominium, she began to write in her diary remembering the times of her relationship with Terrance. She began seeing that all of the things that used to make her happy, now made her sad. She began seeing the portfolio that they made together from their first date to their first fight. They had shared so many good and bad times that there was not a moment when they did not remember being in each other's lives.

The incident had occurred on Friday evening, it has been four days, and she had not been to work or talked to anyone. Dalia secluding herself began drowning her sorrow in alcohol. Tuesday, she finally got out of the bed, took a shower and did her hair. She felt better than the last couple of days but was still very depressed. She wanted to reach out to her friends, but did not know how to reach out to them. At this point, she does not know how to feel or what she should do next. So, she began to pamper herself just so that she could clear her mind.

She first began to light candles all throughout the house, playing soft jazz music with all the lights off in the house. Dalia was a big John Coltrane fan; her father collected most of his music. She played normally when she had a long day at work or when she had problems in her life that she couldn't seen to find the solutions to. The house, now smelling like cinnamon and apples, began to bring a certain ambiance to the house which was able to mellow her mood from the unrest and emotions she would soon have to face.

She went into her outhouse and pulled out three big tubs. She always kept her outhouse bolt locked because it was a part of her that she did not want to share with anyone. She wanted to save herself from criticism or remarks that anyone would make against what she stored in her outhouse. As she pulled the tubs one by one into her living room, a sigh of relief came over her face. She got a knock at the door unexpectedly. At first, she ignored the knock, but it continued so she could no longer ignore it. She yelled at the door, "I don't want any company, so go away". She had forgotten that she had invited her cousin from New Jersey to visit with her. When she opened the door, her cousin, Shawn, was excited to see her. She saw how Dalia looked and knew instantly that something was not right.

Shawn, the cousin she looked up to since she was a little girl was 28, successful, and married to a wonderful man. She married straight out of college, moved away to start a new life with her husband and has been living the good life according to Dalia. Shawn, not as extravagant as Dalia, but very strong minded and ground never had to work hard for what she wanted. Things just seemed to come naturally to her. Dalia envied this from her cousin, but respected that she was able to accomplish so much. At first, Dalia did not want to share with her what just happened, but it was apparent that something was wrong. Dalia trying to be the strong one told her cousin that she had a rough day at work and needed some time to herself. Shawn did not really believe what Dalia told her, but decided to respect her wishes and let it go. Shawn began to question Dalia. "Why are you playing this sad music and why do you have these God forsaken tubs out her, what is in this?" Dalia immediately removes the tub from the living room and puts them back in her outhouse. Dalia blows out her candles and turns her music off, telling Shawn, "Damn, I can't have some me time!" Shawn replies to her saying, "Whatever works for you, Cuz." Dalia rolled her eyes and began straightening up her house so her cousin could have somewhere to sit down.

Shawn was in town for a conference with her job. She was the Sales Director at one of the largest car dealerships in New Jersey. She had been working this job for two years, and she loves it to death. They planned to enjoy the evening. Dalia wanted to take her mind off everything just for a little while. She did not want to burden her cousin with her problems or place herself in the position to be judged about her relationship with Terrance. The question was whether Dalia was going to call her girls or not even bother. She did not want to go through all the trouble because the one thing that she could not do was hide her true feelings from them. Dalia had not left her house in four days and now she has to face the world when she goes out for dinner with Shawn.

Dalia makes reservations to one of the nicest restaurants in the area. The women get all dressed up for the dinner and start sharing old stories from when they were kids. Reminiscing about old times, took Dalia's mind off everything that had her at her lowest.

Shawn brought up the time that when they were little and Dalia always kept wedding books with different wedding designs. She always wanted to be a wedding planner, and she kept several books with beautiful pictures of wedding gowns and bridesmaid dresses. They both continuously laughed about the old times. Only her cousin Shawn knew about her aspiration of wanting to become a wedding planner. For years, she collected different images of wedding designs and color formations in several different portfolios. She kept them in a secret place that only she knew about. As they kept reminiscing, Shawn asked her about her wedding books to see if she still had them or if she threw them away. She began telling her, "Remember when you came in and you saw the boxes and tub?" Shawn replied, "Yeah, are you telling me you kept them all of this time?" Dalia began telling her that she didn't think it was possible to make a career out of it or that it would not make enough money to support herself. Shawn explained, "Well, with the support of Terrance, you can do it". Dalia took a deep sigh as a response to what Shawn said, and Shawn noticed her reaction. She didn't make a comment, but she noticed her instant reaction to it.

So, after a couple of hours sitting in the house and drinking a bottle of wine, Shawn asked about Terrance. She noticed that he was not there when she arrived and Dalia had not mentioned anything about him. Dalia responded, "Terrance is out handling some business out of town." Shawn knew that wasn't the truth, but she accepted it and asked when he was coming back to town. Dalia stated, "I'm not sure. I guess once he finished handling some running around". Shawn knew it was a touchy subject, so she left it alone. By this time, they had drunk a whole bottle of wine. To avoid anymore questions about Terrance, Dalia jumped up and said, "We are going to be late for our reservations if we keep talking." Shawn replied, "Let's go then. I was here catching up with you, chick". As they were getting ready to leave, Dalia turned her cell phone on for the first time in four days. Just as soon as she turned it on, she had over 20 messages and text messages. Shawn asked her if she was going to check her voice mail because she heard the ringer go off on the phone. Dalia responded, "Its nothing but work. I will talk to them tomorrow. I don't feel like dealing with those cartoons." Shawn laughed, being so used to Dalia's sense of humor, she kind of felt that Dalia was finally acting like herself since she had first arrived. As they were walking to Dalia's car, Shawn noticed something on the car. There were a dozen of roses and a card attached. Shawn thought it was the most romantic thing that any man could do for a woman. Dalia was enthusiastic about the roses. She assumed that the roses were from Terrance. Before Shawn was able to grab the flowers, Dalia threw them on the ground and told her to get in the car, with much emotion attached. Shawn looked at her and wondered where all the emotion derived from. Dalia exclaimed, "I don't feel like talking about it, so don't even ask. I don't ask you about the mini episodes that occur in your life that I've noticed, so I expect the same thing back from you, k cuz?" Shawn replied, "What in the hell has you in mood swings?" "You have been jumpy since I got here. You have been acting like everything is ok and then you snap when you see the flowers on your car. I wasn't going to say anything, but you need to tell me something to make me think that you don't need to be committed!" Very upset, Dalia states, "Why does it matter to you, in a couple of days, you are going to go back to your perfect little life and get clear like you don't even belong to a family or like we don't have a name." Shawn wonders where is all of this built up anger is coming from. Dalia asked her

9

if she still wanted to go to dinner or not. Shawn stated, "If you are up for it, then I am all game, but I did think it would be nice for me and my favorite cousin to have a nice visit since you don't have the time to visit since we have such busy lives." Dalia stated, "Whatever." As they drove to the restaurant, the entire drive was quiet as hell. Neither one of them wanted to look at each other nor make a sound so the other person could hear it.

They arrive at the restaurant, which is very elegant; so much of Shawn's style. Shawn immediately told the host that the have reservations for two under Shawn. "Right this way ladies," said the host. Looking gorgeous as ever, Dalia did not notice anyone in the room. She held her head high and walked proudly through the restaurant. Little did she know that her co-worker — the one she caught in her house with Terrance happened to be there with her husband having their three year wedding anniversary dinner and not sitting too far from where she and Shawn were sitting. Dalia sat down and immediately asked the waiter for a glass of their best wine. Shawn didn't want to say the wrong thing, but she kept looking and watching Dalia's every move to see if she was going to come out and say what was wrong. It had been ten minutes and Dalia had not looked up from the menu. So, Shawn, being bold as she had always been from when they were little asked Dalia, "Is there something that has been bothering you? Did I come at the wrong time, and you haven't given me a straight answer about Terrance either." "Please let me know, cause I haven't cussed a black man out in a long time and I need to renew my membership in the angry black woman's club." Dalia began to laugh at her cousin because she instantly got mad without knowing anything. To Dalia, Shawn showing such emotion to her feelings made her feel just a little warm. Finally, Dalia opened up to Shawn, but she does not quite fill her in completely about what happened. They order appetizers and their meal while Dalia vaguely explains that she has some things going on and that she needed some time alone to sort some things out. "It is nothing that you need to get all upset about. It became a time where I needed to figure out what was best for me and it just happened to be today. It's nothing so serious that you have to bring your ghetto back or anything, just trust me when I say I am fine. I just need some me time". Shawn stated, Bull shit, bull shit, bull shit, is all I am hearing right now, but because you are family I am going to let it slide for right now. For the most part, I want you to have a good time and take your mind off of everything that is going on with you, whatever the hell it may be." "Thank you Shawn, for being there for me, I needed to hear that and I need a break from everything, even if it is just for tonight." Shawn states, "That is a load of shit, and you know it. When did you become sentimental about your feelings, like that? I guess time does bring on a change." They both laugh and continue eating dinner.

Out of the corner of Dalia's eyes, she happened to get a glimpse of her co-worker while she was enjoying her dinner. She almost dropped her fork out of her hand when she looked at her firmly. She wanted to put the fear of God in the co-worker, but she also wanted to keep her composure in front of her cousin. The co-worker did not want Dalia to get up and come to her table and say the wrong thing to her husband, but Dalia being the grown woman that she is was sitting calmly thinking how she could fuck her and maintain her dignity at the same time. Little did this woman know she had messed with the wrong one. Dalia took a napkin and wrote a note on it stating, "Meet me in the restroom, or the next bite you take will be your last." Dalia nicely called the waiter over to the table and asked, "Can you give this note to the nice woman at the table across from us?" The waiter said sure ma'am, not a problem. When the co-worker received the note, she knew what it was concerning. When she read the note, she ran to the bathroom and Dalia made up some excuse to leave the table telling Shawn, "I will be back in a minute; there is something that I have to handle before it is too late." Shawn thought it was a little weird, but she did not say anything. She nicely waited until Dalia returned.

Dalia walked into the bathroom and the first person she saw was Carmen, her co-worker and the first thing she did was slap the crap out of her. She told her, "If I ever see you again, I will fuck your shit to another country." Carmen yells back to her and says, "You do not even know, do you?" Dalia states, "I don't need to know anything, I know what I saw, and that was enough. I came into my house and saw you all over my man. So, do not make it seem like you did not know or that you happened to fall on his dick. Shit does not happen like that. What do you have to say that is so important that you have to tell me that will make me think or feel any different about you right now? And before you say anything, I want you to know that there is mace in my bra and a knife under my tongue." Carmen began crying emotionally saying, "There is nothing that I can say to make this any better, but I think that you should talk to Terrance before you jump to any conclusions." Dalia grabbed Carmen around her neck, and slammed her against the wall and held her there tightly. She made dangerous threats to her trying to instill fear into her. Instantaneously, Dalia snapped forgetting where she was and what she was doing. She let Carmen go, dropped her hands, thinking, "What is happening to me?" Dalia tried to compose herself so that she could return to dinner without seeming as if something was wrong. When Carmen returned to the table with her husband, she told him that she did not feel well and wanted to finish their anniversary celebration at home. Her husband, with an astonished look on his face, immediately got her coat, and walked her out of the restaurant. By this time, Dalia is walking out of the restroom, running into her cousin who is worried that something is wrong because she had been in the restroom for more than fifteen minutes. Dalia told Shawn, "I felt a little faint and I needed to put a wet, cold rag on her face to get myself together, but I am ok, nothing to worry about." Shawn thought immediately that Dalia could have been pregnant, but little did she know what went on in the bathroom.

When they returned to their seats, they waiter asked if they were ready for their checks and they both told him yes. They both expressed how much they enjoyed the evening. They left the restaurant as if nothing happened well, to Shawn's knowledge. Dalia apparently felt a sigh of relief for just a moment; however, the building pressure of deceit and betrayal was beginning to overtake her thought process of what actually made sense to her. As the ride home, seemed longer than usual, Dalia daydreamed about the good times that she and Terrance shared. He was her first love, first lover, and first man she had ever lived with. Terrance had been the best in everything according to today's standards for men. He helped cook, clean, wash clothes-- you name it he did it. He supported her in everything that she did and even encouraged her to do more. As she daydreamed about pastime events, she recalled a time when they went to the beach for a week. He surprised her after taking finals their junior year in college. He had everything planned from the plane tickets to the reservations at the restaurants. He cherished her in every way you could have imagined. Do not get it wrong, he made his mistakes, but his good sure enough did outweigh his bad. He pampered her and made her feel special all the time. She could always look forward to coming home to him and he could brighten her day. This time, he dampened her day if anything.

When they arrived back at the condominium, Dalia showed Shawn to her room and helped her with her things. Dalia looked at the pictures that she had put up on the wall, which was a picture of Shawn and her husband; Dalia adored how happy they looked. Shawn stood beside her looking at the picture saying, "It takes a lot of work to get there, trust me". Dalia did not make a comment nor did she pay it any attention. All she could see is that Shawn had it all. She then asked Shawn about her husband, Darrin. She told her, "He was fine, getting on her nerves every second". "But it's a delight, right? You love being married and the goodness of it"? Shawn began telling her that "It is wonderful being married, but it takes a lot of work to keep that happiness and excitement going in the marriage. Dalia states, "I understand that, but you guys had something to build on and you kept that steady for such a long time". Shawn did not seem to understand where all this chatter about relationships talk came about. To her knowledge, Dalia was always secure and happy with her relationship with Terrance, but she could tell that something more serious was going on that she was not willing to discuss. Therefore, Shawn asked Dalia, "Is everything ok with you and Terrance? Are you happy, or have you found someone else that is making you happy?" Dalia smiled and told her, "It is nothing like that. I just wondered about my cousin and her husband that is all. It is not like you to come out here without him." "That is the trick of marriage; you do not have to do everything together to maintain a healthy marriage." "Has the kids' conversation come up again?" asked Dalia. "Of course, Darrin could not be Darrin if he did not bring it up at least once a day. I bet he is going to call me in a minute asking about it." Dalia chuckles. She thinks that it is funny how it seems to annoy Shawn just a little to know that her husband is that much interested in having kids. By Dalia laughing, she makes Shawn laugh with her. Shawn's cell phone rings and it is her husband. Dalia is laughing so hard that by the time Shawn answers, Darrin can hear Dalia on the other end laughing so hard that she is turning red in the face. Slowly getting defensive for no reason, Darrin asked Shawn what is so funny. Shawn told her husband, "She is just laughing at something that we were just talking about, nothing serious, just a joke I made." Darrin states, "I hope I wasn't the joke." Internally, Shawn wants to laugh because she thinks that is such a coincidence that Darrin happens to call just as soon as she and Dalia were talking about him. Darrin tells Shawn over the phone that he had been waiting for her to call to see if she made it in ok. She apologizes to him and states that she forgot. It was nothing intentional. "I lost track of time once I arrived at Dalia's since she had not seen me in a while." Darrin responded, "I understand, Babe, but you could have called as soon as you got off the plane. Do you know how worried I was starting to get when I did not hear anything from you?" She apologizes again to her husband who reassures her that he was just worried that he had not heard anything from her since she left. She began telling her husband about her flight; while on the other hand, Dalia is listening to her voice mails.

Each message had a different apology from Terrance proclaiming how he was so sorry and that he just wanted a chance to explain himself to her. As she listens to each of the messages, all she could think of was how she caught him in the act. The more and more she heard his voice, the more apparent the image came in her head. While checking the last couple of messages, she had a beep on her phone. When she looked at it, she saw that it was an incoming call from Terrance. She did not know if she was going to answer it or ignore it. Dalia always thought that ignoring calls was the rudest thing anyone could do to another individual. Therefore, she answered the phone, trembling like crazy. She did not get the opportunity to say hello before he started talking. The first thing that came out of his mouth, "I'm sorry Babe." I don't know how it happened, just let me explain". Very calmly, Dalia states, "I am sorry, right now I have company that I need to entertain and you will have to reach me at another time and she disconnected the call." Terrance called back, "You have to let me explain, you have to talk to me, you can at least give me that." "I don't have to give you anything, you have given enough, and I don't want to deal with it right now," replied Dalia. He asks her, "When will you be ready to deal with it, because I am not going anywhere until my wife is ready to talk to me and work this thing out." Dalia became enraged with the look that she had in her eyes. She began to grind her teeth, "Now you want to give me a title. You did not think about any other title when you were handling you business when I got off from work". "Ughhhhh, states Terrance, "Can we just talk about this in person?" "Why, so we can just have makeup sex and everything will be milk and honey. I don't think so. Like I said before we will have to talk about this later, I have company." He says, "When Shawn leaves, we will handle this." Dalia hung up the phone and with despair; she could not believe that he remembered Shawn was coming visit.

Dalia and Shawn hung up the phone at the same time; however, while Dalia thought Shawn was too busy to over hear her conversation talking to her husband, she did hear the tone that Dalia was using with whoever was on the other end of the line. Shawn asks, "Is there anything you want to talk about?" Dalia states, "Nothing important, that is worth talking about." Shawn states, "I don't believe you, but I am not going to say anything. I am going to bed; I have a long day ahead of me. She asked Dalia what were her plans for tomorrow. Dalia had not thought about the next day, but she knows that Wednesday is usually a day that she meets the girls or catches up with them if they had not talked the whole week prior. Because of their busy schedules, they had not talked, so, she knew what treat was in store for her on tomorrow. Dalia told her, "I was going to catch up Lauren, Jayden, and Blake tomorrow." "That is our set day off from work set aside for girl time. Regardless of what we have planned, we made a solemn vow to make time for each other." Shawn states, "I wish I had a great network of friends who cared so much that they would have a designated day to devote to friendship. Y'all bitches have too much time on your hands." Dalia laughed at Shawn because she knew that Shawn really meant what she said about friendship. They both said their goodnights and went bed. As Dalia laid her head on her pillow for the first time since Friday, all she could say was, "This is the first time that I have laid in this bed without him. How can I do this without him?"

Chapter 2: Blake Lowry

"Good Morning all!" said Blake as she walks into her department at the Marketing Firm. Enthusiastic about this Good Friday morning, Blake walks past her assistant's desk who hands her the agenda for the day and her messages. She walked into her office and began gathering her notes for her first meeting; in the meantime, she receives a beep from her assistant. "Ms. Lowry your nine o'clock appointment has been moved back to noon. Mr. Sellers wanted me to let you know something came up that had to be handled." "Ok, thank you Tina." Blake being so anxious about this meeting was upset that this happened. This could set her career in a different angle. She runs through her planner and sees that she had a lunch date scheduled with this man that she met at a conference last month. She quickly thought for a minute how this man seemed so much different from any other man she had met. She remembered that he introduced himself as Michael Lansford, a representative from Lansford & Son, a company that his grandfather started. He was tall, dark, slim, and handsome just how she liked her man. He had nice teeth, good hair, a nice physique, and he smelled like a god. Blake was looking forward to this encounter. She did not want to be negative, but she truly was interested in him.

Her phone rang and it was Lauren, "What is up, Blakie?" Blake started telling Lauren about her morning. "My boss moved the most important presentation of my life back two hours." "So what was the problem? That would give you more time to prepare and get yourself together. I tell you what, how about you go get you some of that high price coffee that you like and calm down you are panicking over nothing," stated Lauren. "Look, whenever the top dogs around here move a meeting backward or forward, it is never a good thing", states Blake. "What do you think it means for you," Lauren asked. "I don't know what it is, but I can't afford to have anything like this to happen to me right now in my career," Blake retorted.

"Don't put that much pressure on yourself. "You have worked too hard for anything bad to happen. I say knock them dead when you go in there."

"Ok, you are not in one of your promotional meetings, this is your girl you talking to. I need to pray that this is just an emergency and that it has nothing to do with me." "Well, you know that is how we got through college," reminded Lauren. "I think these people at this job are getting to me. I think that is where these words are coming from." "You know that don't work with me. Blake how many times this year have you called me with this same conversation?"

"What the hell does that matter, each time should be a rehearsal for the real one." "Girl, you are stupid as hell." "Hey, I got to go; I have to meet with my team to discuss this new group we just got on broad."

"Is that the one you were telling me about last week at dinner with the girls?" "Yeah, that is the one," responded Lauren.

"Ok, call me when you get done."

"Alright, I will if it doesn't take too long."

"Oh, call Jayden and Dalia. We are supposed to meet up next week. Make sure everything is still good with them."

"Your fingers must not dial those numbers." "But you sit at your desk more than me." "Are you trying to say I don't do any work?"

"No, I am saying just what I said." "Gr-eat, how about you call Jayden and I will call Dalia and I will touch bases with you later this afternoon."

"Cool, gotta go." "Bye".

Blake checks her watch and notices that it is now ten o'clock. She needed to prepare some briefs that she promised the Marketing Director of her department. She intercoms her assistant and asks her to find the file for the briefs. She reminds her that she left those briefs at home. She took them with her when she went home last evening to finish them there. "I could kick myself for leaving them there." "Was there anything else you need?"

"No, that will be all"... "Oops, Tina, can you hold my calls? I have to run home and get those files. David is going to be expecting those today and they have to be ready."

"Sure, Ms. Lowry, are there any calls that you are expecting that I should be aware of?" "Not any that I know of at the moment, but if anyone calls and says it is important, forward the call to my cell."

"I sure will."

"I'll be back in time for my appointment at noon." Blake began gathering her things.

During the ride home, she tries to run the rest of her day in her head. She remembered that her meeting moved back to noon. She had a lunch date with Michael, the new man. She had to call Jayden to see if the girls' night was still on for Wednesday. She needed to make sure that she set up a meeting with her team before the end of the month. She also had several projects that she was overseeing and was very prevalent to her career. Blake came to the company very motivated and ambitious to elevate within the company. While all of this is running through her mind, she forgets to turn her cell back to the ringer. Her company has very strict rules about cell phones; however, Blake decides to either turn the phone off or place it on vibrate. Today, Blake has it on vibrate and she has it in her purse; She forgets to take it off even though she asked her assistant to forward any important calls that she may get. Blake arrives at her home, which sits on an acre. It is four bedrooms with four bathrooms, living room, dining room, great room, game room, pool house, home office, basement, workout facility, and her own private salon. In a short couple of years, Blake has managed to make a good life for her self; nonetheless, the trust fund that she came into once she finished college and turned 21 helped greatly. Very appreciative of what she had, she never thought she was too good for anything and anybody. Maintaining high standards for Blake was a way of life. Privileged more than others, she worked her way up from the bottom at this Marketing Firm and she was proud of it. Blake took more pride in her work than in the material things she possessed. She felt that she truly deserved every good thing that happened to her on this job. She knew her parents had no part in it.

Upon arriving at her house, she could hear her phone ringing in the house. By the time she was able to get into the house, the phone stopped ringing. It went to the answering machine. Blake did not stay around to listen to the message. She ran upstairs to her office to find those files. While in her office, she happened to look at the caller id and saw it was her mother calling. She figured that it was one of those routine calls that her mother makes every Friday to ask her why she had not gotten married and had any children yet. She thought to herself that she would call her back at the office. Blake found the files and was so happy and relieved that she finished the report. She hurriedly ran down the stairs, placed the files in her briefcase, and headed for the door. Before getting out of the door, her phone rang again. Something told her to turn around and check the Caller ID. She saw that it was her mother again. She debated back and forth whether this call was for serious or was it her mother being motherly again. She decided to come back in the door and answer the phone. She picked the phone up and on the other end; she could only hear screaming in the background. Instantly, Blake became frantic about what was going on. Her mother called her name, "Blake honey, are you sitting down?"

"Yes, ma, I am now, what is wrong?"

"I have something that I need to tell you."

"Ma, what is it?"

"Your father, he died this morning"… "What? How did that happen, why didn't you call me, I can't believe this is happening to me!" Blake instantly dropped the phone and just sat in the chair by the kitchen door. She did not know what to do. Aware of how her daughter was going to react to the news, Mrs. Lowry sent a car to pick her daughter up and drive her to the airport so that she could come home with the family.

As she arrives at the airport, she receives several calls from friends back home who were giving their condolences. After a while, she stopped answering the phone. Unable to deal with the grief, she turned her phone off until she arrived at her parents' home. The plane ride was relaxing, but not enough to ease the hurt and pain she was experiencing. She did not know how she was going to be able to go home with her father not being there or him greeting her at the door. She pulled out every picture that she had on her that included her father. All she could think was that she didn't get the chance to say goodbye. She kept trying to trigger her mind to see if she had forgotten or missed something that he said that would let her know something was wrong. As much as she tried, she could not think of anything that gave her the sign that he was sick, disgruntled, or unhappy with something. She knew that this was not going to be an easy time for her family. Her father was the backbone of the family. This was the time in her life where things like this would not be a problem. Unable to pack anything, she realized that she was so unprepared with paperwork, checkbooks, credit cards, and her prized possessions. However, for once in her life, she realized that none of that mattered.

Instantly, she remembered that she had an important meeting at noon and lunch with Michael. She did not know how she was going to manage it all with what she was now facing. She knew that using her cell in the air would not be the safest and smartest thing to do. She was going to call Tina just as soon as the plane would hit the ground. She did not know what position this would put her job in; however, it was something that she could not worry about right now. "Michael." Many things were running through her mind right now. She had decided that she would call him and explain that he had a family emergency that needed her attention. She also recalled the briefs that she ran home to get that were supposed to be in ASAP. She had so many things running through her mind, and she did not know what to do and how to handle things. The only thing that she could think about was calling Lauren. She knew that anytime things got sticky, she could always turn to Lauren for help. She would know exactly what to do. She felt some sigh of relief knowing that she had one person in her life who knew her well enough to help her through this. The Captain comes on the system and declares that they will be landing in twenty minutes. She knew that once that planes hit land; the world that she knows would soon be a harsh reality that she would have to deal with. She looks for her Blackberry and turns it on. She sees that five missed forwarded calls from her mother's cell and home. Apparently, just as soon as she left the office, her mother was calling to give her the news of her father. The plane lands and she phones Lauren and it goes to voice mail. Obviously, her meeting ran longer than expected. Now, she has to think on her own and figure out what she is going to do. She called Tina, stating, "I have a family emergency. Can you contact Mr. Sellers and let him know that I will have to reschedule my meeting for a later time?" "Tina asked, "What is going on? It is not like you to be out of the office unless it is life or death."

"My father passed this morning, so can you rearrange my schedule for the rest of the week?"

"If the execs want to speak with me forward them to my cell and I will handle it."

"I will handle everything on this end, don't you worry about it. Sorry about your loss and give your mother my regards."

"Thanks Tina, I will be in touch." "Ok, I was able to handle everything with work, now I need to call Michael or should I just not show up. He does not know me anyway; it would not hurt for me to miss the date. He will understand. I will call him anyway". She begins to locate his number in her planner as she waits for the driver to come pick her up. She finds it; takes a deep breath and began dialing his number. He did not answer, which to Blake may have been a good thing to avoid an awkward conversation. She left a voice mail, "Hi, Michael, this is Blake. I am going to have to take a rain check on our lunch date for today. I have a family emergency that caused me to have to fly out of town for a couple of days. I will call you as soon as I get back to town". She hung the phone up, thinking that she did not leave a great voice mail. She was thinking that she sounded like she was giving him an excuse to not go out rather than putting him on notice that her father died. The driver arrived; placed her bags in the trunk; and told her to get in the car.

She had not been home in a year and to come home to a funeral was the last thing she would have thought would bring her home. Her mother came to the door when the car pulled up to the driveway. Her older sister was there already helping their mother make arrangements. Nothing had changed about the house; everything looked the same. Her mother asked her about the plane ride and the trip. Blake could hardly talk about anything because she had so many unanswered questions. She did not know where to begin. All she wanted to do was see her father. Her mother told her, "He died at the house earlier this morning. He passed away in his sleep, a massive heartache." The only thing going through her mind was, "I was not here with him." He always wanted his two girls to run his firm.

They quickly finished the arrangements because Blake's mother did not want them to have to endure the grief that long. The funeral was on Monday morning. All of his friends from school and acquaintances he made throughout his career were there. The only thing that made the time seem so long was that Blake's father knew so many people, and it took a long time before they were able to get the news. It was like each time they called, Blake had to relive his death all over again, especially when talking to those that he dealt with on a regular basis. It was all happening so fast none of her friends were able to attend.

"I did not get the opportunity to call them; and even if I did, I was not able to get back in touch with them about the details for the funeral," Blake thought.

"I wanted to be alone; I did not want any contact with anyone outside of my family." This was something new for Blake; she did not know how to handle this grief besides being close to her mother and sister. She scheduled to leave on Tuesday evening.

Blake had to get back to her life; there were some unresolved issues back home. Her father had a will in which she was not too interested in who he left what to. Blake's mother wanted her to stay, but she did not see the need to. The reading was going to be at her parent's house. The lawyer scheduled the meeting for early Tuesday morning, right before she was to leave for the airport. Not to think any technicalities would be an issue with the will,

Blake took no interest in hearing it. Her mother thought out of respect for her father that she should attend. Blake agreed to do as much.

The lawyer arrived; he handled many of the family's affairs since Blake's mother was a young woman. An older man, who was very prominent in his field, was always very professional. He began the reading promptly at eight o'clock in the morning. The three of them-- Blake, her mother, and her sister-- gathered around in her father's office while the lawyer began reading the will. Blake's mother automatically gained the rights of the estate and all the properties that they obtained while married. He also gave monies to staff and relatives. Blake's sister gained control of the company with her mother having controlling interest. While they came into their trust funds at 21 upon graduating from college, there was also an amendment to it. Blake would receive an additional two million once she got married and her children would have trust in holding as she and her sister did. I never discussed family with my parents, but this is what he had planned for us.

Just when they thought it was over, the lawyer stopped them from departing to tell them that it was more to the testament. "Wait a minute ladies, there is more". With an astonishing look on our faces, he announced that my father had another child before he married my mother and he left her a house and a quarter of a million dollars. As shocked as I was, there was nothing I could say. From the looks of things, her mother already knew about this other child, but not my sister and me. I wanted to ask questions, but I had too much going on to think about it.

My sister, Blair, understood how I felt. She knew something was not right, but she could not put her hand on it. She would have never thought of this. I told my mother that I would be back to visit next week. She stated, "It would be nice to have the company since your father is not here anymore. I was hoping to see Lauren and the other girls when you came."

"I did not get a chance to inform them of daddy's death or of the funeral"... "When I return, I will be sure to bring them back with me."

"Ok, I will be looking forward to hearing from you soon. Love you, dear."

"Love you too, Ma." Blair drove me to the airport later that afternoon after the three of us had lunch together at the house. On the way there, we caught up for a while. I frequently talk to my sister about work besides that we do not share too much. She took the career path after our father and I took a completely different road to success. I did things unexpected for the daughter of a well to do lawyer and college adjunct professor. I began telling my sister, "I did not even know what I wanted to do when I went to college and Daddy helped me so much to make a decision with what I wanted to do with my life."

"I do not know how I can survive at the firm without his guidance and assistance. He has always been there to help me make the best move."

"We will be fine. I am sure of it".

We arrived at the airport just in time for me to catch my flight. It seemed like I was going back to my life as if my father was never here. When I got to the line to check my luggage in, I received a call from my sister. "Hey, I got some information on your long lost sister. Her name is Carmen Dennis, twenty eight, and happily married. Been married for a couple of years."

"Do you know where she lives?"

"It looks like she lives in your town, Baltimore, Maryland."

"You have got to be kidding me."

"No, I am so serious; let me know if you happen to run across her there. We could meet her and get to know our long lost sister."

"Ok, I am about to board the plane. I will call you later to get the rest of the details."

"Have a safe flight." "Thanks".

The flight back was smooth and relaxing. I looked through my planner to see what the rest of the week was going to be like. "Today is Tuesday and I haven't talked to my home girls in days. Where is my Blackberry? Oh God, where could it be? I hate to have to buy a new one when I get to town. Ok, I cannot worry about that. I am not going to think about anything until this plane lands. I need a moment to myself, so I will take a nap until I arrive back to my place of residence." The captain awakes me, "The plane will be landing in thirty minutes. Please fasten your seat belts and prepare yourselves for landing." I knew that was not going to last long. When I got off the plane, I could not wait to get to my car and go to my own humble abode. I pulled in the driveway and something seemed strange. I was tempted not to go in, but I did anyway. Just as soon as I turned the knob, there was Lauren, scaring me half to death. I asked her, "What are you doing here?" She stated, "I got your message after my meeting and then when I tried to reach you at your office, Tina told me that you had a family emergency. I could not figure out what would make you leave work and leave town without letting any of us know."

"So, how did you find out everything?"

"When I could not reach you on your phone, I happened to catch up with your sister and she filled me in, but this was after the funeral and all.

"But, she did not mention anything to me about you calling."

"I told her that I would be here once you got home." "

Ok, that makes sense of how she went along with me coming back here."

"Yeah, she knew all about it."

"Have you talked to Jayden or Dalia?" "I have been trying to reach Dalia, but she has been out of reach for a couple of days. Jayden went out of town with her father and her stepmother for a couple of days. Apparently, her phone does not have any reception where she is."

"Let us not worry about that. I want you to tell me all about your trip and how you are doing."

"I am ok; I guess the reality of it all has not hit me. I want you to do me favor." "You name it, I am there."

"My mother wants the four of us to visit her in Jersey for a little while."

"I guess I can move around some things and come for a little vacation."

"Thanks so much."

Lauren goes into the kitchen where the wine cellar is and she gets a nice red wine and pops the cork on it. As she opens the wine, I am sitting in my chair in the living room reminiscing about my father. "I just cannot believe that he is gone."

"I know, honey, it is going to be ok. We are all here for you." Lauren grabs two glasses of wine, brings the bottle in the living room, and places it on the table. "You know, you don't think about death until it happens. My father was such a healthy person who loved his body. He always watched what he put in his body and how it was proportioned."

"How did he die?" asked Lauren.

"He had a massive heart attack in his sleep and he died early Friday morning."

"I know whatever I say is not going to make your pain go away, so let's drink some of it away."

"I am all for that". They toast each other, sat, and drink the whole bottle away. While drunken by the alcohol, Blake began to share what she had just learned about her long lost sister. "My father had a will, you know, and I did not see the need for me to stay until my mother insisted that I did. I found out that my father had a daughter before he married my mother."

"Are you serious?" exclaimed Lauren.

"He left her a house and a quarter of million dollars. I do not know if she even knows about her new inheritance."

"Who is she, where does she live and have you met her?"

"Her name is Carmen. She is married and lives her in Baltimore. I would love to meet her, but I do not know if I can deal with a new sister right now."

"Carmen, that name sounds familiar, what is her last name"?

"I think it is Dennis."

"That name really sounds familiar to me, but I can not think where I know it from though," stated Lauren.

We end up falling asleep on the couch in the living room. The next morning, we woke up, Lauren left, and I began to get my life together and prepare myself for work. It was going to be a rough day back to work and I did not know if I was ready to face my co-workers. I debated very seriously, if I was going to call in or just take a half a day. I pushed myself to go on. I began to run the shower and tie my hair up. The phone rings and I ran into the room to answer it. It was Tina, "Good Morning, Ms. Lowry, I wanted to touch bases with you", Blake rolling her eyes. Sometimes I think that Tina takes her job too serious.

"Good morning, Tina, I will be in the office today. I will be arriving in about an hour."

"I have an early appointment for you with Mr. Sellers that I could not reschedule any longer for you. Also, there is a message here for you from a Michael, Jayden, and Dalia, stated Tina.

"Ok, thanks. I will get those messages when I get there. Oh, Tina, take the forward off the phones and tell Dave that I will have those files for him today."

"Not a problem, see you when you get here."

"Note to self, meeting with the girls today," thought Blake.

Chapter 3: Lauren Daniels

"Breath in and breath out, good job ladies, nice work, we will pick this up next week same time, same place," stated Lauren's Yoga instructor. It is Friday morning and Lauren has just completed her Yoga class for the day. Friday is the day that she takes for herself. A very organized and professional woman, Lauren loves to have everything planned out from day to day. Looking in her planner Lauren makes a note to herself, "After Yoga class, go home, take a shower, and get ready for my ten o'clock appointment at the spa." Lauren leaves the gym in her brand new BMW that she worked very hard to get. Lauren approached her home, which has three bedrooms, four bathrooms, a workout room, a large dining room, breakfast room, a den in the upstairs and downstairs, a living room and a den sits on an acre of land outside of the city limits in a very good neighborhood. Lauren has worked very hard to get where she is and is very proud of her accomplishments, and has just celebrated her 26th birthday. But--she has one thing that she worries about which she cannot change nor has any control over-- getting married and having a family.

Lauren rushed into the house and jumped into the shower. She tried to check her voice mail since she got up at dawn; she did not get a chance to see any missed calls or messages that may be pertinent for next week's work schedule. She has five messages; one from her boss, Kevin, who has re-assigned her three new clients. Second, a call from her mother, who knows that Fridays, is her free day to handle those things that she did not get a chance to do during the week. Third, a guy calling from another Accounting Firm trying to get in touch with her about an employment opportunity. Fourth, it was Blake calling to see if she had made the plans for next Wednesday for all the girls. Lauren took a long well deserved shower until she ran all of the hot water out. She began preparing herself for her day at the spa. Normally, this is something that she liked to do with the girls, but they had other things planned for next week. At the spa, Lauren pampered herself with a pedicure, manicure, facial, and a massage. This is normally her day.

Then she goes home, balances her checkbook, and returns all the phone calls of family and friends. Lauren never makes Friday a stress day. She loves to focus on herself and make herself happy. She has made it prevalent that a man is not on her list of things to indulge her time.

Currently not in a relationship, she does not desire to lower her standards just to say that she is involved with someone. Lauren has not been in a relationship since she and Jason broke up in senior year in college. A long relationship that ended abruptly without any hesitation of reconsideration, it would sometimes run across her mind when she gets lonely, which is not too often. Lauren consumed her time with work, friends, family, and pampering herself, which was plenty for her to keep track of, since she did not have any companion to share any alone time with. Lauren never brought up the issue of being alone or showed any despair about it. She had not talked to her ex since college; nonetheless, they shared a magical connection that everyone close to them saw. Jason after graduation moved to Washington, D.C. where he took the job of being a technical engineer. Lauren kept up with what Jason was doing through college friends that they still mutually share. On several attempts, their own classmates have tried to rekindle their flame, but because these two independent individuals wrapped themselves in their careers, they would never take the time to try to make it work. Focused more on the childhood dreams, Lauren always thought there would be time for marriage and children. The most important thing that Lauren did everyday was focus on her self and making sure that she was happy before doing anything else. Of course, she was able to prioritize the most important things in her life; she knew how to balance her friends, family, work, and pleasure. Men were the farthest thing on her mind; however, every once in a while she wondered what it would be like to be in a relationship filled with love and compassion, but there was a second voice in her head telling her that she did not have the time for it.

By noon, Lauren had returned all the calls she planned to make for the day. She had touched bases with Blake, who was very busy with projects at work and her very important presentation. She also talked to her mother, who was also busy at work with her Staffing Agency and she needed Lauren's help with interns. She caught up with some friends from college and she finished running through her schedule for the rest of the week. Lauren felt that she had completed all she set out to accomplish. Exhausted from her filled morning, Lauren decided to take a well-deserved nap to relax even more. Before lying down, Lauren turned off all connection with the world; she turned off her house phone, laptop, and cell phone. Before she knew it, she slept until late evening. Upon awakening from her nap, she ran to her clock to see if she had missed her dinner date with a colleague. Her clock showed that it was four in the evening and her dinner date was at six. Without turning on her cell or house phone, she began preparing herself for dinner. Lauren was a stickler for whatever she put on her body. It would take her hours to get her attire out, regardless of where she was going. She made sure, when she designed her house, that her closet was the main thing that was customary for her. She had two walk-in closets with mirrors on both sides; a vanity where she could lay out all of her makeup to match exactly what she was wearing. Two hours would give her just enough time to get herself dressed and ready. Going out to dinner was an event in itself. She ran the shower, pinned her hair up, and turned on the stereo. A long lasting shower was just enough for Lauren to feel even more relaxed and refreshed from her nap. Without a thought, she had not realized that there had been no contact from anyone. Finally dressed to her satisfaction, Lauren leaves the house and forgets her cell phone.

At dinner, she enjoys stimulating conversation about politics, economics, and money, some of her favorite topics for intellectual human beings. Of course she was able to be more versatile, but every once in a while, she likes feeling that college feel again, so she would entertain her self with someone that could think outside the box and broader her horizon. She spends hours at the restaurant and then at the coffee house with her friend. She leaves her friend feeling that her day had been more productive than usual. While away from her house, she does not realize she is missing the most important calls of her life. When she gets home, she changes into something more comfortable. She watches some TV, gets some ice cream and curls up on the sofa in her den. It is about ten at this time, and she is mentally thinking about what she has to do tomorrow. Unexpectedly, she gets a knock at the door. It is late for visitors at her home, so she hesitates to answer the door. She asks, "Who is it". The visitor states, "Delivery for a Ms. Lauren Daniels." She thinks to her self, "Who in the hell delivers this late at night, you have to get to be kidding the flip out of me."

"Ma'am, I am trying to make a delivery before my shift ends."

"Leave it at the door and I will pick it up".

To her self she thinks, "He must be out of his mind to think that I was just going to open the door." Lauren is saying this while peeping out of the door to look at the delivery person. She waits until she sees him pull off in the car before she opens the door. Scared to death, Lauren runs upstairs to her bedroom and gets her gun. "Lord, I have never shot this thing, but I will use it if I have to, better believe that."

When she opens the door, she is looking for a big brown box. She looks down and sees white paper wrapped around something, but she does not know what it is. She is afraid that I might be anthrax. She reacts as if she is going to lose her life if she opens the package. She says a small pray to her self, "Lord, remember me in paradise." When she finally opens the packages, she sees that they are white roses, her favorite. She looks around to see who had sent them, even though she knows the deliveryman brought it. There was a note attached with the message, "I called you today, but I could not catch up with you. I have been thinking of you for a long time. I just want to show you how much I care." Lauren has no clue of where the flowers came from. She immediately runs upstairs to check her voice mail. This is when she realized that her laptop, cell, and house phone were off since earlier that day. Adoring the flowers, she puts them in one of her favorite vases in the house. While listening to her answering machine playing all of her messages, she hears the message from Blake, who informs her that her father passed. Instantly, Lauren stops preparing her flowers and stops the answering machine. She calls Blake, but she gets no answer. Her cell phone rings while she tries to ring Blake again. The call is from an unknown number, so she hesitates to answer. When she answers the phone, she hears a voice that she had not heard in years. Too scared of what to say or do, she hangs up the phone with no hesitation and she sits on her bed in shock. She sits there for a minute not knowing how to respond to the call that she just received.

She remembers that she needed to finish listening to her calls again. She had a message from Jayden telling her that she just arrived at the mountains and that her phone did not have good reception, so she would call when she got a chance. She wanted Lauren to give her regards to the girls for her because she could only make one call and she knew that Friday was Lauren's at home day. The next message came from her doctor's office about the test taken at her doctor's appointment. She did not seem worried about that call because they would have stated if it was urgent or not, but it just seemed like everything was normal and they wanted to let her know that the results were in. She received a call from Sandra, another accountant from her job, who wanted to let Lauren know that the company gained ten new accounts and they were up for grabs. Lauren saw that as more work and more stress, but she was up for the challenge. Lauren stopped the messages; she did not want to hear anymore. She had a mindful at this point. Her phone rings again, she answers it abruptly. The voice on the other end states, "Hello, how are you beautiful." She responds, stuttering her words, "I-m doing fine, how are you?"

"I had something delivered to your home tonight, did you get my package?" the voice asked.

"If you are talking about the roses, I got them…very nice, you remembered." "How could I forget"? Instantly, her voiced elevated, "Where did you come from all of a sudden?"

"You have been on my mind for months now." Lauren takes a deep breath and asks, "So, you called me to tell me that?"

"No, I called you because I wanted to see how you were and doing." Shocked as she was, she was speechless, without anything to say. She stated, "Well, I am fine. Nice to talk to you," with this clueless look on her face.

He responds, "So, it is like that between us now?

"You act like we have been out of touch for only a couple of days. Earth to Jason, we have been out of touch for a couple years!"

"So, what are you saying?"

"It is not what I am saying; it is what has been said for years now."

"Wow! You sound a little upset."

"I am not upset; I am fine, better than ever". As they continue their conversation, Lauren keeps up this wall, as if she does not want to let Jason into her inner self. Jason keeps the conversation circled around certain issues like work, pleasure, limiting to general talk, so that he does not have to face the real issue why the both of them are sitting on the phone. Not once did they talk about each other's personal lives. That would be too much for them to handle. In the background, Jason's pager goes off, which is the pager that has him on alert to come in the office. As Lauren hears this in the background, she easily found her way out of this conversation. She felt unprepared and lost for words. She tells Jason that she will talk to him later. Hhe tells her that he will definitely call her back. Is she ready for that? Alternatively, can she take the pressure of knowing that she has to deal with her feelings and emotions where Jason is concerned?

So stunned with everything, Lauren lies down for the evening and thinks to herself, "What just happened?" She is too overwhelmed to even think straight. When she wakes up Saturday morning, she tries to forget that last night even happened, but it is hard for her to do. A full day ahead of her, she gets dressed and goes to her appointment at the salon. Lauren's cousin, Sandra is getting married in Pasadena today and she had to look her best. She wanted to make sure that all her old friends and family members saw that she had made it. Leaving the beauty salon at noon, she hurries home, packs her bags, and hits the road for the wedding. The ride was relaxing for Lauren; she continued saying to her self that she was going to forget about the individual who called her last night. The problem is that this individual is far from her mind and she is far from his mind. She arrives at the brunch that was prepared for the wedding party and family at the Hilton. Dressed for the occasion, Lauren instantly stops traffic with her persona. Her aunt, Delores, very excited to see her niece ran to her with her arms wide open, asking about her mother. Lauren explains that her mother had to fly out last night to handle some unexpected company business. Lauren's aunt states, "That woman don't know when to stop working. I hope you don't end up like that. You have to make time for yourself and people."

"Aunt Delores, I make time for all of that, but work is important. Everyone can not look for a man to please and satisfy every desirable need."

"Oh, so that is why we have not been to your wedding yet."

"What is that supposed to mean."

"Just what I said. You will learn dear."

"So, is that what Sandra did?"

"No, if it wasn't for me, Sandra would not be marrying this wonderful guy."

"Does Sandra really love him?"

"She adores him and his bank account."

"That is not nice, Aunt Delores."

"It is the truth; money does not hurt, but broke does."

They both laugh at that comment. They both head into the dining all with the rest of the guest. Lauren is reacquainting her self with everyone at the brunch. Her aunt mingles with the crowd and shows everyone how happy she is for her daughter.

After the brunch is over, Lauren is confronted by a really, nice eligible man, Josiah, an old classmate from high school that her cousin invited who shows interest in her, but Lauren does not seem to remember him right off. He called her name to get her attention. She turns around and she sees that there is a really, fine man standing in front of her who wants her attention. She has no clue who this man is. Josiah was very quiet in school, a geek, who wore thick glasses, and hung out with the weird crowd. He was no one that she would remember from school. When he jogged her memory of who he was, she was so shocked and stunned that she did not know what to do. To sum up the conversation, Josiah is now a successful architect, who has his own business in a town nearby. Apparently, he designed the building that Lauren works in. Lauren catches him up with the girls and tells him what is going with each of them. He began telling her what the other classmates were doing with themselves. He asked her out for drinks later after the wedding and quickly she accepted. She had not even realized that the words had come out of her mouth, but then she thought, "Why not." Rushing her way back to the church, she realized that her cousin asked her to help with her makeup and hair. Lauren's cell phone rings, which her aunt is asking her whereabouts and what was taking her so long. She told her that she would explain later once she saw her. She takes a nice ride to the church. As she approaches the church from afar, her heart flutters for some reason. She does not know if it is her fear of getting married or her fear of thinking that it would never happen for her. She kicked the feeling, grabbed her things out of the car, and rushed into the educational facility of the church to help with her cousin. When she gets in there, she sees the entire wedding party preparing themselves for the main event. Lauren greets everyone, and looks through the room for her cousin. She finally spots her cousin in with her wedding planner, who is looking beautiful, like a bride is supposed to on her wedding day.

She and her cousin share tons of stories about growing up as she helps with her hair and gets her into her gown. The wedding gown is so gorgeous and immaculate, that it takes them about twenty minutes to get her into it. Lauren states, "Jesus, where in the hell did you get this runner."

"Ha ha ha, your aunt and I found this when
New York this past summer. I actually had m
from another company, but when I saw this one,
mind."

"I bet it did blow your mind and your pocket.   ....
you pay for this?"

"It was a nice penny, trust me, but, worth every penny for my
Chris."

"I want to see him take you out of this. He is going to need
room service and some to find you inside of it."

"You so silly, what am I going to do with you."

"You are not going to let me buy a dress like this that by the
time I walk down the aisle, I will need a nap."

"I guess it will be worth it, huh cuz."

"Oh yeah, especially when it is a one time thing, no second
rounds, you hear me Lauren?"

"Why are you saying that to me, I have not been married once?
You are starting the trend; I should be saying that to you."

The director enters the room and gives the party the queue that
it is show time. Sandra starts to get nervous and anxious. I guess
it is wedding jitters. She looked so beautiful from the tiara on her
head to the jewel laced shoes she wore; I would never imagine
that this day would come for her. As the wedding party entered
the church, I noticed a set of eyes gleaming back at me--Josiah. He
was making me feel so uncomfortable that the palms of my hand
were starting to sweat. I could not even take pictures like the way
I wanted to because I could feel his eyes staring so hard. The
ceremony went smoothly, and I was glad to see it over. I felt like
the pressure was on me to get married and I was not prepared to
have those conversations today.

The reception was just how I like: a full bar, seafood, good
music, and good-looking men just to get the party started. The
first thing I did was grab a glass of champagne. I was yearning for
that since the wedding started. It is something about formal
events that make me feel like champagne is necessary or maybe I
am just the alcoholic.

As the bridal party entered the room and I saw Sandra and Chris together for the first time as husband and wife, it warmed my heart. I could not wait to get back home to tell my mother what a wonderful wedding she missed. My aunt could not help her self; she was so emotional throughout the ceremony and at the reception. I really enjoyed myself at the wedding, but I was not in a hurry to have one anytime soon. Weddings to me, add the pressure of questions like "When are you getting married? When are you going to have children?"

"Oh, my God, why do I have to do those things to be happy or to be successful in life?" I think that marriage is a sacred and mutual thing that should come naturally, not a goal set out to achieve when you become of legal age. If it is meant to be, it will be. "Damn, I am starting to sound like the old, bitter women that I hated being around when I was little."

We began taking pictures for my personal photo album. Since my mother was unable to attend, I want her to feel like she did not miss anything. Everything turned out great. While I was gathering my things, preparing myself to leave, Josiah came to me and asked, "Where did you want to meet up?" Completely forgetting that I promised him a drink after the reception, I quickly told him that I would run to my aunt's house to change and take a shower. That extra outfit came from the overnight bag that I always keep in the car. I called my aunt to find out where the spare key to the house was. I exchanged numbers with Josiah and I told him that I would call him once I had refreshed myself. Arriving at my aunt's house, I was thinking to myself, "What do I expect out of this, just conversation or does he think this is going to lead to something...or maybe I am reading too much into it...yeah, that is it...reading too much into it." I called him while I was putting on my makeup and we decided to meet at a nice bar and grill not too far from my aunt's house. Somehow, he got there before I did, and his face lit up once he saw me. It is always a good feeling for a woman when the man you are with face lights up when he sees you. Your confidence climbs at least ten notches up the chart. We sat at the bar, opened a couple of drinks, and had great conversation. I could not believe my eyes that Josiah had turned out to be one of the most eligible bachelors in Maryland. You have to be kidding me! This was definitely a number going into the book. Before I knew it, I invited him up to Baltimore for dinner one night. He caught my interest, so it was something I wanted to pursue. It would be good company and someone I could share nice conversation. We sat at the bar for a couple of hours before I had to leave and head back home. He begged me not to go, but to stay and share with him some more, but I knew that I had other obligations on Sunday. "Good evening, talk to you soon."

"You sure will Miss Lady". He is watching me as I walk away.

On the way back to the house, I felt that I accomplished a lot on this trip. I even accomplished some things that I did not set to achieve today. I wanted to pat myself on the back for that. When I got to my house, it was at least nine o'clock and I was exhausted and woozy from the drive. I just threw my things on the floor just a soon as I entered the room. I ran upstairs to get my clothes together for church tomorrow and checked my voice mail. When I played my messages, it was strange that I didn't have any important missed calls. The one thing I thought was strange was that it had been a couple of days and no word from Dalia. "Mmm, that is not like her to be out of touch this long…she could be working overtime at the hospital…yeah, she does have to do that a lot…maybe I should ring her before I do anything else." I picked up the phone and dialed Dalia's number and it went straight to voice mail. That seemed strange to me, but you never know what everyone else has going on in their lives. "I really need to get in touch with Blake". I called Blake again and no answer, so at this point, I am thinking, "What the hell is going on. No one wants to talk to Lauren today?" I turned on my stereo and ran my bath water. My music lets me mellow out. That was always something that the girls and I could share, music, regardless of the genre.

After enjoying my bath, I went downstairs in my robe to grab a late night snack. I shut down everything downstairs and started for the stairs. Just as soon as my foot hit the first step, there was a knock at the door. Hoping that it would be one of my girls checking in since I had not heard a word from Dalia or Blake, when I opened the door, I fainted. When I came to, it was Jason. How he found out my residence, I do not know. Still a little tipsy, I kissed him and the next morning I woke up with Jason beside me. My words were, "What have I done?" I did not want this and I did not plan this. Jason looks at me with such passion in his eyes and me, I am afraid of something happening that I cannot control and I feel like this is something I cannot control right now. "This morning is startling, so wrong in so many ways; I do not know what to do. First, I wake up to my ex lying next to me; second, I am late for church…what else?"

"So, you are regretting what happened last night?"

"I am not saying that, I do not know what to say or think. Can you leave right now? I need to think and be alone."

"Ren, I want to be with you."

"What do you mean, you want to be with me, and you have not seen me in years. You do not know the person that I am now; you know me from college."

"You have not changed and it does not matter if you did or not. I just want you." "Oh Lord, I need some time to think about this, can I at least get that"?

"Alright, you get that, but do not make a fool out of me."

"You took that chance when you came all the way here without calling me."

"I just needed to see you."

"What if I had company?"

"That would have been a simple glitch in the plan."

"Are you serious, ok, I really need time to think and be alone. Good Bye". I cannot believe what I had done. I was so out of it that it took a day for me to get back to myself. Monday, I did absolutely nothing productive, which is not like me. Could I get out of bed? "No". I felt like someone had hit me in the head with a hammer non-stop. Tuesday came too quickly. I woke up with my regular routine of reading my daily bread, listening to the radio, checking my email, and then getting ready for work. When I get into the office, I have a message that I am going to be in meetings and briefs all day about the new clients the company is obtaining. There is no rest for the weary I can tell you that. Unable to think about what all had happened to me this weekend; nonetheless, I had enough work to keep me busy and occupied. My whole day shot to hell from the moment I walked through the door until it was time for me to leave for the day. Upon completing this day, all I wanted to do was go to bed. Tomorrow was going to be another full day with the girls.

Chapter 4: Jayden Miller

"If you don't get your ass off this phone so I can finish packing. Yeah, I hear you, but I cannot change the damn world in a day...If I miss my plane, I will personally kick your ass, thank you...good bye, talk to you later" as she gets off the phone with her little brother, Jordan, before leaving on her trip with her father and stepmother.

Jayden is getting ready to go to the mountains for a family trip. Not too favored by her stepmother, Jayden's father asked her to join them on the trip. Not too fond of going out of town with her father and his wife, she agrees because she knows that it will not hurt for her to try to develop a good relationship with her stepmother. Having a close relationship with her father meant the world to Jayden. Never wondering why her parents were not together, she did not want to seem like she was in competition for his attention. However, for some reason, her stepmother seemed to dislike her because she felt intimidated by her mother. Everyone who know Jayden's father, James, knew that Jayden's mother was the love of his life. So many issues separated her parents that it was never a thought if they were going to get back together. Jackie, Jayden's mother, never calling or coming to the house unannounced, still felt threatened by Jayden's presence.

Jayden drives to the airport, praying that this trip be worth the while that her father hopes it will be. Jayden being not too sure about that just agrees with her father and is willing to try it. As she turns in her luggage and her ticket information, she looks for her cell to call her mother to tell her that she was getting ready to board the plane. Her mother does not answer the phone, so she leaves a detailed message for her describing her feelings and emotions of this trip. Wanting to give it all she has, she continues to stay positive about it all. She hears the overhead announcer saying that it would be a fifteen-minute delay boarding the plane, so she decides to go to her favorite place to clear her mind, Starbucks. Even though her father has fussed at her repeatedly about drinking this expensive coffee, she just seems to keep the fetish going. As she sits in the café, she thinks why she is really going on this trip and why it is important to her. Not alone that she needs to get to know her step-mother and she does not want to have a raft between her and her father, but personally she has a lot on her mind.

"I hope this isn't a mistake, but who the hell cares. I didn't have to pay for anything and it is time for me to connect with my other family besides my mother." Jayden says several things to herself trying to be positive, but deep down she is prepared to take a detour on this trip if things do not go the way they should. She hears the call to board the plan; Jayden makes her way to the gate and finds her way to her seat on the plane. Jayden loving the ride of a plane is looking forward to a relaxing trip. She almost forgets that she was supposed to make an important call. She takes out her phone and calls Lauren to tell her that she was on the plane and would call her once she is settled. Lauren does not answer the phone so she leaves a message sounding so delighted to be away. When the plane takes off, Jayden thinks about her job and the responsibilities that she leaves behind. Always so concerned about her stores that she manages, she never takes time to enjoy what she has worked so hard to obtain. The only time that Jayden does not consume her time with work is when she is with the girls. Being very close to Dalia, she has been out of touch since her promotion. Normally, she and Dalia will meet for coffee after work just to talk and release some stress. With more duties and tasks to fulfill, she has very little time for anything else. This trip was something that she had to fight for especially with the high demand at work. Trying to get her thoughts together in her head, she ends up sitting next to an older man who wants to talk the whole flight. Jayden wanting to let him have it, thought about how the man could have been her father and she would not want anyone to disrespect her father like that. Quickly, she looked for headphones to plug into her IPod, so that she would not have to resort herself to his type of conversation.

Jayden ends up taking a nap for the entire flight. She woke up when the flight attendant advised the passengers to prepare for landing. She realized that her phone was off and that she needed to turn it back on so that her father could call her to find their location. Once the plane landed, she saw her father texted her to take a cab to a resort twenty miles outside of the town. Shocked as hell, she was thinking, "Where in the world am I going to find a damn cab." Her father sent another saying, "Cabs are right outside the airport. Have the cab driver bring you to the Kingdom Resort, which is twenty miles outside of the city limits…love you"… "What in the fuck? Twenty miles outside of the city limit, I bet I will not have a signal on my phone out here." Jayden easily sees a cab just waiting for her and she gets in the cab gives him the same directions that her father told her. She was surprised that he even knew what she was talking about. The ride to the resort was so nice. "The mountains were so beautiful; it was like I was in a dream or something. I am trying to figure out where the old man found this place. That ride did not even seem like it was twenty minutes." When I arrived, it was like a two story house. My father and my stepmother came out of the house and they looked so happy to see me.

My father helped me get my bags out of the car while Karen, his wife, pretended to be happy that I was there. "She got one time to say something out of the way."

She begins to carry conversation with me, "So, how was your flight?" "It was good, how was yours."

"You know we only go first class, so that is always good". To her self, "She is such an ass. I do not know what my father sees in her." Apparently, they had the whole trip planned because they wanted me to hurry up and changed for dinner. Thinking to myself, "Who in the hell changes clothes for dinner unless they are going to an expensive restaurant. I am not trying to spend a paycheck on one meal. They have got to be smoking trees or something to think I am going to be up for this shit". Being the team player that I am, I ran upstairs to a vacant room to change my clothes and I could not believe how beautiful this place was. I did not change into what they were wearing, but I felt quite fine with what I had on. Karen was dressed in a navy blue pants suit. My father was dressed in a sports coat, dress pants, collar shirt and dress shoes. I am thinking, "Where are they going, to a church meeting or something." I am wearing my favorite Apple Bottom Jeans and shirt with my denim boots. I guess I do not fit in with what they have on, but mine is authentic. The ride to dinner was irritating to me. We went to a lavish restaurant where nothing on the menu was what real black people eat. Ever since my father married Karen, he seemed to have changed what he eats, the places he likes to hang out, and the clothes he likes to wear. It does not bother me, but I do not like how he knows this is not me and he wants me to feel comfortable with what his wife has forced on him. "It ain't gonna happen to me". Karen did try to help me figure out the menu, but I think it made her feel good because in this case she had the upper hand.

Dinner was ok, but I would have rather ate at Church's and get some biscuits from KFC. Not saying that I do not know how to take it a step up, but you do not have to go all out all the time. Nevertheless, when it comes to Karen, it is going all out or not going at all. We were discussing our plans for Saturday and Karen wanted to go shopping while I wanted to go sight- seeing. We were in another state that none of us had been to, wouldn't you want to see how beautiful the place was. Apparently, she just wanted to shop the whole time. Do not get me wrong, I love to go shopping, but I felt that there would be plenty of time to do that. Therefore, my father decided that we would get up early and go sightseeing first thing in the morning and once we finish that, we can go to a mall. I was pleased and so was Karen, hallelujah. Since the house was so beautiful at night, my father stated, "We should know something together as a family." I was gamed for it because the atmosphere at the house was very cozy. Karen suggested, "We should play a family game and open a bottle of wine." That was the first thing she said the entire time today that I actually thought was a good idea. "Monopoly, it will last long enough and I can beat the both of you," which was my suggestion. My father laughing continuously, knowing that I used to play that game all the time when I as small. Karen loved the game. She played that with her kids when they were children. The problem that we had was that no one had the game. Luckily, there was a general store about five miles away, but we were ready to go. Karen and I went together to go get the game from the store, which was Karen's suggestion, and I was wondering what kind of stupid things she was going to talk about in the car. When we got in the car, Karen stated, "This is nice that we can do something together."

So, I said, "What do you mean?"

She stated, "We don't get a chance to do things together and I think that this trip will give us the opportunity to build a mother, daughter relationship."

"Oh really and how are we going to do that?"

"First, we have to be able to have a civil conversation."

"I can do that, but I do not need to feel like it is a condescending conversation for the both of us to communicate." At this point, I feel like the conversation is about to move in the wrong direction. She then states, "That would be the way you interpret what I say."

"Excuse me; you should not say things condescending to anyone because that is disrespectful regardless how you look at." Trying to avoid her further explaining herself, we arrived at the store and she jumps up and says, "We are here. I hope we can find the game her." I had a puzzled look on my face. I just knew then that she was going to piss me off for the rest of the trip. I got out of the car and went into the store to try to find the game. I located the games first and I told Karen that I had it. She offered to pay for the game, but I told her that I would pay for it myself. During the ride back, I wanted to avoid a weird and frustrating conversation, so I called Lauren again and told her what was going on and pretended that I was having a better time than what I actually was. After phoning Lauren and leaving a message, I called my job to check in with the other associates from the stores. That took up the time from the store back to the resort.

When we arrived back at the resort, my father had the bottle of wine opened and three wine glasses waiting on the coffee table in the living room. He had this look on his face like he was so excited to see all of us together. "Hey, dad we got the game so get ready because this is going to be a quick game." Karen stated, "I do not know about all of that, your father seemed to have stepped his game up with Monopoly... "He must have been practicing."

"Oh, he has been doing a little something". We sat on the floor while I began passing out the game pieces and the money. My father and Karen began talking about the rooms in the house; they really liked the design and structure of them. They did not bore me as much as they usually do. Everyone was very enthusiastic about the game. It really made me think that there could be a possibility that Karen and I could find some common ground. The only thing that I wanted to avoid with her is drawing my father into some silly little conflict that would be uncalled for. We played the game for hours. Once it was over, we departed and went to our rooms.

Saturday morning, I woke up with a better feeling about the day. I was ready at eight o'clock in the morning. Karen knocked on my door to tell me that breakfast was ready. As shocked as I was, I could not believe that she cooked. She did not do that before. I really wondered what brought that on. There was a part of me that thought she was trying to go out of her way to please my father or me. I just could not seem to put my hand on it. Breakfast was great, but after I ate, I was ready to hit the road. Slowly moving that morning, Karen and my father decided to leave the house around eleven for us to go sightseeing, which was too late to do any of the things that I wanted to do. That was killing me. By leaving the house late, especially when we have a full day ahead of us, made me feel like we wasted a day. We missed some of the tours that were going on that morning and the museum had already closed. Not too disappointed about the events missed, I knew that there would be more time later to do them. Thinking to myself, I had not head from Dalia at all. That did not seem right for some reason. I did not have a good signal on my phone, so I had to wait until we went into another town or somewhere other than the resort.

We went to a very nice mall. Not sure how my father ended up finding this, we ended up having a great time there. The mall had a very nice restaurant also a bowling alley, wine tasting store, and a wide variety of stores. Somehow, we had a good time, altogether. We spent most of the day at the mall, which did not turn out to be a bad thing. My father wanted us to cook dinner together one night, but he did not say which night that was going to be. Karen jumped up and stated, "We should all go to the grocery store later this evening to buy dinner." I am rolling my eyes right now because Karen loves to be the authoritarian and the one to run every situation. I go along with the fairytale of us as a family going out together. "They are killing me". My father asked, "Jay where would you like to eat dinner tonight?"

"I would like to eat where there is some southern food. Do you think we can find that?" James states, "I think we should be able to do that baby girl." My father had the tendency of calling me his baby girl ever so often. We shared a connection. Karen not looking so happy about the decision for dinner, just remained quiet the entire time that we were looking for a good, southern restaurant; my father knew this would've a change of scenery from what we had been doing since this trip started.

We finally found a place about thirty miles away from the resort, we were staying. Karen looking unpleased with the restaurant that we chose did not look happy at all. We walked into the restaurant and the hostess who stated, "How many is it going to be tonight for you folks"? I immediately stated, "It is a party of three". The hostess says, "Right this way". It was a family owned restaurant in an all black neighborhood. Karen still looking uncomfortable states, "The tables are extremely small in here". I responded to her comment, "There is nothing wrong with the tables in here. It is nice and family oriented. Isn't that the theme we are going for on the trip, right"? "Well, it was more of your father's idea".... "What are you trying to say, stepmother"... "I am trying to say that if it were up to me, we would not have come here and it just would have been your father and me on this trip. Do you know how long I have planned this trip for me and James"? Therefore, me being the person that I am, responded to her, "That is not a problem, I can take the first flight out of here just like I came. I only did this damn trip as a favor to my father. I could give a shit about you and this trip." "Jay, watch your mouth," my father states. "But, Daddy did you not here what she said or are you just going to ignore that."

"I heard what she said". He turns to Karen, "Where do you get off telling my child that she is not welcomed on this trip. It was my money that paid for the damn trip in the first place."

"Your daughter is disrespectful and needs to learn some manners."

"My daughter is a grown woman and has a lot of manners for adults. She has done nothing but been nice to you and you seem to turn your nose up at her."

"See, this is why I was not for her coming on this trip. We always tend to argue or disagree when she is around."

"It is not her, it is you. You change from being the good person that you are whenever she is around." The waitress came to the table and asked, "What would you folks like to drink tonight?" Karen and my father both stopped for a second. My father stated, "Give us a minute. I am not sure we are going to even be eating tonight."

I am just sitting here patiently, not sure whether to leave or just be quiet. I remember when my parents would argue and if I jumped into it at all, the argument quickly turned on me for some reason. They would always tell me that a child should never be in grown people's conversation. At 25, I still do not belong in grown people conversation.

When the waitress left, my father continued with Karen, "I do not know what it is that you have against Jayden, but we are not leaving this state until we handle this."

Karen makes a big issue by saying, "You always put her first."

"Put her first, you planned this trip. I thought it would be a good chance for my wife and my daughter to establish a relationship or to try on work on building one."

"Well, you thought wrong."

"There is something else behind this and it better be well worth it for you to cause a scene in front of my daughter."

"Your precious Jay, do you ever see any wrong in what she does?" "Tell me what she does so that I can get her, but if you keep treating her like she is the enemy, then you make me your enemy." "I do not think we should be having this conversation in front of your daughter." I jumped in, "Dad she is right. The two of you should be talking this out in private." Therefore, Karen jumps in and says to me, "I bet you would want this to be in private, since your father is all on your side."

"That has nothing to do with it. You have really lost it. I do not care what you and my father do, I have my own life." My father interjects, "Jay that is enough. You do not need to make things worst. You stay here and have dinner on me."

"I think I would feel better if I just took a flight back home". My father tried to convince me within the timeframe of his wife having at temper tantrum, but I would not stay there, what would be the point in that. "Jay, at least come back to the house tonight and you can catch a flight in the morning, on me, and I will know that you will be safe."

"Dad, that sounds nice, but you handle your marriage and I will see myself back to Maryland."

"Baby girl, I hate that this trip did not turn out to be what I hoped for."

"Dad, don't worry about it. I will talk to you soon."

"Call me and let me know that you made it safe."

"I will, love you!"

By this time, Karen has stormed out of the restaurant, upset that she has not gotten her way.

My father and Karen left hurriedly; I was thrown for a loop by all of this turned out. While I left a tip for the waitress, I noticed a guy staring at me. I went to the counter to order some food to go. Even though the night turned out a disaster, it did not mean that I was not hungry. The woman at the counter asked, "What can I get for you dear?" "I would like to order baked chicken, white meat with candied yams, fried okra, and mashed potatoes to go please."

"Ok, Miss Lady, I will put that in for you and it should take about fifteen minutes." "Thank you!" By this time, I could see someone coming towards me. When I slightly turned to my left, I noticed a very nice looking man looking at me saying, "What are you doing out here alone?" I looked at him, "Are you serious?" He goes on with his lines, "You are a beautiful woman, and you shouldn't be out here alone."

"Really, where should I be alone?"

"I guess you have heard all of that before?"

"Yes and your version is the worst." "And your name is…"… "Unknown, Unknown Jones"…

"Wow, are you going to be like that?" "You walked over here and you expected me to be real submissive, ain't gonna happen with me, maybe with the next chick"… "I like you though"… "But, I don't know you to like you. Look, I am not interested and I don't want you to think that I am trying to play hard to get, I am not interested."

"You are just fire, aren't you"? "No, I am for real."

The woman came from out of the kitchen, "Ma'am your order is ready. Your total is eleven dollars and fifty nine cents." I handed her a twenty-dollar bill and told her to keep the change, this was just to get away from that monster in the restaurant. Of course, he wanted to walk outside to see me leave. "You have got to be smoking."

"Is there anyone I can call you or get your name?" "Sweetie, this is going to be the most conversation that you are going to get out of me, I am not interested." "Can you at least tell me your name"? "My name is Jay"… "Jay, Jay, that is nice. I will not forget you Jay, and by the way, my name is Kevin"… "Ok, I have to go, nice to meet you Kevin. I was ready to get out of there.

I took a cab back to the resort. I wanted to eat, sleep, and wake up the next morning to head back to my home. "I just knew that this trip would not be all it was cut out to be". While I was riding, I began thinking about Brian, the man that has been in my life for four years now. Dating on and off, I cannot seem to live with him or without him. Due to so many changes happening at work, I cannot seem to deal with my personal issues with Brian. Lately, I have not been able to tell if he loves me or is in love with me. For months now, I have chosen not to think about this issue, because I am not sure what I want right now. Work has made me focus on my career more and less on a man. Brian means the world to me, but I will not deal with that kind of drama right now. "My phone has no damn signal out here, what kind of flipping place is this". When I arrived at the resort, it was very dead. I did not see the car that my father and Karen were in nor did I see any lights on in the house. There was a note on my bed once I went into my room stating, "Dear baby girl, I will not be returning tonight, don't worry about me, I am fine. Have a safe trip back home. Love Always, Dad". I am reading this note repeatedly trying to get a complete understanding of what this really means. I am trying not to make too much of it, but I don't know what else to think. Before I knew it, I fell asleep on the bed.

When I woke up Sunday morning, I was so ready to get out of that place; I packed my bags so fast that I turned around twice because I forgot important things. There must have been something keeping me in North Carolina, but I could not figure out what it was. My father and Karen were still out wherever they were, but I did not know. I really did hope that the both of them were fine. I took a cab to the airport to catch my flight. I wanted to get there early since they had Starbucks Café in this airport too. I needed something to calm my nerves. Again, this drive was at least an hour to the airport, but I needed the time to think and sort some things out. I never wanted to see an airport so bad in my life, than this moment right now. This was the worst trip I had taken in my grown life. I hurried inside because it was cold here. As soon as my foot touched the inside, I could hear over the intercom, my flight delayed for three hours because of the weather conditions. Just my luck, North Carolina was about to experience one of the worst winter storms ever. I am just standing here in one spot, cursing continuously to myself because there is nothing else I could do in this situation. I had two choices; one, I could stay here and wait the delay out, or two go back to the resort where it would be more comfortable for me. However, with that one, I could risk being stuck with Karen again and I really do not have the energy for that.

I decided to stay in the airport, it was closer to me getting out of there rather than staying at the resort. I wanted to call my mother, but at the same time, so much had occurred that I needed to take some time for myself and be alone. This trip was supposed to be like a vacation for me, but it turned out to be more stressful than my job. Family, they are the worst ones to deal with sometimes. I really did not mean to cause problems for my daddy and Karen. He just finally saw what I had been telling him for a long time now. It has been a couple of hours and another announcement comes that they are going to begin loading the plane. I am so anxious that I can finally get out of this place. I did not even get the chance to enjoy myself here, but I will have to return with the girls one day. Finally loading the plane, I did not get a chance to go through the whole airport. The plane ride back was much smoother than the one going to there. When I landed, I felt so relieved to be back in my own atmosphere that I did not know what to do with myself. Just as soon as I was able to claim my luggage, I headed to the parking garage to claim my car. Driving home, I called my mother and clued her in on the disastrous trip. My mother did not want to make a comment about my father and his wife; she did not want to say anything negative to me that would affect how I treat either one of them. Nevertheless, she just listened to what I had to say. I guess that is what a good mother does.

I pulled into my driveway and I felt sleep falling on me just because my body knew I was home. I could hear my phone ringing when before I got into the house. I hurried into the house to catch the phone; I could barely make out who was on the other end. The caller stated, "This is Logan from Rocky Memorial Hospital, calling to inform you that your father has been in an auto accident and wanted me to inform you". I was instantly frightened, "Can he talk...is he ok?" "He is fine and is going to stay here for a few hours for observations and after that he will be released to come home"… "I want to talk to him"… "Give me a moment and I will put him on the phone"… As much as I hated being at the mountains with my father and Karen, I was ready to go back to check on them both. My father came to the phone and reassured me that he was ok. It was nothing serious and he should be leaving soon. With me being the oldest child, I knew it was detrimental for me to be there at those moments. My father insisted that there was no need for me to jump back on a flight. The hospital was going to release him within a couple of hours. Most of the night, I was unable to sleep wondering if I made the right decision or night of not going back down there. Before I was able to go to bed Sunday night, my father called to say that they were back at the resort and would be catching the first flight out on Monday morning.

I decided to unpack my things and settle myself in for the evening. I did not want to talk to anyone because I just was not in the mood for conversation. Since I already had Monday and Tuesday off, I decided to have some time alone to think. With no days off since the promotion, everything in my house was a mess. Well, Brian has something to do with that. When I woke up Monday morning, I changed into some lounging clothes, something relaxing, turned on my T.I. cd, lit some incense, and pulled out my planner to sort out some details for the rest of the week. I know that I have not talked to the girls and I am going to hear that on Wednesday. I have not checked on my managers to see if everything was running smoothly. I even did not have a chance to pay my bills before I left. I had many things to do personally and after I thought some, it was not such a bad thing that the trip was short. While I am chilling, I get a knock at the door so, I asked, "Who is it?"

"Why don't you answer it and find out?"

"Oh Lord, I know who that is, didn't I just get finish saying that I wanted to be alone". I opened the door and there was Brian, I do not even know what to call him. We have been on and off for a while now, so, it is what it is. "What are you doing home?"

"What are you doing here if you knew I was supposed to be out of town"?

"I was just riding by to check on the house for you."

"Boy, stop, you don't even just stop by to check on the house, you were being nosey as hell!"

"So, what if I was?" "What the hell" as I laugh at him. He has something to say for everything. "Look, I am trying to handle some business right now."

"I am trying to handle some personal business of my own. Brian moves closer to her, as he is trying to go in for a kiss. Jayden backs up from him. "Didn't I tell you that I was trying to finish up something here?"

"You have time to do this shit later."

"How in the world are you going to call my business shit? I don't do that to you."

"Oh Lord, here we go."

"You right, here we go." "Look I did not ask you to come over here". As Jayden talks, he kisses her and she drops everything that she has in her hand, hits the floor and they go at it none stop. Their lovemaking is so passionate that it shows the deep connection and emotion that they both share for each other. This is exactly what Jayden is afraid of with Brian. She wants her first love to be work and love second. She continues to have that challenge. Two hours later, she wakes up and realizes that it was four o'clock. She could not believe it. She wakes Brian up and he pulls her back into the bed and makes her lie back down and relax. Never wanting to face the reality of her relationship issues with Brian, she tries her best to avoid them. Keeping his cool for the first time in their dealings, he convinces Jayden that she will have all the time in the world to plan her schedule but the one thing that she cannot plan is happiness. Apparently, that statement bothered her, so she contently lay next to Brian without a word. Brian ended up spending the night. Whatever they ate, they did it in bed. If they watched television, it was in bed. Jayden had a smile so wide on her face as if she was in the fairytale of her dreams.

She explains to Brian that she has to handle some business with her job. "I really have to check on my managers or I won't have any managers to check on"… "Handle that and then I want you to come back and handle me". Jayden giggles at the comment that Brian made. Jayden afraid to open her heart and soul to Brian, she enjoys his company and companionship. Never once did she really express her feelings and the future of their relationship. When she finished making her calls, Brian tells her that he wants to talk to her about something. Unexpectedly Brian states, "I want to talk about us and our future". With a nervous look on her face, Jayden responds, "What did you want to talk about"? "I have been thinking that we should be monogamous, seriously"… Why do you want to discuss this right now?" "I feel that now is a good time. In college, your priorities were in other places in which I knew were more important. I have taken the back road for long enough and I want you."

"I want you too, but I don't know if I want something that serious right now."

"Huh, what the fuck do you mean, you don't want something that serious right now." As Brian really gets angry, he gets out of the bed and puts his clothes back on. Jayden, not knowing what to say, just watched him get dressed. She wanted to tell him how he felt, but the words just could not come out of her mouth. Brian grabs his things and heads for the door saying, "Call me when you ready for something serious". Again, Jayden does not have anything to say and the words just would not come out of her mouth. "All I want to do is cry because I knew I let my husband walk out of the door. I just did not know how to say it." Jayden crawled into bed for the rest of the evening. "Not only do I feel bad about Daddy and Karen, I feel bad about what I did to Brian. I just keep messing things up." Before Jayden lay down for the evening, she sent a text message to Lauren, Dalia, and Blake to meet her at Starbucks at nine in the morning. Before she could wait for a response, she went to bed feeling down about her weekend and especially about what happened with her and Brian.

Chapter 5: I Need My Girls

Arriving one at a time, Dalia, Blake, Lauren, and Jayden all got in the line to order their coffees. They sit at a long round table where they are staring each other in the face. Curious to see who was going to break the ice first, Jayden jumps up and says, "Where in the hell have all of you been when I was going through shit and Brian ass getting emotional with me? Y'all know I can't deal with that shit." Everyone burst out laughing at what Jayden says, but it breaks the ice. Therefore, Lauren asks Jayden, "What in the world? Brian getting emotional, what did you do to him?"

Jayden replies, "Nothing. I think he is going through a damn mid-life crisis or some shit and it came out of nowhere!"

"Well, if you think that is bad, I slept with Jason the other night and it was great," states Lauren. Everyone's reaction is like, "What!"

"Where did he come from?" states Blake. "That is what I was thinking to myself." "How did he find out where you live?"

"I do not know, but he showed up at my door...?" Lauren stops in the middle of her sentence noticing that Blake and Dalia had very little to say.

"What is the problem, why are you looking like someone died?" states Jayden. "Do you want me to tell them"?

"Tell us what"... "Blake's father died last week and she did not tell anyone." "What do you mean, not telling anyone? I don't get that. We are supposed to be your girls. Honey, how are you doing", replies Jayden.

"I am as best as I can be right now. I just need to be around happy faces and friends."

"Well, you know that is us and we are they", states Jayden. "I told you that they were going to cheer you up," states Lauren.

Jayden turned to Dalia and realized not a word has come out of her mouth since they got there. "What in the hell...?"... "Not today, ok, I am just not in the mood for that," states Dalia. "I want to know why you sitting here like you looking for attention or some shit!"

"Nothing, I thought I could do this, but I can't". Dalia gets up out of her seat and leaves. Jayden is looking surprised because she has never seen Dalia act like that. If anyone knew Dalia, it was Jayden. They have a connection that runs stronger than the other women that sat at that table. Their past has built an every lasting relationship between the two of them and created a bond stronger than blood. Trying not to draw too much attention to Dalia's scene, Jayden continued talking to Blake and Lauren. Being as curious as they are, "What is wrong with Dalia?"

Is she going through one of her moments?" asks Lauren. "I do not know, but I will be damn sure to find out before the sun sets in this muthafuka." The girls laugh at Jayden; they know she has a crazy sense of humor. The girls continue to catch up with each other.

Lauren not thinking much of her situation wonders how Blake is dealing with the death of her father; she begins to focus all of her attention on Blake. Being as close as she was to her father, it had to be taking a toll on her. Looking sympathetic towards Blake, she asks, "What are you going to do?"

"There is nothing for me to do but work my ass off right now. All I can think about is what I am going to do for the holidays. What am I going to do on him and mom's wedding anniversary? Who am I going to call for advice? Who is going to tell me I knew you could do it? Who is going to walk me down the aisle when I get married? Who is going to be there when I have my first child? I just don't know what to do right now and it feels like a bad dream that I cannot wake up from." By this time, Jayden and Lauren are consoling Blake. Blake becomes very emotional, being that her feelings and emotions are all over the place, she began telling some true feelings that she was feeling. She told the girls that she only used men for the things that she wanted because every guy she met did not measure up to her father, so, they were not important. She depended on her father, which made it easier to dismiss all the men in her life. She finally confessed of wanting to settle down, but she did not want to settle for less to marry. The girls understood what she was saying because they all have demands when it comes to men. Running low on beverages, Jayden got up and got Blake another Vanilla cappuccino, which was her favorite drink. To Lauren, Blake states, "I do not want to forget to tell the girls about going to visit my mother in Jersey, don't let me forget."

"I gotcha, I won't let you forget," replies Lauren.

Jayden returns to the table with her drink, asking Blake, "How is your sister Blair? She knows she is too cute for the clothes that she wears!"

"Stop, you know you wrong for that, Jayden," states Lauren. "You know I am telling the truth and Blake knows how her sister is."

"When you met her, she did act a little snooty, but once you get to know her she is the best," states Blake. "But, she is fine. She is doing much better than me, I think."

"Girl, you know she could not wait to take over that company." Quickly, Lauren kicks Jayden under the table. She knew she had gone too far too soon for Blake to be able to deal with. Noticing what Lauren did, "I saw that and it is cool. I wonder myself if that is what my sister's intentions from the beginning. Because I am not there, I do not know what Daddy was thinking before he died, or his relationship with Blair. Oh, before I forget, my mother wants all of us to come for a visit."

"You mean to tell me that your mother wants me there, she don't like me," states Jayden. "Oh Lord, who told you that my mother has never said anything negative about you," states Blake. "So, when are we going to be taking this trip, and does Dalia know about this yet?" asks Jayden. "I was going to mention here today, but she left before I could tell you all. And what is wrong with her?" Agreeing with Blake, Lauren is curious what has Dalia all in despair to make her skip out on the girls' day.

While the girls are still enjoying themselves at Starbucks, Dalia returns to her home sobbing about her trials. Not able to ignore what has been bothering her anymore, she actually hit rock bottom on Wednesday. She has really resorted to the bottle to solve and ease the pain instead of dealing with the issue at hand. Putting on the front with everyone has made today one of the worst possible days that she has faced. She is now putting everything that she worked so hard for at risk. She does not even realize it. Her performance at work is starting to suffer and her superiors are thinking that she is just slacking off while Carmen knows the whole situation, but she cannot say anything to anyone. Playing her jazz again, she opens a bottle of wine and pours a glass for herself as the tears roll down her face slowly. She goes to her outhouse again and pulls her tub out looking for a particular portfolio of wedding designs. Something else that she kept a secret is that she dreamed of getting married to Terrance, but she never discussed it. In this particular portfolio, she had everything planned and described out of how she wanted everything. She had the color of the maid of honor, bridesmaid, junior bridesmaid, groomsmen, flower girls, and ring bearer attire. Her colors were cinnamon and chocolate brown. These were not her favorite colors, but for a nice fall wedding, she knew that those colors would coordinate well with her and Terrance. Flipping through ever page, she wanted to drown herself. Without wondering why she left her girls, she just kept pulling herself away from them when she knew she needed them the most.

Her job calls and she tries to compose her self to answer the call. "Hello... "My I speak to Dalia Little?"

"This is she."

"This is Tiffany from Bartland Hospital. I was calling to see if everything was ok. We haven't heard seen or heard anything from you in a couple of days. We know it is not like you to miss work."

"I apologize, Tiffany. I have been dealing with something for the past week."

"Is it something medical or something that we need to be aware of? If you need to take a short leave of absence, I can fax you the paperwork now and you can fill it out and send it back to me, if you like."

"That would be a great idea; I could really use the time".

"That won't be a problem; we can always do that for our management".

"You are a life saver, Tiffany. I will get that back to you." No, thank you Dalia, we want to make sure that you are ok". "Thanks". They both hung up the phone. Dalia thought to herself that they were only concerned about the job and not about her.

She began to check her voicemail and all she had were messages from Terrance. Still ignoring his calls, she deletes the messages and acts as if she did not get them. She does this while she is still going through her memory box of wedding plans. She began tearing up again thinking that if she continued to cry it out, it would soon get much easier to deal with and the pain would get better. Drowning in her sorrow, she moves from looking in her wedding portfolios to looking at all the pictures that she and Terrance took together thinking about all the good times that they had together. Confused as she could be, she did not know what she wanted to do with her relationship, leave it, or fix it. Thinking about how distant she was with the girls, she felt bad about how she acted because none of them had clue of what was going on with her. She thought about calling them and explaining, but she was in no shape to do that. Then, she thought about sending them text messages to avoid a phone conversation that would lead to questions and more questions that she did not feel like giving answers to. She decided not to do anything, not hoping that they would reach out to her, but that she needed space to get herself together. With Dalia being such a strong person, she did not want anyone to see her at this point, feeling vulnerable, emotions all over place, and confused.

Meanwhile while the girls are at Starbucks, Terrance happens to walk in, so being friendly as they were, they called him over to the table. They all hugged him and asked him how he was doing. "Hey, how are you doing man, haven't seen you in a while," state the women. Terrance, who has this shocked look on his face, does not know how to react to this because he does not know if they are being sincere or sarcastic at this point. He responds, "I am alright, trying to make it that is all". They reply, "Yeah, I know what you mean." "Oh, you do, that is surprising," states Terrance. Now, the girls are confused because they know something isn't right but they do not seem to know what it is. Blake wants to leave it alone because that is just the person that she is. Jayden on other hand thought, "Hell no, there is more to this than what he is was saying." Lauren interjects, "I think we should check on our girl to see what is up cause something is not right." Terrance goes to get his coffee; the girls are having this conversation trying to figure out what was going on. They are all watching Terrance like a hawk and he notices it. Therefore, Dalia being curious as hell asks Terrance, "How is Dalia?" He replies, "She is good". Jayden looks like she doesn't even know. Something ain't right, which is what she tells the girls after she returns to the table after talking to Terrance. He leaves Starbucks and tells the women goodbye. Blake wanted to let it go until Dalia said something to inform them. Jayden disagreed while Lauren said she would rather know before she got involved in her business. "Y'all bitches are crazy 'cause this is our girl and you know something is wrong. It is not us being nosey; it is trying to figure out why Dalia is acting weird as hell. Don't ask unconcern 'cause then I would think that you all don't give a damn and I hope that is not the case."

"Girl, you know that ain't the case. I just don't want to pry where Dalia don't want me to," states Blake. "Well, that may be true, but this kind of fell into our lap. He walked in here looking guilty as hell. I am with Jayden on this one. Something ain't right and it is our duty as the home girls to find out". Jayden hi-five Lauren and tells Blake, "Get with it cause you going with us too", states Jayden. "Where are we going and do we have to do it today, right now", asks Blake. "We are going to Dalia's house to check on her," says Jayden, "Ok, let's go since you won't let this go," replies Blake. "Yes, ma'am, if it were you, we would be doing the same thing. You just be glad that I wasn't here when you came up missing to go to Jersey", states Jayden. They all left Starbucks and headed to the car. They decided to ride with Lauren since her car was the closest. While riding Blake brings up the trip to visit her mother, "No one said if we were all going to Jersey."

"And you didn't say when you wanted this trip to take place," coming from Lauren. "Well, I knew we were going to have to work around everyone's schedule, so I wanted to see what we guys wanted to do."

"I am in, states Jayden, what about you Lauren."

"I already told Blake that I was ready to take a vacation, you chicks have taken trips, and mini vacations and I haven't been anywhere."

"And whose fault is that?" asks Jayden.

They arrive at Dalia's condominium, they see her car in the garage, but it is dark. Hesitant about going up to the door, they look at each other wondering who was going to get out of the car first. Blake looks at Jayden, "Since you were so anxious to come over and be nosey, you should be the one to go to the door." "No, we are all going up there together; don't punk out on me, we are supposed to be girls. How many times do I have to remind you of that?"

Lauren states, "We are here, aren't we. We are going in and we are going to find out something, but we can't make her take, we can only ask," looking at Jayden. Lauren knows how aggressive and determined Jayden can be when she gets her mind set on something and she doesn't want her to take it overboard with Jayden in the house. Lauren knocks on the door and they wait. No one comes to the door, so she knocks again. Lauren looks at Jayden, "Don't say anything, just wait a minute."

"You know I am trying to compose myself, 'cause this shit don't make any sense for her to act like that with us," states Jayden. She began getting louder outside, so anyone in the vicinity could here what she was saying, "Open the door D, we know you are in there". They finally see her shadow coming from the other room.

Dalia opens the door looking like hell. The women's mouths drop open. The first thing Blake says, "What the hell is wrong with you, you ditch us this morning and when we come here to check on you and you look like you lost your best friend." Dalia walks away from the door and the women come in the house and shut the door. Observing things closely, they notice the wine bottles and one glass. They see how dull the house is and that something more serious than what they thought was going on. Surprisingly Dalia opened the door to let her friends see her at her lowest, she doesn't say much to them at first, she just has the sadden look on her face as she sits on the couch watching whatever was on the television. The women glanced at each other for a moment, but the only one willing to break the ice was Lauren, "Honey, what is wrong, talk to us."

"I just have a lot going on right now and I just want to deal with it my way," states Dalia. Quickly, Blake turns to the Lauren and Jayden, "See, that is our queue that we need to leave and let her be." Jayden states, "After seeing all of this, you know we ain't going anywhere."

"I agree with you, Jayden." Lauren looks at Blake thinking what is wrong with her. Again, Dalia does not respond to her friends. She just sits there and stares at the television. Dalia, wanting to try another approach, gave Blake and Lauren the eye, which meant for them to back off and let her try in her own way. Jayden gets close to Dalia sitting on the couch and asks, "What is wrong? Did someone die? Did you lose your job? Are you sick?" All these questions running through her mind, she is trying to figure out what is wrong with Dalia, 'cause she is giving complete silence. Dalia looks up at her lightly and states, "He don't love me anymore".

Trying to figure out whom exactly she was talking about that would have her like that. Looking up at the bar where the girls were, she caught the glance from Lauren who whispers, "Terrance."

"Shit, you have got to be more careful," states Jayden. She looks at Dalia and asks her, "Are you talking about Terrance? Can't be 'cause we just saw him at Starbucks." Thinking about what she just said, she is recalling in her head how weird he was acting with them when they asked him how he was doing. Dalia tells Jayden, "We broke up". Curious to know what would have been so detrimental for them to end their relationship, Blake and Lauren moved in closer to the living room asking "Why". Dalia now wanting to open up looks at all of them, "He cheated on me".

With disgust on Jayden's face, she comes out, "What the fuck. Tell me you lying" Confirming it Dalia states, "I caught him in here. I came home from work and caught him the house with another woman in our bedroom". Instant Blake feels so bad for wanting to let it be, she goes into the bedroom to find Dalia some clothes. The women knew that they were not going to let her stay there by herself and deal with that alone. Lauren looks for Dalia's phone, purse, and planner, Jayden asks Lauren, "What the hell does she need with her planner... to plan when she is going to cry, get that shit outta here". Dalia tells them quietly that she doesn't want to go anywhere, but they pay her no attention and continue getting her ready to leave the house. Jayden tells her, "Yes, you are leaving here and you are coming with us. We are going to have a wonderful day to take you mind off of this". Jayden walks off for a minute and says softly, "That son-of-a-bitch, if you gonna do your dirt, why in the hell would you do it in the same house as your woman". Over hearing what she said, Blake says, "I would have killed him and made her watch". "High-sedity, you would have done what", chuckling at how Blake is reacting to the situation. "I would have forgotten that I was a professional that day"... "Girl, I would have paid to see that, continues Jayden.

They gathered everything including Dalia and headed out of the door. First, stop to the spa. They could all use that. They didn't want to ask questions, so they resume on with plans of having a good day at the spa. By this time, they had done Dalia's hair, makeup, and clothes. Her face and mindset not ready for mingling or smiling, she knew it would be good for her mentally to get out and do something different. Upon Lauren's suggestion, they went to her favorite spa that she only goes on Friday. They signed Dalia up for the works; an hour-long massage, manicure, facial, and time in the sauna. Without thinking about how much of all that was going to cost, the women knew that it was something that they had to do with Dalia for the sake of friendship. Starting with the massages, they could only go in pairs in the same room. Blake volunteered to go along with Dalia in the room. She grabbed her hand and they went with the masseuse. They changed clothes in a private room and they went into door number one, which had candles lit and coffee already prepared on a table. The ladies fixed their coffee to their liking and chatted while they waited. A voice response came on which frightened them, "In fifteen minutes, your massage will begin. In order to receive the ultimate service, clients must be lying flat on their stomachs with towels removed. Thank you so much and your patience is greatly appreciated". While the ladies heard this message, they continued drinking their coffee. Since they were alone, Blake wanted to ask Dalia what really happened. Without having to ask anything, Dalia began, "I don't know what happened. We were fine one day and the next he is cheating on me". Not knowing what to say, Blake responded, "Have you talked to him to see why it happened?"... "Talk to him, I don't even want to hear his voice or his name"... "Hey, my mother wanted all of us to come to Jersey for a visit since she is alone now. I think it would be a good trip for you to take with us. It will give you a chance to clear your mind and think about what you really want to do 'cause throwing in the towel is not the answer. You have to decide if it is worth fixing or if you don't have anything left to give to the relationship". Dalia responded, "You are right. I am ready to pack my bags". They hug each other and this was the first time that Dalia actually smiled in over a week. They received their massages and they moved on to the sauna. There, they linked up with Lauren and Jayden, who also enjoyed their massages. They discussed what they were going to do after they left the spa. "There is life outside of this place", states Dalia. They all laugh together. "Things are finally feeling normal again, states Lauren. "We all know we are far from it, states Jayden. "But, we still have this unit with each other and that is all that matters", states Blake.

Leaving out of the sauna, they took showers to refresh themselves and prepared for their facials. They all chose to have different types of things done to their faces, but linked up again for their pedicures and manicures. Leaving the spa, Blake made the suggestion to go to the mall to get new dresses for dinner. Jayden and Dalia both state, "Why do we need new dresses for dinner"? Blake states, "It is a part of the ambience for our girls' day out". At the mall, they found nice dresses that characterized their personalities. Lauren found a nice light, short beach dress with spaghetti straps that complimented her long legs and her honey tone complexion. Blake chose a cranberry, pencil leg dress coming right beneath her knees, they complimented her small figure. Jayden, who likes earthy tones, picked a black simple dress where she was able to accessorize with jewelry. That was more of her style. Dalia could go either way with her style. She chose to wear a camel turtleneck, sleeveless, pencil skirt dress with a leopard print belt to compliment it. When Dalia tried this dress on, the only thing that Blake could say, "Damn, you look like a model. How come we don't get to see you dress like that regularly"? Dalia states, "It is because I don't have the need to. I work in a hospital with sick people, so I wear scrubs most of the time. Then, when I do go out, I tend to stick to nice pants and a top". "Ima need you to break out of that and do you", says Blake. The rest of the women agreeing with Blake admire Dalia's look.

Leaving the mall, they decided to go to a nice restaurant for dinner. Lauren called ahead to make reservations for the four of them. They had to decide whose house they were going to go to so they could change for dinner. It was a girls' night out and they wanted to get cute. Blake offered her house up for everyone to come back to. Dalia asked aloud, "Who picked up my phone from the house"? Lauren stated, "I have it, I don't think I brought it in the store though. It may be in the car". "I need to check that", states Dalia. "Are you trying to see if Terrance called you", states Jayden. "There are other people who call me besides him", replies Dalia. "I was just asking", states Jayden. "Are you ready to go, cause we are going to be late for our reservation. You know we are going to need time to do hair and makeup. I know how long it takes Blake to do her hair", Lauren states. "I can't believe you put me out there like that when you are more worried about your hair than I am", Blake interjects. "It doesn't matter, we just need to put a move on", states Lauren. "I am ready, how about the rest of you"... "I am ready too"... "Alright, let's check out and head to Blake's house. At the counter, Jayden could not find her checkbook and her credit card was in her other purse at home;

nonetheless, Blake told her privately that she would pick up the tab on her dress. Feeling uncomfortable, Jayden tells Blake that she will pay her back once she gets her ATM card. Blake tells her not to worry about because she did not buy her anything for Christmas. They laughed, gathered their bags, and left the store heading to the car.

Enjoying the ride in the car, Blake whispered to Jayden, "Don't worry about dinner, just add your meal to my tab". She whispers back, "I don't feel comfortable doing that". They go back and forth about the issue, which turns into a full-blown conversation that is no longer a whisper. Lauren and Dalia are not wondering what they were talking about. Not trying to drawn anymore attention to their private conversation, Blake just told them, "It is nothing, just Jayden being hard-headed like her normal self. "Oh, don't we know about that", as Dalia puts that out there. "What is that suppose to me", Jayden feeling offended. "It means that you don't listen to us sometimes, and you do what you want to do"… "Isn't that what grown ass people do, do their own thing", Dalia arguing her point across to her friends. Lauren being quiet in this conversation does not have much to say. "Grown people don't always have to object to every opposition", states Dalia. "What in the hell, are we going to continue the whole ride talking about how I don't listen to you guys", states Jayden. "Don't think this conversation is over", states Lauren. They pulled in the driveway at Blake's home. Blake has not lived in this house long, but she has managed to decorate it down to every room with her own liking. The women adore the moderations that she has made over the course of months to her house. She does not want to boast about her house; Blake just loved having her own space.

Getting dress together was an event in itself to these women. They would take turns trying on each other's makeup and exchanging tips that they learned. Never jealous of the other, they admired the likes and dislike each woman had to offer to their friendship. Taking over an hour to get dressed, there is a knock at Blake's door. Not expecting anyone, she runs downstairs in her robe to answer the door. She asks, "Who is it?" She opens the door to see Terrance standing there. Looking suave as ever, he politely asks, "Can I see Dalia". Trying to be quiet Blake states, "I don't think now would be a good time. All of us are here Lauren, Jayden, and Dalia. You don't want this to turn into something big". Not caring, Terrance becomes very persistent about wanting to talk to Dalia. Trying to repeatedly explain to Terrance that now wasn't a good time; Dalia comes downstairs asking if I had a lipstick to match her dress. Instantly at the top of the stairwell she sees Terrance. You could tell by the look in her eyes that she was still in love with him. Immediately, Blake leaves the two of them alone so they could talk. Dalia continues coming down the stairs, "What are you doing here and why would you track me down at Blake's house". He responds, "It is Wednesday and the four of you would have to be at someone's house. After all the years we have been together, it wasn't hard to figure it out. I just want you to hear me out, give me a chance to explain myself". Listening to him says this, Dalia looks at him, "Why should I give you the opportunity to explain yourself. You have said enough with your action. Terrance having a look of compassion on his face, "I want you and only you". Dalia becomes emotional and this is what she wanted to avoid until she would be able to handle it. Noticing that her makeup and hard work of getting ready to go out with the girls had gone down the drain after talking with Terrance, she did not want to let the girls down nor did she want to go back to that dull feeling she had. He wanted to have his time to talk with her, but she was not ready for that, as Blake saw her emotion raged when she saw Terrance from the stairwell. Dalia did promise him that she would talk to him later after she spent the evening with the girls. Accepting the invitation back to the home they shared later that evening, Terrance handed her the flowers he brought, which were the same flowers that she and Shawn saw on her car when they left out of the house on their way out for dinner. Taking a little time for herself before returning back upstairs, Dalia went into Blake's sunroom, which was dark and quiet just like Dalia's mood at this moment. Blake stealing away from the other women knew that Terrance's presence would have that affect on her.

When Blake comes down the stairs, she looks for Dalia in every room only to find her in the sunroom looking out the window with tears coming down her face. Lauren and Jayden noticing that Dalia had been gone for a while began calling for her throughout the house wanting to share some cleansing tips that were experimenting with. Coming down the stairwell, they did not hear anything, but they did end up finding Blake and Dalia in the sunroom. Dalia in Blake's arms, crying her heart out. Lauren and Jayden not knowing what happened quickly assumed that she was letting out her anger that she felt for Terrance. Blake tells the others, "Terrance was just here". Instantly, Jayden remarks, "What? Why did he come here and what did he do to her". Blake answered, "It wasn't anything that he said directly to her, this is something that she needs to deal with alone, you here me Jayden". "When did you get a backbone", asks Jayden to Blake. Lauren turns to Dalia, "Do you still want to go out, we can stay right here, order take out, drink wine, listen to jazz, and let you vent it all out, if you want". Not hesitating, Dalia states, "I want to go out with my girls and have a good night. We promised not to let anything come in between our Wednesdays and that was a solemn oath. Don't you all remember that?" Instantly, the room became overwhelmed with Dalia's statement. They knew the symbolism of what Dalia was getting at, so they complied and got themselves prepared to leave for dinner. Lauren took Dalia upstairs to do her make up over, Blake, and Jayden took a moment of remembering what struggles and sacrifices they made to create the bond they now share.

Getting ready to leave, Lauren called the restaurant to let them know that they were going to be late. Everyone grabbing his or her purses and cell phones, hurried out of the door eager to enjoy the night. They have all focused so much on Dalia that they almost forgot about the issues they we are facing. The friendship that the four of them share is very rare and yet they do not regret anything that they have done for her. The gratification that Dalia felt comfortable and was able to wear a smile this Wednesday made a world of difference to these women. They arrive at the restaurant, anxious as ever, Lauren let the host know that they had reservations. Scrambling to their seats, they all shared a smile across the table all through the trials they faced the week prior, from death to infidelity. They managed to maintain their dignity and respect. First thing they wanted to order was a good bottle of wine. Not knowing how much Dalia has drawn herself to alcohol, they ordered this bottle of wine and Dalia's face lit it. The women ordered from chicken to steak, some of the best on the menu. They began discussing their trip to New Jersey. Blake gets excited that all of her friends are going back home with her. "Are we going to drive or fly", asks Blake. "Girl, don't nobody fly from New Jersey to Maryland when the drive isn't that long", states Jadyen. "Well, what do the rest of you want to do", as Blake makes the remark to the rest of them. "I wouldn't bother me either way that we do", replied Lauren. "Dalia what do you think", states Lauren. "I would like the ride better. It would give me time to think". "Then, we are going to drive there", states Jayden. "Ok, this is my question. What in the hell are we going to do there and how long is this trip supposed to be", states Jayden. Blake looking around the table, "Well, I thought we could stay there for a couple of days"... "And how many days would that be, 'cause you know some of us have jobs that we can't be off that long, you know", states Jayden. Everyone else knowing that Jayden was going to have something to say just let Blake answer her questions. Blake responds, "Three of four days at the max if that is ok with you, Jay"... "I guess that is fine", states Jayden. The waiter comes to the table and asks if anyone has room for dessert and they looked around at each other and they all said, "Why the hell not". Blake and Lauren ordered Caramel Cheesecake, which was their favorite while Dalia ordered a Chocolate Mousse Cake, and Jayden ordered Tiramisu. Since these desserts were in large portions, they had to get a box to take it home.

While eating their dessert, Lauren looked to Blake and asked her, "How are you doing?" Not expecting that, Blake stated, "I am making it". "That is the same thing that you have been saying for the past couple of days", says Lauren. "I don't know what you want me to say"... "Ok, I will let it go", replies

Lauren. "What she is saying is that you lost your damn Daddy and all you can say is that you are making it", interjects Jayden. "Stop, Jay, you always go too far," states Dalia. "That is because you all don't say what you mean. Everyone at this table knows the kind of relationship Blake had with her father. She just don't want to open up to us", states Jayden. Everyone turns and look at Blake, "Is this true, Blake. You don't want to open up to us, why, is this the reason for this trip to Jersey?" asked Dalia. "Look, I don't want to bother you all with my issues. My father is dead and gone. He is not coming back. There is no need of me bringing him up and talking about him all the time", Blake states, as she gets frustrated. "We all need our time to grieve and deal with issues, but can't keep these kinds of feelings on the inside", states Dalia. "Hold the hell up, Blake does this have anything to do with what you told me" says Lauren. "What do you mean? Do you know something I don't know, states Jayden". "I don't know anything", states Lauren. "Then what was the statement all about if you don't know anything", states Dalia. "I just found out some things when my father died", states Blake. "You are acting like that is supposed to change your feelings for him. He was still your father who took care of you and made you the woman you are today," states Jayden. "I just don't want to talk about it right now. Is that fine with you", states Blake. The table instantly quiet. The waiter comes and asks if they were ready for the checks. Blake answers the waiter, "Yes, and you can put mine and Jayden's on the same ticket. The women pay their tab and leave the restaurant. It was now time for them to go back to their own houses alone and deal with their own issues.

Departing from Blake's house, they all exhaled because they had to leave their little boxes of friendship that they surrounded themselves with every Wednesday. Lauren, on her way home, checked her voice mail, and had two messages from Jason. She was not excited or looking forward to having that conversation with him. She wanted to avoid that it happened and it appeared to her that Jason wanted something more of out one night. Somehow, she felt like she had moved past that part of her life and on to something new. Glad that the conversation at dinner did not surround her, she knew that she was not in the mood to discuss Jason. Blake would have loved to talk about that all night. Thinking about how to plan her Thursday, Lauren received a text message from Blake telling her thank for not mentioning her long lost sister, Carmen. Lauren replied to her, "Not a problem, but you know they are bound to find out sooner or later". They text back and forth until Lauren gets home. By that time, Blake text her last text before falling asleep she was exhausted from her day with the girls. Lauren planned her mind "First, check email. Second, set up time to meet with new client, Albemarle, schedule second interview with job in Canada, and remember don't tell the girls until I know for sure that I am going to take the job". Lauren applied for several jobs recently not because she was not happy with her job, but she was running from the one thing she could not control in her life, marriage, a topic that she didn't care to discuss with anyone. Her life was getting so normal that the only new adventurous thing for her to do would be to settle down and since Jason has appeared into the picture, Lauren wanted to run far away. As confident and together she appears to be with her friends, she hides this part from them, but little does she know that it is all going to come and not in the best way.

Jayden, on the other hand, thinks about her actions prior to her going out with her friends. She contemplated if she overreacted with Brian or if she didn't take him seriously, when he was being honest. Taking the long way home, she stopped by a bar closer to Blake's house just to clear her mind. Jayden, the bold one, was never afraid to face her fears or challenges head on. Somehow, when she walks into the bar, her older cousin Gerald is there. They talk for a while and he sees the fucked up look that Jayden has. He looks at her, "You better fix it". She responds, "How do you know that I need to fix something". "Girl, I have known you all your life and you only have that look when have fucked yourself. Fix it", states Gerald. Jayden leaves the bar in a hurry with her mind on Brian. She heads over to his house. Not thinking about calling before she goes over there, she pulls into the driveway, runs up to the door, uses her key to go in, and surprisingly she finds a woman in the house, but Brian is not there. Instantly, she thought about Dalia's situation and thought that this was his new chick he was messing with. She asked the woman who she was. She responded, "Who are you". Getting even more enraged, she goes into her pocketbook and what do you know, Jay has a piece on her. The other woman in the house began to look frightened. She looks at Jayden and states, "You have until I count to ten to get the fuck out of this house or there will be polka dots all over these walls"! The door burst open, "What the fuck is going on in here"; Brian walks through the door. Jayden turns the gun towards Brian, "Please tell me you are not messing with this half ass woman". Brian moves in closer to Jayden with the gun directly on his chest, "Who's your man? You know I like all woman in one woman". With tears starting to come down her face, "Then, who is this chick?" Rubbing his head, "She is Dre's cousin. She spent the night hear cause she is going to school up here". Looking embarrassed and relieved at the same time, Jayden states "She does look a little young", she apologized to the girl and she drops the gun out of her hand. Brian kisses her and hugs her saying, "Don't come into my house acting stupid again, but it turned me on". He began taking her clothes off in the living room, kissing her all over her body. She moans and moans louder and louder. She began taking Brian's clothes off beginning with his shirt and then his pants. He picks her up and takes her to the master bedroom. He laid her on the bed kissing her from head to toe. Jayden thinking to her self that she had reached heaven as Brian kissed her navel then he moved down until she reached the climatic stage of their lovemaking. For hours, the two of them make love until the sun comes up.

Dalia walks into her house and she could hear the door creeping. She felt better today then she did the last couple of days. Before she is able to put her pocketbook down, she gets a knock at the door, forgetting that she promised Terrance he could stop by to talk. When she opens the door to see Terrance sobbing horribly with flowers in his hand, she could feel the pain he was going through. Without saying a word, Dalia invited Terrance in the house. She began to explain to Terrance, "I don't know what I want right now so, there is no need for us to talk about that". Terrance looking empathetic towards Dalia explains to her, "I want to give you your space, but I don't want you to push me away". Dalia tells him, "I don't think you want me to talk about this right now". Dalia thinking about what she did to Carmen in the restaurant. Then, she thought about it again. To her self, "I attacked the wrong party in this case. I should have killed him instead. He is the one who betrayed me in this situation". Dalia's look changes and Terrance saw this in her eyes. He tells her, "I will call you tomorrow". Dalia does not react to anything that Terrance says at this point. When he leaves out of the door, she throws her vase at the door smashing it to pieces. She is thinking how she could have been so stupid all these years to put her trust in someone who would have betrayed her in this way. Dalia did not want to fall back into the same rut she was in before she went out with her friends. She grabbed her bag, turned off the lights, and headed for the door. When she opened the door, Terrance was standing there waiting for her to open the door. He looked Dalia in her eyes, "Baby, I love you with all my being. You are my world and I would give the world just to be in your presence again. You are my everything and my reason for being. There is no one I would rather be with but you". He grabs her hand, "Terrance, I don't want to go there tonight", states Dalia. "What do I have to do to make you see that I am sorry", as Terrance pours out his heart to Dalia. "You don't have to do anything as I need time to get myself together and I don't need you around while I think". With a bit of pity on his face Terrance explains, "I don't have anywhere to go, babe. I have been staying with a friend and my time as ran out. I don't have anywhere else to." Dalia looks with disgust on her face, "Are you serious? After all that you have done, you want to stay here". "This is my house, dammit and I can stay here if I want to", Terrance began to raise his voice of frustration towards Dalia. "You can sleep in the other bedroom or on the couch, but not in my bed", states Dalia. Not replying to Dalia, Terrance goes to get a blanket and pillow so that he could go to sleep. As angry as she was, she tried to go to sleep, trying not to think about Terrance. The hardest thing was how she could get him out of her mind when he is in the house with her. Dalia lays down her bed, "Another day, Lord", and she goes to sleep.

Chapter 6: New Jersey: I Can't Wait

Thursday morning and the women are ready to face a new day. The day before they leave to go to Blake's house, they have many loose ends to tie up. They most worried about the trip, Jayden, ponders all day about what they are going to do and if Blake's sister is going to be there. Dalia wanting the getaway to clear her mind, packs way ahead of time; Lauren wanting to take this vacation because she knows she would not be able to do it on her own. Blake knowing that her father's death has been harder than what she has led her friends to believe awaits the trip just to see how she could coup with her father not being there. Early Thursday morning, the women talk on three way arranging last minute plans. They ended up renting a sizable SUV so that everyone could be comfortable with themselves and their things. They planned to depart Friday afternoon. It would be a change for everyone to work and tie loose ends.

While at her home Thursday evening, Jayden was on the phone with a girlfriend of hers from back home talking about when they were going to hang out again. While doing so, Brian walks in the door anxiously waiting to see Jayden. He walked through the house looking and calling her name, not knowing she was on the phone. Very private about her relationship with Brian, she immediately, hushed him so that he friend on the phone could not hear his voice. Jayden continues her conversation on the phone while Brian turned on the television and watched Jayden packed. Clueless about the trip, Brian waits for her to get off the phone. She finally hangs up the phone and the first thing that Brian does is kiss her continuously telling her how much he missed her from the other day. Then, smoothly he asked her, "What are these bags for? Are you moving and you weren't going to tell me about it". Jayden stops him and tells him that she, Dalia, Blake, and Lauren were taking a trip to Lauren's family house for a couple of days. Brian not being too satisfied is thinking that she was going away with the women who were going to make her change her mind about their relationship. He does not say this aloud to Jayden, but he wanted somehow to let her know that he wanted her in every way. Before he is able to say, anything to her, his cell phone rings and he gets a very important phone call that he had to take. He walked into her living room to take the call while on the other hand; Jayden calls Blake to see if there was anything extra that she would need to pay for the trip.

The number one thing that Blake wanted the women to bring was their bathing suits for the hot tub and Jacuzzi that her mother had installed not too long before her father passed. Not too fond of bathing suits, Jayden packed it anyway thinking what the hell. Brian returns to the room, he asked Jayden to come to him and without hesitating, she came. He hugged her, told her that he loved her, and that he hoped she has a safe trip. Jayden had a boggled look on her face, "You are saying that like you aren't going to see me again". Brian replies, "I didn't say that... "But that is how it sounded, Brian. "I just love you, damn! But, you don't see that" Brian walks out of the room and out of the door. Jayden feeling a little down, but surprised at the same time at how Brian is reacting all of sudden. Thinking hard, Jayden continues to pack trying to keep her mind off everything.

Lauren on the other hand, so organized, wrote down everything that she needed to pack and buy for the trip. Using her Burberry luggage set that she only uses on special occasion, she went into her outhouse to get it. That shows how much she has special occasions. Listening to the messages all Thursday evening about the new job offer that she has failed to mention to anyone, she runs toward the trip as a scapegoat. Putting all negativity out of her mind, she plays her Raheem Devaughn cd on her stereo in her room. Thinking about moving to a better job, which would be good for her career and then thinking about what happened with Jason. She didn't know which one had her more confused. Playing that cd and packing kept her mind occupied for the next couple of hours. Planning her outfits out down to every activity she could think of for every day she would spend in New Jersey, Lauren knew she had herself prepared for it all. While placing her toiletries in her handbag, she called Dalia to see how her packing was going. Little did any of them know that Dalia had returned to work, Lauren called Dalia at her work phone asking her if she had packed her bags. Dalia didn't have anything planned or packed. Lauren couldn't deal with the disorganization got off the phone with Dalia and just told her to get it together because they would be leaving on Friday and that they were not waiting on any late comers. Dalia not really considering that she didn't give the trip a second thought, resumed back to her normal schedule trying to take her mind off her relationship and focus on something else. Too much for Lauren to handle at the time, she turned her music back on and finished making the final touches to her wardrobe for the trip.

Blake on the other hand needs to face and deal with the grief of her father's death. She was ready to see her mother and sister because they don't get a chance to do family things together. While looking at old family photos, she could not seem to fine one picture without her father in it. Blake only planned to work a half a day on Friday because she wanted time to get the rental car and not feel rushed for the day. Blake forgot to phone her mother to tell her the details of what she and the others were planning to do and when they were planning on come up to visit. Not wanting to really bond with her mother and sister, she really wanted the rest of the crew to come with her. Well, it wasn't as if they were not used to going to Blake's house because they did that a lot when they were in school. Blake had the more relaxed household. Her parents were very sociable. Every other weekend they had something at their house whether it is her father's colleagues or her mother's country club members. Very proactive with social and work groups, they bestowed strong religious values in Blake and her sister Blair. Blake shared a very strong bond with her sister, but most of her mature, adult life she kept away from her father most of all. Her mother not knowing too much of the woman she matured to be, assumed from things that she did and what she got from her father. As the women take this trip to New Jersey they will be surprised at how much this trip will affect them.

It is Friday, and the women are preparing themselves to leave for New Jersey. With all the loads they are carrying with them, it will not be a surprise if this trip won't be a life-changing event for all of them. The women arrive one by one at Blake's house. Since Blake is in the gated community, they all know that her house would be the safest to leave their vehicles. They all greet each other and somehow they seemed to all be thinking the same thing. They all were out of character on a weekday. Lauren is dressed in jogging pants and a tee shirt with her alumni. Jayden dressed similar, had on jeans and a tee. Dalia dressed with a cute denim outfit, the only one that actually looked like the professional along with Blake, was prepared to hit the road for a relaxing vacation. While on the road, Blake wanted it to be like their college days by playing loud music and singing the songs the whole ride. Lauren quickly reminded her that they were out of college, their worries were carefree in college, and they were far beyond that. "We are not going to be quiet for this whole drive to Jersey" Blake states while driving. "But you ain't about to make us relive college all over again, like we teenagers", openly states Jayden. "What are we going to do for the drive", as Blake reiterates. Why do we have to do something? Why can't we just enjoy the ride without all of the talking?" states, Dalia. "You all are going to make this trip boring" as Blake tries to find something to listen to on the radio. Headsets are in and each of the women zone out to themselves thinking about the decisions they have to make to the things they have to work through. Two hours into the drive, Blake stops to the gas station to get some snacks. Dalia asleep does not realize that the car has stopped, awakes once everyone gets out of the car.

Dalia looks at her cell and sees a missed call from Terrance. Wondering whether she should return the call or not, she just continues to look at her phone in dismay. Lauren enjoying the ride gets out of the car looking around as she goes into the store with her earplugs still in her ear. Jayden, the first one in the store with Blake, gets snacks for everyone else in the car, calls her father to check on him to see if everything is going well with him. Unfortunately, she ends up getting her stepmother, who does not care to speak with Jayden. Keeping her cool, she politely asks how her father was and if she could speak with him. Karen states, "your father is sleeping and he asked not to be disturbed." Knowing that was a lie, she just said ok and hung up the phone. Angry and furious all at the same time, Jayden just went back to the car, stuck her earplugs in her ear and closed her eyes. Looking all over the store for Jayden, Blake just checked out and brought the snacks herself to the car. The women got back into the car and prepared themselves for the road again. Lauren, still amazed with her surroundings, asked everyone if they remembered the time, when they were in college and they took the trip to Florida for spring break and how much fun they had, boy did the ear plugs come out then. They all sat up and had blushed on their faces, "yeah, we did not tell anyone that were leaving for the weekend", states Dalia. "I am surprise you even remember that, inserts Blake. "Tell me something that I don't know", that was a memorable trip, but let's not talk about that too much, because that might bring up too many memories", states Lauren. "I am not embarrassed about what happened to me", states Jayden. "I know I met the wrong guy and he wanted the wrong thing. Are you guys going to ever let that go or are you going to hold that over my head forever". "What I think is that all of us need to deal instead of steal all the time, states Dalia. "What the hell does that mean" Jayden interjects. "We are always running away from the issues that we cannot solve instantly, so we don't deal with it, and then by running we rob ourselves of the opportunity to move past what has been bothering us, Dalia states while looking at all of them in the car. Jayden waiting on the opportunity for someone else to say something, looks around, "I know you all are not about to let Dalia kick some knowledge to us like she is doctor fix it or something."

The ride only being a couple more hours, each of these women are expecting a different answer from this trip in regards to the minor issues they are battling. Dalia, trying to figure out if

Terrance is really, what she wants and if she can live without him. Blake, dealing and facing the death of her father and what is in store for her life next. Jayden, who is trying to learn that not everything is negative and not her future can be as prosperous with Brian as if she sees with her other friends. Then there is Lauren who risks losing herself in her issues of commitment, marriage, family, and children, who tries to runaway from facing those issues by taking a new job far away. Looking to Jersey to be thee sanction for their unanswered questions, they take refuge in Blake's family home for peace and quiet, which will be time away from their normal lives. As they arrive at the house, Blake enters the code to get into the gate to enter the grounds of the estate. As fabulous of life that Blake has, she has managed to keep an array of friends and to maintain a level of the average woman, which would entail of working hard for what one has obtained and not feel that things are given. This one thing has kept these young women grounded for such a long time. Even though, they think they are reaching pivotal points in their life to decide about marriage, children, and careers, they place a lot of pressure on themselves to make decisions that should not be their focus.

When they walk into the house, Blake's mother is not there, but she has left a note just in case that she would not be there once they arrived. The note follows:

Good day Ladies, It is my pleasure to have all of you here to visit with   me.   I hope this time will be valuable and memorable for you. I do have some things in store for all of us to do. Since the loss of my husband, it has brought light to me that I need to give back in other ways than through my charities in which my husband and I have done for so many years. I know at this point, you are wondering what silly thing I have in store for you, but I am sure that you will enjoy. I may be out for a little while, but Lou is there to help you get situated and entertained until I get back. My darling Blake, glad to see you home, love you and I will be there in a little while...Oh, and ladies, make yourselves at home. After reading the note, the looked at each other wondering what that note meant and then Lou approached them. Blake not being too familiar with Lou, because her parents hired her once she went off to college, so there has been no connection between the two. "Good evening, I have been advised to escort you to your rooms. Follow me please." The women followed Lou. Exhausted from the ride, they did not make any comments about it. They just followed Lou, as they were anxious to settle themselves in their rooms. In each room, there was a personal note. Not too detailed about their lives, just thanking them for the visit from Blake's mother was sitting on the nightstand. Jayden thinking to herself, "These privileged ass people have too much time on their hands, and if I didn't know any better, I would have thought this was Lauren's mother", as she laughed to herself. Dalia looked out of the window of her room is thinking very hard about her relationship with Terrance. She is not at the same place she was a week ago, but still trying to figure what she wants as a grown woman. Blake is staying in her old room looking at all the things she acquired as a child and thinking about the woman she evolved to become. Very proud of herself, she feels a void because her father died. Lauren immediately pulled out her planner thinking how she could make each day productive.

Lou came on the intercom and announced for supper within the hour and that they need to prepare themselves as supper was going to be very casual. Blake forewarned everyone that her parents were very particular about dinner and very organized with everything that they did. It was how they apart of their growing up so they made it important in she and her sister everyday living. By this time, Blake's mother, Barbara Lowry entered her own, looking very lavish as always. She looked so excited to see the faces coming downstairs for supper. She greeted each of them and ran to the other room to freshen herself for the meal. No one wanting to say anything, Lauren the only one bold enough to make a comment. "Blake, is your mother always like this"? Smiling back at Lauren, "You know my mother is a character and this is what makes her happy, let her do it. "Hell, I don't know if I can take all this happiness", states Jayden. Before Blake could respond, Dalia had a few words to share with Jayden, "You are not going to spoil this trip for us. This has to be one of the nicest vacations we could have in this beautiful home, spacious, and comfortable. You need this time just like the rest of us. If you didn't, you would be home with Brian instead of running from the one good man in your life". Looking at Jayden's face, you could see the rage steaming across the table; the food came and so did Blake's mother. She asked if everyone settled in ok and if anyone was uncomfortable with anything. No one had any comments and especially not Jayden sense Dalia blasted out something about Brian that was new to everyone else at the table. Apparently, the issue with Jayden and Brian was something that they talked amongst each other.

Some of the down- home favorites that they all liked in college were on the menu. Baked chicken, fried catfish, mashed potatoes, rice & gravy, string beans, baked beans, steamed broccoli, and for dessert, there was a variety to choose from; apple pie, cheesecake, chocolate cake, and carrot cake. Blake's mother wanted to make sure the girls enjoyed the dinner. They were all shocked at how much she remembered about them. This even put Jayden's attitude to rest. They laughed and talked all throughout dinner. "I never knew you were so down to earth", states Jayden. Blake's mother stated, "You never gave me the chance, remember". Not knowing what to say, Jayden just smiled and let the conversation flow. After about an hour went by, Barbara got the ladies attention, "Hey ladies, hurry and finish up. I have something else in store for you that I think you are going to like." Wondering what she had planned, Lauren stated across the table, "I am ready to see what momma Lowry has yet". She looks at Jayden, "What do you think about our vacation now". Looking back at her, "I never said that this was a bad idea"... "But, you weren't the first to initiate this trip either", states Dalia. "Ok, so that makes me a bad person, "Get the hell out of here", inserts Jayden. "No, I think you were afraid to admit that this evening was better than what you thought it was going to be, states Lauren. While the women are having this conversation at the table, Blake and her mother excused themselves from the table. Barbara wanted to show Blake something that was concerning her father. When the two returned to the table, Barbara told the women to join her in the family room for a glass of wine. "Blake how did you mother know that was my thing", asks Dalia. "My mother is a big wine collector. I didn't want to tell you all too much about my mother. I wanted you to get to know her like I do", states Blake.

"Hurry up ladies. Grab some rug and gather around. We can talk and have some girl talk," states Barbara. "I don't know if you want to hear our problems, they might be too much..." coming from Dalia. "Honey, you will be surprised what I have done and been through to get what I have", states Blake's mother. "I bet it was nothing like climbing a pole or standing on a curb", inputs Jayden. Dalia nudged Jayden in her side to get her to stop talking and saying things to Blake's mother. Barbara returned to the room with a bottle of wine and glasses for them all. While preparing to sit on the floor, Barbara began "I am so happy that all of you decided to come visit me. I am not sure how Blake was able to get all of you here this weekend, but it doesn't matter". Lauren looking at the picture on the mantle of Barbara and her late husband caught Barbara's eye. "That picture was of Bernard and me in Paris before we had any children, with no care in the world. We went there for a vacation. Your father had great charisma. He'd been working at least twelve hours a day at the firm, going out of town on business every couple of weeks, coming home late for dinner at least four nights out of the week, he would miss dinner reservations, you name it he missed it. By this time, we were only married for two years. He was trying to get the business off the ground, but in the process, he was abandoning me. In my early 20s, I was losing my mind. I did not get married for this man to leave me at home alone in this two bedroom condo". Blake asks her mom, "You and dad lived in a condo". "Yes, not long, but that is just one more thing you thought you knew about us.

While the nights got longer, I got lonelier and the lonelier, the idler my mind became. I decided to find a hobby so I took a cooking class and a wine tasting class. Now, the wine tasting class turned out to be one of the best things, it helped when we were out of town and I could put my expertise to use. Even though the classes kept me busy so did the people in the classes. I met a woman in that culinary class who befriended me early on in the class. Her name was Evelyn and she was a very classy woman, who looked like she came from a well to do life. The first day of class, we all had the opportunity of introducing ourselves and telling our reasons for taking the class. When it came to be her time, she said that her name was Evelyn and that her husband enjoyed home cooked meals and she didn't know how to do that, so she wanted to surprise him by taking the class. When it was my turn, I told them that I needed something to occupy my time while my husband was picking up more work with his job. At first, it seemed that we had a lot in common and we shared some things that others in our class did. At the end of the class, she came to me and said, "My husband works a lot of long hours too. What does your husband do?" I told her that he was starting his own business and it is taking a lot of his time right now, so I needed something to keep me busy for a little while. She told me that her husband was an ER doctor and he was on call more than he was off call.

For weeks, Evelyn and I partnered for every activity in this class. We had some kind of connection, but Bernard never met her. It wasn't intentional; the moment just never seemed to happen for them to cross paths. We became close over the time of the class; we even talked about taking another class together. Therefore, we signed up to take a defense course. It wasn't nothing that we needed, it was something positive to keep our minds focused on something else than being alone. During this class, I noticed that Evelyn started to act a little funny. I never picked up what it was because I didn't want to seem like I was prying into her personal affairs. The talk around was that she and her husband were beginning to have some problems and it wasn't getting any better. I didn't want to pay it any attention because I thought that if it were that serious, she would have mention something to me.

"Ok, why do you think she would have told you about her marital affairs", asks Dalia.

"We shared some things about our lives and I think that if they were on the verge of breaking or splitting, she would have mentioned something to me. Weeks went by and she did not say anything. There was even a time when she called me at the house and said that she wasn't going to make it to class because she did not have a babysitter for her child, which I did not believe because she talked about her nanny and maid all the time. I figured she didn't want me in her business. One day when I came home, there was a note on my door, very mysterious saying, "There is something very important that I need to talk to you about, you don't know me but I did not know any other way to get your attention without you thinking I was insane". At this point, I didn't know if this was a stalker, an ex, or just some crazy person.

"Who did it end up being", asks Lauren.

"I'm getting to that part in a minute. Now I didn't pay attention to the note, I wanted to act as if I never got it. The next day, I get a mysterious voice mail on the house phone, "This is Evelyn's husband, and there are some things that you need to know."... At first, I didn't know how to respond to it. I looked at my phone for at least an hour. Something told me to call their house because I did consider Evelyn a friend and he could have been calling me to tell me something about her. When I called the house, the phone did not ring twice before he picked the phone up. This man filled my head with so many things at one time that I did not know what to do or think."

"What did he tell you?" asks Dalia. Blake on the side looking like she really did not want to hear it in one sense and then on the other hand, she wanted to know because this story seemed like something that her parents didn't even shared with her or her sister. She did not want to say anything to give her mother the impression that she was not interested or judgmental.

Her mother continued; this man began to tell me that after all of these years his wife has managed to trick him to move to same town as her baby's father and somehow slid her way to get close to the wife. At first, I didn't know what this man was talking about and I even told him that if he didn't explain himself, I would call my husband to handle him.

He said, "Ma'am, my wife is Evelyn Morris and she slept with your husband some years ago. They had a child together.

So, instantly, I went on the defense. I would have never thought that this would happen to me or he was telling me the truth.

I said to him, "You must have the wrong person. Evelyn and I are good friends. We take a culinary class together and are enrolling in a self-defense class next month.

"No, that is what she wanted you to believe. Let me tell you something. Do you remember about four years ago, Bernard went out one night to the strip club with some law students and he didn't tell you about it, but you ended up finding out about it the next day?

"I don't remember that", I told him even though I did, but I didn't want to believe it. He continued on,

"He met my now wife, Evelyn before she met me. They went into a private room where who knows what happened. I do know that they spent the night together and next thing you know she got pregnant. From the story that she told me, she called him when she found out she was having a baby and he ignored her."

My first reaction to him, "I don't understand. You are telling me that my husband had a child with your wife over four years ago and this woman came close to me just to get close to my husband". At this point, tears where coming down my face because I didn't know whether to yell at him on the phone or call my husband. I had all kind of mixed feelings going through my head. This man goes on to tell me that,

"My wife named the child Carmen."....Instantly, Dalia remembered that name and starting twitching her eyes looking at Jayden, who she told could recalled telling that name to. Dalia as curious as she could be asked Barbara, "Do you know where this Carmen person lives now?" Barbara answered, "From what I have heard, she is married and lives in Baltimore where you girls live and she is married with children". Instantly Dalia blurts, "You have got to be kidding me. Do you mean to tell me that you half sister is the bitch that slept with my man in my house." Blake looked confused at Dalia not knowing what she was talking about.

Blake asked Dalia, "Carmen is the woman you caught in your house with Terrance. That can't be so". Looking furiously Dalia states, "Why? You don't even know her and you don't know the kind of person she is.

Barbara interjects into the conversation, "What are you all talking about". Blake began telling her mother, "One of the reasons we came down here for a visit is because Dalia caught her boyfriend Terrance in the bed with a woman name Carmen, who happens to live in Baltimore and his married with children too" Barbara looking really shocked at the news. Jayden began telling her, "And this is not some random chick, she even works with Dalia at the hospital". Reacting as mother would Barbara goes toward Dalia, "Honey, I am so sorry that happened to you and that it had to come out that way". Dalia not knowing how to feel, hugs Barbara crying her eyes out. Barbara began saying to all of them, "I know something wasn't right when you all got here and I knew it was a matter of time before it came out, but I didn't expect nothing like this. I want all of you to sit down and I want to tell you something about life.

By this time, the women all moved into the dining room. Barbara asked the house cleaner to get another bottle of wine to bring out. She looked at all of them, "Let me tell something about men. They will only do what you let them do to you".

Blake looks at her mother, "But you stayed with Dad even though he had a child with another woman and he never told you". She looked at her daughter, "You are right, and it was something that we had to work through together. One, he had this child before we got married. Two, marriage is for better and for worst. God never tells you ahead of time what the worst is going to be. He only promises the worst will come. Three, Women are vindictive and men are weak. I am not making excuses for the things that men do, but if you look at the circumstances and not the mistake, you can heal and the relationship. Young women, we have to find within ourselves what makes us happy and then we have to figure out to ourselves what is the happiness worth." Looking at her daughter, "Your father gave me the best years of my life. I could have been angry about that for the rest of my life and you know what would have happened. We probably would have been divorced and another woman would have come in, accepted that child, and lived happily ever after. We are all human and we all make mistakes. See, what I know that Evelyn and her husband didn't know what that Bennie could not pass a single test in his classes the second year of law school. He was contemplating quitting and being a paralegal. I encouraged him to keep going, get through, and the one thing he told me he would do once he graduated was to show his appreciation. I did not know what he meant by that. Little did I know he wanted to marry me and give me everything and more?

You don't want to give up lifetime happiness for short term satisfaction. Do not give up the sight of the long-term goal for the short-term reaction. "So, what happened between you and your husband once you found out he had a child", asked Lauren. "When he came home that day, I was waiting at the door. He thought I wanted something else, if you know what I mean. I was so furious and upset, I could have walked out of the door and never looked backed, but I didn't want to. He asked me what was wrong. I told him what I knew and about Evelyn and her husband. He looked at me and tears began to roll down his face because he thought he lost my heart. He told me, "I love you with all my heart and I made a mistake a long time ago that I knew was going to regret. I looked at him and said, "Why didn't you feel that you could come to me". What I realized it that I was more hurt about this other woman having his first child before, you, me, the wife was able to do, but that was something that I had to get through on my own, before I was able to deal with my husband. In the meantime, we worked through it because only two are a couple and three is a group. If I continued to let Evelyn and her husband contribute to my household, it would have taken a told on my marriage and I wanted more for my husband and myself. Are you listening to me? I doesn't seem like you all are taking heed to what I am saying.

The first to say something was Jayden, "I understand what you are saying, but I can't speak for anyone else when I say this, but I know what I am afraid of. I feel like me giving my all to a man that I partly feel may leave me one day is not what I am willing to do.

Barbara looked her in her eyes and told her, "Honey your problem is with you and not with this man. You have not decided yet if you want to give a part of yourself to someone else or if you want to be single. You need to ask yourself that question. Are you ready for a solid, committed relationship? If you are, then it will be okay for you to let yourself be happy and involved with the man that you love. I am not saying that you will make dumb choices and stupid decisions, but you will be able maintain your individualism while having a healthy relationship."

"Ok, but what if you feel like marriage and children are the worst thing ever and…" inputs Lauren.

"What do you mean hate?" I never knew you felt that way, Blake.

"Well, now you do. I am afraid of being too involved and attached. I think children are good for other people, but I get a nasty feeling when I think about another person coming out of my body. I could not imagine that, expresses Lauren.

The women all shocked at what Lauren put out on the table that they did not know what to think or how to react. Not really a look of dismay, but shocking to hear that family was never a part of her future. As their looks became even more strange to Lauren, she did not know if she made a mistake by telling her true feelings of family and children or if it was a good thing that she told her friends how she really felt. Barbara, being the one at the table with the most experience and knowledge of young women, since she is a college professor of women's studies did not seem to have a different reaction. Instant Barbara reacted, "There is nothing wrong with having the fear of family and children". "There has got be something wrong with anyone who thinks that motherhood is horrible thing", implies Jayden. "I do not think it is a horrible thing. I just don't think it is for me", replied Lauren.

"What you all have to understand is that you mind and body undergoes some many changes and challenges in your twenties. It is a very hard balance between work and home. Some of you will have a home and no work while some will have work and no home. It does not say that you are bad, weird, or dumb person for feeling the way that you do. When you block certain things out of her mind, they become something imaginable to you because that is what you have built in your mind." Barbara stated this while really focusing the statement on Lauren. Feeling much better about opening herself up, Lauren was beginning to understand her negative feelings of marriage; on the other hand, Jayden felt a little ignorant for jumping down Lauren's throat about her feelings.

The phone rings and Barbara leaves the table to answer it. Sitting at the table, Jayden looks to Blake, "I did not know your mother was cool as shit". Laughing hysterically, "You did not give her a chance. When you see her, she is work mode, in which she looks to be something that she is not". At the other end of the table, Dalia is in a world of her own. She is still wondering how one of her best friends could be the half sister of the woman she caught in her house with Terrance. After a while, she was thinking repeatedly about everything that happened over the past couple of weeks. She recalled the incident at the restaurant with Shawn when she was in the restroom with Carmen and she remembered her saying, "You just don't know why he did what he did". She was thinking that maybe Terrance was out to get her, but after hearing this news, she wonders if Carmen knew all along whom she was and she was trying to get back at her. On the other hand, maybe she thought Terrance was Blake's man. All of these things were running through her head. She gets sidetrack when Jayden asked her cross the table, "Chick, you have been sitting there in a damn dream for the past thirty minutes. What the hell are you thinking about"? "Nothing, just thinking that's all", replied Dalia.

Blake states, "I do not think my mother is going to be coming back anytime soon and this wine is kicking in pretty strong". They all agreed to turn in for the night and prepare themselves for the weekend. While walking up the stairs, they all share comments about what they want to do in the morning. Blake inserted "my mother loves breakfast at the table in the mornings, so count that plan out. We are probably going to be here for breakfast". "As long as I can get a morning swim in that nice pool, it wouldn't bother me none", states Lauren. "Who swims in the morning?" asks Dalia. "You must think you white...Oh, I forgot, you are one of those beige mother fuckers" states Jayden. She and Dalia both laugh as they make a joke out of Lauren wanting to swim after breakfast.

Barbara returns to the table after taking her call and sees that the girls have all gone to bed. She stands behind one of the chairs thinking about the love and warmth that was in the room. It was a long time since she had that many young, energetic life in her home. She thought about each of the girls and the issues they were all facing. She looked at the chairs thinking about all of the beautiful faces that sat in those chairs, wondering how in some way she could help them or give them the advice they needed. She saw all the potential and strength in all of them. With a smile on her face, she turned away and walked upstairs to go to bed.

Saturday morning the women woke up at about ten, feeling refreshed, none of them thinking the wine had anything to do with it. Lou comes over the intercom inviting the women to breakfast that would be ready in fifteen minutes. Jayden was in a deep sleep until she heard Lou's voice says aloud, "Who the fuck is that so damn early on a Saturday morning". Dalia in the next room was enjoying the treatment, "I haven't had treatment like this in years". Blake, down the hall, woke up at eight in the morning, going through her old things, "Wow, I remember all of this. Where did the time go"? Lauren, whose room is across the hall from Blake, was already up writing in her planner and organizing the day so that no time is wasted, "It is such a beautiful day, which bathing suit should I wear this morning". First, to arrive for breakfast Blake and Dalia, they walk downstairs to see the feast prepared for them. Dalia in complete shock, Blake thinking, "I can't believe my mother is going all out like his". Barbara was already in the kitchen making sure everything was going according to plan. She asked Dalia and Blake, "Where are the rest of you". Dalia states, "I know Jayden is still in the bed and Lauren is probably planning the whole day and she will not show her face until she has completed making her notes." She imitates Lauren while she is saying this to Barbara.

"Barbara asked them, well, what do you have planned for the day?" Blake talking to her mother, "Lauren wants to take a swim". "That would be nice. All of you should do that. You are supposed to be relaxing from what I heard last night. Dalia honey, you need to enjoy yourself and take your mind off things. If you keep your mind in Baltimore, this trip will be pointless", states Barbara. "Maybe I will go swimming and then go sightseeing", replied Dalia. "Girl, we are going shopping. I haven't been able to do that in a while", states Blake. "You know I can't do that", Dalia speaking to Blake on the side. Barbara barges into the conversation and asks Dalia, "Would you ever consider relocating to another state?"... "I haven't thought about. There was never a reason for me to do so. I was always happy where I was"... "Well, think about it and let me know something before you all head back". Dalia and Blake both looked very surprised, as they didn't know where that comment came from or what it meant. Just to entertain the question, Blake asks Dalia herself, would she think about moving here, and she responded, "I don't know". By this time, Lauren comes downstairs with her bathing suit on and a towel wrapped around her waist heading to the table for breakfast. "Are you revived", asks Dalia. "Of course I am. I am off from work on a mini vacation and I am not going to waste any time enjoying it," states Lauren. About an hour later, Jayden comes downstairs and she is not interested in breakfast or mingling with the rest of the crew.

They all gathered for a moment to decide their day plans. They decided after the swim to get dressed to go to a local wine tasting, which is something that Lauren and Blake decided to do. Later that day, Dalia and Jayden would have their way. At poolside, the sun was blazing down perfect over the water. Lauren lays on a beach chair with her shades on enjoying the sun. Dalia decides to refresh her swimming skills by taking a dive in the pool. Blake sits on the side with her feet in the pool reading a magazine. Jayden comes to the pool as if she is at the beach. She has on her flip flops, a beach towel around her waist, boggles, and the whole nine yards. They all laugh at her, but you know she does not care what they think cause Jayden is going to be Jay all day regardless of what anyone says.

Lauren, without moving an inch of her body, as Dalia when she comes up from under the water, "Have you heard from Terrance sine you been here"? "I don't know. I haven't really had my phone on"... "Aren't you at least worried, concerned, or something. Don't you want some answers."... "I want a fresh start"

Jayden laying her towel down beside the pool, asks Dalia, "You have got to be kidding me?" After the news, you just found out, it should have answered some questions and make you think about talking to him. No, I know what this is all about; are now feeling guilty about something.

"Why does someone always have to be guilty to you? Ever since...." states Blake.

"Don't go there. We all did things and we regret them. Just let it go", implies Blake.

"None of you should get all righteous now. It's done, but don't act all high and might with Terrance. You did what you had to do then and he did what he had to do", states Jayden.

"Are you trying to condone Terrance fucking some chick in my house to me cheating on my nurse's exam", states Dalia as her voices raises.

"Why are we talking about this here? You two can do this later, states Lauren.

"Regardless of how you see it, we all clicked, clocked and docked our way through school. Why does it matter now when we got what we wanted", implies Jayden.

"I didn't get what I wanted", states Dalia... "Well, you incident did happen at a bad time"

Lauren on the other hand is sitting in her chair thinking and reminiscing about her college days. All she could do was think about this professor that changed her world. Lauren secretly had an affair with her college professor that she only shared with Blake. The love affair lasted a very long time until this man decided that he wanted more from their relationship.

This little love affair became a problem when Lauren became pregnant with her professor's child.   While trying to hold everything together, Blake was a student of his and he began to make a move on her.   Not knowing that the two of them were friends and roommates, they both decided to plan something for the professor.   With the detective skills that Jayden had, they brought her in on a plan to help with the demise. While planning to take the professor down, he threatened to expose her and her friends if they tried to do anything to him.   In order to save their college career and not to disappoint their parents; the professor gathered all of fellow colleagues that were sleeping with their students and black mailed Dalia, Jayden, and Blake into relations with one of his friends in order to pass and eventually graduate.

Each of them forced to sleep with the prestigious faculty members, which happened to be good friends with the professor that was forcing Blake into this affair.   At the end of the semester, all of them made straight A's, graduated top of their class and were placed on the best jobs.   They kept it all a secret and swore to never tell anyone about the tragedy they resorted themselves to. Dalia and Jayden were never really close to Blake, but they knew they had to help get rid of the stalker that impregnated Lauren and seducing Blake.   They later respected Blake and looked out for her just as Lauren did.   They respected her for making the sacrifices and risking her integrity Lauren's sake.   Blake being such a beautiful young woman, she was loved by men for many reasons; forced to go to events, pose for pictures, wear very provocative clothing, and entertain at their pleasure.   She managed to excel the best that she could under the circumstances. When any of them would ask her about these incidences, she would refuse to give details.   So embarrassed at what she resorted herself to do, she would refrain from talking about with the rest of the girls.   Feeling bad also because she knew that her best friend, Lauren really had deep feelings for this man and expecting his child, only to find out that he seduced not only her, but every young, beautiful woman he became close to.   Learning the information that this man was evil and nothing she could see herself with, she told him that she wanted an abortion;

unfortunately, this was his plan all along. He planned for her to have his child so he could use it as collateral if ever she decided to turn on him. Secretly, Lauren had an abortion. She disappeared for a weekend and she returned to school after, she completed the procedure.

Lauren, at the pool, jumps out of mind with the scandal. As her life had become such a routine and simple thing, she could not believe that she endured all of that. All of this going through her head while at the pool, the ambiance circled all of them. Dead silence speaking a lot at this moment because they all shared this dark secret that they grew to regret and despise themselves for not making better choices. All the other problems that they brought with them this weekend disappeared just for a moment and they remembered what kept them grounded and what brought them together. No one has really spoken about college just because they were all so happy when they graduated. It took a lot to get to that day and when they did, they vowed not to discuss what it took to get the piece of paper in their hand that they longed for since they were children. Blake's phone goes off and she reads the text aloud to everyone, "Hey, we can go to the tracks and watch the race like we used to in college, someone just sent it to me"…"Are you sure that is going to be fun", states Dalia. "Well, if we don't like it, we can always leave," replied Blake. While gathering their things from around the pool, Barbara comes outside to tell the women that there is a White Party going on tonight that is sponsored by the ABA, which is the All Black Attorney's Association that Blake's father founded.

"What is the White Party", asked Jayden. "Oh, my goodness, it is one the best parties in town. Everything is white; drinks, clothes, food, games, and cars. You wear all white, you drink white drinks; like white wine, white liquor, and whatever you mix it with has to be white. The lawyers all wear nice white linen suits, it is like a ritual, and they drive nice white cars. The women who are present there compliment the party with the white attire and you have the honor of being dazzled by some nice, romantic gentleman."… "Why didn't you ever bring us to this before", asked Jayden. "Why would you need something like this, you have a good man", states Lauren. "Did you hear what you said? I have a good man, not husband," implies Jayden. They all laugh because Jayden always has an answer for everything. Instead of going to the tracks, they decide to get themselves ready for the White Party. The one thing these women love to do is pamper themselves, and this party gave them the excuse to go all out.

Blake calls the spa for them appointments for their manicures, pedicures and a hair so that it will not take all day. They also had an excuse to go to the mall and spend money. They rushed into the house to get dressed excited about the party. The party was only six hours away. They would have to use their time wisely and carefully if they didn't want to be rushed. When they arrived at the spa, it didn't take them long to get their manicures and pedicures. The hair took longer since elegant is not a look that Jayden likes to have, she would rather had a simple, flat look that she can maneuver herself. Leaving the spa, they went to the mall to find white. Of course, it was going to be hard to find, as the most sophisticated people in town will be at the party, which would cut out a lot of riff raff. Going to two different malls, they ended up finding something to suit all of their needs. While getting dressed, they decided they would leave on Sunday because she did not want to be away from work too long. Jayden states, "Just when we are having fun, you want to leave". "My bad, how was I suppose to know that you were going to have such a good time here", states Blake with a smile. Dalia runs downstairs quickly and returned with a bottle of wine, "You know we have to fuck this up before we go anywhere", states Dalia.

"What the hell, why not…we are on vacation, right?" as Jayden opens the bottle and turns it up. They pass the bottle of wine around like it's a forty ounce. They have fun, feel a little buzz, but the most important thing is that their minds are all at ease forgetting about their personal worries and problems that were brought so much anguish to their lives. Not even noticing the cell phones at all, they haven't realized what promising calls they have missed. For the first time, Dalia picks up her phone and notices eleven missed calls and majority of them are from

Terrance. There was one from her job, one from her bank, and the other missed call were unknown. Her voicemail was full and she was not in the mood to check it because she just knew it was Terrance saying how he was so sorry. While on the other hand, Blake is listening to her music, and being as free as a bird with the bottle of wine in her hand. Jayden is retouching her makeup and her hair. Lauren, "just because you have a little time, does not mean it gives you time to check your email", states Blake. "You do what you do and let me be me", replies Lauren. "We all need to get dressed so we won't be late for the party. I want to get good parking", states Blake. "I am about ready. All I have to do it put my dress on, but I do need to check my messages before we go anywhere," states Jayden. "Nah, I do not want to touch my phone until we get back to Baltimore, Blake states as she takes another drink of wine.

Coming down the staircase, Lou compliments the women on how beautiful they look. Once again, they outdo themselves with their attire. Jayden stands out the most with her nice long slinky dress that compliments her figure. They are all thinking to themselves how Jayden has finally come out of her shell. Barbara thought it would be classier for the girls to arrive at the party in a limo so she has one to pick them up from the house. On the way to the party, the conversation starts about the discussion they had last night with Blake's mother. Jayden first to say, "I have no comment and I would rather not say or think about anything serious, I hope they have a lot of liquor because drinking is what I need right now". The others not knowing exactly how to respond to that but Dalia, "Glad you know how to party". Blake and Lauren retouch their makeup so much until they made a mess of themselves. "I think what Blake's mother said last night was really true, but I don't know if I can change who I am right now", states Lauren. "Are you all going to ruin the event by talking about this shit again", Jayden says loudly over everyone. "You are such a sour person", states Blake. "I just want to have fun and you all want to reminisce and be sentimental. You want to cry, then you should go back to the mansion and cry in a pillow, but don't come to a party and talk about shit that makes you depress as hell", states Jayden. "You know I hate to say she is right, but she is", states Lauren.

The party was a blast. The women met many eligible men, but only one of them actually met a potential. They mingled, drank, laughed, danced, and enjoyed the evening. The whole phase of preparing for the event was well worth it and they knew it when Jayden whispered in Blake's ear, "You are my best friend, and you always were". Blake laughed to herself, but at the same time, she was glad that she was able to do something for her friends that made them happy. Blake met a couple of single men, but most of them knew her father and that was all they wanted to know about. They were interested in what she was doing career wise, but not wanting to know about her personally. Lauren came into the party just to have a good time. Still used to putting her guard up with every man, which is the vibe that she throws off majority of the time, she was able to let that go at this party. While sitting on a bar stool at private table, a man walks up to Lauren, "Hey, you don't look like you are from around here". She looks up and all she could see was wedding bells. This feeling never happened to her before. She heard people talking about it, but she never experienced it. The only thoughts that ran through her head were, "this is my husband, my soul mate". It was a moment before she could even respond. He introduced himself, "My name is Kendall, what is your name"? She finally speaks, "My name is Lauren, and no, I am not from around here. Originally, I am from Georgia, but I live and work in Baltimore". He responds, "Very nice. I know you hear this all the time, but you are beautiful and I did not come here to meet anyone, but there was just something about you". Blushing so hard, Lauren did not know what to say as she felt the same way about him just by meeting him.

Instantly Lauren asked him, "Would you like to get out of here and talk"? Immediately, she was ready to go along. While leaving the party with Kendall, she texted the girls and let them know what she was doing. Jayden was having so much fun that she did not have her normal responses to situations. The party had such a great effect on everyone; things just seemed to be going in everyone's favor. Jayden enjoyed the nice company, good food, nice surrounding, and great music that she was able to escape everything she left back home. Dalia was able to let go and have fun for once in weeks. Thinking hard about the career opportunity that Barbara offered to her, she was really considering changing her surroundings and starting over. Blake knew that this scene would be better for her friends than for her. She gave up trying to mingle because her luck was running out. She decided to go to the restroom to freshen up. On her way there, her phone goes off. She thinks it is a text message from Lauren again talking about this guy she met; instead it was a text message from someone else, which stated "You look so beautiful right now. I wish I could have you all to myself". At first, she was shocked that someone actually knew her personally there that would send her a text message. She responded, "Who is this and where are you?" The reply, "When you come out of the bathroom come into the second ballroom to the bar". Anxious to see who it was, she hurried out of the bathroom. As she walks into the other room, she sees Michael at the bar. "What are you doing here?" "A friend of mine knows your father invited me to this. For some reason I knew you were going to be here. I am so sorry about your father; I heard he was a well accomplished man, looks like he passed that down to his daughter." Blake is blushing from ear to ear.

Michael did put together that was the reason for her postponing their date. He asked, "Is there anyway that I can get my date before this evening is over?" Blake responded, "I don't see why not. I just have to make sure that my friends have a ride back to my mother's house". "You handle that and I will make reservations somewhere for us", states Michael. Smiling on the inside, Blake quickly runs towards Jayden, who was the closest, to tell her about Michael. Finally, Jayden was excited for her and told Blake to give her the keys, "Have fun, you guys are finally on vacation like I told you before". Jayden then asked Blake before she walked off, "Have you seen Dalia?" Blake turned looking around the grounds, "The last time that I saw her, she was drinking a cocktail at the bar outside". "Okay, I will look for her and you did get the text from Lauren", ask Jayden. "Yes, I did. I hope she is having fun". "I bet she is unless she would not have left this party. Okay, see you at the house this evening", states Jadyen. By the time Blake walks off, Jayden runs into Dalia, who looked refreshed for some reason. The two of them together decided they were ready to leave the party and go to a small local club where they could dance, which is not too far from the house.

Chapter 7: Getting Right

Its Saturday night, Lauren is out on her date with Kendall. Blake is out with Michael. Dalia and Jayden are at the grown and sexy club, Desire, having so much fun that they don't know what to do with themselves. All of them are reaching a turning point in their crisis. The choices they make at this point, will determine their futures. Jayden knows her heart belongs to Brian, but she did not know how to let herself go so she can be happy with him. She has been thinking hard about what Barbara said to her last night. Dalia really considering making the move to New Jersey is getting used to the idea of changing her scenery. Her only issue is the T-word. Lauren finally met the one had her thinking about commitment Kendall. Blake is finally getting the one date that she awaited for weeks now. She did not think she would have the opportunity to be in his presence again.

Lauren and Kendall go to a cozy restaurant that has dim lighting. At such short notice, he arranged a private room with a bottle of wine, candles on the table, and white chocolate fondue with every fruit you could think of. The hostess asked the both of them to take their shoes off and have a seat on the pillows. Unexpected to what was head for the evening; Lauren took her shoes off and sat down with Kendall assisting her while trying to sit down. The waiter came and brought the fondue closer for them to feed each other. This was his idea of getting closer to her and getting to know her on an intimate level. This was like a dream come true for Lauren. They would take turns feeding each other fruit. She asked Kendall, "How did you know I liked white chocolate?" With a smooth smile, "I did not know, I just went on instinct," stated Kendall. They spent hours talking and sharing. Kendall expressed to Lauren that he was lawyer, but it was not his ultimate career goal. He would love to run for a political office, but he did not want to do that until he was married and had a more stable life with the woman of his dreams. He told her without asking how he had been single for two years. He did not have time to get involved with a serious relationship because he had some serious cases that took up all of him time, but allowed him to make a name for himself as a successful lawyer. So interested in what Kendall had to say, she did not want to mention her all so organized life, but he was more than interested to here about it.

He asked, "You seem so together. I want to know all about you. What do you do, your hobbies, what turns you on, what turns you off, just keep talking and don't stop". Lauren was getting the feeling that Kendall was so into her that regardless of what she told him, he would still see it as a positive and something he would love about her. She felt so comfortable talking to him, as if she could tell him anything. The one thing she kept thinking to herself, "did I finally meet the one"? She began, "Well, I work at an Accounting Firm as a CPA, which I have been there for a couple of years. I am very organized. I like to plan everything, nothing unexpected. I like to spend time with my friends and be involved in social groups. I am in a book club with some people from within the community. My friends and I hang out every Wednesday as a girls' day. I like what I do and I take it very serious. I haven't focused on men in a long time because I just felt like if it was meant to be it would". While she is talking, Kendall is glazing into her eyes, enjoying everything that she is saying. As they sit enjoying the fruit and chocolate together, they look like a match made in heaven. Not wanting to take over the conversation, Lauren asks, "Why are you looking at me like that"? He compliments her on her nice skin, beautiful teeth and natural hair. Never thinking she was as beautiful as Kendall is describing her, she actually thought that this guy was looking at her inside appearance and not her physical features. Not only did she admire that, but also she adored him for doing so.

They spent time going back and forth discussing their likes and dislikes with everything from under the sun. They stayed so late at the restaurant, that the manager locked the door on the two of them. They discussed things from religion to politics; they differed on some, but were able to respect and understand each other's point of view on everything. The one thing Lauren lacked in her life was the stimulating conversation and company of a man in her life. As she thinks of her past while looking into his eyes, she daydreams about every negative and sour thing she experienced. She also thought about the agony she endured in college and how she secluded herself from men regardless of the situation. She even thought about that gut feeling she got when she went to her cousin's wedding that made her feel that she missed out on her husband years ago. She even thought about the conversation she had to Blake's mother, that she needed to hear at that moment. She never thought Blake's mother would be that influential in her life.

As the conversation continued between herself and Kendall, the one thing they overlooked was residence. Not to think about that she was on vacation with a friend, she met the man of her dreams who did not share that with her. He lived in New Jersey and her residence was in Maryland. She realized this when he kept talking about his job and how it was within minutes of the restaurant. If it was one thing that Lauren did not like, it was long distance relationships. She felt they were tolerable in college, just because the collegiate years are for exploration, but once you become an adult, those things changed. It was a personal preference that she lived by regardless, which is another reason she and her ex did not make it. With him in Washington and her living in Jersey, it was going to be hard to maintain that relationship. Quickly, she states to him, "Kendall, I live in Baltimore. I can't relocate. I have my job, house, friends, my world, its all in Baltimore. I can't think about moving or changing my life right now, just when everything seems to be on track". He stops her, "Whoa, babe...I would not want you to change anything about you just for me". He grabs her hand and looks into her eyes intimately. She feels him in her heart, an unimaginable feeling. "Then, how is it going to work if we are living in two different states". He begins to smile, "I have been looking for houses in Baltimore. My company just opened a new firm downtown Baltimore and I will be there to find staff for the office. I am relocating there in a month". So excited, Lauren puts her hands over her mouth to hide away her emotion, but you can see the tears forming in her eyes. Kendall wipes the tears from her eyes and he answers the question that was in Lauren's head without her saying it. "Yes, I want you and only you. When you leave tomorrow, just think about me being on the next flight there", Lauren hugs him with all her might as if she does not want to let go. He helps her up from the floor and they hold hands as they walk out of the restaurant with such joy in their faces.

When she gets in the car, she checked her phone only to see a text message from Blake that she was on her way back to the mansion. Not even thinking about replying, Lauren closed her phone only to capture the moment with Kendall. In the car, Kendall puts the key in the ignition and he hesitates. In Lauren's mind, she was thinking of him just making love to her like the movies, but she knew that would not happen. Two grown people in a car making love would be so uncalled for in her world, but the one thing she has learned is that love is not something controlled it is enjoyed. Kendall leans in towards her and kissed her like no other kiss she ever had. They stop in the moment and instantly read each other's mind. Without saying a word, Kendall drove off and took Lauren to his condominium. It was so beautiful Lauren was speechless. He lived not too far from Blake's family home, which you could tell the neighborhood fully surrounded with those of the same liking. He pulled in the driveway, opened Lauren's door, waited until she got out of the car, opened the door to the house, and immediately kissed her. Not hesitating, but going with the flow, Lauren opened his jacket, trying not to rip the buttons off; he rubs her body, as it is a treasure. He runs his fingers through her hair while he kisses her neck. She moans for more as she opens his pants first by unbuckling his belt. He stops to look at her and he picks her up and takes her upstairs into the bedroom. When the reached the top of the stairs, she sees the master bedroom and how gorgeous it was. He lays her on the bed, she kisses him, and he zips her dress down slowly, kisses her down her back. She lays there with her eyes half way closed, in dreamland, grabbing the sheets as he touches every spot on her body. He turned her over and began kissing her again from her neck to her breast down to her stomach; she pulls him up slowly to her lips as he bits his bottom lip. They ended up making love for hours. Not for one second did she think about sleeping with this man on the first day meeting him.

On the other hand, while the romance heated up at Kendall's house, Blake is having her long awaited date with Michael. He appeared to be the man she was looking for temporarily in her life, but after going on the date, she thought that he might be something long term. The only problem, she did not know if it was something, she was willing to give right now while she felt that she was in the peak of her career. Everything was falling into place on the date; Blake saw this being more than what she bargained for. Surprisingly, she never imagined being at this point of not wanting what she thought she wanted. Always accused of thinking too deep in any situation, she was doing it again. She thought about it and began enjoying her night with Michael, the long awaited date. They went to a nice Lebanese restaurant about twenty minutes outside of town. Very high maintenance and sophisticated, which was just how she liked her men. They talked for hours about law and business the entire evening. He even offered to set up a meeting with her company as a new client prospect. He thought it could be a good business move for the both of them. She agreed and they exchanged the numbers of their assistants to set up something.

She then changed the subject, "I did not know you lived here". He responded, "Yeah, I moved here a few months ago, trying something new. I needed to get things off the ground here for prospects. I have been trying to expand the company and prove to my grandfather that I am in this for the long haul. "So your grandfather is giving you a hard time on the job," asks Blake. "My grandfather is a character within his own. He started this company as a young man and he feels that everyone should have the same passion and desire that he had", states Michael.

Blake chuckled at the comment Michael makes about his grandfather. Michael asks, "I did not know that Bernard Mowry was your father. I have admired his work for many years. He has won major cases and broken barriers that many other attorneys could not do". Blake smiles, "My father did a lot of things, but it took its toll on everyone. I try not to be as busy as he was, but somehow I end up working the long hours, not taking vacations, and taking away time from family".

"There is nothing wrong with working hard. You have only yourself to worry about; you don't have children or a spouse that you are missing out on, you can focus solely on your career", implies Michael. "But, I do have my friends, my mother and my sister, who care about me and expect to see me more, but I cannot because of the demands and expectations of my job", states Blake. "I bet you are so good at your job, that they couldn't manage without you being there"..."I don't know about that". Trying to divert the conversation to something else, Blake wondered to herself if her job was the only thing that she did alone. Not wanting to let Michael know this was on her mind, she pushed the conversation back on him quickly. "So, what do you like to do in your spare time"..."Sometimes, I like to go fishing with some of my college friends. We will rent a cabin for the weekend and go fishing. Don't ask how we starting doing it, it was a tradition we started years ago and somehow we can't seem to break it". Michael has this look on his face as if he is ashamed of fishing for some reason. He does not know how Blake is going to react. She reassures him, "Why would you want to break a tradition like that; there is nothing wrong with that. Let me tell you my girls' and I do every Wednesday. We either take a day off or make sure we are available to spend the day together. We begin the day by going to Starbucks, and then we may go to the spa for a facial, pedicure, or manicure, depending on how we feel, and that is for starters." Fascinated with the glow Blake depicted when she talked about her relationship with her friends, Michael could do nothing but admire it. "Wow"! Was the only expression he could have after hearing what she had to say? "I don't want to tell it all, but you should never be a shamed of what you do for enjoyment or the bond you share with your friends, especially if it makes you happy".

The manager of restaurant began locking the doors and the wait staff began vacuuming and cleaning the tables, kicking the two of them out. As Michael helped Blake up, she thought to herself of the lovely evening she had with him. As they were walking to the car, Blake had this glow on her face that she only got when she brought in a new client with her firm or made a deal with a company. She was actually thinking that this could lead to something, and then she stopped herself from thinking too much from just one date. While driving her back to her mother's house, neither one of them knew how they wanted to end the evening. In her head, Blake was contemplating if she should kiss him or let him make the first move; while on the other hand, he was thinking, should I kiss her or just escort her to the door.

On the other hand, Dalia and Jayden are returning the club, wasted as ever. They had so much fun; they don't know what to do with themselves. They barely make it out of the car. As they help each other across the lawn, they landed on the chairs outside near poolside. While laying there zoned out, Dalia opens up to Jayden that she is considering staying in New Jersey, "You know, I have been thinking since Friday night, that I need to make me happy. For years, I have been happy through someone else and I need to do something for me". Dozing in and out Jayden replies, "Are you saying that you are going to stay here? I hope the incident with Terrance has nothing to do with your decision to move here because running away is not going to solve the problem, it is going to create chaos". Listening attentively Dalia responds, "I want to do something else in a different place. I want to try it"..."Whoa, whoa, what about Terrance", Jayden asked. "What about him". Dalia thinks to herself for a moment while Jayden is talking, "So, you are just going to give up on him after all you heard this weekend" states Jayden. "What I heard this weekend has nothing to do with his commitment he made to me, which showed it was nothing"..."I never wanted you to give up on him; I just wanted you to see past the hurt and not give up on life, cause there is life after a breakup. But, it sounds to me like you already have your mind made up". Dalia turns toward Jayden, "I think I have". They finally get up to help each other make it through the side door.

When Blake and Michael arrive at the house, Blake jumps out of the car and thanked Michael for a nice evening. She realized that she did that without waiting to see what he was going to do; she felt that she messed up that moment. He jumped out of the car to walk her to do the door; he leaned in to give her a kiss. This is what she was waiting for, a romantic ending. He kissed her and she melted. He told her he would call her later and made sure she was okay before returning to Maryland. She smiled and went into the house. By the time she opens the door, who does she see coming from the other end of the house but Jayden and Dalia. They nearly scare each other to death. Jayden a little more aware than Dalia looks to Blake, "Help me get her up the stairs". Blake assists with getting Dalia up the stairs and she quietly asks Jayden, "Is Lauren already here"..."I haven't seen her since we got here and we have been here for a minute". By the time they get upstairs, Blake has this worried look on her face. "She is probably with Kendall still", implies Jayden. "Hey, but she would have called or texted by now and we haven't heard anything. I am going to text her". Going back downstairs, Blake sends Lauren a text message checking to see if everything is ok with her. Minutes went by and still no response from Lauren. Jayden runs downstairs to get a glass of water and asks Blake if she heard anything from Lauren. "Not a word. Maybe we should go looking for her"..."Lauren is ok, she is just getting her groove back, oh, wait a minute, she never had one. She is just getting her groove on". Jayden laughs to herself while Blake is in a nervous wreck. Finally, she gets a reply from Lauren, "Hey, I am fine. See you guys in the morning and I won't be late, promise. Love you!" As soon as she gets the response, she turns in for the night.

Back at Kendall's place, Lauren is having the time of her life. Never thinking she would even have a good time on this trip, she has met the man of her dreams. It is about 2 AM in the morning and Lauren looks at her cell, "I didn't know it was this late. I have to get back to the house or my girls are going to think something is wrong". While opening a very expensive bottle of wine, Kendall reassures Lauren that is everything is ok since she sent the text message to Blake. Kendall pours Lauren a glass of wine and she turns on soft music. He hands her the glass and the talk and sip the wine for another two hours. It is now 4 AM and Lauren begins finding her clothes so that she can return to the mansion without anyone seeing her come through the door. Kendall takes her home and he tells her that he is going to fly out Monday evening to see her. So delighted that she didn't have to mention them seeing each other, she smiles back to him while getting out of the car. "I can't wait to see you". She closed the door and headed toward the house. Lauren is able to get in the house without anyone knowing. She gets upstairs and into her room to change her clothes, but little does she know, Dalia is drunk as hell and Jayden is wide open in their rooms, so not much is going to get past them.

Lauren throws her pumps on the floor and her pocketbook on the bed. She flops on the bed thinking of her evening out. She gets a soft knock at the door. She tries to ignore it so the person could go away, but a little voice says, "Let me in. I know you are up and I heard you creeping in here like no one could hear you". Lauren ran to the door, opened it, and snatched Jadyen in. Out of all the people to catch her, it would be Jayden. Knowing that Lauren is not used to moments like this of meeting a guy and sleeping with him after just knowing him for a couple of hours, Jayden just wanted to make fun of her because she know Lauren was going to feel uncomfortable. "What happened? Who is he, where is he from and what does he do? You aren't saying anything. Did he turn you out or did you turn him out" Jayden is asking all of these questions while she follows her into the bathroom. "I would say something, but you have been talking a mile a minute since you got in here"…"Well, it is not everyday that "Miss plan-it-all" does something that is not on the agenda". Rolling her eyes at Jayden, she knew she was right. She loved to plan everything and punctuality was her middle name.

"Jay, I have met a man that I don't even know how to describe. I feel like I have known him all my life. He makes me happy and he is so into me. He is my match". Surprising to her this come out of Lauren's mouth, Jayden looks at her, "Are you sure he didn't put anything in your drink when you weren't looking or something". Smiling, Lauren states, "I am sure. He hasn't done nothing, but touch my heart and I don't even know how he did it". Jayden kind of frowned her face. "Ok, this is a little spooky for me. So, you are telling me that you think this guy that you have only known for a couple of hours, maybe the one"? Lauren turns on the shower. "I don't think, I know he is the one for me". Too astonished to say anything, "I can't believe you are telling me this right now. We came to New Jersey for a visit, a vacation, and you done fell in love. This is too much for me. I know it is time to go home where shit makes sense". Lauren still on a cloud nine says to Jayden, "You are in love too and you have the man of your dreams, but you are too afraid to admit it, but close the door so I can finish washing". With a dumb look on her face, Jayden thinks about what Lauren said to her and she closed the door and exited her room.

While walking out of the room, Jayden runs into Blake who asks if Lauren was ok and Jayden gives Blake bits and pieces of Lauren's love story. Blake asks Jayden, "And tell me again, why are we up at six o'clock in the morning". Blake and Jayden look at each other and they head back to their rooms. "I want to lay down for a couple of hours before Lou wakes all of us up for breakfast"..."Good night", coming from Jayden. Dalia finally came to life for a quick moment only to regurgitate in the bathroom, which each all of them could hear in their rooms.

They only slept for a couple of hours before they awoken by Lou's voice over the intercom system in the house, "Breakfast is ready to be served". They all pull their heads from under the covers like they were teenagers being waken for high school, but in this case, they partied like there was no tomorrow. Barbara running through the halls was excited to have her house full of life with the young, ambitious women, as she thought of them. She wanted to discuss all about their night at the White event. None of them was too excited to discuss that kind of talk with Blake's mother, but Barbara couldn't resist herself from trying to get something out them. Little did she know that one of them had some news of their own that she was going to be very excited about hearing? While getting dressed and preparing themselves for breakfast, Dalia finally sober was in the mirror reassuring herself that this was the right step to take. "Something new", right. She kept saying that to herself the entire morning, but the only other person she told was Jayden.

Coming down the stairs together, Jayden and Lauren were conversing about the first thing they are going to do once they got back home. "Good Morning   ladies, I am going to hate to see you leave. I enjoyed the company. You all should come back and visit again". Smiling from ear to ear, Jayden and Lauren, as Blake and Dalia come downstairs. "Thank you for having us stay at your home", states Lauren. "It looks like someone is going to be staying permanently". Jayden gets a shrug in the arm from Dalia for spilling news before she does. "What news" asks Blake? "I have decided not to go back with you all. I need a change and I think now is a good time to do that". The eyes and mouths of Lauren and Blake are so wide open; they are shocked and confused at the same time as Dalia tells them she is staying in Jersey. Immediately, Lauren is thinking to herself, what about our Wednesdays? It will never be the same with Dalia missing. Blake's mother, smiling from ear to ear, stated, "You have decided to take my job offer?" Blake not knowing what her mother is talking about, asks, "What job offer?" Barbara began explaining to Blake the private conversation that she and Dalia had about her moving there and how she could have a new start and a new job working with her. Blake looks at Dalia, "Are you sure this is what you and want and you are going to be happy"? Dalia answers her as confident has she can just to avoid any questions from any of them.

"Everyone sit down and enjoy Lou's breakfast. I tried to get her to fix some of everyone's favorites. I know you all are going to want to leave early to get back, but I wanted the breakfast to be memorable." While she is talking, they are all taking their seats at the large dining room table. They were all sending their signature of approval to Dalia through smiles from across the table. The closest to her, Jayden, gave her the warmest hug. The table was filled with pancakes, fruits, grits, eggs, ham, bagels, bacon, sausage, cereal, hash browns, toast, waffles, etc, you name it, and it was on the table. They discussed when they were leaving and the nice time they had on their visit. Lauren, of course, stated she would definitely return. Dalia seemed so revived even though she should have had a hangover from her eventful night with Jayden. A cell phone went off and Jayden knew it was hers, so she ran upstairs to answer it. Just as soon as she left the table, Dalia brought Lauren out. "I think someone else has some news at this table, since Jayden wants to bring me out, I am going to bring someone else out"…"Damn, do any of you keep anything to yourself, states Lauren. "The guilty always speak", laughing to her self, Dalia was waiting for Lauren to share her news. Now everyone is anticipating Lauren to share something but, "well, what happened? What do you have to share that is so important", asks Barbara. Lauren began to grin, "I met a guy last night". You could hear the moans and groans all across the table. "Shut up! I am serious. I think he is the one. Have you ever met anyone who can complete your sentences and your thoughts? It's like you get a feeling in your soul that tells you to let go and tells you it is right. I don't know, I can't describe it to you." Lauren throws her hand to them in frustration that she can't describe the feeling she has for Kendall and continues to eat her breakfast. Barbara breaks the ice, "Honey, I know what you are feeling. It is an uncontrollable thing. When you start talking, you tell things you don't mean to say. You can ignore anything around you when you engage into each other's eyes. The wrong seems so right and most of all, the LOVE words just wants to jump out of your mouth". Barbara was so feeling what Lauren was going through that she was beginning to give herself the chills, but Lauren understood where she was coming from. They have their little moment at the table while the others enjoy their breakfast.

On the other hand, Jayden is upstairs trying to get to her phone and when she answers it, Brian is on the other end. He sounds very calm even though she hasn't talked to him in two days. Somehow, the tone in his voice seemed that he understood this time away was not to bring distance from the relationship, but mentally time away with her friends and the rest of the world. Not knowing where this conversation was leading, Jayden started, "Hey, babe, how are you? I have been thinking about you a lot". Before she is able to say another word, Brian interjects, "Beep this, I haven't heard nothing from you in two days. So, you done went to Jersey and found you a new man, huh". Jayden's mouth dropped on the phone, "What are you talking about? We have just been busy; I was coming straight to you once I got back". All she could hear was Brian breathing hard on the phone. Finally, he says something, "Man, do what you do like you been doing for the whole damn weekend". Jayden knew he was more than mad, so one sat on the bad, to soothe him out, but she was unsure if she was able to do that over the phone and not in person. "Bee, are you serious? You have always been my ace. Why would I come here and find someone else". By this time, her voice is getting louder and Blake is beginning to hear her just a little bit, but she starts conversation to keep the attention off what is going on upstairs. "I will talk to you when I get home and don't do anything stupid by the time I get there" She hung up the phone in frustration, but she didn't want to let everyone else know that Brian bothered her that bad. She took a moment to compose herself and then she went back downstairs to finish her breakfast.

Back downstairs, the conversation rose with Dalia moving again. "I am going to come back in about a week to resolve some things; like with my job, condo, and pack most of my things." Blake states, "I will help you with that, it won't be a problem because it will give me a chance to see Michael..."Michael" asked her mother. "Yeah, I met him on a conference that I had with my job a couple of months ago. I ended up seeing him again at the gala last night and we went out for drinks"..."What firm does this Michael work for?" asked her mother. "His grandfather owns the law firm, Lansford & Son". Barbara began to read her newspaper and then she looked up, "I know them and your father used to mentor Michael. He is a very nice man. I hope he is nothing like his father, putting it likely so that it won't dampened the impression that Michael made on her. His grandfather is a very sophisticated man. He came from a wealthy family"..."What do you mean like his father, asks Blake? "Child, his father has so many children all over the place, I don't think he knows all of them"..."I don't know him that well to know what kind of man he is and he didn't mention anything about his father to me", Blake saying with a smile as she drunk her coffee. Jayden not saying much once she returned to the table, so Barbara directs her attention towards her. "Honey, you haven't said anything since you took that call upstairs"..."I am fine, I just need to get back home and straighten some things out". Dalia rolled her eyes, "You know what that means..."yeah, she and Brian got into it and when they get back, they are going to make up like always", states Lauren. "I would have a few words to say to you, but we are in the presence of wise-ness so I won't blast none of y'all right now", Jayden grinds her teeth to the rest of them as she speaks. "Anyway, when are we leaving, Blake"..."Uh, I about an hour we are going to hit the road. We should be all packed up right when we finish breakfast", Blake looks at her watch to figure out the tine frame for finishing breakfast, pack and be ready to hit the road.

Lou enters the room and the women thank her so much for all her hard work including the rest of the staff for preparing the breakfast. They all began getting up from the table. They were all chattering to themselves while going upstairs to pack their bags. Barbara had this sad look on her face as if she did not want them to leave, which she didn't really want them to leave, but she knew they weren't going to be there forever. Looking up the staircase, Barbara asked aloud, "When are you all coming back to visit". The response back, "Huh, I am not going anywhere, so you will have to tell me when you want me to leave". Barbara knew right off hand who that was from, Dalia, and for a moment she almost forgot that she was staying. As she laughs to herself, she hears the side door open near the pool, "Hi! I am back and I am so tired. Why don't we go get some breakfast"? Instantly, Barbara turned and saw that Blair entered the room. "Honey, what are you doing here? I did not expect you until another week or so". She ran towards her giving her a hug. "Who do all of these bags belong to?"... "Oh, your sister is upstairs and she brought some of her friends with her for a visit. You missed them". Blair began looking a little displeased because to herself she was wondering if Jayden was one of those friends. That was her least favorite friend of Blake's. For some reason, the two of them could not get along. Out of all the people to come downstairs, Jayden runs down to put her things in the SUV. As soon as she came down the stairs, she runs directly into Blair. She looks, "What the hell" before she was able to catch herself. Barbara trying to smooth things over, "Girls, it is so good to have all of you here". She was trying to come up with something to avoid a nasty mingle between the two. Jayden forgot that she was in her mother's house and she comes out of her mouth as if she doesn't belong.

Blake runs downstairs, "Hey, we need to leave in an hour if we want to get back before it is dark". As Blake continues to talk, she sees her sister in the doorway. She runs towards her and gives her the biggest hug. Barbara stands to the side with joy in her eyes as she watched her daughters embrace each other. Jayden goes on to the car to load her bags and then down come Lauren, who seems to be Blair's favorite friend of her sisters'? They catch up for a while and Blair invites Lauren back to the house for a visit. Lauren began telling Blair about the guy she met and that she will be back soon to visit and she would love to stay at the mansion if it was okay with Barbara. Barbara intercedes, "Of course you girls are always welcomed here". Blair states, "There you go. When you come back, you are going to stay here and we are going to have some real fun. I know Blake did not know where to take you". They laugh and share jokes with each other. Somehow, Blake is distracted from the schedule she had for them to get back. "Mother, has some news that she needs to share with you", states Blake. "What!" states Barbara. "Dalia is going to be staying here. She decided to move here." Blair's mouth dropped when she heard the words coming out of Blake's mouth. With her very possessive persona, she did not know how to react and of course, Barbara was afraid that her eldest daughter would once again act as if she was a teenager. Unfortunately, they did not get the show they hoped for; she embraced Dalia with open arms and welcomed her to the house once she came down the stairs. Blair whispers in her sister's ear, "Whose shock now", there was nothing to say; there was a lot they wanted to say but they left well enough alone.

"This is good and all, but we need to get home. Ma, love you. Lauren, Jayden, come on if we are going to make it back in time to do anything tonight", as she is pulling her bags out the house to the car. Dalia already is feeling left out of everything, but she knew it was something that she had to get used to since she was relocating. "Dang, I wish I could come with you all. Where are you all going tonight", asks Dalia. No one wanted to answer her because it would not have mattered if she knew or not, but at the same time it would spare her feelings from missing them so much. "I will call you once we are on the road friend. I am going to miss you", Jayden hugs Dalia again before she walks out the door. "I will be back here soon chick and we can catch up then", Lauren states as she walks out the door. Reality hits Dalia when the door closes. Now it was time for her to get her life on track like the way she wants it.

Chapter 8: Lights, Camera, Action

Jayden pulls in the driveway of her home, checks her mail, opened her garage only to drive her car in slowly, so that she could make a nice entrance into her home. When she opens the door to her house, she only takes her pocketbook and her small carry on bag that she loved so much. She did not notice anything at first, so she took several small trips to her car, to get all of her bags out. After getting the last bags out of the car, she turned off the garage lights and on the kitchen lights. Still not noticing anything, she took a couple pieces of mail and her pocketbook down to her room. She opened the door to her room, "What the fuck"; Brian was in her room waiting for her to return from her trip. Shocked to see someone in her house, "What are you doing here and why didn't you call...and where is your car, because it wasn't outside?" asked Jayden.

With a very serious look on his face, Brian stood up, "I need to talk to you and you weren't answering your phone or my text messages, so I didn't know what that meant", states Brian.

"My phone was turned off most of the trip and I just turned it back on when I came back to town", states Jayden.

"So, there was no time in there where you felt that you should have called me or let me know that you were ok". Jayden has this pathetic look on her face because she knew that Brian was right and there was no excuse for her to be out of touch for the whole weekend. She refrains back to what she know she could control,

"You didn't answer my question, where is your car"... "My car is in the back yard...."So, you were trying to sneak up on me, what did you think you were trying to prove by doing that? Jayden tries to divert the conversation to something else in order to distract Brian off what is important.

"I parked my car where I always park my car when I come over here. If you start paying attention to me more often, you would notice that". He walks past her in frustration to the other room in the house. Jayden follows behind him, "What is

119

wrong with you? I was hoping to return from my trip and have a good evening with you, but that can change too". At first, he did not want to pay her any attention, but when he heard "But" come out of her mouth an instant reaction to the average black man, "What the fuck is that suppose to mean". Of course, he did not scare her with his words, "it meant just what I said. You in my house with an attitude"..."Damn right", states Brian. "I came here for a reason and you pissing me off". Jayden stopped for a minute and for a quick second Barbara popped in her head and she could remember the conversation that had. She evaluated the situation before making a comment, "okay, I apologize. Let's just start from the beginning. What did you want to talk about?" At first Brian did not want to say anything to her because she pissed him off, but he did not know how to react to this new revised Jayden. "Uh, sit down; I want to talk to you about something". He grabbed her hand as she walked to the couch to sit down. He sat across from her with a very serious look in his eyes. She was waiting patiently only because she remembered the advice Barbara gave her.

"I mean, you mean the world to me. I don't know if you know that or not, but I love you and I really care about you". Jayden interrupts him, "Babe, you can tell me anything. Just go ahead and say it". He takes a deep breath, "Will you marry me?" Brian pulled a 2 carat ring out of his pocket and placed it in front of her. Jayden was so shocked that she did not know what to do. She was frozen for a moment. This shocked her because they were arguing non stop for a couple of months. Even though it was bringing them closer, the bickering was keeping them a part. She knew how she felt about him, but she did not always show it. Somehow he knew how she felt. "Hey, are you going to say anything. If you aren't going to accept you can just tell me that. I am a man, I can take it". She stops him in mid sentence, "Yes, yes...I will marry you". He kisses her nonstop for about fifteen minutes. She stops him to put the ring on her finger and he looks at her, "You ain't going no where tonight if I got anything to say about it". He kisses her again leaning backwards on the couch. Just as the moment intensifies, her phone rings. Brian whispers to her "let it ring". She ignores it for a minute, and then she panics, thinking it could be an emergency with her mother or with her father. Because she did not want to ruin the moment and she did not want Brian to think his word did not mean anything, she did not answer her phone. Was it the smart thing to do? It was a missed call from an unknown caller, so it was difficult for her to trace it, but she figured if it was important, they would leave a message. She continues the rest of her evening with Brian on the couch, in the bedroom, in the living room, all over the house. It was a memorable moment for the both of them. She would never forget the night Brian proposed.

Lauren walks through the door of her house on the phone while trying to carry her bags at the same time. She drops on of her bags while turning the key into her door. She is on the phone with her mother telling her all the details of the trip and the nice guy she met. She wanted her mother's reaction and her opinion. Even though it would not matter at this point because Lauren's mind was set, she still wanted the support of her mother in the process. Her mother was interested in meeting the dream man instead of hearing all the good. She continues her conversation with her mother while checking her mail. She goes upstairs to her office and sits at her desk talking to her mother. She began to yawn on the phone. She realized how exhausted she became from the trip and discontinued her conversation with her mother. Hanging up with her mother, she turned on her stereo in her bedroom and laid down on the bed for a nap. She slept for about an hour. When she woke up, she checked her voicemail, which is normally what she does on Friday mornings. There were three messages from Kendall, a mysterious message from Jason and a message from Terrance. Lauren saved that message because she did not know how to handle it. She wanted to wait until she spoke with Dalia before doing anything and she knew if she asked Jayden it would be a quick meaningless response, "Don't call him back". She knew that would be her response so it would be no reason to mention it to her. Lauren noticed it was getting late, so she began unpacking her things and organizing next week's schedule. She called Kendall back and of course; he was excited to here from her.

"Where have you been," Kendall states in a very smooth, deep voice. "I was calling you, babe"... "I fell asleep while talking to my mother," explained Lauren. "I have been missing you like crazy. I want to see you". Lauren gets chill bumps whenever Kendall talks. She expressed her feelings in return. He asked again, "Are you sure you miss me and you want to see me?" She responds to him, "What do I have to do to show you how much I care about you and that I want to be with you". Kendall tells her to come downstairs and when she walks down there, he was standing at the door. Lauren was so shocked that she did not know what to do. She did not want to seem selfish by asking him to come so soon, but somehow he read her mind. She opened the door and ran into his arms. The first thing she noticed it that he did not have any luggage with him. "Honey, where are your things? I know you did not fly here without anything". Looking down at his arms, "I did not think about bringing anything, I just wanted to see you. Clothes were not important". Lauren hugs him again and assures him that he does not have to worry about clothes; they could always go to the store and get more.

She instantly thought about work. Shockingly, she looked at Kendall, "What are you going to do about work". He responds, "Work is fine. I will have that handled. My casework isn't high right now. I just want to be with you". Kendall being the romantic that he is carries Lauren up the stairs, into her bedroom and they make love to a Billie Holiday CD. As he laid her on the bed, he pours honey on her stomach while it was warm. Slowly, he rubs it from the top of her stomach to the top of her inner most private section of her body. He licked her stomach from the bottom to the top, moving upwards toward her right breast, then her left breast. Lauren enjoying herself, moans slowly and softly as her hands grab the headboard tightly. While he continues to kiss her moving upward toward her neck, she rubs his back from bottom to top, letting him know how pleased she was. He wanted to show Lauren how deeply he felt for her and that his feelings were real. In response, she made sure that Kendall got the same response from her. The lovemaking continued on for about an hour when Lauren's doorbell rang. Not expecting anyone this late in the evening, she grabbed the closest robe to her, and ran downstairs. "Do you want me to come down with you?" Kendall stilling lying in the bed while Lauren grabbed her robe, Lauren assures him that she will be ok and who ever is at the door will get pushed out. "Coming", she yelled as she ran down the stairs. She opened the door and it is Terrance.

"What are you doing here", asks Lauren. "Hello, how are you? Where is Dalia? I need to talk to her, but she will not answer any of my calls nor will she call me back. I don't know how to get to her, and I know you could help me". Looking very anxious to get back upstairs to Kendall, "Look, Terrance, you really should be talking to Dalia about this and I don't want to be caught in the middle of it. I wish I could help, but I can't". Terrance let himself in through the door trying to convince Lauren to help him. "Terrance now is not a good time. I am busy". As Lauren is trying to politely tell Terrance that she has company, Kendall makes his presence known by coming downstairs to check on Lauren, "Is everything ok down here"? The thought still not running across his mind, he was fixated on Dalia and trying to get in touch with her. "Terrance, when I talk to her, I will tell her to call you, I promise". She knew that would be the only way to get him out of her house. "Thank you, Lauren; I knew I could count on you". He walks toward the door. "I cannot promise you anything, but I will try".

When Lauren closes her door, she knew Kendall was waiting for some of explanation, not that he deserved one because he just came into her life. "Kendall that was Dalia's ex. They broke up right before we came to Jersey. I guess he hasn't talked to her since, about a couple of weeks, so he came here to get in touch with her?" Listening carefully to the story, Kendall has this look on his face that is was trying to wrap his mind around why Lauren's girlfriend's ex would show up at her door wanting help and insisting on getting her to help him. Kendall sits up in the chair, "Tell me, they broke up because of a simple disagreement and not infidelity". Bending her lips, "Well, let's just say no one didn't have to tell Dalia he cheated, she saw it". Kendall's mouth dropped as if he was lost for words. "Are you serious? How long were they dating?" Not wanting to share more details than necessary, "They were together since high school". You could see the change in Kendall's face when he heard the longevity of the relationship. "That is too long for someone to be in a relationship for something like that to happen". Laughing to herself, "That is the same thing Dalia said. I really think that is the reason why she hasn't returned any of his calls or reached out to him." Kendall stands up, "Can we focus on the two of us right now?" She walks toward him, "I thought you would never ask". The two of them go back upstairs, but before going, Lauren makes a trip to the kitchen for some strawberries and whipped cream. She brings them upstairs and she could see the excitement on Kendall's face. They lay together and shared for the rest of the evening until they fell asleep.

While Lauren is enjoying the surprise trip from Kendall, she forgot about the arrangements she made with the girls to go out. Apparently, Jayden forgot also since she is in her romantic mode with Brian because of their recent engagement. Blake, on the other hand, tried to contact her two girlfriends, but could not reach them. She found herself alone, without something to do. She tried calling them, but of course, they were unavailable. At home, alone, in her gorgeous house, she decided to call Michael. She wondered why she didn't think of that earlier. When she phoned him, he was so excited to hear from her. He just walked in the door from having dinner with his father, so, he was free and available, just how Blake liked her men. They talked for an hour about life and goals. She saw something different in Michael that she didn't see in Jersey. She realized he could be a good friend, or he could be something serious in her life. She didn't want to think more into it because this was some guy that she jus met, "I am going to take the Jayden approach with this one. Let it be what it be". Who does that sound like, her girl Jay. That was always how she approached the situation with a man, sad, but true. Jayden was so hard on men that she would beat them at their game, which was something that none of them could ever model from Jayden. She would consistently remind them of that on occasion.

Blake decided to fix herself a glass of wine. She knew if there wasn't anything else she could do, she could do that. She pulled out her laptop and started searching on the internet. She thought to herself, "I could decorate my office here since I haven't had the chance to do so in a long time". She went to Macy's web site and looked for a while, but she didn't see anything appealing. She then searched through overstock.com and boy, did the time slip away from her. Before she knew it was midnight and she spent most of her evening on the web searching for God knows what. When she saw the time, she jumped up and realized she didn't prepare herself for work. She looked through her closet several times, but she couldn't find anything to fit her mood. She finally decided to wear her navy blue suit that always seems to bring her good luck. She took a long hot bath, climbed in the bed, turned on her television, and to sleep she went.

Dalia, on the other hand, finally retuned Terrance's called. After her well-deserved weekend with the ladies, she felt that she reached a point where she could have a normal conversation with him. When she called him, he sounded like hell to her. He was shocked to here from her, so, of course, he assumed that she was at home.

"Hey, I just wanna talk to you. Can I come by are you up, is it ok?" She slowly responded to him,

"No, I am not at home and I won't be. I decided to make some changes and I did".

"What do you mean you made a change"? Terrance is now yelling on the other end of the phone. He realizes that not only is Dalia not willing to talk to him, but she has moved away.

"I decided to move to New Jersey and that is where I am at now. I wanted to call and let you know".

"So, you didn't think I would like to know that before you decided to move. What about the house we had together and all the memories? You can't just throw all of that away". Tears started to roll down Dalia's face because she never saw him react or show so much passion for anyone. She thought he loved her before, but his true feelings were just exposed.

"I needed something different and I need to do something for me". She took a deep a breath, hoping that he would understand. On the other end of the phone, Terrance is trying to swallow all of this, because in his mind, it doesn't make sense why she would do such a thing.

"Look, I don't know what happened to you or why you are running from me. You ain't ever done that before. I know your friends aren't telling you to do me like this, cause they never got in our business before, so, what is up. Did you meet someone else, or have you really given up on us altogether. Please, let me know something".

"Why do I have to meet someone to move on"... "So, that is what it is, you have moved on now".

"You are twisting my words"... "No, I am trying to understand what the hell you are telling me. For all of these years, I have made you my world. I messed up and I want a chance to fix it. I can't get that, damn."

There was a pause because Dalia was not prepared for him to lay it on her like that. She didn't know what to say to him,

"You don't have anything to say. You had a lot to say when we first got on the phone, but know you mute. Where are you staying?"

"I am staying with Blake's mother until I get some money saved to get my own place. She offered me a job and I decided to take her up on her offer". Terrance waited a moment before he said anything to her, but he just couldn't help himself.

"So, you are going to leave your home, that is yours, to go out on a venture, when we were starting a life together, that don't make sense to me".

"Apparently, a lot of things don't make sense, if that was the case, I would know why you felt the need to run to the arms of someone else. Since you have so much to say, let's talk about that then". On the other end of the line, there was absolute silence. Apparently, he didn't expect for Dalia to come out like that, but they haven't had that conversation yet.

"Eh, I want to talk about this, but I am not going to do this over the phone. Are you going to come back here, or do I need to come there. It don't make me no never mind". She didn't know what to say to that, but there was a part of her that felt that she owed him the opportunity to explain himself, or at least here him out.

"I will come back there since I need to make some phone calls and do something with house".

"Do you know when you will be coming down?"

"Since, today is Sunday; I may leave out on Monday or Tuesday. I will have to buy a plane ticket or a bus ticket, not sure, but I will figure out something."

"Don't worry about it, I will book you a plane ticket for in the morning, and I will pick you up from the station and we will go back to our house and talk about this, dammit"

"Are you telling me what to do, how you know I want you to pick me up".

"If you ever loved this dick, you will be at the airport in the morning and ready when I come get you tomorrow".

Terrance hung up the phone without saying another word to her. Boy was he mad at her. Somehow, Dalia was not surprised because she knew how determined he could get once he has his mind set on something. There was this little voice in the back of her head telling her that maybe she should give the relationship another try, but then there was another voice telling her, hear his side first. She was indecisive, but she knew for sure that she couldn't just leave the relationship with everything unresolved. Surprisingly to her that Terrance didn't try to come back to the house sooner, since they did share the condo together and they purchased it together. Standing beside the bed in the guest suite of Barbara's house, Dalia stood there stunned about her conversation with Terrance. She started packing her bag, but she contemplated for a while because she did not know how long she was going to be gone or how quickly she would return.

She stopped packing for a moment to go to the intercom system to see if Barbara was at home. She answered to her and Dalia asked her to come to her room so they could talk. Barbara decided to rest for the rest of the evening once she came back from church. She was watching a lifetime movie eating her favorite yogurt in a silk robe her late husband bought her for her birthday last year.

When she knocked at the door, Dalia gave her the ok to come in. She began explaining to her that she was going to tie up some loose ends in Baltimore. When the first sentence came out of her mouth, Barbara took a seat on the bed.

"So, you talked to Terrance, didn't you?"

"How did you know" He called and I realized that I never gave him the chance to state his case or here his side of the story".

"I don't know what you want to hear, you saw it all. What you want to do is see if it is worth saving and keeping. Good men are hard to come by and that doesn't mean that good men don't mess up. I think that is something that young women seem to forget. Everything is not going to be good and grand all the time. Sometimes things are just bad, but it's the person on the inside that makes all the difference. I doesn't matter what anyone else thinks, look at your heart and if you can find a part of you that will forgive him and move on, then you do so and live happy, but if you can't, then you can cut your losses and move on."

"I hear what you are saying and you are right. Maybe I do need to let him explain or to just hear him out. Okay, I just wanted to let you know that I am leaving in the morning and I am not sure when I will be back, but I am coming back. It all depends on how quick I can get everything squared away"

"Honey, take your time. I know you have to get your life together there before you can move on to something new. You only get one life and you should live it with no regrets"

Dalia finished packing her bags as Barbara walked out of the room. She ran downstairs to grab something to eat before she ran out to get some things for her flight tomorrow. While going downstairs, her cell phone rang and it was her mother. She hasn't spoken to her in about a week at the most. She wanted to check on her to see how everything was her. Someone spilled the beans to her about her break-up with Terrance. "Mommie, I will have to call you back, I am in the middle of doing something right now"…"Ok, baby, call me as soon as you get a moment". Dalia ended the call as soon as she could because she didn't know what kind of message she was going to get right now and she definitely didn't feel like hearing it.   Lou was in the process of fixing some club sandwiches as a snack for herself, so she made one for Dalia too. It was the best sandwich she had in a long time. She took the sandwich upstairs so that she could go online and see if Terrance really bought her plane ticket and sent the information to her email address. Just as soon as she opened her hotmail account, there was her confirmation and flight detail. "Wow, I can't believe he really did it, you have got to be kidding", which is what she was saying to herself. She printed the information off the printer and confirmed all the information. Once she got everything she needed, she placed it with her bags and left the house to run some errands. Of course, she didn't know many places to go by herself, so she previously asked Blair to take to the post office and to the ATM. By the time she walked outside, Blaire was in the driveway on the phone talking to a friend. She jumped in the car and the ladies went about their business. It didn't take long for them to handle everything since, Blair was just checking to see postal rates and addresses. She went to the ATM to get cash and check her balances so she wouldn't have to do it in the airport on tomorrow. Once they finished running the errands, they decided to stop to a bar for a drink before they turned in for the night. They talked for about an hour before they Blair brought her back to the mansion. When Blair dropped her off, Dalia went straight to bed because she knew she had a long day ahead of her.

Chapter 9: The Let Go & the Look UP

"Good morning, babe. Did you sleep ok"? Jayden rolls over after a wonderful night with Brian.

"It was good especially since I am waking up to my husband to be". Brian loved the sound of that, he laughed to himself.

It was about seven o'clock in the morning and Jayden didn't have to go to work until noon. Since she monitors so many stores in the area, today was a visitation day, where she is scheduled to make an appearance at one of her stores to see if it organized according to company policy. There really was no rush for her to get up, but Brian on the other hand was working a different shift than she was this week. Normally, he works very early in the morning and is done by noon. He changed his schedule for someone who needed to switch with him.

Brian got out of the bed to get dress for work. He received a call from his supervisor that they needed him to come to work earlier than what he planned. While preparing himself to leave Jayden's house, he shook her so that she could wake up.

"I have to go into work early. Mike just called me and told me that they are backed up, so I have to go in". Halfway sleep and wake at the same time, Jayden just nodded her head to Brian.

"Jay, you heard me"?

"Yeah, I heard you babe", as she lay back down to go to sleep.

"Come back over here when I get off tonight. Love you, babe"

"I love you too. Brian closes the door and leaves for the day.

About thirty minutes later, Jayden wakes up and gets herself ready for work. It finally hit her that she was now wearing a ring on her left hand. She never thought it would happen to her especially with all the mess she Brian was going through lately. As she was getting dressed, she got a text from Dalia,

"Hey, I am coming to down for a couple of days. Terrance is going to pick me up from the airport today. I will be staying at my place. Will call when I get there! Answer your phone."

Jayden didn't know what to say. She knew if she did a three way with Blake and Lauren, she would be late for work. But, Lauren was probably already at work, but this was important news to share because I know the rest of them didn't know any of that. "She is letting Terrance pick her up from the air port. Lord, Jesus, I am trying not to curse this early in the morning". Jayden didn't want to lose her motivation and momentum she woke up with so, she just responded back, "Ok, keep me posted", when she really wanted to know what the fuck was going on with her when they just saw her the day before.

Jayden then jumped in the shower and turned on her radio. She was praying to God to bless her union with Brian. She knew that some things they struggled with were her fault and she was willing to change, but she reached a different level when that ring slid on her finger. Nothing else in the world meant more to her at this moment. She began thinking to herself, what should my colors be, where will we get married, how many bridesmaids will I have, who is going to be my maid, and how much is all of this going to cost? She was thinking too much in depth too soon. Quickly, she deterred her mind to work and focusing on this horrible store she had to visit and inspect. While walking out of the door, she called the store manager of store #0809.

"Good Morning, this is Ms. Miller. I just wanted to know if the store was prepared for my visit on today or if you needed more time."

"Good Morning, uh, I know you have been wanting to come here for a couple of weeks, but we have been short staffed and it has taken me longer to get things organized in the way I know you like it to be done." Normally, this would piss her off when a store manager doesn't try to impress her. She thought it was a part of their job to keep their store in a certain way, especially if the visits are planned the same time each quarter. But, today was a different day for Jayden; she decided to reschedule the store's inspection for another week just to give the manager time to get what she needed done.

"Well, I will tell you what I can do for you this one time. I will reschedule your visit for a week from today. I will call you later with the exact time, but I want everything spotless. Do what you have to do to get this job done, ok". The store manager was so happy; she didn't know what to do.

"Thank you so much. You don't know how much this means to me and I won't let you down, I promise".

"Well, I hope not, but do what you need to do to get that store together". Jayden disconnects the call. She really didn't want to go to this store today. She wanted to daydream about her engagement and of course she would have time to do that with her girlfriends. So, instead of going downtown to the store, she headed to her office so she could check her messages, email, and write up reports to turn in to her boss. When she walked into the office, her colleagues quickly noticed her ring. Jayden didn't wear rings, but she did accessorize a lot. Kim, the other regional manager, ran out of her office to admire the ring. Jayden somewhat considered her a friend because they had the same background and shared some of the same goals. Jayden continued walking into her office with Kim right behind her.

"Chick, tell me how you did it. The last time we talked about men, you were on nigga status with Brian".

"Girl, I cam back from Jersey and he was on the marriage kick. I don't know what happened, but it did.

"Jay, I need to tell you something". Kim closes the door to Jayden's office so she couldn't be heard by anyone else in the office.

"They are creating a new job for regional managers and they want you to do the job"

"That is a good thing, right?"

"Jay, the job is located in Connecticut. The money is good, better than good. They will set you up with housing, car, and an allowance with this, but it's a long way from here."

"How do you know about it?"

"The candidates were you and me. I couldn't do anything because of my little girl. I don't wanna switch her to a new school and then I need to be available in case the school needs me. It would be a great career move for you, but since you came in here with your carats and all, I didn't think it was going to be good anymore".

Jayden began pacing around her office contemplating about the news Kim told him, but she was thinking to herself, "They haven't offered me anything yet. They may not offer us the same thing or they may have another candidate in mind". She was trying to come up with all kinds of things in her mind to make this seem easier than what it was, but she didn't know how to turn this one. Then, she started thinking how she could break the news to Brian without him thinking she didn't care about his feelings. But, on the other hand, it would be a good career move for her, "That would be selfish to make that decision by myself". Just as Jayden was in her daydream, she was buzzed her in office by her upper manager, Ron, who asked her to come to his office just as soon as she got a minute. When she answered back ok, she was looking directly in Kim's face. Kim, looking back at her, "Girl, I told you". Jayden took a long deep breath before she walked out of her office. She knew she had time to get herself together since upper management was on another floor from her.

When she got upstairs and knocked on Ron's door, he was delighted to see her. It was just the two of them in his office. He asked her to take a seat,

"I want to talk to you for a minute. First, I want to let you know, that I love what you have done for these stores and I hear nothing but good things about you from your store managers, which means a lot to me. You have been here for a little over two years and you have worked the hardest out of my regional managers. But, the company has decided to make some changes, which some that I am not proud of. We had to discontinue some jobs to cut back and save the company in the process. From saying that, Jayden we have to let you go. We have a wonderful severance package for you and as soon as things pick back up, you WILL be the first that I call back. Before you say anything, I want to let you know that you will receive $30,000 for your loss and suffering with the company. I had to fight to get that for you, but I hate having to tell you this news. Your health insurance will cover you for the next six months. I do apologize for this, but it was out of my control. It came down to the board and you know how that goes."

"What, this doesn't make any sense to me? One minute you are telling me that I am such an asset to the company and the next you are letting me ago after all the long hours and hard work that I put into this company. Then, you want me to take this severance package that is no where near my salary. How am I supposed to make it on this?"

"Jayden, I did all I could do. Hey, if I get a whiff of anything extra coming I will let you know, but right now, there is nothing that I can do".

Her heart was broken. This job signified an image that she worked hard to maintain with her family and friends. Humility all over her face, she didn't know how to accept the disappointment or what her next step would be. She knew she had a lot on her plate in the near future, but now it may have to come to a halt. Jayden sat in Ron's office for a few moments just to let everything settle in, by this time, Ron walked out of the office giving her a few minutes to get herself together. In just a short while, he returned with some documents in his hand, which guaranteed her severance, insurance, and some other documentation including professional references and the terms of her severance. Still in a daze, she accepted everything, thanked Ron for her time with the company and she headed to the elevator to return to her office. Just as soon as she got off the elevator, Kim was there waiting for her to here the news about her meeting with Ron.

"Alright, what happened and I want all the details, oh, and let me tell you, Brian called while you were upstairs. I told him I would tell you to call him later, but I didn't mention anything about your meeting. Hello, you aren't saying anything"

"I got laid off". This was the only thing that came out of her mouth. She was speechless, embarrassed, and hurt, all at the same time. Her feelings were all over the place. While walking to her office, Jayden explained everything to Kim the best that she could. Kim didn't know how to console her friend without sounding redundant or a jackass. Jayden began packing up all her personal belongings in her office as quick as she could. At this point, she couldn't stand the site of being in that place any longer. Kim offered to assist her and so she did. She walked Jayden's belongings to her car and back down to the garage as many times at Jayden needed her. What bothered Kim the most, is that there was no mention in the company of their being a cutback, not to say that there wasn't one, but she didn't want to mention that to Jayden as she could see how hurt she was. Kim reminded her that she needed to call Brian, so that he could be there for her, but she wasn't sure if she was getting through. Kim didn't want to call Brian herself because she thought it would be crossing the line. Jayden would call when she got ready to do so.

While Jayden was experiencing the low blow of losing her job, Lauren was at work taking everything head on. She found herself unable to concentrate and take thing seriously since her encounter with Kendall. She was late for two of her meetings this morning, which is so not like her and it didn't seem to bother her. She felt like she needed to rethink things and not put so much pressure on herself like they way she was doing. So unlike Lauren, she didn't even complete her schedule for the rest of the week, nor did she schedule her book club meeting, which she was suppose to handle as soon as she got back from her trip. What a difference a man can make in your life? Just as soon as she decides to block all distractions while sitting at her desk, her phone vibrates and it is a text message form Kendall telling her he missed her. When she looked at her phone, she saw a text message for earlier that morning from Dalia telling her that she would be in town and hopefully her schedule would permit her to take a break. She knew she was a little off balance, but somehow she didn't see it as a bad thing since she never had spice in her life.

"Lauren, I need those reports on my desk by Tuesday evening", states Lauren's manager. "Oh my God, I didn't realize that those reports were due already", Lauren said aloud to herself.

She plundered through her desk looking for the documents for this project, but she didn't remember where she put everything. She knew she had them, but she couldn't figure out if they were at home or in her office somewhere. She walked down the hall in her storage room to look for the files she needed for the project, but no luck there either. This project was very important to her and it would show the superiors within the company that she could do more work, deserved more, and especially deserved better pay. Since nothing seemed to be falling into play like she expected, she was beginning to panic like never before. She was beginning to think that she could have prepared herself better and how she hasn't been focused on the important things in life. She then thought again to herself, "I can do this and have a man. People do this all the time. I just have to find my balance between the two". She took a deep breath and began thinking of exactly where she stopped working on the project. When she did that, she found the documents she needed in her locked drawer. She asked one of the Administrative Assistants to get her a cup of coffee from the lobby downstairs and bring it to the conference room.

Lauren gathered her team of bookkeepers and her files and went into the conference to prepare the project for the presentation. So quickly, she was able to get herself together and focus on work.

"John, I need you to gather all the numbers for each employee for this group in 2008. Jack, I need you to give me a collective revision of the expense accounts given to each employee. Terry, I need you to give me a total of what the executives spent on luxuries versus company expenditures. Before she knew it, it was noon and they had accomplished so much, the project was near completion. She checked her watch and saw that it was 12:01. She ran to her office to check her phone to see if she had any missed calls or text messages. She had a missed call from Jayden, "Dalia is in town, not sure if she sent anything to you all, but I don't think I will be able to hang out for lunch. I will talk to you guys this evening. Love ya!"

Lauren had this puzzled look on her face because one, she didn't know who this "y'all' was in the message that she was referring to. She assumed that the other person must have been Blake. Two, "Dalia is in town, for what" and three, "If we all are suppose to go out, why can't Jay make it with us and then she says, will talk to you this evening. Something about that don't sound right". Lauren put her cell phone down and used her desk phone to call Blake to see if she knew what was going on for lunch. Blake answered,

"Ms. Daniels speaking, how may I help you?

"Hey, it's me. What is going on for lunch?

"What do you mean, I have been hear non stop working on a new proposal that is due Friday and I have the slightest idea of what this is going to be about"

"Did you get a text from Dalia or Jay today"?

"I haven't checked my phone today. I have been really busy."

"Girl, I got a text from Jay telling me that Dalia was going to be in town and that she wouldn't be able to hang with us for lunch and she would catch up with us later. Look at your damn phone. You are missing everything". Blake looked for her purse to see if she had any messages from either of them and she did see the texts from Jay and Dalia.

"Oh yeah, I have a text from Dalia that she was in town to get some things together and that Terrance was going to pick her up from the airport"

"Pick her up from the airport. When did they get on speaking terms?"

"The hell if I know, but if you all are going to do something for lunch, we need to make a move, because if I sit here any longer I am going to die, Blake was still staring at her computer screen.

"Hold on, I have a beep on the other line. "Good afternoon, Lauren here, how can I help you?

"Hi, it's Dalia. I hope you got my text this morning. Meet me at Olive Garden in twenty minutes if you are available.

"I have Blake on the other line. Have you talked to her today?"

"I was getting ready to call her".

"You don't have to do that; I can click over and tell her to meet us there because she was just talking about leaving for lunch".

"Ok, I will see you all there". Dalia disconnected the call and Lauren clicked back over to Blake. All she could hear was typing.

"Blake that was Dalia, we are going to meet her at Olive Garden in twenty minutes".

"I will be there in two. I am so hungry and y'all are procrastinating. Alright, I will be there in a minute, call you when I get there".

"Ok, bye!"

Lauren didn't want to go into detail with Blake or Dalia over the phone because she knew it would prolong them from going to lunch. She figured everything would come out at lunch. Lauren went back into the conference room where Jack, John, and Terry were getting the project together for her presentation. "Ok guys, we are going to break for lunch. Since you all have worked so hard and consistently, I am going to give you an hour and fifteen for lunch today, but I need you back before two today to wrap this up". The team broke quickly just in case Lauren decided to change her mind. They knew how she could get when her mind was focused on getting something done. She doesn't know when to slow down or take it easy. Lauren grabbed her things and headed to her car to meet up with the girls.

When she arrived at Olive Garden, Dalia was outside talking on her cell phone. Soon after, Blake arrived, driving fast as ever. They walked into the restaurant and were seated by the hostess.

"You can be nice all you want, but I am just going to ask, what are you doing here and what do you mean Terrance picked you up from the airport? You didn't even ask us if we could get you, states Lauren.

"He called me yesterday and he yelled and fussed about how I was moving and I didn't talk to him about it. Then he went on to say that I didn't give him a chance to explain or even talk about our relationship. He was acting all crazy."

Both of them looked the other way when Dalia started talking about Terrance's reaction. From the looks of things, they understood Terrance's frustration. They knew that Dalia didn't give the guy a chance to explain and then, after she heard the intentions of Carmen, she still didn't think about talking to him.

"Why are you looking at me like that", asked Dalia.

Neither one of them wanted to say anything. Usually, that Jayden's job to turn the awkward situation, but she wasn't there this time to regulate the conversation.

"Did you talk to Terrance, since that is your primary goal of this trip", as Blake.

"Dang, you all are riled up today", states Dalia.

"No, I think you need to decide what you are going to do and do it. Stop playing with him, before you lose him", implies Blake.

"Who said that I wanted him?"

"Then, why are you here? I don't know what you are trying to prove, but you ain't getting nothing solved by traveling up and down the airwaves just to talk. You have to go to be smoking."

"So, I am wrong for wanting to talk to Terrance".

"No, you are wrong for not giving him the chance to state his case"

"What case? I caught him in our house having sex with another woman. What I saw was enough for me to let go and let it be"

"Well, she got a point there", states Lauren.

"Don't agree with her. You are lucky that Terrance has stuck around this long. I don't see why you didn't talk to him before you made the decision to move"

"I don't get why my personal life seems to be your focus"

"Whoa! You will not argue about this bullshit", implies Lauren.

The waiter comes to the table to take their order. Lauren was ready to order her food because she knew that she had a lot of things to accomplish for the day and one of those things was not to argue with Dalia and Blake about what Dalia was going to do with her personal life at this point. Trying to maintain a good eating habit, Lauren ordered the salad special with a sex on the beach drink. Blake looked at her like she was crazy. Not only was Lauren going to be nutritious, she was going to have a buzz when she returned to work. Blake ordered the Alfredo and salad with water. Dalia was the only one out of three of them who ordered this large meal. You could feel the tension at the table, but no one wanted to break the ice.

"Are you going to sit here and not say anything to me? No one is going to ask me how everything is going", states Dalia.

Blake looked at Lauren across the table without acknowledging Dalia's question. For some reason, Blake was not in the mood for Dalia; hopefully it would get put out on the table before lunch was over.

"How is everything going with you? Are you planning to work with Barbara or are you going to go on a venture", asks Lauren.

"I was hoping you would ask me that", Blake rolled her eyes as Dalia starting talking. "I am going back to school and before either of you say anything, you know how much I wanted to be a nurse and I didn't pursue that dream back in undergrad."

"Wow! I would not have thought you would have made that decision. When did you make that decision?" asks Lauren.

"Wait before you answer that question. What about Terrance?" asks Blake.

"You like to put a damper on things, don't you? Terrance has nothing to do with my decisions about my career. You have your career in Marketing, which is what you wanted to do. Lauren has her career in Accounting, that she enjoys getting up and going to everyday. Then, Jay has her business ventures in retail that she kills for, but what did I have"

"I will tell you what you had that the rest of us didn't have. You had a home with a good man, a good job, and a future. You didn't know how to deal with the strife of the relationship. Since I knew you, you were with Terrance and he makes one mistake and you through him to the curb. I don't get that. If I was Terrance I would have moved on to someone else"

"Let me tell you ass something. I have taken enough shit from you today. Terrance cheated on me in my house and in my bed. After all those years, you just don't do shit like that. Yeah, I had a man, but I lost focus after my parents divorced and I just feel like I am getting it back. Why are you so negative?"

The Upside Down of Things

"You are calling me negative. Every time you do something stupid, we always support you and your dumb shit, but this time, I won't. Get your shit together and let me know what it is and how it is before you start dishing shit out. You are twenty-five and this is supposed to be the pivotal time, where we are peaking ourselves. You are trying to wish and hope on things that you are unsure about.

"Whoa, let me just say this; why are you made about the choices that this grown woman wants to make". Laurens interjects as she looks at Blake. She also addresses Dalia just to squash the quarrel between the two. "And you, I am glad that you have decided to do what you want, but how you are handling this thing with Terrance is wrong. You can do better". By saying that, Lauren had the most serious look on her face of disgust that she had to interject the conversation between these two best friends. Dalia and Blake having so much pride would rather overlook the tension and talk about something else and so they did.

"Has anyone heard from Jay since the text she sent this morning", asks Lauren. "I haven't heard anything from and why isn't she here? That is not like her", states Dalia. "She didn't tell you. Something must be wrong, states Blake. Everyone was thinking something, but they didn't want to suspect the wrong thing out loud.

The women began to wrap their lunch up as each of them had promising afternoons. They departed from Olive Garden making plans to meet up somewhere for dinner since Dalia was now visiting in Baltimore and they really didn't know when they were going to see her again with their busy schedules.

Chapter 10: And It Keeps Getting Better

"Hello"

"Where are you?"

"I am leaving Olive Garden. I was getting ready to go to the house for a minute".

"Would you like me to meet you there?"

"I guess that fine"

"Alright, I will see you in a bit"

Dalia has a very short conversation with Terrance as she is getting ready to leave the restaurant with Blake and Lauren. She tells Terrance that she is going to meet him at their condo. She was nervous even though he picked her up from the airport, she desperately tried to avoid having any kind of serious conversation, but now she won't be able to avoid it. She knew by telling Blake and Lauren what their instant reaction would be, so she kept it to herself. When they asked what she was going to get into later, she just responded that she was going to tighten up some loose ends. Of course she had other things on her mind, like the fact that she was using the money she saved for two years to support herself, but it didn't matter because she was happy with the decisions she was making. Secondly, she needed to decide what to do with her house and her belongings she left in the house. Third, she didn't know how this conversation with Terrance would turn out.

Lauren and Blake head back to work and Dalia heads over to her house. Dalia pulls in the yard and Terrance is there waiting in the driveway. She tried to act as if she didn't see him sitting in the car so she went pass the car hurriedly and opened the door. Of course, he couldn't go into the house with the keys he had, because Dalia had the locks changed soon after the incident. She walked into the house and left it unlocked but closed so Terrance could come in. Before she was able to close the door, Terrance walked in the door. Before being able to turn around and turn the light on in the living room, Terrance grabbed her and kissed her with all tongue. For a few seconds, Dalia enjoyed the kiss because she missed it, then reality hit, "You must have lost your mind", along with that was the hardest backhand she could give. "What was that for?"… "That is for thinking you could come in here; get a fuck and everything would be good". He touches his face and turns away from her. "What, you think that is what it is all about? How long have we been together, so it shouldn't matter? I have been with you forever and you go through that in my face". "You making this all about you and it's about me this time". "Ok, what about you?" "I am doing me. I am going back to school to become a nurse and I am going to have a fresh start for a chance."

Terrance had a very confused look on his face. "So, you saying you couldn't do you while you were with me?" There was complete silence. She knew how she wanted to respond to that, but she knew it was not the time for games. "Look, what you did was the last thing I suspected from you, but it was a wake up call". Terrance moved in closer to her. You could tell all the sexual tension between the two. Mind you that neither one of them had been intimate with each other nor anyone else for a while. As Dalia continues to talk about her feelings of pain, she started to tear up and Terrance wanted to seize the opportunity to get back with his girl. The only question was whether Dalia was going to let that happen. He began moving closer and he didn't notice any resistance from Dalia. He touched her face to wipe her tears and she looked up into his eyes, speechless. He leaned in to kiss her and for a moment she remembered all the good times.

Both of his hands were on her cheeks as he was kissing her as hard as he could. Dalia was taking it all in slowly, but surely. He backed off for a moment and she grabbed him by his shirt, pulling him closer to her to kiss him again. They stood there in the doorway kissing passionately. Terrance didn't want to make an abrupt move again and repeat what just happened. He wanted Dalia to take the first step and boy did she. Slowly, she started kissing on his ear moving down to his neck. She knew that this was Terrance weakness. She started unbuttoning his shirt and his hands moved all along her body. Forgetting the past couple of weeks, they made love for the rest of the day. Time flew by for the both of them. Terrance forgot the other obligations he made for the day while Dalia lost control and didn't get a chance to accomplish what she wanted either. They both fell asleep afterwards and once they awoke, they realized the day slipped right by them. When Dalia finally realized what happened, she was lost for words. "What the hell did I do", she said softly to herself while rubbing her hair. She needed a minute to get herself together. As Blake told her at the table, she needed to figure her life out, and for a moment, she thought about everything Blake told her was right. She was confused, lost, and hurt all at the same time.

Terrance came to, rolled over to her, and placed his arm around her as he always did. She didn't know how to react because she had mixed feelings, well at least, she didn't want to admit that she was still in love with Terrance. "Babe, you are all I need, but there is something that I have to tell you". Just as soon as Terrance was beginning to tell her something, Dalia had this funny look n her face. She felt nauseated for a moment, but she thought it would past because of the mixed feelings she was having over the past couple of weeks. "Hold a minute; I need to go to the bathroom". Dalia jumped out of the bed and ran to the bathroom, only to make herself dizzy as hell, thinking that she needed to regurgitate; she got a warm feeling out of nowhere that became overwhelming. Something didn't seem right to Terrance so he went to the bathroom to check on her. He knocked on the door, and Dalia couldn't respond because by that time, her face was in the toilet bringing up all that she could. Once he heard the noises of her throwing up, he had his answer, so he returned back to the room and lay in the bed until she returned. Dalia tried to get herself together so she would know how to handle this situation with Terrance, but she knew this wasn't going to be a quick fix.

The Upside Down of Things

Dalia walks out of the bathroom in much better shape than she walked in and her phone rings. Actually, it was a text message from Jay. "Hey, I couldn't make it to see you today, but there is something that I have to tell all of you. Can you all meet me at my house in about thirty minutes if you aren't busy?" Dalia's first thought was that Jay should have been at work and she wanted to meet at her house, that didn't sound right. Dalia responded to the text, "Sure, not a problem, I will be there as soon as possible". She really didn't know how to react and for Jay to make an announcement to all of us that she needed to talk. Now, somehow Lauren knew something was up with Jay since she wasn't able to meet for lunch so she went by job only to find out that she had been laid off. Lauren was so shocked and hurt for Jay that she didn't know what to do. By that time, she decided to get with the girls; Jayden sent all of them a text message. Just as soon as Lauren received the text, she turned her car around in the direction of Jayden's home.

While back at Dalia's condominium, Terrance had a big smile on his face when Dalia entered the room. "I don't feel too good, but I have to go. There is something up with Jay"

"Don't you think this right here is more important than your friend?"

"Terrance I don't have time to pick and choose between my friend and ex-man right now"

"Don't walk out of that door. We aren't done with this". His voice rises, as he gets even madder that Dalia once again puts her friends ahead of him. She assures him that they are going to finish their conversation before she leaves out of the door. Dalia leaves out of the house, jumps into her car and headed over to Jayden's house. While riding, she was thinking about what happened with Terrance. Her feelings were changing and the sense of stability of being with him felt comforting to her. She didn't want to focus on that because she knew there was something serious going on with Jay for her to call all of them there. Dalia was maybe twenty minutes away from Jayden's house so she knew it wouldn't take her long to get there.

In the meantime, Blake was just wrapping things up with her conference call about the project she was working on. She got good news that there was going to be an extension on the marketing project due to the company making some changes to its board at the time. She checked her phone after the conference call to see that she had a text message from Jayden telling her to meet at her house in thirty minutes. Blake needed to get away, so she didn't' hesitate leaving the office. She tried to call Lauren, but she didn't get an answer. So, she stopped by Starbucks on her way to Jayden's house. Since she really didn't know what she about to get into, she just picked up everyone's favorite drinks before she headed over. Blake was caught in the line at Starbucks for fifteen minutes. She didn't think it was going to take her that long. She finally was able to leave and she knew she was late and everyone was looking for her. She was shocked that she didn't have any calls or text message.

When Lauren received the text message she was wrapping everything up with her team who was assisting her with the books that were due like yesterday. Lauren knew it wasn't good, so she wasn't in a rush to get there. She was concerned for Jay, but she wanted to delay hearing bad news. Lauren slowly gathered her things because someone she knew she wasn't coming back in for the day. She sent an email out to everyone in her area that she would be working from home for the rest of the day. While walking out of the building, Lauren received a call from Kendall, who wanted to see how her day was going. Lauren was so excited to hear from him. She gave him an earful of how her morning was going. She didn't mention anything about going to Jayden's house because she really didn't know how personal the issue was; she would rather keep it to herself. She talked to Kendall the entire ride to Jayden's house, which took her about thirty to forty five minutes to get there from where she worked.

While Jayden waits for her friends, she was sitting at the house destroying all the plans she had for the company; ways to help them manage their stores and other plans she was working on to make her stores a success. She became even more sadden by the loss of her job. Just as soon as she was about to sulk herself into misery, Dalia pulled into the driveway, talking on her cell phone. She waited until she saw another car pull up so that they could be on a united front. Somehow that seemed to be the way they handled all of their situations, while sitting and waiting, she thought about the time when Jay and Blake came to see her when she had the fiasco with Terrance. She remembered how supportive they were to her and she knew she had to return the favor to Jay regardless of what she was going through. Beginning to tear up in the car, Lauren pulled up in the driveway wide open. She jumped out of the car, "Why in the hell are you still sitting in the car, and why aren't you on the inside checking on Jay?"

"I was actually waiting for the rest of you to show up", states Dalia.

"You are really starting to be a peace of work, but I didn't say that", Lauren states with a pissed off look on her face.

Lauren walks to the door without another thought. She knocked on the door and Jayden opens the door with bags under her eyes. Without asking anything, Lauren hugs her and walked into the house and Dalia falls into play forgetting about her own problems.

"Ok, I don't like being all sentimental unless I know what it is all about, so I'ma need you to talk, tell me something, so I can stop trying to figure out Dalia's shit for a change", states Lauren.

"Where is Blake, I don't want to have to tell this more than once", states Jayden.

"Well, I know she is on the way", states Dalia and Lauren, looking at each other.

Just as soon as they were talking, Blake pulled in the driveway, taking forever to get out of the car. When she entered the house, she had coffee, lattes, and cappuccinos for all of them. Delighted as they were that she thought of them to bring Starbucks to Jayden's house, there was too much on Jayden's mind to even pay that any attention.

"Ok, you all don't have to look like the world is over or did I miss something", asks Blake.

"No, we are waiting for Jay to tell us what is going on", states Dalia as she looks at Jayden.

"I lost my job today", states Jayden as calm as she could be.
"What do you mean you lost your job", asks Lauren.

"They called me in the office and told me that my job ended
because of budget cuts and all this other bull shit that I didn't
want to hear. I went completely off in the office. They gave me a
good severance package, but I don't want no package, I want my
damn job", states Jayden.

"Whoa! They gave you a severance. Oh, I would be straight,
next! I wouldn't even be stressed about that", states Dalia.

"Of course, you would say that cause you are all over the
damn place with your life", states Blake with an attitude towards
Dalia.

"I wish the two of you would chill the hell out and stop
arguing all the damn time", states Lauren.

"But, that ain't it. When we got back from the trip, Brian was
here at the house"….the door closes. "Who in the hell"?

'Babe, who are all these cars in the driveway", Brian walked
through the door while Jayden was about to tell her friends that
they were engaged. She had this shocked look on her face hoping
that Brian didn't come out of his mouth wrong. Before she could
say anything, she looked down at Brian and saw that his gun was
pulled out and loaded. Jayden jumped up, "Why do you have this
thing out and in your hand like you are about to do something",
Jayden trying to talk to Brian softly while grinding her teeth so no
one could hear her. She excused herself from the girls and pulled
Brian into the other room. While Jayden and Brian went into the
other room, Dalia became light headed for some odd reason. She
excused herself from the girls quietly and went into the bathroom.

"Why the fuck are you home and not at work and then all
these motherfuckers in the house like y'all up to something",
Brian getting real agitated really thinking something was up.

"No, No, No, I was going to tell you when you got off. I didn't
want to call you at work and tell you some bull shit that could
wait until you got off, and then I didn't know how you were going
to react, so I was giving myself time to get myself together",
Jayden is pacing back and forth trying to gather herself to tell
Brian the news.

"Babe, why are you pacing? I am your man; didn't we have this talk last night? It don't matter what it is, just say it", Brian finally put his gun down on the dresser in the room.

"I lost my job today"

"Huh, are you serious? FUCK! Jayden was startled at first, because she didn't know if he was mad at her or mad at the situation. "Is that why they are here? You were going to tell them what happened or about the engagement?"

"I was going to tell them both, but you came in right when I was going to tell them about the engagement, they know about the job. Hold a minute, why are you here?"

"I left my lunch and my debit card. Babe, it is going to be alright. I'm your man and you are not going to want for anything, you here me?"

"Yeah, but Brian, this was my career, my life. I can't get let this go."

"I didn't say all of that". He grabbed her and brought her close to his chest. "Your life now is me and our marriage. You will find another job. I need to get back to work, but I want all of them gone when I get back so we can work this out together".

"Wait! What about our wedding plans and all?"

"Didn't I tell you I got this? I put money aside for this, babe. Don't worry about a wedding. We will talk about this when I get home tonight.

"Hey, if my friends happen to be here when you get back, you better chill the hell out. I got you and their time won't interfere with your time, okay."

"You and your damn friends." Brian comments while shaking his head walking out of the door to return back to work.

Before Jayden walked out of the room, she sat on the bed, grinning because she knew that Brian had her back regardless. But, besides the sadness, she was engaged to the man she loved and nothing could take that away from her. She walked out into the living room where her friends remained. Dalia was just coming out of the bathroom.

"Where the hell have you been, taking a dunk", asks Blake.

"I just didn't feel well. I am dizzy. I think I ate the wrong thing at lunch", states Dalia.

"Whatever you say", states Blake.

"Is everything ok with you and Brian", asks Lauren.

"We are great. Like I was telling you before he barged in, he proposed the other night and I said yes". They were all ecstatic for her except Dalia. She only replied with a measly, "Congratulations".

Lauren and Blake had the look of disgust on their faces after the reaction Dalia had to Jayden's news. To each other, Lauren and Blake, "I can't believe she is jealous"…"no, this is suppose to be your girl, regardless of what is going on with you, put that bull shit aside and be happy for her". The two of them, talking out of the side of their mouth so that Jayden wouldn't hear it, continued to hug and congratulate Jayden on her good news.

"Have you decided on your colors or any plans yet", asked Blake.

"No, not since I got the news about my job", answered Jayden.

"Well, now you will have time to plan it", states Lauren.

"I don't know. We may not go all out since I am not working", implies Jayden.

"Mmmm, have you ran that by Brian yet", asked Blake.

"Why! Um, don't think I am going to be one of those wives that does everything her husband wants her to", states Dalia as she gets her attitude back like they know her to have.

"You know that is not what I am saying. But, you do have to be submissive to him, dang", states Lauren.

While Lauren and Blake are happy for Jayden, you could barely tell that her best friend Dalia could not share with her happiness. For some reason, she seemed to envy what Jayden has or moreover, she wanted Jayden to be at the same place she was, lost. Jayden at this point didn't know if she should be happy or sad. She was having mixed emotions, but she knew she would be safe with her girls to back her up and Brian by her side. She didn't have time to entertain Dalia's mood and nine times out of ten, she knew something was up with her, because she wasn't acting like herself.

"Excuse me, I have to go to the bathroom", states Dalia as she brushed passed Blake to get to the bathroom in a hurry.

"What is her deal? Y'all better get her before I lay into her ass", states Bake firmly.

"What has gotten into you lately, you've been a little hood lately", asks Jayden with a smile.

"She has been like this since she and Dalia got into it at Olive Garden for lunch today", states Lauren.

"What! What happened, and don't leave out anything", states Jayden

"I can't tell you in front of her", states Blake.

"You better tell me about this later then", states Jayden.

They all laughed because hardly anything bothers Blake, but for some reason Dalia was getting on her nerves. Maybe she was starting to see how unbalanced she was in college through the things that Dalia was doing. Dalia returned from the bathroom looking horrible and flushed. If no one else didn't notice the way she looked, Blake noticed and the thoughts that ran through her head were not the thoughts you would have about a friend. Jayden on the other hand peeped that something wasn't right.

"Dee, you good", asked Jayden.

"Why do you think something is wrong", states Dalia.

"Maybe cause I have known you for a very long time and you don't normally act like a donkey unless something is up unless you moving to Jersey has turned you out already".

"I am fine", implies Dalia.

"Then, why do you keep running to my bathroom. Are you bulimic or something, cause you can get help for that?" Lauren is listening to this conversation between Dalia and Jayden and something clicks in her head.

"Bitch, are you pregnant?

"Why would say something like that", states Dalia.

"Girl, I lived with you in college and I don't even remember you throwing up", states Jayden.

"You lived with me for a couple of months and you think that is long enough for you to know that I don't throw up", states Dalia.

"Okay, prove me wrong then. Take a test, then we will all know the truth", Jayden puts it out there for everyone to suspect that Dalia is pregnant.

"If that is the case, it would explain a lot", states Blake.

"Congratulations Jayden, but I am done being interrogated about having a baby. I have some errands to run before everything closes. I will catch up with you all later. Holla!" With the quickness, Dalia got out of there before they could think anything. She couldn't wait to get out of that house. She stopped suddenly once she got outside the house, "What if I am pregnant and with Terrance's baby? This would mess up all kind of shit." Dalia started whimpering like a little dog thinking that it was a good possibly that she could be pregnant. She got into her car and headed to the drug store for a pregnancy test.

Back in the house, the girls started making plans for Jayden's wedding.

"Do you know when you want to have the big day", asked Blake.

"Brian and I haven't decided on anything yet. He just proposed last night when we got back, but he did say that he wanted to discuss the details when he gets off today", states Jayden.

"Cool, then you can call us over here once you all have decided on that", states Blake.

"Lauren, you are quiet over there, who are you texting on that phone", asked Blake.

"My boo, Kendall, who else would I be talking to"

"Hell, at one time I thought you were fucking that job of yours", bursting in laughter with Jayden. They all loved to tease Lauren about her job because she brought everything home with her no matter when she went.

"And I know you aren't talking about me and my job. You have an office at your house that is set up just like your office at work. What can you say about that?"

"I can say that I work hard and I damn sure play hard", comments Blake as she still laughs at Lauren. Jayden is sitting back laughing at both of her friends as they make a mockery of each other. The only thing that was bothering her was that she didn't have a job anymore that she could talk about, but she knew deep down that there was more to life than her job.

Chapter 11: What Do I Do Now?

"Hey, it's me. I wanted to see if you were in town, maybe we could hang out or do something, hit me up when you get a chance. Talk to you later, bye" Blake leaves a message on Michael's voice mail. She hasn't talked to him since her trip to Jersey and she was getting really bored with herself, so she figured she could call up a friend to hang out.

"Dang, what is he doing, that he is not answering his phone. He should be at work; maybe I should call that number. No, I don't want to seem desperate since I already left a message on his cell phone. I will just wait for him to call me back, and if not, oh well, I will find something else to get into or get on top of tonight."

After leaving Jayden's house, Blake wanted to head back to the office, but she realized she had enough of that for the day. Just as soon as she made her mind up to go home for the day, Tina called. "Ms. Lowry, I hate to bother you while you are out, but Mr. Sellers has chosen to reschedule your meeting this afternoon at four"

"At four Tina, are you serious?"

"Yeah, that is the call I got just now"

"Did you tell him that I was out of the office for the rest of the day?"

"He didn't ask any of that, apparently it didn't matter."

"Okay, Okay, uhhhhh, do you remember where all the presentation things are, right?"

"Yes, ma'am, I learned from the last time."

"Aww, great, you are the best. We should look into giving you a raise or something for all the hard work you do."

"Blake, you don't have to kiss up ok. I have it, just get in here for your presentation and don't forget your coffee."

"I have you beat; I am drinking my latte right now. I should be there in about thirty minutes."

"Ok, see you in a minute."

Blake heads to her house, which she was only a couple of minutes away from; she wanted to pick up a file she left in her office at home. While pulling in her yard, she was thinking about Dalia for some reason. "What if that fool is pregnant for real, what is she going to do? I hope she gets that under control and I wonder if she will tell Terrance. She knew how Dalia could be sometimes." Blake ran into the house picked up her file and headed for the door. While locking the door, she noticed the red light flashing on her phone letting her know she had messages. She couldn't imagine whom they could be from, so she decided to wait until she got back to work to check them from her office.

When she got back to the office, Tina and Marci were waiting for her. She could understand why Tina was waiting for her, but not Marci. She greeted everyone who was in her presence and Tina knew it was her cue to come in Blake's office so she could prep for the meeting. "Hey Blake, when you get a minute, I would like to talk with you", states Marci. Blake wanted to ignore her because everything that Marci has her nose in is nothing but trouble and she didn't want any part of that. "Ok, get with Tina to see what time I have available this week and we can talk", stated Blake back to Marci. "Not a problem. I got her extension", replies Marci.

Tina wasn't a big fan of Marci and she wasn't looking forward to that call from her either. Marci had been with the company for a long time, and she was jealous of any young, black educated woman who walked through the door. Not only did she despise Blake when she started with the company, but she hated that Blake had her own and she didn't need anyone's help. As nosey as she is, she went on the internet searching under "Lowry" to see any dirt she could find on Blake. Her goal was to find out things about Blake, but she ended up finding other unexpected things that she didn't want to know about Blake. For about two years, she has kept it all to herself because she was afraid of what may happen or what her findings would bring about, but she knew from then on to stay clear of Blake.

As Blake made the final provisions to her presentation for the board members of the project, Jared walked by, "Good luck, I know you can do it." He winked his eye at Blake as he knew the high expectations Blake set for herself. He knew that would just put her over the edge and give her the confidence she needed. While walking out her office, Tina handed Blake the additional copies of her presentation to hand to the board members. "Good luck, boss", stated Tina. Blake said to herself, "I don't know why she calls me boss. She is my assistant and I have told her that over and over." "Ok, thanks". Blake leaves the area to the elevator heading towards the boardroom.

"You have got to be kidding me", Lauren checked her messages on her blackberry from work, "Urgent! "There has been a corruption on all files in the system and all work has been lost if it was not saved on an external drive. I know this may be an inconvenience to all of you, but I apologize for this. Once the repairs are completed, files may be available. Thanks, Jeff of Technical Support".

"I can't believe all of my files are lost. Wait, my files may not be affected, but if they are, we will be doing some serious overtime this week. I am not in the mood for this today!" Lauren screams to herself in her car while riding downtown. Her phone rings and it is Kendall. "Hey, how are you", Lauren answered the phone with the lower range of her voice, which prompted Kendall to ask her if anything was wrong. "What's wrong babe?"

"I just checked my work email and our systems went down and the project that I have been working on all day is gone."

"Calm down. I know you saved your information to an external drive in case of this disaster."

"No, I didn't. We have only had this issue once since I have been with this company."

"Ren, if it can happen once, it can happen again."

"I really don't want to hear anything, but my work is on my computer when I click on my personal drive."

"Didn't you tell me that you did your work from home sometimes?"

"Yeah, I worked on it when I got a free minute."

"Then, you should be able to pull it up from your computer at home. I will show it to you when you get home."

"What do you mean you will show me when I get home"

"That is why I was calling you. I just got into town about an hour ago and I wanted to take you out to dinner tonight. I have a new case that caused me to come here for a day or two, not quite sure how long yet, but have some sources here that I need to check out."

"Babe, are you serious? So, after my day today you are here to take my mind off it. You are the best!'

"Yeah, I may be done a little late though, depending on how these interviews turn out."

"Not a problem. Call me when you get done."

"I will. See you tonight."

Lauren felt some relief that she had a distraction at least for tonight. She only worried if she would be distracted by Dalia or Jayden since they had so much going on, then she thought to herself, "The only one to worry about is Dalia because her shit will fall apart. Jay on the other hand can keep hers together and tell us later. I just better not turn my cell off today."

Back at the Johnson & Pole Marketing Associates, Blake began her meeting and everyone seemed very pleased with all the hard work and effort she placed in her presentation. All the VPs were surprised and astonished that Blake was capable of doing such impeccable work. While back on the second floor, Marci began doing database searches on Blake and her family. All she wanted was to find some flaw in Blake that would break her in front of everyone at the job. Of course it wouldn't be easy for Marci to do, but she was going to try her damnest to make it happen. Running out of ideas of what to searched, she remembered that Blake went to an all black college, but she couldn't think of the name. Then, she happened to make herself to walk past Blake's office where her degree was proudly hanging, "Morgan State University, perfect". Smiling to herself, Marci walked swiftly back to her desk to start searching, hopefully this would be her key to getting the dirt she needed. She went on the school's website and typed in Blake's name under student search. Unfortunately, she couldn't find what she was looking for, but she could get the email address that Blake still used every once and a while. Before she knew it, her boss walked up and filled her desk with a pile of work that would take well into the next day to finish, but she wasn't done with Blake Mowry yet and she would make sure that she'd get what was coming to her.

When Blake came from her meeting it was taking all that she had to keep her composure from jumping for joy as her meeting better than expected. She nailed every question and explained everything with the proper research. There was nothing left unanswered. She was feeling at the top of her game. Tina saw Blake coming from a distance so she ran straight into her office ahead of her so she could get the news first hand.

"Hurry up and get in here, I want to know what happened"

"Close the door, you know they are nosey."

They both start screaming as soft as they could so that they wouldn't draw attention to Blake's office. Then Tina stopped, "Wait! What am I jumping and screaming for, you haven't told me anything."

"They loved it all. I covered everything. They didn't even have to ask me any questions. Everyone was speechless and they loved it."

"I am so happy for you, so what does this mean." Tina asked the question as if Blake should be promoted for doing such a good job with her presentation, but Blake really didn't know what to say. She felt that she made a big accomplishment in her career. She always wanted to feel like she belonged and she earned her paycheck, well today was the day that she set the record straight with that.

"I have accomplished something today, but I couldn't have done it without you"

"Yes, you could. You did all the laborious work. All I did was help you find it." Tina left and closed the door behind her because she knew she had work to do and her phone was ringing. Blake was so happy that she turned her seat around facing the window behind her desk. Nothing else in the world matter to her right now, not even Michael and that fact that she seemed empty in her personal life. Just as she went into a daze, there was a knock at her door.

"Come in Tina", still with her back turned.

"Are you Miss Lowry, there was a Fed Ex that was overnighted for you," states the messenger.

"Okay, thanks!" Blake took the package and opened it. There was a business memo on the inside from her father's law firm:

To: Miss Blake Lowry
From: Executive Board Members

There will be a tentative board member meeting held for next Monday at 10:00AM. You attendance will be greatly appreciated. It is imperative that you are in attendance as major decisions regarding the company are at hand. Thanks so much for your continuous support.

Yours truly,
Mowry Law Associates & Company

"What the hell is this all about?" Blake couldn't pick her phone up quick enough to call her sister. She knew it was something that she was up to, "Like she couldn't call me over the phone with this, why is she so technical all the time". As she was dialing the number, she was receiving a call on another line that was from one of the board members. Just as soon as she looked up and Tina was standing in front of her telling her to answer the call, it was John form upstairs. "Damn!" She flipped over to the other line, "This is Blake, how can I help you/"

"Blake, this is John. I wanted to let you know that you did a superb job this afternoon, excellent work."

"Thank you so much! I put a lot of work into that presentation."

"And we all could tell. Listen, I was just talking with some of the board members and we have decided on some new changes around here. We would like to schedule a meeting with you first thing tomorrow morning."

"Great. That will not be a problem."

"I will send you an email with the details."

The call disconnects and Blake has this dumbfounded look on her face. She didn't know whether to be excited or frantic, but she wasn't going to panic until in the morning. She was concerned about the memo she received from her sister. Blake decided to call the company instead of trying to reach Blair on her cell.

"Good Morning, Lowry Law Firm, how may I direct your call?'

"Hey, April, this is Blake. I was trying to get in touch with Blair this morning."

"Uh, Blake, your sister has been in meetings all morning. I thought she would have called you by now. I am going to lose my job for saying that."

"Saying what, you haven't said anything. Tell me April. I will make sure that your job is safe."

"I don't know if you can." At this point, Blake voice starts to elevate. Not that she is mad at April, but the fact that something is wrong and no one has filled her in on it.

"Godddamn! Apparently, the half sister that you two have is trying to come in and take control of her shares in the company. She went and talked to the board members and kind of got them on her side as the poor outside child who was lost and forgotten. Somehow they fell for it and she is trying to take over the company. Wheww! I have been holding that for the past couple of days and it was killing me."

"Why hasn't my sister called me?"

"She has been trying to save this company so that you and your mother wouldn't think she was a failure."

"Why in the hell would we think that, she has no control over what someone else does or says."

"Put me through to this damn meeting now!"

"Hold for just a moment and I will put you through." Blake is now standing up on your headset in her office pacing back and forth. She was ready to get on a plane and handle this business if her sister couldn't.

"Yes, I am in a board meeting, this will have to wait."

"Blair, this is Blake!"

"I am in a meeting right now"

"Take me off the speakerphone now; I have to talk to you." Blair picks up the handset to talk to Blake while the other board members become impatient.

"Look, I will have to talk to you about this in private. I tried calling you this morning, but all of your numbers were going to voice mail."

"Why is this half sister trying to get part of the company?"

"Well, it's more like her and her husband, but I can't answer that. The only thing I can do is try to fix it."

"Blair, her husband, who is he and what does he have to do with the company."

"I thought you knew all about it since you were hanging out with him a couple of weeks ago when you were visiting. Things are almost worst, so you might want to help straighten out this mess you helped created. I know your job is important to you, but this is important too. I have to go, talk to you later." Blair disconnects the call and thinks to herself, Blake was hurt. The words from her sister struck straight through her. She was trying to figure who her sister was referring to. She began thinking about her trip to Jersey and who she was associating with that would come back to bite her like this. Of course, Michael did not run across her mind. It is past five thirty and Blake is still in her office contemplating and trying to figure out what went wrong.

While Blake is having a family crisis, Lauren on the other hand returned to work to find out that on her way back to the office, the company's entire system crashed. The only recovered files were things that were placed on the old back up system that sometimes worked and they stopped using that over a year ago. Lauren's day turned from promising to horrible all in a matter of hours. She was no longer looking forward to a romantic evening with Kendall. This vice president of their new accounts division sent a mass email stating that everyone was dismissed from work until they were able to get the system working. He instructed the account managers to work at the clients offices until the systems were straight there.

"What kind of crap is that? What about those who are hourly? How are they going to be able to make a living if we are off indefinitely", Lauren asked the director over her division.

"Lauren, your job is fine. You can't worry about things you can't change. You can't take on everyone's burdens. The account managers are set up with offices in the client's facility. We made sure of that in case of situations like this. The hourly people are not account holders and they don't solicit accounts either. They will be fine, don't worry about it"

Lauren was so pissed off she didn't know what to do with herself. All she could do was contact her personal clients to inform them she would be in their office for the next couple of weeks. The only downfall that Lauren dreaded of working in their offices was that everyone would walk around on pins and needles because they seem to think something is wrong when the account is in the office. They assume someone would lose their job for embezzling corporate funds, which is normally not the case. By the time she finished with all of her contacts, it was near six o'clock. Not noticing the time that she was suppose to meet Kendall, back at her house, he sat there waiting for her. While he was waiting for her at the house, he grew impatient. He walked into her kitchen looking for some kind of alcoholic beverage to cool himself down. The phone rings and Kendall thinking that it may be Lauren calling, but then again, "Why would she call her house phone for me when she could clearly call my cell." Kendall ignored the rings, when he noticed that it wasn't from Lauren. Her voice mail comes on, "Hey baby, I really enjoyed our night. I wanna make this think work this time. I know it is not like you to let your guard down like that, but you felt so good, it made me remember what things used to be like. I am coming back to town, if you still want to see me, call me, you have my number." Jason hung the phone up and the voice mail stopped.

Kendall became mad as hell from the message he just heard. The only thing that ran across his mind, "I really enjoyed our night". The one thing that Lauren knew about Kendall was that he was a real man, gentle, and kind, but the one thing she didn't know was that he temper could get the best of him at times and this was one of them. "Did she cheat on me," was the question running through his mind. Then he thought again to himself, "Ain't no nigga gonna leave a message like that over some pussy he got weeks ago. This had to be recent as hell and I couldn't tell this shit. You have got to be kidding me." Kendall's instant reaction was to take his anger out on everything in Lauren's house, but he realized that would be disrespectful. He decided to leave the house and turn his cell off, but we wanted Lauren to know he heard the message without her thinking that he was being nosey. He decided to leave a note;

Lauren,

I decided to wait for you as if any good man would, but in return I over   heard a very important message that I am sure you didn't want to miss.   So that I won't be in the way of your rendezvous, I will give you the   privacy that you need. When you ready for the real deal, you know my number.

Kendall

Lauren couldn't believe what she was reading. She read the note several times until she could actually figure out what message he heard. It then hit her to check her voice mail. "Damn! The girls told me one day this was going to come back on me." When Lauren played the messages, she heard Jason's voice "this nigga is making this sound like we hook up all the time. Shit! Why would he leave a dumb ass message like that, now I have to figure out where Kendall went."

When Blake goes home for the day, she has so many messages on her voice mail that it was blocked. There was a message from everyone who worked at the company who knew her, but nothing from her mother. Blake called her sister again, but she couldn't get through. She decided to get a ticket and go to Jersey, "Oh shit, I have that meeting tomorrow." Blake left puzzled and confused of what to do.

Chapter 12: What's Next?

"Congratulations, baby. I hope he makes you happy", states James as he hugs his daughter Jayden. "How is everything? You have been a little out of touch the past couple of days."... "Daddy, I lost my job yesterday to budget cuts."... "Well, your husband to be can take care of you until you get back on your feet." Jayden looked away from her father because of course she didn't like what her father was suggesting. "I am not going to live off of him. He has his own things and I have mine. I don't want to share all my things with him, states Jayden. "Baby girl, what do think having a husband is all about"... "I was hoping it was about having a lifetime companion who cares, shares and loves me no matter what, implies Jayden with as much passion as she could show. "It's all of that and more. A grown man takes care of his and home, remember that and if he can't do that, then you need to think twice before you make such a commitment", her father implies. "I never said that he wouldn't do it, I am just not about to bring it up to him to take care of me. I know you mean well, but I didn't work this hard to give up because one job laid me off". James shakes his head because he sees so much of himself in his daughter that it was unbearable for him to see it.

"How is Karen, even though she doesn't care about me to ask".... "Baby girl, you have to stop this. You are going to get a long with her like she is going to get along with you", states her father very firmly. James was never one who loved misery or confrontations. He always respected his daughter's decisions, but he also expected the same thing from her. "Have you talked to Jordan", asked Jayden. "Yeah, I did. That crazy son of mine said he would be back in town in a couple of days. He hasn't called you; he said he was going to a couple of days ago." Jayden looking at her father knew what that meant, especially if he was asking if Jordan had called her. "He probably wants to stay here on his break". James looked at his daughter with a grin without replying to her. "All the money he makes, he wants to stay with one of us".... "You aren't going to tell him no, you never do". "I can't help it, he is my little brother".... "I know he is and that is why you are going to let him stay here. I have to make some appointments today, I just wanted to come by and check on you since I haven't heard anything from you. "Daddy, I will call you later if I hear from Jordan"... "Okay, baby girl, I will talk to you later". He gives Jayden a hug and heads out of the door.

Crying to herself, "What am I going to do now?" is what Dalia was thinking as she looked at the pregnancy test. The door slams, which scares Dalia too death as she sat in the living room of her condominium, Terrance burst in and notices the test in Dalia's hand. Shocked, as he could be, "Is this for real"... "As real as it gets", stated Dalia. Terrance walks into the room, letting go of the door, he pulled Dalia to him as she cries, "It's going to be alright. I am here and I am not leaving. We can do this together, babe". All she could do was hug him back as she cried her eyes out. He wiped her eyes, kissed her passionately, and then he began rubbing her all over. Even though Dalia didn't initially want to go back to Terrance like that, at this point, this was the only person she felt close to that understand everything about her. It was starting to feel like old times to the both of them. He made love to her all through the house. Dalia could tell by the way Terrance handled her that he hadn't had a piece in a while and neither had she. There was a lot of sexual tension between the two and they were releasing it on each other.

Even though Terrance made a mistake, Dalia didn't see the mistake as being forgivable, but now there was more to take in consideration than just her own feelings she had to think about a baby. They went at it for more than two hours from the kitchen to the living room, and finally to the bedroom. Before, Dalia couldn't bear to be in that bedroom because it reminded her of Terrance being in there with Carmen. In the middle of her making love to Terrance, something came over her. "Carmen, that bitch knew exactly what she was doing." She didn't want to ruin the moment with Terrance, but just this connection with Terrance brought everything back to perspective for her, but now she had to figure what her next move would be. "First, I need to move back here, I don't belong in New Jersey when my heart is here. Then, I have to get this bitch back. Finally, I will make things right with Terrance, but I have to tell my girls. Now, I see why Blake was acting like that with me. What was I thinking all this time, why didn't I talk to Terrance or let him tell his side?" She rolled over and looked at Terrance looking so peaceful beside her like it was suppose to be until Carmen appeared in the picture. Dalia was going to make it her business for some getback.

"Sis, what it is, nigga!" "Hey, Jordan, where are you?" Jayden talking to her brother who is on a plane to Baltimore, "I am about to take off on this plane, on my way to holla at ya"... "And you weren't going to call me and let me know you were coming. I could be having a big orgy here or something". Laughing on the other end of the phone, "If that fine as Lauren is going to be there, I will bring my camera so we can make our own flick"... "You so damn nasty"... "Hell, you were the one to bring it up"... "But, you didn't have to say all of that". Jordan loved to piss his sister off and he did a good job of it every time he talked to her over the phone, which was their main way of communication nowadays.

Jordan Miller, big time football player at USC, who loves his sister to death. This was his third year off at school and Jayden missed her brother every time she saw the local football players whenever she was out. Jordan, always wild; he was into parties, drinking and having a good time, but never disrespectful. Not every influenced by his father not being with his mother just like Jayden, he shared a close relationship with both of his parents. The one thing he didn't like was that his step mother would disrespect his mother every chance she got. Jordan made it his business to stay away from Karen and her evil ways. Even though, he didn't come much because of his hectic schedule, he always seems to make his presence known for the little while he was home. He didn't like to stay with his mother because of the strict rules she had for him. He had to be in the house a certain time, clean up after himself, and no loud music after nine. A young college boy like himself couldn't take that, so he decided to stay with his older sister Jayden.

When Jayden got off the phone with Jordan, she began looking at his most recent football pictures. The one thing she feared the most was her little brother going pro. She knew it would be too much fame for him, but it would be a great career for him since football became his life at an early age. The first thing she had to do before Jordan came to town was tell Brian her brother was coming to stay. Even though Jordan didn't come too often to visit, Brian would still lose him mind because he would assume some other nigga would be at the house. Sometimes Brian couldn't be reached at his job, so she would send him text messages and he would call when he was available, so she sent him a text, "my brother would be in town later this evening and he is staying with me. Let me know if you want me to come to your house tonight or you are going to come over here after work. Love you, Jay".

In the meantime, Jayden really didn't know what to do in her free time since she didn't have you job to focus on. It was getting late and she wanted to cook a special dinner for her brother. She phoned her mother and father inviting them to her house. She was shocked they didn't oppose so she knew it was too good to be true. She figured it would give her the opportunity to tell her mother about the engagement and at the same time welcome Jordan home. She went to the store to pick up a few items and while on her way there Brian called. "Hey babe," states Jayden. "I saw you text me earlier, but I couldn't get to my phone, what's up"... "I wanted to let you know that my brother is coming to town and he is going to be staying with me and I didn't know if you wanted to still come over here after work or if you wanted me to come to your house", it was hard to hear anything since there was a lot of noise in the background. "Babe, pack you stuff and come to my house. Let your brother have your house while he is here and you can be with me", states Brian. "Are you sure about that", Jayden implies since she knows how possessive Brian could be about his things, especially his house.

"It will give us the time we need to discuss our future. I was meaning to talk to you about some things anyway, so it's cool," states Brian.

"I should be over there late because I want to have a dinner here at the house tonight for Jordan with the family" states Jayden.

"You gonna bring your momma and James in the same house for dinner with your lil' brother", asks Brian.

"Shut the hell up! It is not going to be that bad. My parents can act cordial for one evening."

"What the fuck ever. You know your daddy is going to act hard cause he loves the hell out of your mother, then your mother is going to try her best to ignore your daddy cause she know damn well he loves her back." Jayden laughs on the other end of the phone because she knows deep down that it's the truth. Her parents were crazy about each other since they were young, but life led them in other directions.

"First of all, my mother doesn't want a married ass man, for your information. Second of all, my mother can flaunt all she wants, James Miller married who he wanted, didn't he."

"Someone getting a little angry about their parents", Brian began laughing at how serious Jayden took him about her parents.

"You make me sick."

"I bet I make you happy too."

"Ugh, just hang the hell up, I will talk to you when you get off"

"Oh, so I am not invited to the festivities."

"You are just going to laugh and make fun of me, so NO, I don't want you here. Just be ready for me when I get to the house tonight."

"I will be more than ready." The call ends.

Talking to Brian took longer than expected. Time was running out for her and she knew that she needed to go to the grocery store and she hadn't started anything with dinner. When she got ready to open the door, "Hey, Baby, I talked to your father and he told me the news", Jayden's mother was talking so loud that she was blowing her hears up.

"Why in the hell couldn't you call and tell me you were engaged. You know your mother should be the first person to know about these things. I tell you, children, you can't teach them enough sense. Ooo, I like what you have done to the house, everything looks nice". Jayden is rolling her eyes behind her mother because she knows how extra she could be at times, but on the other side, she was her ace when he came down to it. She thought to herself, "yeah, I could have told her first, but damn, my mind wasn't on it. Hell, I lost my job and ain't nobody say, why didn't you tell me that first. But, what can I say, this is my mother. She would have something to say regardless."

"Ma, why are you going through all of my stuff? Alright you gonna find something you don't wanna see", Jayden shaking her head at her mother.

"You think you are the only one here with some business. Girl, I had business when you didn't know what business was."

"OH MY GOD, every time....we got to go through this. Where are your son and your ex?" states Jayden as she backs away from her mother. She knows her that her mother is touchy when she refers to her father that way.

"That man is your father and that is how you can continue to refer to him".

"Why are you acting like he isn't your ex. Dang, you had two children with him".

"That was before I was smart. I was young and dumb".

"Really!" Before Jayden could go into details with her mother about her father, the doorbell rung and through everything off balance, "dang", Jayden said to herself. Her mother was looking with such relief on her face.

"Ma, get the door so I can put my food in the oven". When she opened the door, it was Jayden's father, James Miller.

"Boy has it been a long time since I have seen you", states Jayden's mother looking at James from head to toe.

"Yes it has", states James returning the same look. Even though Jayden missed the initial reaction, she knew there was still some chemistry between the two.

"Hey, Dad!" shouted Jayden from the kitchen. "Hey, baby girl. It sure does smell good around there", states James as he takes off his hat and shades.

"Jackie, you sure are looking good girl," states James.

"Thanks! You are looking quite swell yourself, if I might say", states Jackie.

"I wonder when this boy is going to get here. Why didn't your wife join us this evening," asked Jackie.

"She had a meeting she had to attend with the ladies from her job," as James answered quickly.

"Did she know your son was coming home and hasn't been home in a long time," Jackie asks with a slight attitude.

"She is excited to see him too; she just couldn't make it tonight."

"No, what she couldn't make was seeing me here and being up close to me."

"Wow! That is what you think."

"That is what I know. Your wife treats my kids like crap because she thinks deep down that I want you back", Jackie voiced raised as she stood up stating her point firmly to her ex James all the while Jayden is still in the kitchen not hearing a word. James stood up close to her, "Do you want me back", ignoring all that Jackie said, he wanted an answer to her question. He moved in closer, staring into her eyes just when the doorbell rang.

"Can someone get that for me" asked Jayden from the kitchen. Jackie and James gather themselves before answering the door. Just when they open the door,

"Momma!" Jordan hugs his mother with a bear hug. "What's good pop", as he shook his father hand firmly.

"It is so good to see my baby. Come sit down, I want to know all about your trip and how school is treating you."

"Ma, school is good and I don't want to talk about it. Where is my sister so I can bother her?"

"She is in the kitchen preparing the food", states Jackie. Jordan walks into the kitchen. Jackie and James are left in an awkward moment. Soon after, Jayden brings the food out with the assistance of her brother as they all sat down to enjoy dinner. They laughed, talked and reminisced about old times. Jayden shared her news with her brother that she was engaged and that she lost her job. Her family sympathized with her and showed their support. She offered her house to her brother for his stay while she stayed at Brian's house. At least two hours had past before anyone realized anything until James' phone went off; it was his wife calling, checking to see his whereabouts. Of course, Karen was not favored at that table, but everyone there had their reasons. Jackie and Jordan asked Jayden about her trip with James and Karen, but she didn't feel like sharing the news. Jayden was close to both of her parents, but because they were not together, she didn't feel the need to share the details of their lives with each other. Both of her parents had to respect her wishes in this aspect even though her mother wasn't too concerned about James' personal life as everyone thought she was. Jackie always very independent, which is where Jayden gets her personality, moved on after she and James did not work out.

As the evening began to drift away, Jayden began asking Jordan about his plans for the summer and what he wanted to do; while on the other hand, Jackie and James were exchanging looks across the table. Not paying either of them any attention, they were able to share that moment between the two of them. "I have to call the girls and tell them my little brother is here", states Jayden. "Hell, don't tell me you are talking about Dalia, Lauren, and Blake. I haven't seen them since freshman year. Are they still fine", asked her brother. Jayden knocks Jordan upside his head for cursing in front of her. While Jayden is on the phone, Jordan over hears a conversation between his parents that made him feel uncomfortable.

"You are starting to look a little bothered; do you need a glass of water? I remember why you get that look", as James talks to Jackie. She never really responds to him because she wants to respect that he has a wife that he loved and devoted his life to. To herself, "That man, that man, could make me climb walls at one point in my life, but we have all moved on and there is no repeating that. Even though, we look very nice together as a family, there is no turning back". Jackie gathered her composure and cleared her throat, "Jay, I have to go. I have to get ready for work tomorrow and I haven't done a thing to my house. Son, come by and see me tomorrow. James, it is good to see you." Jackie made a hurried exit out of the house because she was more than afraid of what may happen next with her and James.

Jordan had a puzzled look on his face, "Pop, you aren't going to check on ma." James responded, "Your mother is fine." Jordan looked at his father with dismay, "You always check on her any other time I come home and visit. Are you going to stay with her tonight?

"Wait a damn minute, what do you mean, he stays over there every time you visit", Jayden looking very upset at her father. Her brother looked the other way, "Jay, I thought you knew"

"You thought I knew what? Somebody better tell me something before I flip this house inside out," Jayden grinding her teeth together, screaming at both her brother and her father.

James sighs because he doesn't know how to explain to his daughter that he has been sleeping with her mother for the past two years without her knowing, but somehow her brother knew and all of them kept it from her. As infuriated as she was, she asked all of them to leave her house. Forgetting that she promised Jordan her house, she later text him and told him to come, but she made sure that she wasn't there when he returned. The first thing she wanted to do was confront her mother because she never wanted to be judgmental, but it seemed apparent to her why Karen treated her the way that she did and why she felt that her mother was a threat, when in actuality she was and she was taking all the blame for it on the trip to the mountains.

"Knock, Knock, Knock". Jayden heads to her mother's house later that evening after she had calmed down from the sporadic drama at her house after her mother left. She wanted to talk to her mother to see what were her intentions and why would she mess with a married man even though she had him first, it just didn't make sense to her. Of course, it has been a couple of hours since she left her own house, she couldn't rest until she got some clarifications on some things. Jayden felt that she was in the middle of it all since Karen took such a strong approach to her on this trip and then "the gall of my father to ask me to come on the trip knowing that he was sleeping with my mother the whole time. What was he trying to accomplish"? Waiting outside for her mother to answer the door, she noticed that there were no lights on, not even the porch light that she always kept on regardless. Jayden thought something might be going on so she used the spare key that was hidden in the bushes to get into the house. She tried her hardest to be quiet in case someone was in the house that shouldn't. When she entered the front door, there was a chill that swept cross her, which made her even more nervous about everything. She then crept her way through the kitchen and only noticed the oven light on, which was normal for her mother to do. When he saw the hallway, all the doors were closed, which was unusual, so that raised suspicion. She made sure she was extra quiet so that she could catch the intruder and beat the hell out of him. She opened the bathroom door slowly and pulled the curtain back, but there was nothing there. Still being a quiet as a mouse, she moved on to the next door. As she took one more step, she could see a shadow coming from the bedroom, so her suspicions were correct. She slowly turned the knob to the door and took one step in; when she looked up she saw her mother and father in bed together having made sex. She lost all composure when she saw them together. Her father noticed her first and then her mother. Jayden closed the door, "excuse me". She didn't know what to say to either of them, in her head they were both grown and they knew what they were doing.

She was just thinking to herself, "Here I am thinking something is wrong with my mother! Oh, something was wrong, she landed on this married man's dick like it was such a coincidence, never mind the fact that he is married, but you doing it anyway. But, this nigga on the other hand, swore up and down at the mountains that he didn't have feelings for my mother and that he doesn't talk to her. I guess all parents do dumb shit, they just got caught in theirs, but I ain't bitter. They just can't tell me shit and I don't want to have this discussion with them, cause I don't want to be in the middle when Karen flips the hell out."

Jayden talks to herself repeatedly in her car on the way to Brian's house. Her parents wanted to stop her, but what could they tell her that wouldn't contradict all the lies they have told her in the past. They knew Jayden was more like them than Jordan, so trying to talk to her right now would not be the best thing. "James, we just have to hope that she won't say anything and that she realizes we make our own decisions as she has and still does.

"Shit, you can say that because you aren't married and you don't know what kind of mess went down at the mountains. I thought your daughter told you all about it."

"She told me a little about the trip, but nothing in details. Don't tell me that skank had something to say to my daughter?"

"Calm down, your daughter is a grown woman and I handled the trip. There is nothing that would go down with me being there. What kind of man do you think I am?"

"I don't know James. Jayden didn't want to go on the trip in the first place."

"She went, that is all that matters."

"Well, now we have something else to get under control. What are you going to tell her?"

"Why should I tell her anything? I am a grown man."

"What the hell....that is how you are going to handle our 25 year old daughter who just saw her mother and father getting it on in front of her face. James, I don't think that is a good idea, but what can I say you are not my husband. You have to mend your own fences with Jayden."

"You are talking like you have nothing to worry about. Oh, she mad as hell at you too. Don't believe that if you want. She ran out of your house." James implies this as he points his finger at Jackie. In return, Jackie looks back at him furious as ever as she didn't think the repercussion for him would be the same for her, but James informs her differently.

Chapter 13: In the Air!

"We will now board flight 4802 to Atlantic City, New Jersey in fifteen minutes. All passengers please go to gate 31 for boarding instructions." The intercom came on in the airport for the next flight to Jersey. Blake, at the check in point was in a rush to get to the gate in time for boarding because she knew she needed to get home as soon as possible. She turned her luggage in, the little that she had and raced to the gate. She arrived in due time. Upon getting to the gate, "Excuse me, I didn't mean to bump into you".... "Not a problem, don't worry about it." When Blake looked up to see who the person was, she noticed it was Dalia, who was not her favorite person right now.

"Dee, what are you doing here?"

"I have to go handle some business in New Jersey."

"What kind of business? The last you talked to any of us, you thought you may have been pregnant, so what is going on with that situation?"

"I am pregnant, but don't tell anyone yet, I want to be the one to give the news."

"Oh Lord, what news?" That you aren't going to let Terrance be a part of the child's life because he hurt me." says Blake imitating Dalia's facial expressions.

"NO, since you think you know me so well. Terrance and I are going to work things out and we are going to raise this child together. I need to see your precious step sister to whip her ass for messing with my man."

"Clap, Clap, Clap!" "You finally get the damn picture after all this time. I don't know what you were thinking. This is what I have been trying to tell you for the longest. In the beginning, I was with you with being mad and angry at Terrance, but after the trip to my mother's house, I thought you would have regroup and go get that good man you have."

"He is good, isn't he?"

"Jesus, rescue me from the conversation with her."

They both laugh together. "Wait a minute, why are you going to Jersey."

"It's a long story".... "And we have a long flight." The intercom comes on, "now boarding all passengers for flight 4802. All passengers please report to the gate for boarding flight 4802."

Two hours later, Dalia and Blake land in Atlantic City as Blake tries to make a phone call to her mother, but she couldn't reach her. Dalia, feeling queasy from the plane, looked to find some water to clear the dryness in her throat. The plan was to get a rental car and go straight to the law firm. Blake was on a very tight schedule because she wanted to get there before the business day was over. Dalia's plan was to coordinate her life there so she could return to Terrance; little did she know what was ahead for her. Dalia decided to take a cab to Barbara's house where her things were. So, they went their separate ways for the time being. They decided to meet at Barbara's house later that evening for dinner and they would be able to discuss their plans.

Dalia takes the cab to Barbara's house and she tried to use her key to the side door, but it didn't work. Dalia could not get in any of the doors that she attempted to get in. She tried calling Barbara on her cell, but she got the voice mail; "Hi, you have reached Barbara Lowry, I am taking a short vacation, so I will be out of reach for a couple of days. If there are any issues, please leave a detailed message and will try to get back with you as soon as I can. Take care and have a wonderful day, chow!" As furious as she was, Dalia didn't know how to react or what to think. While she was on the side of the house, near the patio, the maid walked by and noticed Dalia and let her in. "Hi Ms. Little, I wasn't expecting you today".

"I bet you weren't, Dalia stated with an attitude like the maid had something to do with it.

"What do you mean, ma'am? Ms. Lowry is on vacation and won't be back until a week from now. I am off that is why I was making the comment, no harm, I promise."

Dalia didn't know what to think since she noticed the locks were changed and she wasn't notified of it since she was staying there for the time being. Once Dalia got her foot in the door, she ran upstairs to check on her things. There was a lock on the door with an envelope addressed to her;

Dalia,

Your items have been removed from the property and shipped to your address in Baltimore. Because of several mishaps and unpleasant events, you are no longer welcomed or may reside at this residence. The locks have been changed. There is no reason to contact anyone in regards to this decision as it has been made based on several suspicions and acts made on your behalf. Sorry it had to be this way. This is no longer personal, but a legal matter.

Take Care,
Blair Lowry

Out of anger, Dalia bawled the letter in her hand wondering if Barbara went out of town for a reason. The one place Dalia knew she could find Blair was at the law firm and so she headed that way in a cab. She tried calling Blake to tell her what happened, but then she thought to herself, "If anyone would know anything about what went down here, it would be Lou". Before storming out of the house, Dalia headed towards the kitchen and ended up running smack into Lou by mistake. "I am so sorry miss, I didn't mean to bump into you", states Lou. "Its nothing, I need to ask you something, do you know anything about this note that was left on my door", asked Dalia. Lou turned partly away from Dalia as if she knew something that she wasn't suppose to talk about. "Lou, what is it, tell me, did Mrs. Lowry put you up to this", asked Dalia pulling Lou closer to her. "I can't say anything or it will be my job and I need my job to take care of my children," as Lou persistently tells Dalia in so many words that she has nothing to do with the note. "Okay, just tell me did Mrs. Lowry leave this note or did that bitch Blaire do it, as she looks at Lou with such sincere in her eyes. "All I can say is that it wasn't Mrs. Lowry", Lou tells Dalia just what she needed to know without telling on any one person in particular, but she knew what to do.

Dalia heads out of the house like a bat out of hell in the cab that was waiting for her. Back in the house, Lou cheers to herself, "I hope that bitch gets what she has coming." Dalia tries to call Blake again on the phone, no answer, but at least it rang this time. She knew from that, Blake was handling some other things that restricted her from answering the phone. Dalia knew the firm was about a twenty minute drive from where the house was, so she had just enough time to get her thoughts together, if she could. What Dalia tried to figure out was the letter. .I knows Blair didn't like Jayden, but I had nothing against her and I assumed she had nothing against me". Dalia started reading the note again to herself in the car, but she was getting puzzled the more she thought about it. Somehow she couldn't put the whole thing together in her head. "Maybe the reason that Blake came up here has something to do with it and it's not about me, maybe that is what it is. Hell, if that is the case, they should all be squashed by this evening. But, wait, she said it wasn't personal anymore but legal. What kind of legalities could have to do with their family? All I did was post at the house for a little while. Damn! I am drawing a blank, never mind, I can ask Lucipher myself when I get there."

Dalia was not far from the firm at this point. She attempted to call Blake again, but she couldn't reach her. She knew something was up with that. "Ma'am, we may have a problem trying to get into this place. There are cops swirling all around this place", states the cab driver. By the time Dalia looked all, all she could see was scene/cop tape around one side of the building like a crime had been committed. She didn't know what to do or what she was about to get herself in the middle of at this point. "Let me out of this car, my best friend is in there. Her car rental car is parked right here in the driveway." The cab driver tried his best to hold Dalia back, but he couldn't do it. Dalia ran to the doorway of the building, as far as she could go in and she was stopped by the detective. "Excuse Miss, can I help you, you can't go into this building. There is a crime scene."

"What happened here? My best friend's father owns this place."

"Really, old man Lowry after he ripped everyone off."

"What the hell are you talking about? He died about a month ago and he was a good man."

"Who's your friend?"

"Bake Lowry is my best friend and her sister Blair we're all here. Where the hell are they?"

"You may want to go to Memorial Hospital."

"Hold up! Before you start sending me around the world, what the hell happened here that you can't tell me?"

"Ma'am, how well do you know these people? They are not who you think they are. Before you go and get yourself all mixed up into something you don't anything about, let it go. Go home and be around your loved ones and forget you were here."

"You don't know what the hell you are talking about." Dalia walked off furious as she didn't want to here more of what he had to say about Blake and her family. Immediately, she starting calling Jayden and Lauren; she couldn't get through to Lauren, but she was able to inform Jayden. Even though she had her own situation going on, she was on her way to be there for Blake. Lauren saw the call from Dalia, but was too busy to take the call due to all the work she had piled on her desk at the moment.

"Let me know what is up when you get to the hospital. Do you know if she was hurt or anything", asked Jayden to Dalia over the phone.

"Hell no and that damn cop wouldn't tell me anything. You wouldn't believe what he said to me, but I will have to tell you about that later. I have to make sure Blake is good."

"I am going to get on the net right now and see if I can catch a flight out. I'll hit Lauren up and get in touch with her. In the meantime, find out what is up at the hospital. Hit me up later."

"Excuse me ma'am, you cannot go into there", the attended said to Dalia as she entered the OR. "My friend is in there and I don't want to hear anything about I can't get any news".

"Maybe you can talk to a relative; her sister is here in the waiting area." Dalia rushes to the waiting area, thinking that maybe Barbara was the relative, but it was Blair. When she entered the room, Blair was standing in the corner with blood all over her body, tears rolling down her face, her hands were shaking horribly. Without even greeting her, "What the fuck happened and I don't want no bullshit." Trying to get her composure together, Blake walked towards the nearest chair, "I didn't know, I really didn't know."

Breathing hard and trying not to lose her cool, Dalia was waiting for Blair to tell her what she had done. "You better tell me something."

"I thought it was a good idea to team up with my sister to get rid of my mother out of the company, so I sided with Carmen and her husband, but come to find out Carmen's husband is the guy that my sister was dating," sobbing continuously, Dalia cut Blair off from talking.

"Whoa, wait a minute, you mean to tell me that Michael is Carmen's husband and he sat out to come between the family, you couldn't see that, so you let greed and envious over your mother and sister get the best of you. I can't believe this shit."

"No, No. I thought all she wanted was to be a part of the family."

"Bitch, you didn't even know this chick or her husband. Why would you want your mother out of the company? She let you run this ship all by yourself", shaking her head while she is pacing down the hallway of the waiting room.

"You don't understand", states Blair.

"No, I don't, but I am not the one you have to explain your case to. You have to tell your sister and your mother."

"My mommie....Blake is never going to forgive me."

"Girl stop! "Tell me what happened at the meeting to that led us here to the hospital." Before she was able to answer, Dalia's phone rang; Lauren and Jayden called her on three way. She couldn't even say hello, before they both starting asking questions.

"Please tell me Blake is not hurt, I swear to GOD I will be up there so fast", states Jayden.

"You just say the word and we will both be there", states Lauren.

"Will you all let me talk? Blair was just about to tell me what happened at the meeting before the two of you called", states Dalia.

"Okay, what did this bitch have to say, I know she did something or had something to do with all of this, I can just feel it", states Jayden.

"She hasn't said anything yet. She is standing in front of me now," states Dalia

"Make that bitch talk," states Jayden over the phone.

Loudly talking, Lauren tells Dalia over the phone, "we are on our way up the quickest way we can, Jay, hang up, and meet me at my house in ten minutes, we are going to catch whatever is at the airport."

They disconnect the phone and as soon as Dalia hits the end button, she notices the doctor coming around the corner in his white jacket.

"I am looking for the family of Blake Mowry," asked the doctor.

"I am her next of kin until her mother gets here," states Dalia as she gave Blair the evil eye like she dared her to say anything different from what she stated to the doctor.

"Okay ma'am. Right now Ms. Mowry has suffered a lot of internal bleeding and we are trying to contain it right now. She was unconscious when she was brought in. That is about all the information that I can give you right now. I have to get back to the patient. I will try my best to keep you posted. Have the nurse page me when her mother arrives." The doctor walks swiftly back to the OR before either one of them could say anything. Dalia turns and looks at Blair, "Bitch, you better pray she makes it out of here on both feet or I am going to break yours."

Out of nowhere, Dalia and Blair here a loud noise and someone walking fast through the hallway, before they were able to see anything, Barbara rushed into the waiting room, demanding answers. She looked at Dalia and Blake, "What happened and where is my baby." Dalia hugged Barbara, "you might want to ask you daughter about that." Releasing Dalia from her arms, she looked at her daughter with fire in her eyes. Deep down Barbara knew that Blair would be the child that she had to worry about if something ever happened to her husband. Even though Blake was unsure of her future, she had a wonderful heart and she loved to live life to the fullest, unlike Blair, who knew what she wanted before she even old enough to get it. She seemed to always be captivated with wrong tidbit of everything. Instead of being involved and shadowing her father to take over the company, she was more interest how someone could ever take over the company or how someone would embezzle money.

Walking towards Blair, "I want you to look me in my eyes and tell me what happened to your sister."

Sniffling like a scared child, Blair could not even have direct eye contact with her mother; she knew she was wrong and partly responsible for what happened to her sister. "It all happened so fast, I don't even remember all the details."

Barbara snatched Blair by the shoulders, "You look at me and tell me what the hell happened to my baby and you better talk fast."

"It was Carmen."

"Carmen!" Barbara's eye stretched out as far as they could. "Why would she be here and why would Blake have anything to do with her." All kind of thoughts ran through Barbara's head. She was thinking of all kinds of answers to the questions in her head, but most of all, she didn't want to know what her own flesh and blood had to do with it. She turned away for a moment to think to herself.

"Ms. Lowry, please calm down, we all have to be positive for Blake, we need her to pull through" states Dalia.

"Pull through; my baby shouldn't have to pull through, because she shouldn't even be in this predicament". After gathering herself together, Barbara turned back to Blair, "You better tell me everything, right now or if God so helps me, I will strangle you with my own two hands."

Frightened as ever, Blair cleared her throat, "I only wanted what was mind. I thought that teaming with Carmen would help me gain control of the company. I didn't know that Carmen's husband was dating Blake and they both had a plan to take the company away from me."

"Am I hearing you right? You turned against your father, your mother, and your little sister, only to team up with a long lost sister, a stranger at that and her husband, all because you were greedy, spoiled and unappreciative of what you have" states Barbara. By this time, Barbara is so angry she could hardly think straight.

"Mrs. Lowry, before you say anything else, I think I should take you downstairs to get something to drink", implied Dalia.

"I don't need anything to drink; I need this bitch to leave the hospital right now before I forget that she is my child", states Barbara.

"Ma, you don't mean that."

"Blair you might want to get out of my sight right now."

As tension grew in the hospital, the three women all stood around weeping and praying that everything turns out in Blake's favor. Dalia, standing alone, was reminiscing of all the good times and bad times that she and Blake shared together. She couldn't bear the thought of losing one of her closest friends. She then thought about Lauren and Dalia and how they would be affected by this. Knowing that she was unable to talk clearly over the phone, she decided to send a text message to them both,

"You all need to make it here fast; things don't look good for Blake. She is in surgery right now and has been there for a while. Things are falling apart for Barbara, and oh yes, Blair is here, so don't make a scene when you get here. Let me know where you guys are....Love you both, Dalia"

Not knowing how else to emphasize to them, that if at any time Blake needed them, now would be the time. She looks over at Barbara, who was bent over the seat with her arms folded with tears running down her face, to see all the hurt in her face without being able to rely on her oldest child. Then, looking across the room at Blair, who never left after her mother wanted her to, looking all confused and dumbfounded like she really didn't think her plan would backfire on her. The waiting room was very quiet and cold. You could hear a pen drop. No one was moving or saying anything to anyone. This was so unexpected and hurtful all at the same time. Blake had been in surgery for over an hour now and not a word from a nurse or doctor. Since I never got a reply back from the girls, I assume they were on their way. I don't want to call them because I may fall a part in the process. I would rather wait until they get here.

"I can't believe we were able to catch a cheap flight this short notice to get to New Jersey", states Lauren.

"Yeah, I can't help but think of how many ways I could beat the hell out of Blair when I get to the hospital", states Jayden, in which she deters from Lauren's comments.

Lauren shook her head because under these circumstances, she knew there was nothing she could do to stop Jayden from acting a fool. "Hey, have you checked your phone to see if you have any messages from Dalia," asked Lauren.

"Oh shit, I forgot to check them before we boarded the plane. Hold up, I will check it now. Aw hell, Rin, Dalia sent us a text, doesn't look good for Blake.

"Let me look at my phone....she sent me the same thing."

The both of them grew very silently. Reality was beginning to look them in the face

Jayden thinks about all of the things that have happened over the past couple of months in her life that she might have dwelled on too long or took too much energy. She began to have a lot of regrets in her mind that she was afraid of admitting to out loud. She thought about her relationship with Brian and how she might be taking him for granted, then her mind ran across her parents. "Am I being too hard on my parents", Dalia was thinking to herself. "Hell naw, he is married and my mother knows better than that. I bet they were lying to me about this shit for a long time...and if it weren't for my brother, I still would have been in the damn dark."

"Rin, did you tell your job that you were going to be out for a while", asked Jayden.

"I told them that I would be out of office for a couple of days, but if we stay longer than that, I will work from Jersey. That won't be a problem, especially with all the system issues we are having. Did you get a chance to talk to Brian", asked Lauren?

"I couldn't reach him at the job. He probably was in the middle of a delivery, but I did leave him a voice mail and a detailed text message on his phone. Trust me, when he gets them, he is going to be calling", states Jayden.

"Man, I just hope we don't get another call from Dalia or text message."

"Who you telling?" I don't know if I can deal with anymore of this. Rin, I am sitting here thinking of the last time I talked to Blake, and I can't even remember". Jayden talking with her head tilted back in the seat, mind boggled of how she couldn't recall the last time she talked to her home girl.

"Yes, you do remember, weren't we at your house talking about you losing your job and your engagement?"

"Yeah, I think you are right....cause she was too upset with Dalia about how she was acting. She was happy for me. Why didn't she tell us something was going on with her family and all?"

"I don't know, maybe she didn't know all the details, which is why she didn't say anything."

"I don't believe none of that crap. You are going to tell me that Blake didn't know this so called sister, excuse me, sisters of hers, you out your damn mind."

"Stop being so hard on Blake."

"Stop being hard, this is reality. When you play with fire, you get burned. How many times do I have to keep telling you all that? No matter who the person is, you can't go around trusting people just because of the title or who you think they are. Its strangers you can trust its family that fucks you over."

Lauren laughs at what Dalia is saying because deep down she sees truth in what she is saying for some odd reason. "I hear what you are saying, but everyone doesn't have the heart of steel that you do, especially not Blake."

"Why not Blake? She knows her parents are well off and that she would have a tough time finding someone because of who she was, which is why she decided to go to school in Maryland in the first place. Do you remember that?

"Of course I remember that. She was so lost when she came to college."

"You got that right. Who brings Burberry luggage to an all black college and expects to be the all around chick that everyone likes."

"Hold up! I had Burberry luggage too when I was a freshman."

"Yeah, but you left it at home and brought that Wal-Mart luggage." They both laugh together, sharing a moment that hadn't been able to have in such a long time.

"But you have to admit Jay; Blake wasn't all seditiy as you thought she was."

"Whew! You are right about that. Do you remember when we went to the house party spring semester freshman year?

"Oh my GOD, yes I do and how loose she got with that alcohol," chuckles from Jayden.

"Please don't laugh at the expense of this underage drinking."

"Well, they shouldn't have had it at the party in the first place."

"Aw, man, how did we get from there to here, you know." The plane was really cold and packed to its capacity. Jayden and Lauren were trying to make the best of the situation. Even though, this was the only flight that they could get in such short notice, it wasn't the best. The seats were crammed together. Luckily for the both of them, they knew each other.

"I can't wait to get off this plane", states Jayden.

"I know the feeling and I am thirsty, where is the stewardess", asked Lauren.

"I really don't know where she went to be honest, probably not out here since you need her", responded Jayden.

"Good Afternoon, passengers, we will be preparing for landing in thirty minutes. Please fasten your seatbelts. This should be a smooth landing, and thank you for flying Delta."

The pilot nicely alarmed the passengers of the landing of the flight, which frightened Jayden the most, since she really didn't like to fly. Lauren, on the other hand, loved to fly because she did a lot of it with her mother growing up. Reality was hitting the both of them harder than expected, Jayden turned to Lauren, "I don't know if I can handle seeing Blake like this."

Lauren put her arm across Jayden's shoulders to comfort her, causing Jayden head to tilt on Lauren's shoulder. "We have to all be strong for Blake and her mother right now, regardless of what the situation may be."

Jayden, the one who always hid her feelings and emotions because she thought showing too much emotion was a sign of weakness and lack of confidence in one self. This was her mind frame growing up and getting through college. This was the one thing she struggled with as an adult, just like the rest of her friends, Jayden struggled with emotions and feelings terribly. What she didn't realize was that she contributed to the gap in all of her relationships, because of the distance she placed in them herself.

"I am so glad to be off that plane right now, I am about to lose my mind. Just as soon as we get our luggage, we can head to the hospital. Call, Dalia while I get the luggage to see what is going on", states Lauren to Jayden.

Ring, Ring, Ring. The phone continues to ring when Jayden attempted to call Dalia on her cell. "Okay, maybe she is in with Blake and can't answer the phone." As nervous as she was, she knew that wasn't a good sign if Dalia didn't answer her phone.

"Well, what did she say, did she tell you what was going on, damn these bags are heavy as hell…..hello, Jay, you aren't saying anything", states Lauren.

"Uh, I didn't get an answer," hardly able to get her words out, Jayden just had a bad feeling that she just couldn't shake, but she didn't know how to tell Lauren without frightening her.

"OKAY JAY, CALL IT AGAIN UNTIL SOMEONE ANSWERS", states Lauren loudly. She was becoming frustrated because it wasn't a good sign since Dalia was answering her phone all along.

"Fuck it! We will just get a cab and get over there. We don't have to wait for her to answer the phone", states Lauren. Tears filled their eyes. A very warm cold feeling ran through them and it seems that time was flying by them while they were at a standstill. Not drawing eye contact with one another, they walked as fast as they could to reach a cab.

"Taxi, this way", as they yelled to the cabs driving relatively fast past their way. Finally, cab stopped who would lead them to the hospital.

"Got damnit, pick up the phone, shit!' Lauren yelled out to her phone as she used her Blackberry to contact the hospital. The line was busy and boy was she furious about that.

They jumped into the cab as fast they could. There hands were trembling. They were never as nervous as they were right now. They didn't know whether to expect the worst or hope for the best. They asked the cab driver to drive as fast as possible to get them to the hospital, but traffic was horrible and the cab drive took every back road possible to get them there. Continuously, they called the hospital and they could get through to anyone. "This is getting on my fucking nerves; I don't get why nobody is picking up the phone. What kind of hospital is that, what if I was in need of some services and shit", states Jayden.

"We should be there in just a minute, looks like the driver is close now. Look, see all the hospital signs. We aren't far from it now," states Lauren has she speaks calmly to calm herself and Jayden down from anticipation. They arrive at the hospital jumping out of the car before the driver was able to come to a complete stop. "Wait, stop right here, this is the entrance, Jay come this way,"

Breathing heavily, "Excuse me, I am looking for Blake Mowry, she was brought in here earlier today through the Emergency Room", asked Jayden.

The nurse asked, "Are you family or a relative"?

Jayden looked at Lauren, "Yes, yes, we are her sisters and we flew here from Baltimore to see how she is doing, do you know something or not"?

The nurse started looking very puzzled as if she didn't know what to say or how to react, "Follow me this way, please."

The Upside Down of Things

Chapter 14: It Ain't Over

"Knock, Knock, Knock, Knock, Knock"
"What in the hell is knocking on this door so gottdamn early in the morning? I'm coming", Terrance yelling back at the person knocking on the door; the door squeals as Terrance slowly opened the door with his eyes halfway open. "Yes, I am looking for Miss Dalia Little or Terrance Ross", said the man at the door. "Uh, I am Terrance, who are you?"

"Sir, I am hear to deliver this notice to you. You have been served." The carrier walked off. Terrance is standing in the doorway with his shorts on, barefoot, wiping the crust out of his eyes. He was up most of the night thinking about Dalia and the new life they were going to bring into the world. It has been a while since he was back into the condo they shared, so he was definitely caught off guard with this carrier at the door so early in the morning.

"Man, this betta not be no bullshit. I ain't in the mood for this shit." He opens the letter; blah, blah, blah.....YOU HAVE 30 DAYS TO LEAVE THE PREMISES. THIS IS AN EVICTION NOTICE FOR NONPAYMENT OF RENT! You have got to be out your damn mind. Wait, wait, wait a minute, let me think. Dee and I bought this condo, we weren't renting it. This shit ain't right. I gotta fix this before she gets back home. Hold up, if we bought this plan, why the evictions notice? Something ain't adding up. I know I got some papers around here with the shit that we signed a couple of years ago. I know what the hell I put my name on, these muthafuckers on this bullshit right now." Terrance looked at the clock while he was searching through his papers and realized it was 9:00. "Damn, I got to be to work in a bit. I might have to handle this when I get off. No, I might want

189

to call in today. Think, think think…..what would Dee tell me." In the back of his head, he is thinking of ever rendition in his head of how this conversation would go with Dalia. "She always told me I didn't know how to prioritize. Wait the hell up, PRIORITIZE my ass….she was hear not me, why did she let things get this bad. You have got to be kidding." All the while, Terrance is running every kind of thought through his head trying to make sense of it all. If he didn't know one thing, he knew that he was about to be homeless if he didn't try to figure this out soon. Terrance got dressed and headed out of the door. While cranking up his car, he headed downtown to the court house, where he knew he could get some answers about the taxes and the ownership on the townhome that he and Dalia shared.

"Get the fuck out of here. I think I got it. I bet she wasn't even going to work when she had everyone fooled that she was. Maybe I really did hurt her more than what I thought or maybe she didn't want to be here anymore or maybe she was planning on moving anyway which is why she let everything get behind. Naw, this shit ain't adding up in my head. Hell, I don't know what to think about this shit, but I do know if I don't fix it, I will be out of a place to stay. Ain't this some shit, early in the gottdam morning?"

Running through the house trying to get his thoughts together, Terrance couldn't fathom that fact that Dalia, who always seemed so together with paying bills and managing her money, somehow fell so far into depression or out of sync that she neglected to handle dealings with the house.

"Nigga, open up the damn door, I know you heard me calling your damn phone." Terrance's friend Trey is at the door to pick him up for work. Terrance forgot that he was car pooling with a friend this week, so that put a wrench in his plans to find out what was going on with Dalia and his house.

"Damn, you early as hell."

"How am I early, if we have to be to work in 45 minutes? It is going to take us about 30 minutes to get there. Man, hurry the hell up before I leave you….and where is Dee? I haven't seen her in a while. I want to mess with her before I leave." Trey starts browsing through the house thinking that Dalia would appear.

"Naw, she ain't here. She is in New Jersey with uh; you remember her friends, Blake, Lauren, and Jayden…"

"Hell yeah, I remember them. That gottdam Blake is fine as fuck. I always wanted to hook up with her, man, but I thought she was too damn expensive. You can look at her and tell, it cost $100 for her appetizers and she probably only eat at certain restaurants. Just high class as hell for no reason", Terrance laughs because he knows his friend is all out of his league, but right to some extent.

"Oh, so I guess you think my girl is like that to."

"Quit tripping; you know well and damn well, Dee has a part of that in her too."

"Actually, Blake is very down to earth."

"What the hell….when did you start saying "down to earth". Trey imitates Terrance saying his words really proper for him to understand. "It's not about acting down to earth; it's what you know to be."

"Nigga, I didn't come here to get a lesson about Blake."

"Shut the hell up! You are the one that ain't ready, as usual."

"Hold up, you are the one, who started talking about Blake and then just like a nigga, you want to criticize her. She ain't asked to be with you or for you to take her out. The smile dropped off of Trey's face.

"So, she been asking about me and you ain't say nothing. That is dirty, man, dirty as hell…." (Trey blows out hot air, just to show Terrance how upset he is that he kept this from him)

"Man, don't you have a chick already."

"Shh, don't say that out loud. You know me and that girl ain't nothing serious."

"I can't tell. You are always with her."

"Man, that don't mean nothing. She ain't nothing like big time Blake, if you know what I mean."

"Hell naw, I don't know what that means. I see Blake like a little sister. I remember when she and Dalia became friends. She was so impressionable and someone always had to look after her."

"Oh, so you think you Daddy now! (Trey laughs to himself, because he thinks Terrance is making himself to be more than what he really is.)

"Chill out. I see her the same way Dee used to see her." Terrance packs his bag while continuing his conversation with Trey. In the meantime, Terrance is still worrying about this eviction notice that he received this morning. In his mind, he is trying to decipher how he should handle the situation. He didn't want to involve anyone else because Dalia didn't like people in her business, but he was running out of options. He decided to go to work and maybe he would come up with something or hell, he could find a way out of this without Dalia even knowing about the situation. Trey and Terrance leave the house for work. When they arrive, they realized that their boss as left a lot of work on their desk for them to complete for the day. They instantly realized it was going to be a long day. They knew it was no way around it and there was also no time in between for Terrance to focus on his personal problems. He would have to figure out another way to get that done some other time without anyone in his business.

"I will holla at y'all later, I have to get to the house", Brian tells his co-workers.

"Oh, so you have to go play house now, huh. I told you, giving her that ring was going to mess everything up", shouted one of the delivery guys at Brian's job.

"I'm no fuck boy, you can believe that", Brian blurted out while reaching in his pocket to check his phone. "Aww, shit, I missed a call from Jay, I wonder what she wants", he says to himself. "I'll catch up with y'all in the AM" he says as he exists the building. "Man, I'm tired as shit. I just want to go home and chill with my ba-by."

Brian gets in his car without checking his messages on his phone. He throws in his Jay-Z cd just so he can blast his music while leaving the parking lot to his job. The entire ride home, Brian is thinking about Jayden all the time and how he is so happy and ready to start a new life with her. Their relationship has been mostly down compared to other relationships. They got along by arguing most of time and spending time apart. Every time they were together, it was nothing but tension and frustration, which was mostly on Jayden's part. She was always hard to get along with, but Brian was always her match.

When Brian pulls up at his house, he notices that she is not there, which is unusual since she is not working. Lately, she is there once Brian gets off because she likes to greet him in her own special way since she is no longer working. Brian knew something wasn't right and he realized that he hasn't heard anything from her.

"Shit, I forgot to check my messages." Quickly, he listened to his voicemail.

"There are three new messages, no saved messages. First message. "Hey Brian, it's me. Sorry I couldn't be there when got off. Lauren and I had to leave and go take a flight to Jersey. I will call you later and fill you in on the details. Don't worry, I am fine. Babe, I love you. Talk to you soon."

Brian didn't know what to gather from that. Just as soon as he heard that message, he closed his phone in furry. "What the fuck going on now? If she said that Lauren and she had to leave, then what about Dalia...."

Brian had a quick thought for a moment that Dalia may be home. Since he knew where she lived, he would stop by her house to see if she knew anything. While getting into the car, he picked up his cell phone and called Jayden's cell. It went straight to voice mail. He wasn't the type to leave messages so he just hung the phone up.

"Wait, a damn minute. She didn't sound like it was an emergency on the voice mail, right?" Brian is talking to himself trying to calm down all at the same time. "She did say that she was going to call so why am I tripping. Damn, those boys were right, I am whipped".....he thought for a minute, "hell, naw. I am going back to the house and wait until she calls me, at least before I have to flip the hell out. The least I can do is go by her house and check on things. Hopefully, her brother hasn't torn up everything.

On his way to Jayden's house, Brian stops by the gas station to get some gas. When he gets out of the car, he notices some guys being loud at the pump across from him. He happens to look up and noticed one of them, "eh, boy, what's been good wit ya?'

"Ain't nothing, trying to get this paper, that's all."

Brian saw Terrance at the station with one of his co-workers as they were getting on their way home from a long day at work.

"How is Dee doing", asked Brian

"She is good, I just wish she would hurry up and get home because she needs to focus on the baby and all, how is Jay?"

"Baby! Dee is pregnant."

"Yeah, man. She early as hell though and she went back to Jersey to move all her stuff back here."

"What the hell, what you mean move the stuff back. You know, don't worry bout it, Jay don't tell me much about her friends in the first place. I don't know why I am shocked to hear all this news. But, I thought she would have told me about the baby, at least. Shit no, with everything else going on, she probably wouldn't."

"Everything else…."

"Jay lost her job a couple of days ago, almost a week and it's been having her down…and, (Brian clears his throat) we got engaged."

"Congratulations, man, I didn't know." They both have a moment and dabbed each other about the engagement.

Trey yells from the car, "Man, you ready?"

"Yeah, I am, gimme a minute".

Brian starts to thinking and asks Terrance, "Is that why Jay left to go to Jersey."

"Uh, Dee didn't mention anything to me about going with the girls up there"…..they both paused for a minute.

"You thinking something ain't right…"

"Exactly, if Dee was taking the girls with her, she would have said something. Hell, she damn near jumped out of my bed to get this shit together…"

"Whoa, wait a minute, and if Jay was only going to help Dalia move her stuff, she would have left that on my voice mail instead of saying that she would call me later…" they are both trying to put this mystery together. "You need a ride home, cause yo man look like he ready…"

"Yeah, I do, you mind taking me."

"Not a problem and we can talk on the way."

"Eh, Trey, Brian is going to take me home, I will holla at you later my man.

Trey responds, "That's what's up! I will hit you up in the AM.

"Terrance, wait I got a new message from Jay, let me check it."

You have two saved messages. First message, (sniffles in the background) "hey babe, it's me, things aren't looking good for Blake. There is a whole lot of mess going on that I can't really explain over the phone. The only thing that I can tell you is that Blake has been shot and I will try and call you when I get more information. I love you!" end of message.

"Shhhhhh-iiiiiiiiiitttttttttttttt" screams Brain

"Man, what did she say?"

"Shit, I think I missed this one earlier today. I got excited when I saw that she wasn't home that I only listened to one of my voice mails. You ain't going to believe this shit here…."

"It can't be that bad."

"You wanna bet…..Jay was crying so bad that I could hardly hear what she was saying. She said that it wasn't looking good for Blake and that she would call me later. She said Blake got shot and that she would call me later and explain the details to me."

"Man, are you serious…nawww, that can't be happening.. That is some TV drama going on…" Terrance frowned his face and shaking his head with confusion. Silence drew amongst both men as they were lost for words as they continue to ride in the car.

"Ok, let me wrap my head around this…so, you are telling me that Blake got shot and the girls are in Jersey right now at the hospital…"

"Yeah, that is what it looks like", stated Brian.

"Man, I got to call Dee and see if she is okay."

Brian reached across and grabbed Terrance phone to stop him from calling Dalia. "No, no, no. I think we should wait until they call us. We don't want to call and get in the way. Plus, we don't even know what is going on up there."

"But, Dogg, I have to check on my baby and make sure its okay".

"Shit, I forgot about that too....yeah, you might want to call. Let me know if you get through", stated Brian.

As Brian pulled up to the house, Terrance stopped waiting for Dalia to pick up the phone because he noticed something strange about the house. He saw a bright pink sticker on the door and something wasn't right about the windows either.

"Oh, crap, that is fucked up", states Brian. Terrance immediately hung the phone up. Terrance jumped out of the car before Brian could put the car in park.

"Gottdamn, I just got the notice today. I can't believe this shit right now". Terrance noticed a note on the door for the furniture pick up and eviction notice again. "Man, none of this shit is adding up to me."

Brian finally got out of the car slowly like he was being precautious to what he was walking in on.

"Man, what the fuck is this shit.....damn, my bad, none of my business. Ugh, I will let you know if I hear anything else."

In total shock from everything, Terrance's mouth opened, looking through all of his and Dalia's belongings wondering through his mind what was going on. He didn't know what to think at that point.

"Bee, you don't have to leave man. We still have to talk about the ladies. I can figure this out later."

"Man, how can you figure this out later if these moving people came here to kick your shit out. That ain't something you want to put off. You might want to handle this, for real." (The phone rings)

"Jay, Babe what is going on? Terrance got a call from Dalia that Blake got shot and she was all hyped and crap. What the hell is up?"

"I had to leave so early that I didn't get a chance to explain everything, but it seems like Blake got caught in a web with her sister and her half sister."

"Huh! *Deep breaths from Brian.* Wait a minute, Blake has a half sister!"

Terrance looks at Brian with dismay. Jayden is on the other end of the phone explaining to Brian bits and pieces of the story.

"Babe, you ain't going to believe half of what has happened. Apparently, Blake's half sister mistook Dalia for Blake and she slept with Terrance thinking she was Blake, but she had the wrong person. So, all along this chick and her husband were plotting with Blair to take over their father's company behind Blake's back....I told you this was some shit."

Brian pulled the phone away from his air, as he was shocked at the drama he was hearing.

"You right, this is some shit here...okay, but how is Blake." *Deep sighs from the other end of the phone.*

Brian sits down as the news is overwhelming even for him...while on the other hand, Terrance waits patiently while Brian is talking to Jayden.

"Oh babe, I wish it was better. Blake took a bad bullet in the chest. The doctor has been working on her for hours. At one point, we thought we were going to hear something, but they are still trying to repair, the last we heard."

"Damn, babe! Is there anything that I can do for you....or Terrance?"

"It would be nice to see you and I am sure my pregnant behind friend could use Terrance too."

"Whoa, wait a minute, I have a question". Brian looked around to make sure that Terrance wasn't paying him any attention and he noticed he was too close to him. Brian decided to walk outside so that he could have a private conversation with Jayden.

"Babe, so you mean to tell me that Terrance slept with Blake's half sister and he is still with Dalia....get the fuck out of here!!!!!"

"You so damn stupid. It's a long story; I will have to tell you about it later"

"Maybe I don't want to know the details of this situation. All I want to know is if my baby is okay."

"I am good now. I guess because I don't know any details and we have been sitting out here for hours waiting for someone to tell us something, but all we see is doors swinging, but no one giving us any details."

"Man that is fucked up babe....just pray about it. I will keep the house straight for you till you get back. You know if you stay too long, I am coming up there."

"Boy stop, you aren't leaving that job for no one...even I know that"...they both laugh on the phone...."hey, tell Terrance that Dalia said she will call him later once she charges her phone up."

"Okay, I will tell him....hey, babe, do you know what is going on with them."

"Whatcha mean? All I know is that they just got back together and she is pregnant and they are supposed to be happy go lucky. That is all I know, for real...don't tell me it's more to this shit. This is too much even for me."

"I don't even want to say nothing. I will let Dalia tell you."

"O Lord, then I don't know how dramatic I may get over this one....okay, babe, I will talk to you later."

"Hey, keep me posted."

"I will."

Brian walks back in the house to tell Terrance more info from what he got from Jayden.

"Eh, Tee, Jay told me that they just have been sitting there waiting for hours. I guess Blake is still in surgery and they haven't heard anything....and Jay told me to tell you that Dalia said she will call you later once she charges her phone up.."

"Cool, man...thanks for the info. Terrance daps Brian in his own way.

"Aight, I'll holla"...Brian shuts the door and leaves Terrance and Dalia's condo.

Part II

"Okay guys, this is going to be one of the biggest cases we are going to handle this year. What I need are my junior partners to assist the senior partners on this one. If we do well with this case, this could be big things for all of us in the upcoming years. Kendall, I want you to head this one if it works in your schedule with setting up the new firm down in Baltimore. You Junior partners, I want you to follow Kendall's lead. He has been with the company a long time so I want you to observe and learn a lot from this man."

Normally they had these meetings once a week at the company Kendall works at to keep everyone up to date with the direction of the company. On aside, Kendall is daydreaming about Lauren and their future together. He hears his boss give him a directive of this new case that is supposed to supersede any other case, but he just can't take his mind off of her. Even though he hasn't seen her in a couple of days, he missed her desperately.

"Hey, I hate to interrupt this meeting", says the receptionist entering the room. "Then, why interrupt", states the vice president.

"No, you have to see this....Kendall, I think you have worked with these people before." Kendall turns his chair and drew his attention to the television;

"We are live from the infamous building of the Lowry Law Firm. There has been a tragic event that occurred hear today. It has been reported that daughter of millionaire Bernard Lowry has been fatally shot and is currently struggling for her life here at a nearby hospital. Blake, a young Marketing Executive has been experiencing some sibling rivalry since the passing of her father a couple of years ago. Evidence at the crime scene has shown that there wasn't a struggle and that Miss Lowry walked into an unexpected situation. She arrived here at the firm earlier today to confront her sister, Blair of a takeover that she was making with the company that Blake disagreed. Blake took a flight out her to confront her sister only to find things in turmoil. No further information has been reported at this time since this case is being handled as an attempted murder case. The mother Barbara Lowry, a former college professor, who was sent out of the country so that this take over could go smoothly was unaware of malicious acts of her eldest daughter, Blair. This is Susan Connerly, reporting live in front of the Lowry Law Firm. It is back to you guys."

Kendall existed the meeting in a hurry. Knowing that he wasn't too far from where the Lowry's stayed, he knew that they had to be at a nearby hospital of the home or law office. While grabbing his brief case, coat, and files that he needed for later, his secretary wasn't even able to get his status for the rest of the day. He ran to his car as fast as he could, reaching for his cell phone at the same time, trying to dial Lauren's number. Of course, he didn't get an answer, but he continued to call hoping that he would get through or that she would answer the phone. Driving through the parking garage and traffic seemed like it was taking eternity for Kendall. He arrived at the hospital in a matter of 20 minutes. He raced into the registration portion of the building where he asked for the family of Blake Lowry. The hospital was given instructions to be discreet and private as possible since Blake could be a victim of homicide or attempted murder.

"My name is Kendall Brockington and I looking for my girlfriend. She is a very close friend of the Lowry family and I really need to see her."

The receptionist looks up at Kendall, while chewing her gum, "Do you mean Kendall Brockington, the lawyer who is always doing the big cases around here."

Kendall clears his throat and responds, "uh, well, yes, ma'am, I do believe that is me, but don't tell anyone you saw me ok." He winked his eye at the receptionist with her mouth wide open like she just met a star. Kendall never thought of himself in that manner, since his true aspiration wasn't being a lawyer, but he was damn good at it and very proud, but in a professional manner. Without speaking a word, the receptionists points Kendall into the direction of the family waiting area.

It seemed as if every angle, door, and hallway was empty as Kendall walked hurriedly through the wing at the hospital. It seemed to him like he as walking for over five minutes without seeing anyone in sight. Finally, he looked ahead and saw what may look like Jayden. He remembered her from the party where he met Lauren. He didn't want to yell, but he called her name out, "Jayden."

She glanced up at him with a mysterious look like he was someone familiar, but she couldn't quite place it. As it grew closer, he noticed, Lauren ahead of him. Not looking her best, she seemed relieved when she saw Kendall coming towards her.

"Lauren, I came as soon as I heard about what happened. Do you know it is all on the news? The receptionist from the job turned on the television so we all could see."

"Come with me, this way, so we can talk. Kendall, I am so scared for her. We have been here waiting and waiting and we just don't know what to do. No one will tell us anything of what is going on..." Lauren sobs as she tells Kendall how she feels about the situation.

"Babe, are you going to spend the night at the hospital because it is getting late and you need your rest. You aren't going to be any good for Blake if you don't get your rest".

Kendall grabs Lauren by the chin to reassure her that he is by her side and there to support her. "Hey, you know you and your friends are welcome to come to my place here if they like. Get your things, I want to take you out and get some fresh clothes and something to eat."

"NO, I don't want to leave her alone."

"Lauren, Dalia is still here and Blake's mother. It is only for a couple of hours, I promise, we won't be long."

"Dee, call me if there is any change or if you hear something", as Lauren tells Dalia before leaving with Kendall, even though she doesn't want to leave Blake's side, there was really nothing she could do at this point.

"I will," states Dalia.

As Lauren and Kendall walked down the hallway, it seemed like the life of Blake was slipping by according to how Lauren was feeling. She didn't know what to expect, but she knew a break from it all would do her a world of good. Leaving the hospital had to be the hardest thing for Lauren to do.

"Kenny, I don't know how all this happened and I can't believe that one of my best friends is fighting for her life in the hospital. This is all crazy to me, for real." Lauren tells Kendall while they are riding in the care.

"Ren, I can't imagine how you feel, but I am here for you and your friends."

Lauren lay back in the seat of the car and closed her eyes for just a moment. She took a deep breath just to make sure that she wasn't dreaming. She then realized that she met the man of her dreams. They arrived at the house and Kendall helped Lauren out of the car and into the house. She went upstairs, Kendall followed behind her. He ran the shower, lit a candle in the bathroom to make it all right for Lauren. He then saw Lauren slowly taking her jewelry off as if she were exhausted. He walked up behind her, slowly touching her shoulder; he unbuttoned her blouse and eased her out of her top. Then, he unzipped her pants, unbuckling her pants. Feeling desperate on the inside for some comfort, she was being guided by Kendall's lead. He softly touched her stomach as he pulled her pants down. The hit the ground and she steps out of them. She closes her eyes to savor the moment.

Kendall grabs her hand to follow him into the bathroom. At this point, the bathroom is steaming hot from the shower running. Lauren pulled the curtain back so she could get in the shower and she turned around as if Kendall was to follow.

"Hey, you not coming", asked Lauren.

Immediately, Kendall got of out his clothes, throwing his very expensive suit on the floor of the spacious bathroom. By the time Lauren was able to blink, Kendall was out of his clothes. Lauren stepped into the shower, the water was steaming hot. She could feel Kendall in behind her caressing her slowly just the way she wanted to be touch. She turned around to face him. He looked her in her eyes and she kissed him passionately while the shower was running. He continued to caress her and she loved it. He lifted her out of the shower and carried her into his bedroom. The water was dripping off of their bodies, not stopping from kissing; Kendall laid her on the bed, rubbing through her hair slowly. Lauren groaned as Kendall kissed her on the neck, slowly moving down to her breast. He began sucking and licking her breast softly. Lauren moaned louder and louder for his touch and he enjoyed ever groan and moan she made.

Lauren phone rings.

"Babe that is your phone", states Kendall.

Quickly, Lauren pushed Kendall from off of her to get to her phone. She assumed that it was something concerning Blake.

"Hello"

"Lauren, its Blake, she is out of surgery, the doctor said everything went okay. They had a scare for a while as she wasn't responding to anything, but they said she is going to have a long recovery back. She may not recognize anyone, but she is going to have to go through a lot of rehab to get to like she was.

Screams....

Lauren screams loudly on the phone as she is amazed her friend survived. Things were not going in her favor when they arrived at the hospital.

"Is she wake now?"

"No, they won't let anyone see her yet. The doctor said he would send the nurse when she is settled in a room and can have visitors. So, it is going to be a while. Barbara said that she wanted all of us to go and take a break and come back to the hospital later this evening or we could wait until the morning."

"Okay, that is great! Oh my God, I don't know what to say, Dee. She made it, thank God. What are you going to do, wait until tomorrow or come back tonight?"

"Hell, I was going to ask you…"

"I know Barbara is going to want to spend time with her first, so I may wait until the morning….Wait! Have you eaten anything? You know you have to eat for that baby."

"Oh wow! I haven't even thought about eating."

"Hello! What are you thinking? Where is Jay?"

"I am going to eat something, just as soon as Jay gets back from downstairs. She went to call her brother and make sure he is not tearing up her house."

In the background, Kendall is whispering to Lauren to invite Jayden and Dalia to come stay at his house until the morning so they can visits Blake in the hospital.

"Hey Dee…when Jay comes back, tell her I want you guys to come to Kendall's house and stay, okay."

"What, Lauren, we don't want to impose on the man."

"You won't be imposing. It makes no sense for you all to get a hotel"

"Okay, I will let Jay know when she gets up here. Send me the address and we will catch a cab over there.

Chapter 15: Six Months Later

"Honey, why are you trying to go back to work? You can stay here with me and we can do mother daughter things together."

"Mother, you still have to talk to her whether you want to or not. I can't neglect my career and job. Do you know how long I have been out of work already?

"You're going to ask me that. I sat at your bedside day in and day out. I think I know how long you have been out of work that is why I don't see the need for you to rush back to it."

"I am fine. I miss my girls and my work. I want to start a regular routine and get my life back.

"Listen to me," Barbara grabs Blake by the arm to get her attention, "You have your life by the grace of God. Do you know how worried I was about you? I don't even want to see you go back to Baltimore."

"Lord, Baltimore is not the reason I was in the hospital; that was all your husband's spoiled firstborn's fault."

"If only you girls talked to me first."

"TALK TO YOU FIRST. I didn't know I needed to wear a bullet proof vest to protect me from my own family. Are you trying to blame me for this, because I don't see this being my fault?"

"Listen, I didn't say it was your fault, what I am saying to you is that if you or your sister had a problem with each other, you could have seek your mother."

"Ma, when did Blair ever seek you for anything only when she wanted something, she always went to Dad? Look, the beach house is nice, but I need to get back to reality and do what normal people do."

"Alright, I will call and get us a flight back." Barbara walks away from her daughter. After all, she had to know this day was coming that Blake would want to come fast to fast with her life and resume things as they were prior to her getting shot.

Blake began walking along the beach thinking about returning to her job and to her friends that she missed so much. She didn't want to face her sister and her half sister even though the subject of where they were or what happened to them ever came up with her mother, she didn't know if she could face it after all. The one thing that Blake realized after spending six months on an island was that she wanted to live life to the fullest without any regrets. All through her life, she did things that were either pleasing to her parents or her friends and some times to whomever she kept as company. No longer did she want to live a life with pretending. She would have to make a decision about her career, love life, family, and friends, but she was willing to do so. She walks under the sun drops and the brisk air picks up. Not feeling any of the chilly air, her mind wondered over everything from family to life, from career to life, from friends to life. No matter what she chose to focus on, it all came back to what she truly wanted since every decision that she has ever made in her life was influenced by someone or something in her life at that moment.

She loved what she did on her job, but was it her passion. She loved living in Baltimore, but was it where she wanted to live. She loved her family, but did she like being around them now that it almost killed her doing so. She liked being single, but was it truly what she wanted. She knew there was a lot going on with her half sister being charged with attempted murder and her sister, Blake being a conspirator a part of the whole part, even though she has been told Blair knew nothing about her being shot. Blair was the last thing on her mind. She just couldn't get over the fact that someone with the same blood as her would shoot fire into her body, trying to kill her. It was all unimaginable to her. Then, being in the hospital, not aware of what was going on or what was happening.

"Only God did it. No one else was able to repair and do all what he has done for me. He has delivered me from the upside down of things gave me a new life." Blake uttered these words as she dropped to her knees, with tears running down her face in despair. Blake stayed on her knees silently praying and thinking of which direction her life should go. She thought by showing genuine desperation for healing and a revelation from God that her problems would go away that she could seek happiness before everything had happened. Unfortunately, things did not turn out the way she interpreted, but once she did get up, she wiped the tears from her eyes and thanked God again for sparing her life and that she was able to see another day.

"Blake", her mother called out to her. Barbara could see her daughter from a distance getting out of sand. She called for her daughter to come to the house.

"Yeah", she called out to her mother.

"You have a phone call that I think you want to take"

"Who is it?"

"Come see, I am not your maid."

As the cool breeze ran through her hair, hitting her face, Blake walked with a fast pace towards the beach house to get the phone. When she reached the house, she noticed the cordless phone lying on the breakfast table.

"Hello!"

"Hi", she heard coming from Dalia, Lauren and Jayden. They were all on the phone screaming to Blake.

"Aw man, where have you girls been? I have missed y'all".

"Well, I am ready to have this baby so I can get my figure back", states Dalia.

"I have been trying to plan out the details on this wedding so I can get this over with," states Jayden.

"And uh, I just came back from vacation with Kendall. We went to Europe for a couple of weeks," states Lauren.

"Hold up, I didn't know he went to Europe with you", Jayden stated before Blake was able to speak a word.

"Yeah, he went with me. I know I told you all that", Lauren stated as she was waiting for the rest of the girls to back her up.

"Girl, you know you didn't tell any of us that", implied Jayden.

"Okay, I don't see what the big deal was in the first place. I don't judge you all about who you do what with", Lauren stated back to the girls.

"You don't have to because I am with Brian, Dalia is with Terrance, Blake is with her mother, from what we know....its been you that we have to wonder and worry about now", Jayden responded.

"Whatever, Blake honey, how have you been," asked Dalia.

"My mother has really helped me get back to my old self. It's funny that you all would call when I was just thinking of coming back to Baltimore today.

"Are you serious? You know we can't wait to have you back. We have a lot of catching up to do", stated Lauren.

"When is your flight leaving and what time will you get back", asked Dalia.

"Are you up to flying, have you talked to your job or anything", asked Jayden.

"Wait y'all; I haven't thought that far ahead. Y'all are asking too many things at one time. I miss you guys so much. Yes, I am up to flying. My mother made the flight arrangements about an hour ago, so the flight should be leaving sometime today. I haven't decided on work yet, my mind is still up in the air about that. I will definitely call all of you when I get to town. Does that answer all of your questions?"

They all cleared their throat or took heavy breaths.

"I guess it does, just call us okay", stated Lauren.

"I would never forget my girls". The call ends and Blake heads upstairs to back her bags.

"Blakey, your plane is going to leave in a couple of hours. I was thinking that maybe we could go grab some lunch and a drink before we leave here", asked Barbara from the other side of the beach house.

"Sure, that will be fine. Just let me know what time and where you want to go. I am so ready to get my life back, it ain't funny", Blake responded to her mother while swiftly walking up the stairs."

While walking out of the living room, Barbara uttered to herself, "Lord, I hope this child knows what she is doing".

Barbara cell phone rings, "Hello".

"Hello, this is Detective Benjamin Stanford, I am calling in regards to your daughter Blair Lowry".

"Yes, detective, what can I do for you?"

"Ma'am, you are a very hard woman to catch up with", the office chuckled.

"Well, I have been spending some time right now with my daughter."

"Yes ma'am, I do understand, but there is an ongoing investigation that we need Blake's assistance with."

"Well, Detective....you said your name was Detective Stanford right..."

"Yes ma'am, that is right."

"I don't see why Blake would be any help to you when you already know the story behind this one. She was shot by a vindictive plot her half sister, Carmen and her other envious sister Blair had against her to steal their father's company".

"Well, ma'am, it may be that simple to you, but from my personal investigation, you had something to do with this as well. See, what I do know is that Carmen's mother happened to be a friend of yours for many years, then you found out something about her, but you kept that to yourself."

"I don't understand what you are getting at and what that has to do with my daughter almost losing her life."

"See Barbara, you don't mind me calling you by your first name do you...I know that this woman was set out to destroy your family and you failed to mention that to anyone. You invited this woman into your house, around your family and you didn't even bother to find out who she was."

"So, you are going to tell me that this is my fault."

"No ma'am, what I am saying is that you have more to do with this than what you are led to believe. But, most importantly, I need to question you and your daughter as soon as you are Baltimore.

"Well, officer, I live in New Jersey, but my daughter lives in Baltimore."

"That won't be a problem. See, I plan to get to the bottom of this conspiracy, because I believe in your own way, you all had something to do with this. The sad part is that one of the conspirators' plan backfired on them."

"Dear, you can think what you want. My daughter and I did nothing wrong in this situation. The next time that you want to get in touch with me, you can call my lawyer."

"Not a problem, I was just waiting for that to come into play. I bet you all love those, which is how this plan all started from the beginning. I will say this before I get off the phone; I hope that you are your daughter plan to tell the truth from the beginning because if there is one thing that I dislike the most is ungrateful privileged people who try to lie and scheme their way out of everything."

"Detective Stanford, my family have been good people and we try to do right by the laws in which we live under, so what you speak of, I know nothing of."

Yes ma'am. You have a nice day, I will looking forward to speaking with you and your daughter very soon."

Barbara angrily hung up the phone with the detective.

"How did he get this number?"

"Hey ma, when are we going to lunch?"

"Uh......." Barbara was shaken when she heard Blake's voice because of the disturbing call she just received from the detective. She hadn't thought about how this would have affected Blake. But, whether she told her or not, that detective appeared to be very persistent and he wasn't going to stop until he got the bottom of things.

"I haven't made the reservations anywhere yet, give me a minute and I will let you know", Barbara answered back to Blake.

"Ma, what are you doing down there and what took you so long to answer me?"

"Nothing dear, I was just doing something. Hey, you might as well pack your things so we can just leave from the restaurant to the airport. We don't want to wait until the last minute and then be in a rush to get back."

"Okay, I had already started doing that. You know ma, I can't believe that Dalia is about to have this baby. I am so excited for her."

"Yeah, I know that you are. I know you girls are going to spoil that baby rotten."

While talking to Blake, Barbara's mind was in a daydream, thinking about all the things the detective mentioned to her. Deep down, she knew she was not the cause of Blake taking that bullet, but she knew that if she had anything to do with it, it would destroy her and her daughter.

She never thought things would be so bad after her husband Bernard died almost a year ago now. He was the head of the family and he has his way of keeping the girls in line and keeping the family strong. Somehow that has all fallen a part now. Barbara hasn't heard from Blair and not once did the cop mention where Blair was or if she was in their custody. They knew Carmen and her husband were caught and in jail just from what she had seen on the news over the past couple of months. Barbara decided to take a leave of absence from the university, but this trip has reassured her that she definitely wants to continue her career.

Barbara and Blake leave the house with the luggage preparing to return to New Jersey and Maryland. They ate lunch at a nice secluded restaurant, where the food is fabulous. Barbara and her late husband ate there many times when they used that beach house to get away for weeks at a time. They mostly used it when Blake was in college and Blair in law school. It was their own time to get a peace of mind and to reflect on their lives together. It didn't take the two of them long to eat. Blake was more anxious than her mother to get back to their lives. Barbara didn't think there was much to come back to. Now, that she didn't know where Blair was exactly, she definitely was in this big mansion by herself. She would only look to having fancy dinner parties and her career to keep her company and busy.

"Ma, you have to walk faster than that to catch your plane."

"I am moving as fast as I can."

"You could move faster if you weren't trying to carry all that stuff."

"I didn't say anything about your things; don't make a comment about mine".

Flight 1340 will be boarding in 20 minutes to Atlantic City, New Jersey.

"Okay ma that is your flight."

"Oh, it is, isn't it? Honey, I am going to miss you. Call me as soon as your flight lands."

"You do the same ma. I love you."

Blake waved to her mother good bye. For the past couple of months, her mother was by her side each day she woke up and each time she lay down for the night. She would have to get used to her mother not being there. Blake took a deep breath, rolled her shoulders back, as she knew moving on was what she had to do if she wanted her life back. She knew her mother was there for her if she needed her, but she needed to get on by herself.

Flight 3460 to Baltimore, Maryland will be boarding in 15 minutes. Passengers please report to gate 11 for boarding.

"I think when I get back I am going to surprise the girls," Blake said to herself.

"Hello"

"Are you at least going to talk to me?"

"Why should I talk to you when you don't listen to anything I say and you just do want you want to do, I don't want nothing to do with that."

"Oh, so now you are mister perfect and shit. Oh, I can remember some thing that you have done that weren't all of that."

"This ain't got nothing to do with and if you want to keep bringing that up, we can handle the baby's affairs thru text and email."

"Damn, you get on my nerves."

"Oh, you can screw up everything with my house, excuse me, our house and everything is supposed to be gravy."

"Hell, I didn't even want the damn house anymore after you slept with some bitch in it in the first place.

"Oh, so this is supposed to be some get back, right?"

"No, but if that is what you make it about, then it can be that."

"These are two different situations and you want to bring one in with the other."

"Terrance, you really want to compare the two, we can."

"I bet you can't wait to do that."

"Look, I didn't even call you for that…"

"Really, then why are you calling me."

"I wanted to let you know that my doctor's appointment is tomorrow and I find out the sex of the baby."

Terrance breathes heavily over the phone.

"Well, aren't you going to say something? See, I knew I should have just gone by myself."

"What! Are you serious? I will be there. Don't ever come out your mouth at me like that. You always trying to make everything all about you. You didn't even know if this was my baby, so don't even go there."

"That was low and you know it."

"Get the fuck outtta here with that. I'm thinking about building a life with you and this is what I get back."

"Please, you are getting on my nerves. We weren't even together."

"So, that is what you are going to tell me now."

"That is the truth."

"Yeah, right. Text me what time the damn appointment is and I will meet you there."

"Aww, you just get on my nerves." Dalia slams the phone down.

"He just gets on my nerves.

"Dee, who are you talking about," asks Lauren.

"I was talking to my baby's father."

"Oh, Lord that again. I don't see why the two of you can't just come together and make this right for this baby. Do you all know that this baby is coming soon and you all are sounding like those hood chicks we went to school with? I don't see what the big confusion is of why the two of you can't get together, my goodness."

"He blames me for everything."

"That much could not have happened while we were in Jersey for him to be acting like that....unless you did something you don't want to tell the rest of us....ump, don't answer, because I have a feeling that I am right and you done fucked some shit up that you didn't have no business doing."

"Oh hell, you doing the same thing Terrance is doing."

"And I bet we both are right somewhere down the line."

"Get ready, we have to meet Jay about the wedding."

Chapter 16: Ain't No Stopping Me Now

"Hi, my name is Blake Lowry, I need a taxi to come pick me up from the airport."

"Sure ma'am. I will send one over to you right way…you wouldn't happen to be the Blake Lowry that has been plastered all over the news, now would it?"

"What does that have to do with anything, you know you what, never mind, I will call another company. I hope you don't treat all your clients like this."

Blake disconnects the call. Apparently, she hasn't seen the fallout from her incident around the city. Little did she know that she was walking into hell returning back to Baltimore. Even though the girls have been separated from Blake for a while, they have been going through their own personal issues that they apparently haven't been sharing with each other. She learns some things about her friends.

For Blake, the days have seemed long and drawn out where she has lost a piece of herself and she is confused of which direction she wants to take her life; however, she is not actually over getting shot and the betrayal of her maternal sister and her paternal sister. Not facing the reality of it all, she tries to go on with her life without giving it too much thought. It appears that since the bullets shattered her mind, body, and soul, for the first time, she is seeing the world in a different light; a light in which she as a grown woman wants to take a different direction that what was and is expected of her. She feels as if she has to start from scratch and realize if this life she lived was for her or to please those around her.

"Dang it, why don't my key work in this door….oops, here we go. It feels so good to be home. My house smells like home for the first time."

Blake walks through her house like she was seeing it in a different light than before.

"Wow! This is me, I did this."

The horn blows…..

"Oh hell, I forgot about the taxi driver outside….I'M COMING".

Blake ran upstairs to get some money for the taxi driver. She noticed that she was short of breath, now she was feeling a repercussion from the surgery and bullet womb. Once she got the money, she ran back down the stairs and out the door, tells the driver how much she appreciated the ride. It appears now, that Blake seemed to be more appreciative for everything around her, even her friends.

"Maybe I should call Lauren and see what the girls have planned for the week."

Blake spends this time in her house checking her email, voice mail to see who was trying to get in touch with her and figure out her next move. Of course, he career was weighing desperately on her mind, but she still didn't quite figure out what she wanted to do. Her mail was ridiculously filled with most of it being held at the local postal office for her next of kin to pick up. Most of the time she left Lauren over her house, emergency contact, and the go to persona over any of her possession while she was out of town or out of reach. She wanted to keep that the same, but she had a lot to figure out. The one thing she didn't do was check with her mother to make sure her job hadn't tried to contact her; maybe they didn't have her job there anymore. She didn't know what to make of it because she planned on making Michael a business partner for her firm. Blake became very inquisitive about Michael. Did his grandfather really start that law firm he told her about or was it all a set up? From the little information that she did know, it wasn't enough. She was eager to find out why did he seek her? What motives did he have? Why would he want to mess with my reputation that I worked so hard for?

Blake was thinking many scenarios in her head. One, maybe he knew about her father's money and he wanted some part of that. Two, maybe he was an old fling that she couldn't remember or three, maybe he was just no good, either way it went, she was anxious to get those questions answered. In mid thought, her phone rang. She didn't know who it could have been or who even knew she was home. She ran to the phone closest to her, "Hello".

Screams came from the other end of the phone.

"On my God, you are home." It was Lauren on the other end. She was calling to leave her a message so that she would hear her warm message when she did get home and had a chance to listen to her messages.

"Yeah, I got here about two hours ago. I have been trying to sort some things out....you know, check my email, my mail, voice mail, etc."

"Oh, girl, why do you want to check all of that? Do you know how happy I am that you are back....okay, let me say this before I forget. We are all about to meet for lunch to talk about Jay's wedding that is coming up. Do you want to come?"

"Uh, I don't know. I have some things that I need to do here."

"Things like what, you just got back and we all have missed you so much. Blake I know you are not going to do us like that."

"Uh, I don't want a lot of attention and I don't want people staring at me. It's the weekend and you know everyone is out and I don't feel like being aggravated."

"Okay, I understand that. What if we all came to you, would that be okay." For a moment, Blake felt like blowing Lauren off, but she knew she couldn't do that. Her friends meant to much to her to do that and she knew them being around again would be good for her.

"Alright, tell everyone to come here. I would love to see all of y'all. It's been too damn long anyway. Let me check the kitchen for some wine."

"Oh hold, can you have wine right now?"

"Rin, do you know how long I have been out of sync with everything? I am pretty sure this won't do me any harm right now."

"Okay, if you say so. Let me call Jay and tell her before she leaves the house. Dee is right here so I will tell her unpacking....awe, shit."

"What do you mean, right there unpacking?"

"Huh!"

"You heard me."

"Um, let's talk about that later okay...talk to you later."

"You better believe it. I will see you all when you get here."

Blake hung up the phone knowing Lauren did not sound like herself when she asked her about Dalia unpacking at her house. That didn't make any sense to her. She knew that some story behind it because it wouldn't be Dalia if it didn't. She chuckled for a bit because she knows how Lauren can get about her space and she and Dalia are two different kinds of people when it comes to space. Even though she didn't mean to change their plans for the meeting about the wedding, she did like that fact that she would be getting the chance to see her girlfriends for the first time in six months. Talking to them over the phone was no comparison to seeing them in person, hearing them laugh, catching all the facial expressions, and just to feel comfortable around them again.

Blake began finishing going through her messages and email until it was time for the girls to come, but her mind could not stop wandering off about Michael. There was something about him that she knew was missing. There were some things that didn't make since to her.

"Wait, a minute, I do remember right before I left to go to Jersey that I talked with Blair and I asked her why Carmen wanted a part of the company and I remember her saying that I should know because I was the one hanging out with him a couple of weeks.....ago......" Blake stops in her tracks and thinks for a moment before the realization came to her.

OMG! I was dating a married man....wait that has to be wrong....and then, this man is married to Carmen...the same chick who slept with Terrance... Now it all makes sense to me. I got played. I was a part of scheme to take down my father's company...but, wait a damn minute, this still doesn't add up for me....why would Carmen sleep with Terrance. He don't have nothing to do with my family. Shit naw, this still doesn't add up for me. Something made Carmen want a part of the company. She already had money when Daddy died. Then her husband, if that is what he is….. Came on to me months ago at a conference….aw, this is sick if my speculations are true."

Blake walks downstairs heading toward the kitchen running everything through her head. Her focused was only on figuring out this scheme. She wasn't going to rest until she did, no matter what.

"I wonder if Michael really knew who I was or if they found out later and they didn't know how to trap me…wait, I do remember the trip we took to my mother's house and Dalia found out that this Carmen thought Dalia was me. How could you get us confused?

Wait a damn minute, I don't think everyone has told me the truth; I bet I will find out once they get here. However, there couldn't have been that much for them to keep from me….aw, hell, I only have one bottle of wine. I am sure we are going to need more. I had better run to the store to get some more before they get here."

Blake picked up her keys and pocketbook and headed toward the door. Her phone rings again on her way out of the door. "Ugh, I will let the voice mail pick up."

"Hi, you have just reached Blake Lowry, sorry I can't come to the phone right now, but leave me a message after the tone and I will call you as soon as my schedule allows me. Have a great one and don't forget to leave your number….beep."

"Hey chick, this is Jay. Lauren called me a minute ago and told me that you were here and that we were meeting at your house about the wedding. I don't know where the hell you could be if you just got back into town unless you are just avoiding me for some reason, but I will see you in a couple of hours at your house….hey, girl, I have missed you so much and I love you. See you soon." Jayden hangs up.

While driving to the store, Blake runs all the scenarios that made sence to her. She was thinking for a moment that she deserved all that had happened to her because of how careless she was with money, men, and all the lavish things she acquired. Secondly, she thought about her sister Blair, that she hadn't seen since before the shooting. She didn't really know why she became so vindictive and envious to want to side with their half sister that neither of them never knew. Then a thought ran across her mind that Blair knew all about Carmen from the beginning and she had been plotting since their father died. Blake wanted to carefully think about everything before she decided to do anything.

Thirdly, she thought about how Dalia had anything to do with her family issues. She blamed herself for the trouble that Dalia and Terrance had when all through college they had the perfect relationship that even she envied at times. Now, because of her relationship with Dalia being such a close friend, it drove turmoil and hurt beyond belief in her life, which could have possibly destroyed her unborn child's family life. All of these thoughts ran across her mind as she was driving to the store. She had forgotten all about the unwanted attention she might receive from her story being blasted all over the news here in Maryland and in New Jersey. She finally was able to experience some of the publicity that her parents used to talk about when they did big things with charity and sometimes the major cases her father won with the firm. Even though, this wasn't something she wanted to face everyday, she knew she couldn't hide from it forever. She knew the most important thing was her health and making sure she recovered like the surgeon advised her to.

As she arrived at the store, which was more exclusive to a certain crowd of people, she did not necessarily drive out into to town to go grocery shopping, but she did stay within the realms of her neighborhood. Not many people were out shopping, but she did get stares. She noticed how some people were trying not to stare, but they whispered amongst her. It was hard to face, but she knew she could not hide for the rest of her life. She thought she was home free, until she entered the check out line.

"Hey, I've seen you before."

"Oh, really you don't seem familiar to me."

"Oh, yeah, I know where I seen you at. You were on the news a couple of months ago, but I don't remember what for..." As loud as the cashier was, Blake was sure that everyone else in the line knew exactly what she was talking about, but no one commented. She was hoping that the cashier could check her out without making anymore accusations about how she may have seen her on television. She smiled at the cashier trying to tell her politely with her facial expressions to drop the conversation, but she knew that wasn't going to work. She didn't know if the cashier was messing with her on purpose or she honestly couldn't remember.

"Hey, I remember you now. It came to me once you got a little closer. You look a little different than you used to. You were responsible for expanding that big car dealership with your marketing company. You were in the commercial shaking the big execs hands and stuff...you still at that job?"

"Uh, yeah, I am. I have been out of town, taking some time off, but I am still there. I am surprised that you remembered that, that was a long time ago and very few people recognized me from that commercial."

"Your total is $31.15, Ms. Lowry right".

"Yeah, that is me. Good memory", Blake smiled back at the cashier.

Blake handed the cashier the money, grabbed her bags and told her to keep the change.

"Have a great day and take care of yourself", the cashier said to Blake as she winked her eye at her while Blake was walking off. Deep down inside Blake knew that the cashier knew more than what she was letting her believe, but she polite enough not to bring it up.

As Blake headed home, she thought about gaining control of her life and how she managed to do so with everything thing that had happened. She thought about her financial statements, mortgage, investments, car notes, and her other financial obligations. Because of the sizable income and inheritance, she was able to stay involve with many investments, start up companies, business ventures, and she wondered if those dealings were tampered with or even kept up while she was away. Not wanting to make any hasty moves, she wanted to take it easy for a while since she was still on the road to recovery. The last thing she wanted in her life was more turmoil and devastation.

Part II

"Have you talked to Jay today and told her that Blake was back in town."

"Yeah, I talked to her not too long ago and told her. You know Jay, she probably done call her and cursed Blake out for not calling her when she got back to town."

"You know she has been uneasy since the time is winding down for the wedding."

"Girl, you know Jay would be that way if there was a wedding going on or not." Dalia chuckled to herself.

"Yeah, you are right about that. I really don't think she can help herself", Lauren replied as she laughed along with Dalia. If there was anything they knew, they knew Jayden and they knew she spoke her mind at all times and didn't care about how anyone else felt, except when it came to Brian.

"You know what Dee, when was the last time we all met up at Starbucks like we used and catch up, or go to the spa and talk."

"Aw hell, Lauren, it's been forever. What happened?" While walking in the kitchen to get a glass of water, Lauren and Dalia are supposed to be getting ready to meet Jayden at Blake's house to talk about the wedding, but they get caught up in reminiscing about the good ole days.

"I mean, with Blake getting shot, your situation, and Jayden being busy with the wedding, we have been too busy to do any of that."

"So is that how you are going to justify something that we have done together for years.....with life issues. We used to hold those things until we met on Wednesdays and talk it out with each other."

"If you can recall, I know sometimes you remember what you want, but the last time we got together, you weren't even there, but we ran into Terrance there. We all asked him about you and where you were, and he couldn't even answer our questions, which was so not like him. Then, he tells us some bullshit and leaves us up in the air. You were acting really weird at the table while we were talking and then out of no where, you told us you couldn't stay and that you had something to handle, that wasn't like you either. That is when we all came to visit to see what was up.

"I do remember that," Dalia stated while making a smug on her face. She knew that was a rough time for her that she didn't feel like revisiting, but somehow she ended up setting herself up for that one.

"Uh, apparently you don't because you didn't even come to us when you and Terrance were having problems. But what got me is that we took the trip to Jersey and you still couldn't even talk to the man," Lauren now in the kitchen fixing some scrambled eggs before getting dressed.

"Oh, Lord…and how long ago did that happen."

"Bitch, don't play. All of this shit would not have gone down, if you had tried to make it right with Terrance when we got back." Lauren was getting frustrated with the conversation.

"Okay, you want to make it sound so simple, when he was the one who cheated on me in our house after all those years invested in that relationship", Dalia bluntly stated to Lauren from the kitchen table.

"Girl, sit you ass down and stop raising your voice in my house. Yeah he cheated, but you found out how all of that went down from Barbara and you weren't even trying to hear any of that. That is what I don't get. I looked at you and you didn't feel any remorse in your heart for that man. You had hate in your eyes, over a setup."

"It is just that simple to you. Let's see if you feel the same way when Kendall takes your relationship for granted and you are in so deep that you can't see your next step without him being by your side or in the picture with you." For that moment, Lauren was at a stand still while scraping the bottom of the frying pan. She was at a lost for words from what she just heard Dalia say to her. She knew that the Terrance subject was very sensitive to

Dalia and she definitely could tell when Dalia attacked her and Kendall's relationship. Although the thought never occurred to her about Kendall taking her trust and loyalty for granted, but her relationship and love was no different from the love that Dalia and Terrance shared.

Dalia walked up the stairs after lashing out at Lauren, frustrated partly because she felt that Lauren was right and the other half that she was still hurting from the betrayal she walked in on a year ago. Even though the hurt wasn't like it before, the pregnancy didn't make her emotions deal with the situation any better. All she could think about was where her life was going and that she was bringing a new life into the world. It was difficult trying to move on without Terrance and then when she got pregnant, things became clearer with what she should have done. She knew she wanted to be happy and that consisted of raising her child with the man she loved and be happily married.

Dalia stood in front of the mirror in the guest room that she was currently staying in at Lauren's house and she glared back at herself. "I got to fix this for me and my baby, but I don't know how to get through to Terrance. I have never seen him this angry." Still glaring in the mirror, Dalia rubbed her stomach as tears rolled down her face. Little did she know that Lauren was standing behind her listening to her inner thoughts and how she was bonding with her unborn child, she empathized with her friend for going through so much.

"Dee, I didn't mean…"

"No, let me talk first."

"I am sorry for what I said. I didn't mean to say anything about you and Kendall's relationship, but I don't think anyone understands the pain and hurt that I have been feeling for the past year."

"Dee, I understand how you feel. I have watched you fall a part day by day because of this guy. I am trying to help you come out of the slump you are in and make yourself happy. Whether that is with Terrance or not, I want you to pull yourself together and get back to living your life and dreams."

"Oh, Lord, I don't know if I can ever get back to that now since I'm having a baby with a man who doesn't even want to hear me talk." As emotional as Dalia was at the time, Lauren was able to look past her emotional state and tell her friend some things that she needed to hear.

"Dee, you gotta pull this together and figure out what you want to do with your life and work towards that, pregnant or not. Lauren takes a deep breath before finishing her thoughts, but she knew since it was the two of them that she would have to be the one to tell her the truth. "Honestly, I think Terrance is the man for you and yeah, he messed up, but you have to be the strong woman in the relationship and work hard for what is yours or you are going to lose it. Then, you will be raising this child alone, dealing with a man who doesn't want anything to do with you."

"You are starting to sound like Jayden. I knew it all was going to come out eventually. None of you know what its like or what I have been going through."

"Just stop Dee! What do you mean we don't know what you have been going through? We have been there the whole time and all we have been saying to you is get through it and work through it. You keep creating these situations. Okay, you and Terrance made up after we came back from Jersey, but something went wrong, and you never told any of us about. The only thing I know is that you called me asking could you come here and it's been almost six months now."

"So, is there a problem with me staying here?"

"I never said that. What I am saying is that you act like you want to be miserable and unhappy all the time."

"Girl, I am here for you, but we are grown now and we try to get our shit together and keep it there. Things happen, but we get it together and keep moving.

"You know what, things are so easy for you and you haven't struggled like I have."

"Is that the excuse you are going to keep telling yourself every time you mess up or every time something goes wrong?"

"It's not an excuse…"

"Oh, so you are going to tell me that Terrance was the basis for your being. You can't think right or do without Terrance, are you serious? I can't believe you have lost yourself in a man. Did you hear anything that Barbara was telling us when we went Jersey?"

"All I heard was some rich, sedity old woman telling me how hard it is to live in a mansion with a man who adored her, but he slipped up and kept a secret from her about having a child before they got married, then that mother of that child later befriended her and caused problems. But, she and her children along with her husband lived happily ever after." As angry as Dalia got, talking about Blake's mother, the more she hated even recalling what Barbara had to say.

"You missed the whole damn point of her talking to us. When are you going to get it and when are you going to learn how to deal with your issues. You can't keep fucking up and expect things to go in your favor, it don't work like that! You know what, let's get dress before we are late and the girls start calling". Lauren walked out of the room down the hall to her master bedroom. She couldn't believe how much she lost her cool like that with Dalia. She didn't know what came over her. She just got fed up with the sympathy card that Dalia plays with all of them all time like she had no part in the issues in her life. Lauren picked her clothes out of her closet, jerking the clothes off the hangers; she carried them into her bathroom's open area to iron them. Unfocused and frustrated at the same time, she was discombobulated and could not get herself together for the meeting. Time was running out and she was all uneasy because of her disagreement with Dalia. While ironing her clothes, she looked up and saw the reflection of Dalia standing in the doorway. She looked at her and started back ironing her clothes,

"Uh, I will meet you all at Blake's house for the meeting. I have something to do before I go there." Lauren looked up at her, "Whatever you say, chick."

"Why it got to be all of that?"

"Because again, you making it all about you, damn, but don't worry about it."

"Man, what the fuck ever." Leaving out the bathroom, Dalia slammed the door, as Lauren jumped to sound of the door closing.

"Ugh, she gets on my nerves with all this selfishness man."

Chapter 17: Welcome Back!!!

"Hi, girl, how have you been, I have missed you so much!"

"Hi, Jay, I have missed you too. It's been too long, I know."

"Well, heffa, are you going to let me in or what"

"Oh, my bad, come in and bring all this crap with you too."

"I noticed that no one else was here yet...them chicks don't know how to be on time for anything."

Blake and Jayden both laugh at the timeliness of their friends. As Jayden brought in her things for the girls to look at for the wedding, she and Blake took the time to catch up since the rest of the girls were not there yet. Blake explained to Jayden how she felt lost and not knowing what she wanted anymore. She expressed how she was ready to come back and be a part of her life again. Jayden showed compassion for her friend as she poured her heart out to her. For the first time, Jayden started to see her friend in a different light. She finally saw that Blake was being genuine and that her own feelings and not the pressures were guiding her from Lauren or her family for a change. She gained a whole new respect for Blake the more and more she talked.

While talking at the table, Jayden reached across and grabbed Blake's hand just to assure her that she was there for her and she empathized with how she felt. Blake was shocked since Jayden is the only one in the group who is firm believer on "sucking up your problems" and dealing with them. However, this time was different, and bonded as if two friends should.

"Even though I haven't gone through what you are going through with your family, I sympathize with you. Family is a mess and if you let them they can bring you down. I know for you, this is your first time going through something like this with your family, but it's going to get better and I know you are thinking that you are alone and no one can understand how you feel and what you are going through, but believe more people can sympathize with than you think. Shit, if I tell you some of things my family has put me through lately, girl; you wouldn't be able to close your mouth."

Jay slams her hand on the table as an expression to Blake.

"Jay, this has really been hard for me." Blake got up from the table, walking towards to bay window near her kitchen table, with her hands on her hip.

"I mean, sometimes I am afraid to talk to people because I don't know what is going to come out of their mouths or who is out to get me anymore. Every time I turn around, I am starting put things together and the pieces are fitting."

With a puzzled look on her face, Jayden asked her, "what things?"

"Well, first off, I am trying to figure out what motive did my sister have to want to team up with Carmen? Then, how in the world could Carmen have gotten me confused with Dalia and if she was studying me so hard and there is something else to figure out about Michael. I spent time with this guy and something just isn't right with everything."

Jayden stood up from the table, "yeah, something wasn't right with him, he was trying to get your drawers and distract you. Blake, he was never interested in his firm working with your company. It was all a part of his plot."

"Wait a damn minute, how did you know that?" Blake asked turning towards Jayden. Jayden released a heavy sign as if she didn't want to tell Blake.

"You know what....these secrets are starting to get old. I am not lying in a hospital bed anymore, I am fine and I want to know the answers that everyone else seems to know."

"First of all, don't raise your voice at me. I mean, hell, I have sympathy for you, but it ain't going to be too much of that....It was all on the news and the detective called me, Lauren, and Dalia to get details about you, your family and the little we knew about Carmen. I thought they would have tracked you and your mother down by now."

"Jay, maybe they did and my mother didn't tell me."

The door bell rang.

"I'll get the door. Get some tissue so the girls don't know you've been crying and get the wine, I know your drunk ass has some", Jadyen stated as she began walking toward the door.

"Hi, how in the world did you beat me here, chick."

"Because your ass don't know how to tell time."

"Shut the hell up, I had an errand to run. Is Dee here yet?

"Hell naw, I thought she was coming with you."

"Well, I don't feel like even talking about that one, where is Blake?"

"Uh, she went to the bathroom. She should be out in a minute."

"Okay. How is she doing," Lauren asked quietly so that Blake wouldn't be able to hear her. "I mean, I talked to her a little while earlier when she just got in and she seemed to be a little all over the place." Lauren began placing her bags on the floor as Jayden assisted her.

Jayden began whispering to Lauren and looking both ways before speaking, "we were talking some before you rang the door bell and she was really pouring out her heart. She is confused about a lot of things...but that damn Barbara didn't tell her shit. She kept her in the dark about a lot."

"WHAT!!!! STOP!! Are you serious? You mean to tell me that she doesn't know all the pieces to puzzle, basically?"

"Exactly! She didn't even know that the detective questioned us and was doing a full investigation that even she had something to do with her own bullets!"

"So, what did you tell her?" Lauren looking curiously at Jayden.

"Hell, I told her, but I didn't really tell her that they were suspicious of her too. I told her that the detective was questioning every motive and intention related to her, her mother, and us. She figured that from what she could remember from before the incident and she is just putting everything together, Rin, you hear me…this is crazy."

"I know, especially if she is getting too carried away with it all." Lauren stated while shaking her head in shock.

"Hey, girl, I missed you so much", Blake went straight towards Lauren with opened arms for a hug.

"I missed you too, girl. How are you?"

Blake looked at Lauren and Jayden together, "I am doing okay. I feel great. I just have a lot to sort out that is all. Hold up, someone is missing, where is Dee?"

Jayden and Lauren both took a deep breath before answering Blake's question.

"Okay, that is the second time that I have gotten the silent voice for asking about Dalia….Oh Lord, should I be mad at her too, does she have something to do with me being shot?"

"Nope, she has her own set of problems going on." Lauren commented as she hugged Blake again.

"Well, does anyone feels like filling me…wait, why isn't she here telling me herself," asked Blake with an attitude this time.

"Look, don't ask me. She told me that she would meet me here, that is all I can tell you," Lauren answered while walking into the den. "I know you brought me some wine, because I am in need of some. Okay, Jay what did we have to meet about today."

"Ladies, please have a sit down so we can discuss this", Jayden asked them with a huge grin on her face.

"Oh Lord, so we are going to have one of those meetings," implied Lauren.

"Shut the hell up. I wanted to talk about the week of the wedding and what I need you all to do. Damn, I wish Dee was here, she needs to hear this, because I am not going to have time to do this over again".

Jayden starts pulling out her portfolio and planner with all her wedding details. Blake and Lauren assisted her and they were all drinking a bottle of wine in Blake den. They laughed about old times and how this day is going to special for Brian and Jayden in which they never thought Jayden would be the first to jump the broom. After a long time of going back and forth with her mother, Jayden decided on cinnamon and cream being her colors, just because her wedding was going to be late summer, but early fall and also she had to pick something that her fiancé was going to wear. Even though he wanted Jayden to be happy, there were some limits placed for her and one of them was the colors he had to wear. By cream being one of the colors, he knew his tuxedo would be cream along with the best man and the groomsmen.

Secondly, he knew that his future wife loved to explore and eat high fluted foods; he had to put his input in on that also. He told her either chicken or steak and he didn't mean rib eye steak either. As excited as Jayden was, nothing could mess up her joy about planning a wedding she never thought she would have. Her portfolio had everything that Brian like and disliked when it came to wedding details. There was one last thing that Jayden began sharing with the girls about some of the things Brian didn't want which was the music. He didn't want sad, slow music in which Jayden tried to explain to him that they would need to have at least two slow songs so she could dance with him and her father. However, she had her way of dealing with Brian and getting him to see things her way and this was one of times where she would have to use her persuasive tongue to get him on her side about that.

Before they knew it, hours had gone by and still no Dalia. Without drawing attention to her, Lauren started looking at her watch. Jayden noticed it, but she was thinking that she was tired of hearing about her wedding plans and her complaining, but little did she know, Lauren was getting more and more furious with Dalia because she knew this meeting was important to Dalia and that she should have been there and be on time for once in her life. Apparently, it didn't matter to her because she wasn't there. Since it was Saturday, Jayden thought it was good idea for them to go to church together and have a girl's day on Sunday. Of course, everyone was cool with it, but Dalia was missing. Lauren knew

232

how much it meant to Jayden to have Dalia there especially since she is technically the maid of honor. Lauren told Jayden several times that Dalia may not be able to stand up that long at the alter in her condition, but Dalia thought that Lauren was being jealous about the whole thing. Even though Lauren was looking out for her in a way, of course she didn't see it that way.

Hours had past and no sign of Dalia yet. It was beginning to piss Lauren off. Jayden tried her best not to make it a big deal, even though she shared the same feelings as Lauren did. Sitting in a circle in Blake's living room, much eye contact shared throughout the room. Without drawing much attention to herself, Jayden continuously looked at her cell, hoping that she would get a text of phone call from Dalia to explain her absence to this meeting that she stressed about for months to all of them. She didn't even expect Blake to be there, because she away resting and recouping, but she did expect her maid of honor to be there and she wasn't there. After a couple of minutes passing, Jayden jumped up from her seat asking Blake did she have anything stronger to drink because the wine she served was not doing the job. Blake expressed to her that she would look and see, but with her absence, she didn't know what she did or didn't have. To all of them, Blake was the wine and champagne queen. She kept a wine cellar to die for; her wine and champagnes were from all different countries and vineyards. It was a personal interest of hers. Lauren somehow found herself enjoying different types of wines too. It started with her going to different wine tasting from the social events at her job to traveling for business trips and exploring with her co-workers.

It was getting late and no one had still yet heard from Dalia. Apparently, this wasn't important to her.

"Hell naw, this is so unacceptable that Bitch didn't even show the hell up. She must have thought this was for one of you," Jayden jumped up pointing at the rest of them making her statement about Dalia's absence. She grabbed her phone and started dialing. Lauren looked at Blake out of the corner of her eyes wondering what excuse could Dalia have for missing something that was important to Jayden. The phone rang and rang until it went to Dalia's voice mail. In the sweetest voice possible,

"Hi Dee, this is Jay, I was calling to check on you. You didn't show up for the meeting today at Blake's, so I didn't know if everything was okay with you and the baby. I kind of need my maid of honor here to help with the details to my wedding since it is coming just around the corner. Well, I am still at Blake's' so give me a call when you get this. Talk to you later." Jayden ended the call and looked up at Blake and Lauren.

"I hope nothing is really wrong with her," Blake commented to the girls.

"Aw, hell, she is the same hell cat that she has been for the past year", Lauren interjected as she got up from the chair walking toward the kitchen to get another glass of wine.

"Whoa, what do you mean," Blake asked with a puzzled look on her on face.

"Do we really have to talk about this right now", Jayden implemented before Lauren was able to answer Blake.

"I wish you would stop taking up for her", Blake slamming her wine glass on the countertop in the kitchen.

"I am not taking up for her, I just don't think that this is the time to draw all of this up, plus Dee is not here, Jayden said directly to Lauren.

Lauren poured a heavy glass of red wine while Jayden was trying to in avertedly take up for the mistakes that Dalia has made with her life since Blake was away.

"When she is living in your house and you have to hear how her and Terrance go at it for the stupidest things and none of it seems to be about the baby, then I will listen to what you have to say," Lauren said to Jayden.

"Wait, she told me that everything was fine with her and Terrance," Jayden with a puzzled look on her face, turned to Lauren for details.

"Let me tell you something, Dee has been messing up a lot and there is a lot that she has not been telling us about this situation."

"Oh, I believe that, but why lie to us when we are her friends." Blake jumped up, "I know I have been gone a while, but will someone care to fill me with what is going on. I really don't have a clue. So, you mean to tell me that Dalia and Terrance are not together, again."

Chuckles come from Jayden and Lauren because it seems to be a repeat event of Terrance and Dalia break up and then make up, but this time was different.

"She just fucked up and she knows it, but instead of fessing up to it, she passes the blame on to Terrance and this time he ain't going for it", Lauren told Blake.

"You don't know what really happened, Lauren, so don't go around making accusations". Jayden picked up her glass while walking into the kitchen to get a refill in her glass.

"I know and you know! Dalia is setting herself up for loneliness."

Wait….a minute, you said Lauren, that Dalia has been staying at your house. Let's start from there, shall we." Blake pulled up a stool to the kitchen counter to engage in the conversation with Jayden and Lauren. "Oh, don't get quiet now. I am so tired of everyone wanting to hear about me and giving me the sob story. I want to know what is going on with you all and what I've missed and from the look of things, I've missed a lot."

Lauren breathed heavily after listening to Blake. Jayden took a sip of Lauren's wine before making a comment.

"Well, let me just say this"…..Jayden looked at Lauren before continuing. "When we came back from Jersey, Dalia stopped paying the mortgage on the condo that she and Terrance shared. Now, you remember they got back together and they were still living in the condo? Dalia claimed she was so out of it that she didn't keep up anything and she planned on moving to Jersey." Blake chimed in, "Yeah, this is when she decided to move in with my mother and leave everything here. Okay, I remember that, but how did that cause her and Terrance to break up."

"Hold up, let me finish". Jayden cleared her voice to continue the story. "So, from the story that Terrance said, he was served with an eviction notice and he didn't know why…then, he finds out that Dalia didn't keep up anything with the house...but, what we didn't know was that Terrance name is on the house and that wasn't a decision that she could have made by herself. Plus, she failed to mention anything about being behind on the bills once she found out she was pregnant and Terrance moving back on."

"Stop, I can't believe this. Does she not know what that could have done to his credit? How do you lie to the man like that?" Blake rhetorically asked the question to see how Jayden and Lauren felt about the situation.

"Uh huh, she ain't finished", Lauren commented.

"Wait, there is more than that. That would have been enough for me," stated Blake as she poured herself another glass of wine.

"If you shut the hell up, you can get the whole story, damn! Now, Blake, I can tell you the rest of it...now, this part is still a mystery to me and to Lauren. Somehow, there was something wrong with the baby or a test had to be done and Dalia had to do a paternity test on the baby because there was a possibility that the baby didn't belong to Terrance".

"GET OUT! I think y'all lying to me. How could that have happened? She made it seem like she was so distort over the breakup that she couldn't even think straight," was Blake's reaction to what she found out about Dalia.

Lauren interjects, "So now Terrance only wants to talk to her when it involves the baby and nothing else. Then, she catches these attitudes with him if he is short with her. C'mon, what do you expect? All out, the blue to tell him that he may not be the father. I'm sorry I couldn't have any part with that. I think that is what started the feud between us."

"Wait a damn minute! I can't believe all of this, Blake stating while shaking her head out of shock.

"Girl believe it, because the drama keeps coming with her. I don't think she realizes that she has a couple of months to get her life together before this baby comes." Lauren turns to Blake and Dalia with a look of disgust about Dalia.

"I just can't believe things got like that. You know, I sympathized with her in the beginning."

"Aw Blake, there was no need for that when your mother explained the whole picture to her about that and she still pushed the man away."

"But Rin, that would be hard to still get that picture out of your head of seeing your man in the bed with another woman in the house that you share with him. I don't know how smooth that would go over me."

"Okay, Jay, we know you would have pulled your piece from the beginning", Lauren barely able to get the words out of her mouth.

"And you damn right. I try not to do too much talking in those situations, because the predicament that you are caught in says enough for me. My problem is that we can work things out after I released my tension."

They all laughed.

Jayden is known for some memorable moments in college and post college years. They all stay at the kitchen counter sharing more thoughts and information about Dalia at Blake's house. She hasn't phoned or come by for that fact. Her presence not being missed at this point, the girls are having a blast without her. Besides, they needed that time to catch up with Blake and fill her in with all the details.

"OMG! Look at the time, its eight o'clock and I don't even have myself together for church tomorrow."

"Lauren doesn't have her stuff together for church tomorrow, I am so surprise."

"Oh Jay, you wanna pick. When was the last time you went to church."

"Bitch, don't try me. You know I am only going for y'all heffas...so, Blake are you going to go with us?

"Mmm, of course I wanna go. Didn't you want all of us to go with you to church anyway?"

"Yeah, I did say that. Great, what time are we meeting up in the morning then," asked Jayden.

Lauren still in kitchen began cleaning the wine glasses each of them used, "It doesn't matter to me. You guys decide and I will be there."

With the inquisitive look on her face, "Why don't we all meet up back here at 9:30 and we can leave from here to the church", asked Blake.

Lauren responded, "It's cool with me, what about you Jay?"

"Oh, I'm good. I just wish Dalia could be here, but I am not going to worry about it. I am going to have a good time with my girls anyway with or without Dee."

"Call her ass again. I don't see why she didn't answer her phone the first time…"

"Me either, Jay", Lauren commented.

"Rin, are you ready to go home because I know Brian is about to lose his mind already and you have to get to Kendall". Jayden grabbed her things and headed toward the door. "Blake, I will see you in the morning, love ya", as she hugs Blake.

"Love you too dear, see you in the morning." Lauren grabbed her pocketbook out of the living room that they were first sitting in.

Lauren and Jayden walk out the house. Door closes.

"Yeah, that is what I missed, my girls…now, things are starting to get back to normal. Maybe tomorrow will be the start of something new for me."

Chapter 18 : Baby Boy Love

"Open this damn door, I know you in there. Keep ignoring me if you want, you will never see this baby burn", bangs continue on the door of Terrance's apartment as Dalia violently screams for him to answer.

"If I have to break this door down I will, I know you in there with your bitch, but you need to come see about your baby", as she continues to bang on the door neighbors walking by as she draws attention to herself. The door swings open briskly, "Man, this shit better be good for you to be banging on my door like this."

"Oh, it's good alright. I had a doctors' appointment today that you knew you had to attend and you didn't' show up."

Terrance wiped his eyes as if he were sleeping, "I had to work". He says very calmly to her.

"And, I don't have a job to go to. You need to be more responsible and stop laying up with this chick that you have been hanging with," Dalia not paying attention to how tired Terrance was at the time.

"Man, I don't have time for this. I have to go back to work in a couple of hours. I will call you tomorrow, alright?"

"So, you're not going to even ask me about the doctor's appointment?"

"Look dammit, if that is what you were concerned with, you wouldn't come here banging on my door like you stupid."

"So now I am stupid?"

"Man look, you need to get your shit together and stop bothering me over nonsense."

"So, your bitch in there, is that why you tripping......YOU DIDN'T SAY THAT LAST NIGHT."

Terrance grabbed Dalia by the arm and walked outside shutting the door behind him.

"You know good and damn well I wasn't with you last night. I was at work, grinding". Terrance rubs his hands through his hair in frustration. Dalia just looks at him hoping that somehow, she has gotten across to him and he will come running back to her, which is what she is hoping for.

"I don't know nothing about your whereabouts lately."

"Exactly which is why I don't see why you come out your mouth like that."

"It's you."

"What about me?"

"You left me alone to raise our baby by myself, not even thinking about the promises we made to each other. I guess none of that mattered to you, then."

Terrance tilted his head to the side with complete disgust on his face.

"Are you serious right now? As I recall, you didn't even know if this baby was mine. You lied to me knowing that you had been with somebody else. After all the years of us being together, you felt the need to keep something like that from me even though we got back together...hell naw, that was some bullshit and you know it.

"Wait Terrance, it wasn't that simple."

"It was simple enough for you to lie to me and make me look real stupid at the hospital."

"How could you look stupid when the baby is yours? I had only been with that guy once. I was with you repeatedly."

"I don't give a damn. This means that you were being unprotected with some guy that you didn't even know and you still came back to me and had sex with me unprotected."

"I had sex with that guy before we even got back together so you can't be mad about that."

"At this point, you put me through it and that is enough said." Terrance turned away from Dalia walking towards his door.

"Wait, what about the baby?"

"What do you mean? I am going to be here for my child, but you and I are done."

"Terrance!"

The door shuts in Dalia's face. She stood outside of the door crying to herself. For some reason, she couldn't reach Terrance like before. Maybe he really let her go this time and he didn't want her back or he was upset and embarrassed that there was a possibility that he wasn't the father. Either way, all she knew is that he was madder with her than she ever seen, but she wasn't going to give up that easily. She had to win him back if it was the last thing that she did.

Dalia got back in the car and noticed that she had several text messages and missed calls from Jayden; of course her mind was not on any of them because her focus was all on Terrance. The phone rings again while in the care, "Hello".

"Where have you been?"

"Who is this?"

"Okay, really, are you serious? Where have you been and why didn't you show up at Blake's house today for the meeting?"

"I had a lot on my mind, sorry I couldn't make it."

"WHAT! You couldn't make it? Then, why didn't you call and let me know? I called you a couple of times and I even texted your ass to see if something was wrong, but I didn't hear anything back."

There was a long pause before Dalia said anything back.

"Hello... Are you going to say something? I don't know what is up with you, but you need to get your shit together real quick."

"Are you done?"

"What the hell? Looka here chick, what is your problem? I know this baby don't have you acting all funny like that."

"No, my baby is just fine. I know that Lauren has filled your head with a whole bunch of mess..."

"Whoa, wait a minute, what are you talking about? Hello, this meeting was supposed to be about my wedding...not about nothing to do with you and Lauren. Where is that attitude coming from? You know it is taking a lot of me not to curse you the hell out right now."

"It don't matter. It's all about me and my baby."

"Hell, I can tell. Look at the way you acting right now. You are really tripping and I don't even know what it is about. I would have thought out of everything you claim you are going through that you would have at least come by to see Blake."

"Shit, I forgot about that."

"Yeah, remember her. The same friend that invited you to stay at her mother's house so you can get your life together and almost lost her life in the process." Jayden implicated sarcastically.

"I mean, are you going to preach to me again."

"Look heffa, I don't even want to talk to you anymore, because this is ridiculous. You are acting as if we are to blame for your problems. Let me tell you something sweetheart, we all have problems, but you don't blame others for your problems. Do you hear the key word, your problems, k."

"I am not blaming anyone. I just don't feel like wasting my energy on other things when I have issues that need to be worked out."

"So, being with us is a waste of time...get the fuck outta here with that. Blake, Lauren and I are the most stable assets in your life and you want to push us to the back burner. Why didn't you just come to us when things apparently got this bad?"

"Hell, Lauren knows what is going on, but she ain't trying to help, all she wants to do is throw her perfect little relationship with Kendall up in my face like I really care what kind of relationship they have."

"Why you being so hard on Lauren, you know she ain't like that, and I know that because if that was the case, then you wouldn't be staying with her, feel me?"

"So, you are going to take her side right?"

"Hell no, I ain't taking sides, but I know you couldn't come stay with me and Brian right now so you have to be considerate of other's peoples feeling regardless of what you are going through. Yeah, things are different than before, but you have to adjust and move along with the program, don't waddle in the distress, because that will add discomfort and more stress. Life is more than that. Do you remember when I came back from the trip with my father and his wife, I could have screamed? But, I knew that it wasn't the end of the world for me. My step mother loves to start crap for me and my father, but sometimes it isn't all about you. Yea, I regret some of the things that I've said to her, but you know how I am. You get what I am trying to tell you?"

"I hear you...doesn't mean I agree."

"Oh, Lord Jesus, what am I going to do with you? How is Terrance doing?"

"See, I knew Lauren filled your head up with all kind of lies."

"Lauren didn't say anything that I don't already know. Why are you blaming her all of sudden? I wouldn't have expected that to happen to the two of you. Anyways, we are all planning to go to church tomorrow together since its Blake Sunday back in town. You should come."

"No thank you. You all are starting to be too happy for me."

"Bitch please. You are supposed to be happy through it all, don't matter what you are going through. Call me back when you finish doing what you doing." Without saying a word, Dalia disconnects the call. On the receiving end of the call, "No, the fuck she didn't. It's best that I don't call her back because that wouldn't be pretty. I am going to go home and take a nice bath and forget that I just talked to her."

"Ouch, damn that hurt. I think I am having contractions." The pains got worse and worst while Dalia was driving the car. Unfortunately, she wasn't able to stop right away because she was on the freeway. For minutes at hand, she had to mange driving while going through excruciating pain. "OH MY GOD! Something must be wrong, I am not far enough to deliver. Dalia decided to drive herself to the hospital. While doing so, she decided to call Terrance and let him know, but he didn't answer. She called him three more times, but he didn't answer so she left him a voice mail. The pain is getting worst every five minutes and it is taking forever for her to reach the hospital. Dalia was headed to the freeway to Lauren's house when the pains started. She had to go in the complete opposite side of town of her doctor's office, and hospital with her doctor's affiliation.

She could barely sit up straight at this point and driving was starting to be more than she could bear at this point. The normal 39-minute drive is now becoming an hour because of Dalia's agony. When she reached for her that was lying on the seat next to her, a pain hit so hard that she didn't have the strength to drive and reach for her phone. When she reached the hospital, she pulled in the emergency entrance horseshoe of the hospital. Unable to control her pains and the reaction, she ran into the back of a parked car in the emergency lane. The hospital staff ran outside hurriedly as if those incidents happened often. When they saw Dalia sitting in the car, her faced was drenched with sweat, even her shirt. Blood began to fall down her legs. Apparently, she didn't see that or noticed that was the reason for her excruciating pain. The nurse ran back into the hospital requesting a doctor and for more help.

'Hurry, we have a woman in labor out front on her car. It looks like she is bleeding, can't tell how far along."

The team of hospital workers ran to the car, taking Dalia out of her seatbelt onto the bed into the emergency room. By this time, Dalia had lost enough blood to take her out of consciousness.

"Hey, she is unconscious; we are going to need a cart to bring her back."

"No, let's see if we can use a smell bottle." All coming from the techs bring Dalia in the hospital. The head nurse walks up, "move, step back, this woman may be experiencing internal bleeding and who knows what else and you want to put a smell bottle to her nose….doctor, we have a pregnant women here, looks about seven months pregnant, apparently she went into shock from the loss of blood, not sure of what may have triggered it, but she was just brought in a couple of minutes ago" the nurse briefs the doctor who approached the scene and begins to examine Dalia.

"Oh my God, this woman has lost too much blood, how long was she in the car." The nurse looks at the ER techs, "Uh, I heard her when she pulled up because she ran into the back of one of the other cars parked here in the ER," one of the techs added.

"What did I tell you about letting people just park in the ER admit, they can't do that because of these types of situations." The nurse sighed heavily with a look of frustration at the techs.

"Kerry, lets go, we are taking her up to trauma. See if this woman has any relatives, spouse, parents, or anyone, she is going to need them right now", the doctor ordered the nurse.

The nurse went back to the ER and asked the techs if they had any information on Dalia. "I have her purse and I will check and see if there is anything in her car."

"Thanks, be careful, this is personal property and we don't want to face a lawsuit here", the nurse added. The tech hurriedly came back into the building, "I found an address book, it has emergency contact.....uh, Terrance Ross is down here. The only thing is showing is a cell number though."

"We have to use it then, if that is all she has for emergency contact."

"I do see a group of other names listed below as sisters."

"Okay, what do those say…"

"Uh, there is a Jayden Miller, Lauren Daniels, and a Blake Lowry."

"Are there numbers or addressed for those?"

"Yeah, they have addresses, work phones and home phones listed here for them, but I don't know who I should call first."

"Well, while I am trying to register her, you can call the first name there and keep calling until you get someone or a relative."

"Yes ma'am, I am on it."

"Hey, don't take your time with this. We don't know what kind of condition she is in, so she may need her family quicker than expected."

"Hey, if she is pregnant, don't you think calling the father would be the best."

"Maybe it's the guy Terrance you mentioned. See what he has to say and if you can get a hold of him, if not, then you have to call her emergency contacts as listed."

"Okay, dialing right now."

The nurse and ER tech work together to get Dalia registered and call her emergency contacts. It was fortunate that Dalia left that information in the car with her. Dalia recently packed a bag just in case she was out somewhere and she went into labor and couldn't get a hold of anyone, everything would be right there with her. It was all Lauren's idea after she and Terrance broke up the second time. Prior to the breakup, Terrance and Dalia had the entire delivery planned out. He came up with all kinds of plans so that either of them would panic or miss anything; unfortunately their plans did not work out, because the relationship ended when she returned from New Jersey and found out that her condo belonged to someone else now. She searched and searched until she found Terrance. By the time she was able to find him, he was so furious that he didn't bother telling her his whereabouts. He moved out with his friend from work for a while and later got himself reestablished and rented a nice two-bedroom apartment, which was 10 miles away from where the condo was located.

His explanation for the two-bedroom apartment was so that his child would have its own room and space. Dalia assumed that the extra room was for the woman that Terrance found to replace her. Unfortunately, it was for his child. Deep down he wanted the family with Dalia and their child, but he couldn't get past all the things and uproar Dalia put him through. Terrance felt he deserved better. Dalia felt that Terrance had an obligation to her and the child because he promised he would be there for her and now he wasn't he was being very distant and cold towards her. This was another side of Terrance that she hadn't seen before. Of course she felt some of it she deserved and she knew she treated him even worst when she found him cheating in their home, but she felt that she wished he would have some sympathy towards her.

"Hello, is this Terrance Ross?

"Who the hell wants to know?"

"This is Melissa from Memorial Hospital. We have you down for an emergency contact for Dalia Little. She was brought in about 30 minutes ago. She started having contractions and some vaginal bleeding. She went into shock and then unconscious. Is there anyway you can come down?

"Wait, a minute, are you serious or is this just a game for her to get down to the hospital?"

"Excuse me sir, Miss Little was brought in here a while ago and she wasn't even awake to even set this up, if that is what you are trying to apply. This woman needs the support of her family and friends if I have the wrong number let me know and you can disregard this call."

"Uh, no ma'am. I do apologize, I'm sorry. Where is she and what happened?"

"Mr. Ross, I can't give any more information, you will have to speak with the doctor and nurse assisting with her."

"Gottdamn, I will be down there soon as a can."

"Thank you sir; I am pretty sure she is going to need you."

Terrance hangs the phone up with the technician in the ER with his mind all over the place.

"How in the world did this happen? Is this my fault? Maybe I should have kept her here and this would not be happening. FUCK! Shit, I have to get to the hospital. Damn, I messed this up, but I can fix it if she lets me."

Terrance leaves the house in a hurry. He can't think of anything else to do but make it the hospital.

"Hello, I am trying to get in touch with Lauren Daniels." Breathing hard on the other end,

"Yes, this is she; may I ask who is calling?"

"This is Melissa from Memorial Hospital. I was calling to let you know that there has been an accident with a Dalia Little and you need to get to the hospital as soon as possible." Lauren on the other end almost dropped the phone.

"Oh my God, have you called Terrance, he is the baby's father?"

"Yes ma'am, I just spoke with him, he is aware of the situation."

"What about Blake and Jayden?"

"Uh, no not yet, they are next on the list for me to call. Do you know all of these people?"

"Yes, I do, don't worry about calling them, I will get in touch with them myself. Thanks for calling." Lauren hung up the phone before Melissa was able to inform her of anything else. She took a minute for herself and sat on the bed preparing herself for whatever she was going to face at the hospital. When she received the call, she was in the middle of her afternoon workout as she always does. She didn't even get a chance to change her clothes; she stopped in the middle of the workout, grabbed her purse and cell phone and headed downstairs out the door. While getting in her car, she called Jayden and Blake, who were supposed to meet her at the hospital.

When Lauren arrived at the hospital, she noticed Terrance in the far hallway pacing back and forth, "Terrance", she called out. "Have you heard anything, how is she?" He reached out to hug her out of worry. She hugged him back, "any news?"

"Naw, I haven't heard anything yet. They won't tell me anything. This is my fault. SHIT!" Terrance pacing even harder, back and forth in the hallway, blaming himself for what happened to Dalia; he began running his hands through his hair and down to his face. Lauren stood to the side, waiting on the girls to show up and on any news from the doctor or nurse.

"Terrance, let me ask you something, when was the last time you talked to Dalia?"

Terrance took a deep sigh before responding, "I saw her about 30 minutes ago. She came to the house, yelling about me having another woman at the house and about this damn doctor's appointment..."

"Wait, she was with you for the past couple of hours?" Lauren had serious look on her face.

"She was only at my house for about an hour and I was trying to take a nap, but she wanted to talk about all this mess that I wasn't trying to hear."

"Terrance, what in the hell happened at your house that made all of this happen? Look, I am not blaming you because I know the two of you have been going through some things, but damn......"

"Lauren, you know I love the hell out of her and my baby, but she did some shit." Lauren cut him off before he was able to say anything.... "Yeah, she did some things and you did too. I just want my friend to be okay."

"So, you are blaming me know."

"I didn't say that. You saying that she thought you had another woman at your house?"

"Look, I didn't even have anyone at my house today. I was trying to get some rest before I had to go back to work. She started banging on the door, disturbing my neighbors and yelling like she hood."

"Oh my God, are you serious? She really went there acting like that" Lauren's mouth was wide open. She knew that things between Dalia and Terrance escalated, but this bad. Footsteps came out of nowhere,

"Hey, we got your message, how is she" asked Blake. Lauren hugged Jayden and Blake, as they arrived together.

"Man, I can't believe I am in a hospital again", Jayden added as she hugged Lauren.

"Terrance, are you okay?" Jayden asked as Terrance had his back toward the rest of them. Lauren pulled Jayden by her shirttail.

"What, I was just asking him a question". Terrance never responded to Jayden. He kept looking outside of the nearby window, blaming himself for what is happening to Dalia.

"I will tell you about it later", Lauren whispered to Jayden. Blake walked over to Terrance, "Hey, are you blaming yourself for this? There is no way you did anything to cause this. Dalia is grown and from what I hear, you guys have been having a lot of disagreements lately, but this is not something you planned, so you can't blame yourself. Just pray that everything turns out okay." With tears in his eyes, Terrance turned and looked at Blake, "Thank you for that. I can see why you and Dee are best friends."

Terrance turned back toward the mirror and Blake went toward where the girls were waiting.

Chapter 19: The Decision

"Is there a Terrance Ross here?" the OR doctor asked with his scrubs and masking still hanging on his face. Quickly, Terrance jumped up, "yes, I am Terrance Ross." "I assume that you are the next of kin to Ms. Little, our records don't show anyone else, but she had you down. Are you the father of her unborn child?" "Yes, I am. How is Dalia? Is she okay, how is the baby?

Blake, Jayden, and Lauren all gathered around to hear the news. "It seems as if she lost a lot of blood on her way to the hospital. She went into shock and we were trying to stabilize her at the moment. She had some internal bleeding that took a while for us to find the root of the problem." Terrance interrupted the doctor.

"What are you saying...?"

"I am saying", the doctor paused. "You have to make a decision between the baby and Dalia at this point. I can't save them both."

OH MY GOD, I CAN'T BELIEVE THIS IS HAPPENING! Shouts came from Blake and Lauren as Jayden just stood there in shock. Tears ran down Terrance face as he couldn't believe the decision was in his hand. He loved the thought of being a father, but he damn sure didn't want to lose Dalia. She was the love of his life.

Terrance kicked the trash can in rage, knocking over the trays of medical supplies, as security walked over, the physician ordered them away as they knew the news Terrance just received. The girls huddled together, crying, wondering which way Terrance would go. They didn't want to harm the baby, but they knew Dalia could always have more children. Each of them were thinking about the last conversation or the last time they spoke with Dalia. Jayden remembered her last time not being so pleasant as she was fussing about the decisions Dalia was beginning to make with her life. Blake recalled not seeing her at all since she returned. She felt that she could reach her in some way. "This is my fault, I should have reached out to her earlier today", Blake cried out. "Honey, no, you had no way of knowing what was going on", answered Lauren. "NO, she counted on me to be there for her. What is her mother going to think," Jayden implied.

All types of emotions ran through the waiting room that they shared. Jayden walked toward Terrance, "You have a big decision to make and whatever you decide, the girls and I are behind you." Jayden rubbed Terrance across his back to assure him of their support.

"Jay, I don't know what to do", Terrance turned around and said to Jay before bursting into tears. He reached for Jay and in return to she hugged him for a long time.

"Oh, crap, we have to call her parents. Terrance, do you want me to do it or are you going to handle it", Lauren asked. While Terrance released himself from Jayden, he wiped his eyes and asked Lauren and Jayden to talk to her parents. He wanted to see if he could talk with Dalia whether she was conscious or not. The girls left and Terrance went to the nurse's station to see if he could go into Dalia's room and talk with her.

"Uh, sir, give me just a moment and I will get the doctor for you," the nurse left the station to find the doctor appointed to Dalia. Terrance stood at the station pacing back and forth thinking every time the door swung open it was the physician to give him some news; it took 15 minutes before the doctor finally came to the door.

"Mr. Ross, how can I help you?"

"Yes, I would like to see Dalia."

"Come walk with me, Ms. Little is not responding to her medication or any stimulates that we are giving her right now. We are trying to make sure that we can at least save her or the baby right now. The next 24 hours are going to be critical to her and the baby. There is really nothing that you or your friends can do right now; just go home and pray for a miracle, son."

"Doc you can't tell me that the woman in that hospital bed is not going to make it. I can't believe that," Terrance began shaking his head. "She was just fine a few hours ago. She was at my house, banging on the door, screaming at me...and the baby, the baby has to make it. That was the one thing that was bringing us together." Terrance grabbed the doctor lightly by the jacket, "You have got to do something to make this better."

The doctor placed both of his hands on Terrance shoulders, "We are going to do everything that we can. You go home, get some rest, and come back up first thing in the morning". The doctor walked off down the hall. Terrance left there standing alone. He could see from the corner of his eyes, Jayden looking in his direction.

"Terrance," she called out. He looked at Jayden with a look of despair in his eyes. He could see her eyes watering up from a distance, "What did the doctor say?" Terrance cleared his throat, Jayden looked up at him, "Lauren is still on the phone with Dalia's mother, she is on way here now, but I want to know what the doctor said to you".

Terrance cleared his throat again, "the doctor said that we should go home because there is nothing that we can do, we will have to wait 24 hours to see if her condition changes. He said because of her bleeding, hell, I don't know...shit, that there is no point in all of us sticking around, we might as well go home and come back first thing in the morning."

Jayden's mouth dropped open, "why would the doctor say some shit like that, I thought all you had to do was make a decision. Now it sounds like it don't matter, the baby and Dalia could both be gone"... "Don't say that, they both could make it", Terrance aid. Her voice rose and frightened Jayden.

"I'm sorry Terrance; I know this is hard for you too. I just don't like how this doctor is saying one thing in one breath and then something different the next minute."

"Jay, don't make a scene, you are just going to make it worst. I can't even wrap my head around all of this. Just a couple of hours ago, I had a baby mama drama thing going, and the next, I could be losing a fucking baby mama and the baby all in one."

"Terrance, we can pray...together. Remember in college, when exam time came and we thought we were going to fail out and not graduate, we got together and prayed....right?"

"Yea, yea, you right. We can pray and everything will be alright." Terrance kept saying this repeatedly trying to convince himself that prayer would be the answer to his problem right now.

Lauren entered the room, "Hey y'all, I just got off the phone with Dalia's mother, and she is on the way here. It will take them a couple of hours to get here. I told them that I would keep them posted if anything changed." Jayden hugged Lauren, "the doctor said that we should just go home and come back tomorrow morning." Jayden shrugged her shoulders in dismay to Lauren. "Are you serious", Lauren gave a puzzled look. "Just a minute ago, he said that Terrance had to choose between Dalia and the baby"...."I know, that is the same thing I said." Lauren grabbed Terrance by the hand, "Hey, You know we are here for you. If anyone knows what you have been going through the past couple of months, it's me. I am behind you one hundred percent."

Blake came from outside, over hearing the conversation between Lauren and Terrance, "HELL NO, are you serious? The two of you are going to let HIM decide whether to kill our friend or that she stays alive." In full rage, Blake headed toward all of them, beginning to make a scene in the hospital. Lauren looked at Blake in shock as if she couldn't believe the words coming out her mouth, Lauren began grinding her teeth, "Blake, let me talk to you alone."

Blake looked Lauren in her eyes, "I don't need anyone to talk to me. Jay, you agree with this too?"

Jayden turned and looked at Blake, "Dalia didn't have you down as her next of kin or whatever that shit is, you can't make the decision, Terrance has to decide, plus this is his baby, not ours."

"This is some bull shit, if I have ever seen it. We could lose a friend and you are really going to leave it in his hands."

"Blake, we can't do anything. Terrance is the only one that can make this decision." Lauren persistently trying to persuade Blake as it wasn't working.

"Hold a minute; you all are too content about this. There is something I don't know isn't it and y'all are not telling me. Just spill it. I don't know what the hell happened to y'all while I was gone, but this shit never ends."

"Gottdamn, you just don't chill out, do you? Alright, since you want to know, Terrance and Dalia got married, damn. They didn't want anyone to know, so Terrance is her husband and he has to make the decision," as furious as she was Jayden blurted out what Lauren couldn't tell her at the moment. In shock, Blake's mouth grew wider and wider, "Why would they not tell anybody?"

Jayden took a deep breath, "Dalia's mother don't know about her pregnancy and before they told them, her wanted to be married first"... "That don't make any damn sense to me", Blake shaking her head. "This sounds like nothing but mess to me."

"Okay, maybe it is, but she is our friend, Blake, chill out and be supportive", Lauren added.

"Hell, that is all I can do right now." Blake walked over to where Terrance was, "I am so sorry for coming off like that. There is so much I don't know, so much happened while I was gone."

"Shit, don't worry bout it. I feel the same way", was Terrance's reaction to Blake. Without anything left to say, Blake made her way back to the girls.

"Well, I guess we should go home and wait for the doctor to call us since we can't do anything here", states Lauren.

"Naw, I am going to stay here until I get some news", Terrance said to the girls. The girls hugged Terrance all before they left, "Let me know if you hear anything or need something. We will all be available okay. We are just a phone call away. We will let you know if here from her mother", Jayden stated..."Okay, I will call if I hear something," Terrance still in a daze. Lauren, Jayden, and Blake all left the hospital together.

Chapter 20: The Case

"Ben, any new leads on that Lowry Case", asked Detective Williams.

"Well, over the past couple of months, I have found some very interesting information. You will be surprised what people with money will do to just get ahead", Detective Stanford laying back in his chair.

"I know you are ready to wrap this one up."

"Uh, not just yet, the more and more I investigate, the more interesting this case becomes.

"What do you meant...?"

"For starters, the half sister who shot Blake, slept with Blake's best friend Dalia's boyfriend thinking it was Blake's man."

"But, if she was trying to get back at Blake, why would sleeping with the boyfriend going to help with anything."

"Now that is the tricky part. Come to find out that Blake just learned about this sister when the father died, so the half sister confused Dalia and Blake. It appears they resemble a lot."

"Whoa, this is like a soap opera."

"But, that isn't the half. Then, there is Blake's mother, who became close with Carmen's mother, but she didn't know her husband had a baby with this woman. Her husband kept this a secret. Somewhere deep down, I believe that Barbara had something to do with this because why not tell her daughters about this long lost sister they have. Why didn't anyone reach out to this daughter? That is a little too suspicious to me.

"Yeah, that would make you wonder, but why Blake and not the other sister Blair?"

"Blair was a part of the scheme to take over the father's company with Carmen. Blair actually turned on Blake because she wanted to have control over the company so she sent the mother on a trip, had her thinking it was something planned, like a surprise, just so she wouldn't know about it and to get her out of the way".

"If that is the case, then why would you think Barbara would have anything to do the shooting of her own daughter?"

"Well, then, why would Blair want anything to do with it either?"

"Did you think that Blair might have been jealous of her sister?"

"Why be jealous of Blake when she lives in another state, she doesn't even study law to run the company, and she is very successful at her marketing firm?"

"Here is the other part. The husband, Michael schemed his way into Blake's life on a business trip she took. She even started dating this guy only to find out that it was her sister's husband."

"Naw, Ben, I think you are going down the wrong road here. It seems as if there is something else about this Michael and Carmen that you need to find out. I think Dalia, Barbara, and Blake are innocent bystanders that were just caught up in the web between Carmen and Blair's scheme to take over the company."

"Why do you say that?"

"Just think about it. Carmen must have just found out that she had right to money when good ole Bernard died so she knew it was going to be trouble getting into it, so what do you do? You work on the weakest link, Blair. It wasn't hard because she wants so hard to please her parents. Since her father is gone, she can do what and how she wants only if she has the power, but she can't do that with her mother having a big stake in the company and her sister. Your two leads would be to find out Blair's relationship with her parents and why Carmen all of sudden became interested in the company."

"Wait, there is another part to this....If I can recall, Carmen worked at Rocky Memorial Hospital and so did Dalia."

"Uh man, I think you have your case solved."

"How?"

"Make a nice trip to see this boyfriend. If Carmen worked at this hospital with Dalia, then there is something else going on. There is no way that Carmen or Michael could have mistaken

Dalia for Blake if Carmen worked with her at the hospital. I think the culprit might be this boyfriend.

"The boyfriend? What could he gain out of the deal?"

"Its not what he could get a deal out of, it's the deal he was probably already getting."

"Are you trying to say that this boyfriend was having an affair with Carmen on purpose?"

"Maybe he had another motive, but he is still in the wrong. When Dalia caught him cheating, I bet Carmen made that intentional, but the boyfriend was thrown off."

"Wait a minute; do you think she was that vindictive?"

"I think she wanted money."

"No, she got money when the father died."

"But, did she get as much as Blake and Blair. How many of these cases have we done where people get greedy and want more? There is still something not adding up with the boyfriend." Stanford and Williams both sat at their desks facing each other trying to figure out the motive behind Carmen and Terrance. As Stanford's mind leaves from accusing Barbara, it began to lean more toward Terrance.

"I got something, Williams, maybe there was something in the deal for Terrance as well. You know I didn't suspect anything from him so I didn't even question him, what the hell was I thinking."

"Your mind just went in another direction that is all. Why do you think you have a partner?"

"But, Williams, check this out, why did Barbara decide to keep this from her daughters?"

"Just think about your mother, would she tell you that your father had any outside children?"

"But, man, times are different now."

"Not for the big time lawyer, Bernard Lowry, who held positions and one of the largest firms in the state. You would want to protect the image."

"Man, you have me thinking of all kinds of things now."

"Whatcha looking at now, I am thinking I should try to get a copy of Mr. Lowry's Will to see I if I can get some leverage there.

What do you think?" Searching through the rolodex on his desk, Stanford made a phone call to obtain a copy of the Will, some inside connection he had that owed him a favor.

"That may answer some questions, but it is not going to explain what this boyfriend had going into this deal."

"Hey, but it would explain the motive and I get the schemer and not the conspirators."

"Hell, they all were a part of a crime and if you play it right, I could get them with corporate espionage and bribery."

"Man, do you know what that would do for me?"

"Wait, are you sure you have thought about every other avenue with this case? You know how anxious you get when you just that close to solving a case."

"I'm thinking right now…so, you think Barbara is innocent all the way around?"

"My personal opinion is that Barbara wanted to protect her children. I read over some of the notes from your case a couple of weeks ago and I remember something coming up about Carmen's mother coming into Barbara's life…" Williams rubs his hand in his head.

"Hey, that is why I was on her track," Stanford rose up in his chair with excitement.

"But, that woman was crazy. Barbara didn't ask to be her friend, she befriended Barbara and this woman wouldn't even come around when Bernard was there."

"But, on the other hand, you wouldn't tell your kids about this woman once everything came out about who she was…?" Stanford looked with this confusion on his face.

"Why would you mention this to your kids…to make them confused about who mommies' friend is and bring up Daddy's past. Heck no! You move on and hope you never have to tell your children."

With a puzzled look for a moment, Stanford thought about what Williams' was saying about Barbara. It all made sense; he just assumed that he wanted her to be guilty when she truly wasn't. "Maybe I should go back to the drawing board and see all my suspects."

"You could do that and you would be wasting time to interview some people. I am pretty sure that Blake is back in Baltimore by now and so is this boyfriend".

"Well, the boyfriend was always in Baltimore, he never came to New Jersey that is what is so confusing to me with believing he was a part of the scheme.

Phone rings at Stanford's desk.

"This is Detective Stanford. Are you sure? Positive? Can you fax it to me, thanks man, I owe you once." He disconnects the phone.

"Who was that," Williams asked.

"Uh, that was my contact in getting a copy of the will. He said that he got it and that he will fax it over to me."

"Man, how did you get a copy of that?"

"Apparently, the family hasn't requested lock and key on it, so anyone with questions can have at it."

"You think you might have scared Barbara when you called her?"

"Probably so, but I needed to get all the information I could out of her."

"You know she could have sued you…"

"Yeah, she could have, but I think she was more concerned about keeping Blake safe."

"Keeping Blake safe huh….what about Blair?"

"Well, what I found out about Blair is that she is very conniving and vindictive. She went to law school, very smart, might I add, but just had that evil side of her. Blake was the lost one that stuck to any and everything that she liked at the time. The parents tried to get her to become a lawyer since she could do anything she sat her mind to, but that didn't work. So, when she went off to college, she met Lauren, her best friend, who helped her along the way. She finally decided that Marketing and Advertising was her thing, so she stuck with it. So, I don't think it was favoritism, Blair chose to be the way she is. But, I guess if the father was living, it would show some difference I guess. Man, you got me analyzing rich people lives and for what?

"Hell, I was just helping you out with this. You know what they say about the rich ones, they are the most unhappy people in the world."

"Well, we are going to find out just how unhappy this half sister really is when this fax comes through." Stanford sees his captain coming through the double doors, as he gets excited about the break he is having with the case. "Hey cap, I got a new lead in the Lowry case…."Good job, I need you to wrap this case up. It's been going on too long and we have been using a lot of resources on these rich people, our tax payers are going to be angry."

"Yes, sir,"

"Hey Stanford, your fax is coming through", another office yelled over the station.

"Thanks!" Stanford picked the papers up and took them back to his desk to share with his partner Williams.

"Man, you wouldn't believe this."

"Yes, I would, try me", Williams answered back to Stanford after looking over the will.

"Carmen didn't get nothing but a quarter of a million while the sisters and mother have equal control over the company and a sizable trust fund. Apparently, Blake already had some of her…just by looking at these documents, Carmen felt cheated, especially since compared to what these girls got and what she got, there is no comparison…but at least money bags left her a house, I guess that wasn't enough for her."

"We knew that all along."

"Wait, Blake got even more than Blair to an extent, maybe because the father trusted her or maybe because she didn't have a stake in the company." I may need to pay Blake a visit myself; she could answer some questions for me too."

"Whoa, whoa, you don't wanna make her feel like she is suspect in her own case. Be careful with that, she may not be the lawyer, but there are a crew of lawyers at that firm that would be willing to take you down for messing with a Lowry."

"Oh, it's going to be a nice visit, I just want to know the motive behind Carmen and the boyfriend, and then it will all make sense."

An officer from behind Williams came up with more documents for Stanford, "Thanks man". As Stanford looked through the documents, there were pictures sent directly to him of Terrance and Carmen together in more than one place, looking really cozy.

"Williams, you aren't going to believe this? Everything that we suspected is right here in color."

"Let me take a look. Oh man, we can just about wrap this case up."

"This explains everything. The two of them were conspiring together. I wonder if Carmen's husband knew about this."

"There is only one way to find out."

"Alright, I guess you have to make a trip there?"

"Naw, I would prefer if you go Williams."

"Are you sure about that?"

"Yeah, make the captain proud. I will stay here and handle the paper work and catch if anything else comes through."

"Okay, I better catch a plane down there now and pay him a visit. Thanks man."

"Hey, bring me a souvenir back", Detective Stanford said to Detective Williams.

"Not a problem", as Williams exits the building.

Chapter 21: The Decision Part 2

"Hi son, how was your flight?" Jackie hugged her son Jordan as he got off his flight.

"Hey, ma, what's good?" Jordan said to Jackie as he picked up his bag from the floor that he dropped when his mother hugged him. Grinning to herself, "Boy, you so crazy".

"Where is Mister James Miller," Jordan asked about his father.

"He had to take care of some business. He said he would catch up with us later"…"Catch up with us later, you going to let him hang with us?" Jordan shocked. "I can deal with your father when I am in the mood"…"Okay, I want to see that happened", Jordan began walking to the baggage claim area. Walking behind him, Jackie began talking to Jordan, "You make sure you call you sister once you get settled in."

"Of course! Did she leave the keys to the house for me," in excitement about taking over Jayden's house. "Uh, she didn't say anything to me, but I don't want you to bother her, so you can come stay with me, k."

"What! I'll just call her."

"Boy, didn't I just say don't bother her. Dalia isn't doing well. She is in the hospital and they don't know if she is going to make it." Jordan looked at his mother with dismay as he couldn't understand what she was saying.

"What the hell happened to her?"

"Watch your mouth son. She started hemorrhaging really bad and by the time she got to the hospital, she was unconscious and they had to stabilize her. I think they had to operate, not sure about that part. Now, they have to make a decision whether to save her or the baby."

"I guess her mother has a decision to make."

"No, not really. Terrance is the only one that can make that decision." Jackie holding back from her son as she felt that it was best to only tell what he asked since he felt close to all of Jayden's friend because they treated him like a little brother too, especially Dalia.

"I don't care about none of that. I want to go to the hospital." Jordan became and more concerned while walking through the parking lot for the car to load his bags.

"Let me call Jay and see when there is a good time for you to go because I think she is in ICU and not many people can go visit." Becoming even more furious, "She is my family, I don't care why no doctor say, just as soon as I get to the house, I am making my way to the hospital." Jackie looking at her son couldn't believe how much emotion he was showing about Dalia. It was first from him, but under her breath she murmured, "I guess anything is possible", closing the trunk to her car.

While riding in the car back to Jackie's house, Jordan started the conversation back up about Dalia, "So, ma, where is Terrance? Aren't they supposed to be getting married?"

"Child, please, you might want to ask your sister about that."

"Dang, it's like that, then I don't want to know about it then. I just wanna see her and make sure she is alright."

"Okay, son that is all good and well, but you haven't said anything about you since I picked you up." Jackie glanced over and looked at her son while driving.

"What do you want me say?"

Jackie glanced over at him again, "how is school boy? I didn't send you all the way out there to mess up. You can mess up here in Baltimore." Jordan held his shirt up over his head, "Oh, ma, everything is good. School is good. Football is good, anything else?" Jordan turned to look at his mother. "Don't get smart with me boy, you ain't too big to get smack in this car, hell, I should do it anyway just for you talking like that."

"Ma, I don't know what you want me to tell you, but I do have a question for you though," he said with a grin on his face. "What...do you want to ask me?"

"Have you talked to Jayden? I heard that she was mad at you and pops. What was that all about?" Jordan turned his whole body in the car facing his mother while she was still driving.

"Don't worry about that. I talked to your sister when she told me about Dalia. And I can tell you another thing, if I find out that you aren't doing good out there in school, I am going to come out there myself and bring you home, you hear me?" Still slightly intimidated by his mother, Jordan turned around in his chair, "yes ma'am. There was complete silence in the car for the next five minutes until Jackie began asking her son about prospects going into the league.

"Son, have you found you a good agent yet?"

"I told you I was going to stick with the same guy I had when you came out there."

"You know I don't like him and I don't think he has your best interest at heart."

"He keeps money in my pocket, a fresh ride, and a nice spot to chill in." Jackie rolled her eyes. "Son, you know that is not what you need to be focusing on, you do not want this man to take all of your money when you are the one running out there on the field."

"Can you trust me to do my own thing? I appreciate you being there, but I am handling it."

"I don't want you to do anything stupid to mess up getting drafted."

"That is a sealed deal right now ma. All I need to do is finish this year out, don't get hurt, and make some spectacular plays. Coach wanted me to take a break and get away from everything for a while. He said over breaks is when the boys get wild and he wanted me out of trouble".

"Hell, I think you should get your coach to be your agent."

"That is his job to be like that. He wants to look good when I throw those balls out there."

"He is still showing more concern than this agent of yours." They pulled in the driveway of the Jackie's home.

"Ma, I think you should give me more credit with handling this. I can do a lot of things, especially handling my agent." Jordan remarked upon opening the door to the car.

"Son, I am just worried and concerned that you aren't taking all the necessary precautions with this. Do you know how many people get screwed in these types of situations? And as soon as that happens, it is going to look bad on me, damn your father, but me Jordan, do you hear me talking to you?" Jackie grabbed her son by his arm to draw eye contact with him.

"Ma, I know you are just concerned, but I got it, trust me. Do you not believe how I run things when I am at school? See, you don't even watch ESPN to see how I get down. When I come home, I want to chill and relax with my people on my break." Using hand motions to express himself, Jordan looked at his mother strongly in her eyes.

Unloading the bags from the car with Jordan, Jackie didn't know what to say to her son. ESPN was nothing something she watched. "Just bring your things in the house," as she was at lost for words on this argument. Thinking to herself, Jackie knew that ESPN would keep her updated with her son, but she knew how Jordan was so she didn't want to watch it and see all the bad things he was doing to his image. She preferred not to watch. Not so much a sports fan, she never thought about watching the station in the first place, she just knew that he was about to embark upon an opportunity that only few people get in life and she didn't want her son to make the wrong decision by trusting the wrong person. But, talking to Jordan made her realize that she needed let him grow up and be the man she and James raised him to be.

As Jordan already walked into the house, Jackie was still outside, trying to make her way to the door, but she was still checking her car making sure Jordan got everything. "Ma, what is taking you so long?" Jordan yelled outside of the door.

"Why you got to act so ghetto all the time yelling?" Jackie answered back to her son.

"You have been taking a long time; I didn't know what happened to you. It's getting late; you shouldn't even be out here like dat."

"Boy, I do this all the time, I am fine." Jordan rolled his eyes. While walking into the house, Jackie was wondering if Jayden called about any news on Dalia. She walked into the house, checking her caller id, but there was nothing. She checked her cell phone, but there was still nothing.

"Ma, did Jay call you?"

"No, no miss calls from her. I am going to call her in a minute if I don't here anything. I know Dalia's mother is coming to town this evening. I may call her and see if she has accommodations."

"Oh Lord, here you go, jumping into stuff." Jordan rolled his eyes.

"How do you figure I am jumping in? I haven't known her for years and I know what it is like to worry about a child that is far from you." Jackie explained to her son with her hands on her hip.

"Ma, I'm just saying," Jordan using hand motions to express himself.

"You just saying what, Jordan! Just go sit down somewhere." Jackie started pacing through the house, just pondering.

"Aight, I am going to B's house to see what he is up to." Jordan grabbed a set of keys off the counter.

"How do you know Brian is at home and that he wants to see you," Jordan not really paying his mother any attention.

"Ma, you worry too much", Jordan kissed his mother on the check. "I'll be back later tonight."

"Naw, you are going to be back quicker than that if your sister is over there," Jackie grinned to herself.

Jordan takes a nice ride through town over to Brian's house, which is in an average area. Once thing that Jordan loves about Brian's house is that it is spacious. It looks like a bachelor's pad, and he has a huge TV in the front room with a nice leather coach that wraps around the room. He always wanted to get a spot like that one day. When Jordan arrived at the house, he noticed a couple of cars in the yard, but none of them looked familiar to him. But, that wasn't knew to him because he had been gone a while, so everything looked pretty much new. Over the past year, Jordan and Brian have become close, one because Jordan is getting older and he fines that he has a lot in common with Brian. Two, he realizes how much Brian means to his sister and he was soon to be his brother in law.

Jordan continued to pull in the driveway in a Toyota Tundra, which was his mother's and his car together. She bought the car so that Jordan would have something to drive when he came home, but she made sure that he was held responsible for the maintenance of it. "Whew, somebody living nice. Bee come out here and check this shit out." There were two guys that walked out on the porch of Brian's house that looked familiar to Jordan, but he couldn't quite place who they were. "What's going on man?" Jordan gave both of the men dap, before walking in the house. "Nothing, but the damn rent," one of them responded.

"Damn, you look just like B's girl." The other guy commented.

"Yeah, that is my sister." Jordan said with a smile as if he were proud to be Jayden's sister.

"B man, where the hell you at ,nigga," Jordan walking through the house.

"Man, hold the fuck up, I know this ain't my nigga Jordan Miller." Brian came from the back of the house with much excitement on this face when he saw Jordan. He walked up to him and gave him dap. "Hell, I see college life is treating you good as hell. What's good wit ya?"

"Ain't shit going on, getting ready to wrap this last year up."

"Have some couch. Man, how in the hell were you able to pull that off....wanna beer or something to drink?"

"Hell yeah, whatever you got is good with me...but, uh, I've just been putting in work and staying focus...no alcohol, no smoking, no partying, just staying focus as hell."

"Damn boy, that's what's up."

"You seen my sister?"

"Naw, she called me about an hour ago, talking about Dalia and shit, man, I couldn't believe that and then she called me back telling me she would let me know when she is on her way home, and that was it."

"Hell, she ain't say nothing about me staying at her place."

"Naw, bro, she ain't say nothing about that.

"Man, I can't stay with my momma or my damn pops."

"You could stay here with me and your sister, but you will have to check with her. I ain't in da mood for her to mess up my high right now, and I am off tomorrow, so I plan on getting bus' up tonight fo sure." Jordan chuckled a bit to himself.

"Eh man, while I am here on break, I thought I would chill with you for a bit."

"Fo sho, that is cool, just don't piss your gottdam sister off, because I don't feel like hearing that shit."

"Who dem niggas out there on the porch?"

"Just some homeboys from around the way; they cool peops. These niggas gotta go before your sister get here tho."

"Man, I know you ain't afraid of Jay?" Brain gave Jordan a look like "nigga please. Let me tell you something about women....if you want peace in your house, you don't initiate a woman to be pissed off, if you know what I mean. You want evr'y thing cop esthetic, because if she pissed off, she is going to piss you off. "

"Damn, man, I didn't know it had changed like that."

"Wat you mean, baby brother?" the other guys from outside over heard some of the conversation and decided to come in the house.

"Lil brother think you don lost it, huh?" one of the guys asked.

"I remember a time where you didn't take no shit from my sister, now it seems like you getting soft," the other men in the room laughed at Jordan and shaking their heads.

"Check this out...I ain't no where soft, but you have to also remember that she is my woman and I respect her more any other woman, next to my momma, ya dig. See, you can't treat your woman the same you treat a hoe out here in the street, shit naw. My man can cosign on that shit." Brian looked to the guy sitting in front of him.

"Wait, wait...what the hell happened since I've been gone", Jordan asked.

"Young boy, when you find that one, you are supposed to treat her right, not mess over her, but you will get there and you will learn the hard way." The other guy interceded.

"Wow, I never thought B would be the one to go down like that." Jordan shook his head while facing Brian.

"Aight, you go mess around and get your head bus up in here, you keep talking like that." Brian in between speaking drinks his beer.

"Okay, answer this for me then, is it that you two are getting married now."

"Hell, fuck yeah. See, I knew your sister was the one for me, but in the beginning, I didn't want that. I wanted to do my thing, even though she knew that. We had some other shit to work on too, but that's another subject. Now, don't get it fuckin twisted, I will still bus a muthafuker head if I have to."

"Oh hell, I can tell that ain't change at all."

"Chill out! I can promise you we still tear this house down about some shit, just because I am me and your sister is her own person, but I don't disrespect her and she don't disrespect me. That makes a difference in any relationship, not booty calls or something on the side, you feel me." Jordan was trying to let it all sink in then the other guy starting talking,

"My old lady put up with me through all kinds of mess. I got locked up, lost my job, and some other bull shit and all she did was support me. Even though, she was quick to jump off about something, she never left me and she always supported me. When I realized that I needed to treat her better that is when she stopped blowing my phone up and accusing me of shit I know I wasn't doing. I regret every time I said something about my woman....oh that is another thing, when you respect her, you never call her your chick: she is your woman because that is how you see her."

Jordan looked at all of them in the room, "Well, I damn sure know I haven't met that kind of chick, excuse me, woman yet. Damn, I need another drink with that shit."

"It ain't nothing. I had to realize some things, but when I did. I had to figure out how to keep it, that is all." Brian finished his beer up.

They heard keys jingling at the door.

"What the hell we got going on here....AND MY BROTHER IS HERE!" Jayden ran to her brother and hugged him.

She hadn't seen him in a while so she was elated to see. She ended up dropping everything in her arms. Jordan hugged his sister while the rest of them watched. Then, she pulled herself together,

"Hey babe," she walked to Brian, hugged and kissed him. The other guys looked at each other giving a signal to leave.

"Hey y'all, what y'all doing?" Jayden looked at Brian's friends.

"Hey Jayden, we were just about to leave. We didn't know it was that late."

"You fine, I am about to go lay down, I am so tired, whew!" Brian began to frown and he jumped out of his seat.

"Whoa, what the hell you mean, you going to lie down," Brian asked Jayden as she was starting to go down the hallway.

Brian's friends grabbed their keys and headed out of the door, "eh man, we'll holla at you later......"Cool".

Jordan felt left out so he grabbed his keys to, "pss, psst sis, I will catch you later, already....B, hold it down" and Jordan left the house.

"Jay, what you mean you going to lie down," Brian asked again, this time sounding sterner.

"I am tired from being at the hospital and all I want to do is lay down. You can come with me if you want."

"Babe, I have been waiting on you to come home and you going to lie down?"

Jayden walked up to Brian and on her tippy toes, she kissed him on the cheek and she whispered to him, "If you give me ten minutes, I can give you an hour to catch up with me."

In his low voice, "Muthafucka, you sexy as hell, alright go lay down and uh, I will let you sleep ten minutes, that's it, then it's my turn." It was a pause before Brian said anything else,

"Oh, I forgot to ask you, how is Dalia?"

"Babe, it's not looking good for her and Terrance has to choose between her and the baby. He don't know what to do. There is nothing none of us can do, just let him make the decision."

"Whoa, what you mean, he has to make the decision, what kind of bull shit is that?"

Jayden sighs

"Talk to me now," Brian is insisting that Jayden be more informative about what is going on.

"Terrance and Dalia got married a while ago and they didn't want anyone to know....." Brian interrupted Dalia, "Say what? Then why the fuck was he tripping all this time about anything, that some foul shit. Aw man, that is mess up for real." Brian started going on and on about all the things he knew that went on between Terrance and Dalia and he became more furious than when he started.

"Brian, I know, but I can't hear all of that right now. All of that has ran through my head too, but it doesn't make Dee better," Jayden began rubbing Brian's face to calm him down. Then she made her way down to his hand and placed hers in the palm of his, "C'mon, lay down with me." Brian followed her to the bedroom. He took his big muscular hands and wrapped them around her waist rubbing his body up against hers as they continued to walk together to the bedroom.

Part II

"Excuse me, are you Mr. Terrance Ross?"

Waking up from a nap in the waiting area, "Yes, that is me, is there something wrong with my wife?"

"Hi, my name is Dr. Cole and I need you to come with me for a minute."

"Okay....."I am sorry to tell you this, but there is no way we can save the baby, we can try our best to save Dalia."

"Wait a minute doc, how did this happen, why couldn't the baby make it?"

"Well, looking at her condition and what happened--stress, tension, and then her blood pressure rose extremely high. Were you aware that Mrs. Ross was not following her diet nor was she keeping up with her appointments?"

"WHAT! Doc, I went with her to some of them."

"Look, don't worry about any of that now. Just pray that we can save your wife right now, she is high risk right now and we need your permission to place her on a ventilator."

272

"Hey, hey, do whatever you have to do to keep her alive. Doc, I need you to save her," Terrance pleaded with the doctor to keep Dalia alive.

"TERRANCE, TERRANCE"

He turned around to see Dalia's mother, Deborah Little.

"How is my baby, I want to see her." Terrance hugged her as hard as he could, not knowing what to say or how to tell her that her only child was on a ventilator fighting for her life and that she lost her only grandchild.

"She, uh, is on a ventilator, the baby is gone and they don't know if she is going to make it."

"What!" Terrance burst into tears and so did Deborah. They consoled each other a long while in the hallway at the same spot Terrance was talking to the doctor.

"I'm so sorry."

"Stop, be a man for Dalia. You know she loves you."

"But, you don't know what happened."

"I don't care what happened, I just want my baby to be alright okay. We are going to stay here and pray until something happens."

"Yes ma'am…."but, I need to call Lauren, Jayden, and Blake."

"Blake, she is back into town."

"Yeah, she hasn't been back long. She was here earlier. The doctor said there wasn't going to be any change so he told all of us to go home and come back in the morning. I'm glad I stayed now. Mrs. Little, there is something I have to tell you."

They began walking down the hall in ICU where Dalia's room was. "Do I need to hear this right now?"

"I want you to know right now." Deborah took a deep breath.

"Okay, Terrance, what is it?"

"Dalia and I got married a couple of months ago."

"That is it. I knew that already."

"Dalia told you?"

"I just know my child. I know more than what you think I know. Aww, Terrance, its going to be alright, we all make mistakes, but it is up to us to learn from them and let that be the best schooling you can get, Mmm, life lessons, what would we do without them? We can call the girls in a minute; I want to see my child first."

Getting near the nurse's station, Deborah asked where Dalia's room was. "Excuse me, nurse, where is Mrs. Dalia Little's room is?"

"Uh, I have a Dalia Ross."

"That is her, what is the room number?"

"Follow me and I will show you. You have to sanitize before you go in and

you have to use mask to cover your faces." They took a couple more steps and they were at Dalia's room.

"OH LORD JESUS, MY BABY! Just before Deborah passed out, Terrance caught her in his arms. She was not prepared to see Dalia hooked up to every machine, tubs coming out from everywhere, you could see the towels where they were trying to stop her from bleeding. Her eyes were glued shut, her body was starting to swell, and she couldn't be recognized. When Terrance carried Deborah to the nearest chair to bring her back, he alerted the nurse to not let anyone see Dalia in that condition as it was unbearable for his eyes as well. Crying consistently, Terrance was at a lost for words of what to think. From the looks of things, there was no possible way that Dalia could survive from this. All he could think to himself was that it was his job to support and take care of her, especially since they said vows to each other regardless of the situation or circumstances they took them under. While Deborah on the side, took a cup of water from one the of nurses, Terrance stood at the door way of her room, too afraid to face her directly, he stared at her body from head to toe with all the machines pumping her body to keep her alive.

"Lord, if you give me another chance, I will make this right. Forgive me for all that I have done, I know I don't deserve this chance. Let me fall for my transgressions and let Dalia live. I know my time will come, but I will gladly go in place for Dalia's health and security, in Christ's name I pray these words Amen."

Tears ran down Terrance's face as he prayed an honest pray for himself and Dalia's sake. He stood staring in the doorway with his hands held to his mouth in the form of a prayer while tears continued to run down his face. He promised himself that he wouldn't leave Dalia's side and he was going to keep his promise.

"Mr. Ross, I hate to disturb you, but we need to take your wife now if we want to save her." The doctor tapped Terrance to get his attention. Terrance had to pull himself together to talk with the doctor.

"Doc, so you are going to take the baby now." The doctor slightly held his head down, "Yes, we have to take the baby now in order to increase her changes of survival. Again, Mr. Ross, I am sorry for your lost. The next couple of hours are critical to your wife's recovery. This surgery is going to take a couple of hours, so it will be early morning before we could tell you anything. You should get some rest. You have been here all day."

"I hear you doc, but that is my wife and I can't be anywhere else while she is fighting for her life in the operating room." The doctor patted Terrance on the back, showing much compassion for him. "I know, I will do the best that I can" and the doctor began with his staff removing Dalia from the room. Terrance was left with his prayer and faith that Dalia would be okay. Deborah still regrouping from seeing her daughter watched from a distance as they pulled her out of her ICU room.

Deborah gathered herself together only to catch Terrance by the hand in despair. "I better call the girls now and let them know what is going on. They will be upset with me for not calling them."

"Yeah, that would be a good idea for you to do so." Terrance walked out of the ICU unit with Deborah still there getting herself together. Terrance decided to get some fresh air, so he stepped outside the hospital to call the rest of the girls. He decided to call Jayden and tell her what was going on. He knew she had just left a couple of hours ago, but she would want to know what was going on with Dalia. At that point, there was nothing that any of them could do, but pray that survived and recovered from this.

Chapter 22: Regrouping

The phone rings

"Hello,"

"Hey, sweetheart, how is Dalia?"

"Kenny, I have been waiting to talk to you all day. Have you been in meetings?"

"Yeah, I am helping the legal team come up with contracts for this new office, and I have to get staff for the building too. I haven't begun posting the jobs anywhere. I am not sure if I am going to get people from the temp agency or recruit from the local colleges. I just have a lot to do and not enough staff right now to do all the work." Lauren quietly listened to Kendall on the phone.

She sighed first before responding, "Yeah, I know you're busy with that.

"You didn't answer me earlier, how is Dalia?"

"I don't even know where to begin with it, Ken. Where are you? Are you in New Jersey or in Maryland right now?" Anxiously waiting for Kendall to respond, she anticipated that he was close enough for her to see him.

"Naw, sweetie, I am in New Jersey right now because I have some paperwork here that I needed to pick up and I needed to get some things from my house, why what's up?" On the other end of the phone, Lauren heart dropped. She felt alone as if she didn't have anyone she could cry her eyes out to. "You keep avoiding my question about Dalia, is she going to be alright? Is that why you are asking me where I am right now?"

"Kenny, Terrance will have to choose between the baby or Dalia. She lost a lot a blood, and there was no way they could save both of them. I just got home from the hospital about a couple of hours ago and I am trying to figure out why my best friend that I was just arguing with earlier today is laying in a hospital bed fighting for her life."

"Say what! Why didn't you call me and tell me that all of this was going on?"

"I didn't want to bother you. I knew you were busy and there wasn't anything that we could do anyway."

"Rin, I don't care about that. I could have postponed some things and come to you. SHIT, man."

"Kenny, don't do that, I just needed to talk to you....wait, hold on, I have a beep, I think it is from Terrance."

"Okay, sweetie."

Lauren clicked over to answer the beep.

"Hello, Terrance."

Softly spoke, "Hey, Lauren, I was calling to tell you that the doctor couldn't save the baby...." Terrance couldn't finish his sentence. Very emotional, on the other end of the line, Lauren began crying also.

"Terrance, what happened?" Lauren asked while sniffing on the line.

"The doctor said there was no way he could have saved her and the baby. She would have a better chance if they took the baby, because she was at a high risk of a stroke about an hour ago. They just took her up to surgery to take the baby." Trying to take in all the information, Lauren was at a lost of words.

"Terrance, I am on my way to the hospital, did Ms. Deborah get there okay?"

"Yeah, she was there when we went to ICU to see her and when the doctor came to get her for surgery."

"Terrance, how did she look? Did she look like Dalia?"

"Lauren, you don't want to see her."

"Oh my God, I can't believe this is happening." Lauren began ranting and raving through her home forgetting that Kendall was on the other line waiting for her to return.

"Lauren, I have to go and call the others to give them an update."

"Wait, Terrance, how is Mrs. Deborah?"

"Lauren, you may have to come get her because she isn't doing well at all. She saw her and she passed out."

"Okay, I'll be in touch and Terrance, she is going to make it, have faith okay."

"Thank you Lauren, I'll talk to you later."

Lauren, then clicked back over the other line.

"Hey, Kendall, I am sorry for keeping you on hold," barely speaking at a normal tone with all the emotion in her voice.

"Rin, what is wrong? What did Terrance say," Kendall on the other line becoming even more infuriated then before.

"Terrance just said that they had to take the baby from Dalia and she is in surgery right now. They have to take the baby so they can save her life." Lauren blurted out in tears over the phone, losing composure like Kendall had ever seen her before. By this time, she had dropped the phone, rocking back and forth, crying her eyes out as she felt that she was about to lose another friend under the circumstance of them arguing earlier that day.

"Lauren, Lauren, sweetie, I will be there tonight. Don't move, I am on my way to you." To himself, Kendall was furious with that he wasn't there when Lauren needed him. He knew that this was a moment if any before; he needed to be there just to support her. Due to the lateness of the evening, Kendall had to figure out the quickest way to get to Lauren. He called the airlines and asked them for any flight that they had they would get him to Baltimore that night. Fortunately, he was able to get one. He knew he needed to be there. "Damn these clothes, I have to be there for my wife," looking at the engagement ring he just bought for Lauren that she had no clue about. Of course, Dalia being in the hospital was not a part of the plan, but he knew now was not the time to ask Lauren to marry him, so he left the ring at his house on the bed.

Sitting on the floor in her bedroom, Lauren sat there thinking about Dalia and all they'd been through as friends. From college, where they met, to now with Dalia temporarily living with her until she was able to get herself together. She wiped her tears, picked herself up from the floor, and began walking down the hallway of her home. She noticed she was approaching the room Dalia was occupying. She was hesitant of going in, but she needed to feel connected to her friend again. Thinking to herself, Lauren was running all kinds of thoughts through her head wondering if she could take seeing her in the condition that she was in.

Her phone still on the floor in her bedroom, she opened the closet door to Dalia's things. She could smell the scent that she loved to wear from Bath and Body Works, Japanese Cherry Blossom that was all over the room. Since Dalia was staying there, Lauren never went into Dalia's room or through her things. She felt compelled to keep reminiscing and pondering through her things as that may be the last things or memories she would have of her.

Knock, knock, know....door bell.

In the midst of her thought, Lauren heard knocks at the door and the doorbell ringing. Even though hearing the doorbell, Lauren took her time walking downstairs. She continuously heard the doorbell and knocks at the door. When she reached the bottom of the staircase, she was hesitant to go near the door as it would be more bad news. She looked closer at the reflection and saw that it possibly could be Blake or Jayden. She swiftly paced her step to walk to the door, "Who is it," as she cleared her voice to project it.

Throat clears on the other end of the door, "This is Detective Malik Williams, and I am here to see a Miss Lauren Daniels." On the other side of the door, Lauren whispers to herself, "a Detective Williams, what could he want with me." She tip toed through the peep hole and she saw a tall, chocolate, elegant looking man on the other end, that didn't come close to any of the guys from Law & Order that she watched religiously. She yelled back through the door, "Uh, what is this about?"

"Well, ma'am if you let me in, I can explain it all to you."

"Hold your badge up to the peep hole." She glanced at the badge that appeared to be legit to her. She unlocked the locks that were on the door and she welcomed the detective in her home.

"This is a very nice home you have here, Miss Daniels." She interrupted, "Please call me Lauren."

"It's a pleasure to meet you ma'am", he held his hand out for a handshake.

"So, you wanna tell me what this is all about? You can have a seat here in the living room, here." Lauren sat in the corresponding sofa across from where the detective was sitting.

"I am pretty sure that you are aware that we have been doing a full investigation on the incident involving your friend Blake. There are some pieces to the puzzle that are missing that I am trying to clean up before," he clears his throat.

"Before what? Are you looking to arrest me, because if that is the case, I will call my lawyer?"

"Calm down. Can you tell me where Dalia is right now?" Feeling uncomfortable about the situation, Lauren stood up from off the sofa, "Look, detective, I don't feel right talking to you about something I had absolutely nothing to do with and plus Dalia is not here right now. She won't even be able to talk with you, so I think you should leave, right now."

"Lauren, I know you want to help your friend Blake, and I believe you can help me. I really want to put away everyone that had something to do with this plot to take over the Lowry Law Firm." Lauren took a deep breath and she thought about what the detective wanted to do. He seemed genuine to her, even though she was not one to trust policeman.

"Okay, detective, what do you want to know? I don't think I would be of much help about this though." Detective Williams pulled out a notepad from the coat pocket of his jacket, "first, I want to know all that you know about Terrance Ross.

With a confused look, "Terrance, what about Terrance, are you tricking me with this conversation."

"Lauren, please answer the questions. If you want to call your lawyer that is fine, but I can promise you that I am not trying to incriminate you, please just help me with this."

"Uh, let me think", Lauren takes a deep breath. I met Terrance freshman year in college through Dalia, they were dating back then. He was always nice, well-mannered, respectable and always supporting Dalia." Lauren began shaking her head, "I don't see where this is going."

"Ma'am, I think there is more to this Terrance guy than what you and your friends have been led to believe."

"Whoa, now you are going to tell me that Terrance is some murderer!"

"No, that is not what I am saying. Can you tell me anything else about him?"

Shaking her head, "No, I can't recall anything else that I know personally about him. I wished a long time ago that I could have found someone like that in college, but it didn't happen for me, so I got over it."

"Okay, what do you know about an incident that happened a year ago between Dalia and Terrance where she caught him cheating in the home they shared together."

"Detective, that is a little personal and I don't see how that has anything to do with this case."

"Your answer, please."

"I need a gottdamn drink, do you want something to drink"...."No thank you."

"I just know that Dalia was really torn about it. She backed up from me, Jayden and Blake at that time. She just said that it was someone from her job and then after taking the trip to New Jersey a week after that happening, we found out it was Blake's sister that she recently found out about."

"Now we are getting somewhere. Did Dalia ever say she talked to this woman or asked Terrance why it happened?"

Pondering through her brain, "good question, let me think....i don't think she ever figured that out. It really bothered her because it was so much out of his character, you know. He was always the good guy, supportive and crap. I know when she caught them, she threw Carmen out and every time Terrance tried to talk to her after that he would say, you don't understand, its not what you think."

"Miss Daniels, do you know what he meant by that?"

"No, but I never thought anything of it. I thought it no more than a poor judgment call on him and some woman who was after Dalia."

"Wait! Do you think this woman, Carmen, was after Dalia or Blake?"

With her eyes wide open, with a confused look on her face, "Why would you say Blake?"

"Think about it. Your friend, Blake finds out she has a sister Carmen that she knew nothing about, then all of sudden, Dalia catches her man in the bed with the sister. I think this is all a plot."

"Oh, my God, I should call Blake. She would want to hear this. Have you called her yet? Have you tried to let her know what you are suspecting?"

"No, I haven't, not until I have evidence and I can prove all of this. There is another part that you are missing Lauren." As Lauren stood up quickly moving toward the telephone to call Blake, the detective rushed towards her to stop her from dialing.

"What else do I need to hear?"

The detective paused for a moment, "I think Terrance could be really dangerous. I want you to stay away from him until we can get this all figured out."

"Excuse me, detective, I can't do that."

"Miss Daniels, are you going to continue to make my job hard?"

"No, you are listening to me; I can't because Dalia is in the hospital on her death bed. She and Terrance are married. They secretly got married a couple of months for whatever reasons, I don't know. He is at the hospital right now, by her side. I can't do that to him and my friend."

"Son of a bitch! He is really smart to marry her."

"What do you mean?"

"I can't say anything right now, but I need you to try and distance yourself away from him; however you plan to do it. Given your friend and her circumstance, just be careful." Lauren could tell by the look in his eye that he was serious. She thought herself if Terrance could really be dangerous or the detective didn't want me saying anything to him.

"What am I supposed to do? I told him that I was coming to the hospital tonight. Dalia was pregnant and they had to take the baby from her, she is in ICU, probably in surgery by now."

"Find someone to go with you, your husband? Someone."

Is that all detective? Lauren became agitated at the demands Detective Williams was placing on her, which was preventing her from being at the hospital like she wanted. She walked toward the front door of her home to escort the detective out, but when she opened the door, she was shocked by who was on the other side of it.

"Hey, I couldn't sleep and I need someone to talk to", it was Blake coming through the front door.

"Oh, my bad, I didn't know you had company." Blake became hesitant to enter the house. She looked at the detective, and began taking steps backward.

"No, Blake you stay, he was getting ready to leave."

Walking toward the door, "Blake Lowry right," Detective Williams said to Blake.

"Yeah, that is me, who are you and why do you know me." Blake glanced at Lauren with a puzzled look since she didn't chime in to say anything to this man standing in her living room. Detective Williams reached his hand out to Blake, "Hi Miss Lowry, I am Detective Malik Williams. I am the investigator on your case with the Lowry Law Firm. You were next on my list to visit."

"Excuse me, this is my house and I said that it was time for you to leave detective." Lauren stepped in front of Blake before she could say anything to the detective's request. Since Lauren always protected her from things, she knew better than to go against Lauren's better judgment. The detective bowed his head to the women, "Miss Lowry, I will be seeing you later. You ladies have a good evening." Lauren gave Blake the queue not to say anything until the detective was out of site. Lauren closes the door hard once the detective leaves.

"Lauren, what the hell was that all about?"

"Come sit down in the living room and I will fill you in with everything that the detective had to tell me." Blake placed her things down at the door, and headed to the den area to wait for Lauren to fill her in.

From the kitchen, Lauren asked Blake if she wanted a drink, "You know this is my second glass tonight. My first one came when this detective was here.

"I wish you would hurry up out that damn kitchen and fill me in. By the way, have you heard from Terrance? I don't know if I can stand another hospital, Rin." Lauren walked into the den with her glass of wine and she sat on the tip of her cream leather sofa. Before speaking, she took a gulp of her red wine, "Blake, there are some things that you need to know."

Laying out completely on the sofa, with her head tilted back with her eyes closed, "Lauren, just tell me whatever it is."

"The detective was here trying to get information on Terrance."

"Oh Lord, has Terrance gotten himself into trouble," with a sarcastic tone Blake asked Lauren.

"Well, you can kinda say that. The detective thinks Terrance has something to do with the plot to take over your father's company that you got tangled with, which landed you in the hospital."

Blake rose from the sofa quickly and she started trembling. Lauren gave her some of her wine to calm her nerves. "Look, Blake, this is serious if what this detective is saying is true." After drinking all of the wine in the glass, Blake stood up pacing back and forth through the den and kitchen area, trying to run all the thoughts through her head.

"This don't make any damn sense to me, Rin. How would...how could Terrance know about Carmen or be apart of it?"

"Listen, the detective suspects it because....do you remember when Dalia caught Terrance cheating, every time they talked she said she didn't understand or it wasn't what she thought."

"Hell, every man says that when you catch them cheating Lauren."

"Think about this, Why would Dalia catch them, he knew when she was coming home and why Carmen, she works with

284

Dalia. There is something wrong with this picture." Both women in the house thinking hard about Terrance and what he has to do with the plot, "Rin, you think we should do something?"

"No, chill the hell out and let the authorities handle it. Something don't feel right though, so I want you to stay here tonight."

"I thought we were going to the hospital."

"Aww, shit. Terrance called and said the baby didn't make it, they had to operate in order to save Dalia."

Tears began to run down Blake's face as she could only imagine what it would feel like to lose a child, especially one that you have carried for months.

"Did he say there was something we could do?"

"Hell, there isn't much we can do. Her mother is there and Terrance. They took her in to surgery when we were on the phone, so they were going to wait until she got out of surgery."

"Damn, Rin, I feel like there is something I am supposed to be doing, but hell, I can't figure out what it is. Plus, this other news you laying on me. I don't know which way to go. I know I should call my mother and let her know what is going on."

"Now, that was the brightest thing I've heard you say since I started talking."

"I don't know all the details. I just hope you will find out once he talks to you.'

"I don't even know if I am looking forward to it."

"Yes you do. You want to know why your body was torn a part by a bullet over money."

"I feel like I have to relive this all over again. Uh, this is some shit. But, if Terrance really had something to do with this, he doesn't want me to find out about it."

"Stop talking like that. What are you going to do? All of this is speculation, let the man do his job." Blake fixed herself a glass of wine and went back to the sofa to think some more.

"I am really wondering...um...I think this detective has been working on this case for a long time and he didn't tell you everything."

"Maybe he didn't, but you know what…." Beginning to look worried, "Kendall said that he was going to come down here and I haven't heard anything from him in the past couple of hours.

"Where is your laptop? I think I want to check on a few things."

"That doesn't sound like you want to google anything. This sounds like you are doing just what you shouldn't."

"Why are you so worried over nothing?"

"Because I know you and that makes me worry."

"How about you go upstairs and call Kendall. I will be down here doing a little research."

"I don't know if I should go along with this or stop you. It don't matter. I am going to check on Kendall. Why don't you call Jayden and see if she has heard anything else since I last talked to Terrance." Blake barely listening since she is on Lauren's laptop researching her own notions of what happened. Lauren ran upstairs to make a her call, leaving Blake downstairs to her research,

The doorbell rang

"Lauren, the door!" Blake shouted up to Lauren that someone was at the door. Apparently, Lauren couldn't hear the doorbell or she felt that Blake would answer the door. Looking up the stairs to see if Lauren heard her yelling, the doorbell continued to rang, "LAUREN, THE DOOR!" Frustrated that Lauren isn't hearing her, she jumped off of the laptop to answer the door. Without even asking who it is, she opens the door hurriedly, "Hey, sweet….Blake, good to see you, where is Lauren?" It was Kendall at the door. Expecting Lauren to open the door, he had no idea Blake would be there.

"Hey, Kendall, good to see you too, Lauren went upstairs, I have been trying to call her since you starting ringing the doorbell, but she didn't even hear me."

"So, she is upstairs?"

"Yeah, she went up there to call you, because she said she hadn't heard anything from you." Kendall walked into the house, looking up the stairs, thinking Lauren would soon walk down, but she didn't.

"Have you all heard anything else from Terrance? No, not yet, we were going to back to the hospital, but we decided not to."

'I told Lauren to wait for me before she goes."

"Hey, if you get her to go, can I ride with you guys?"

"Yeah, I don't have a problem with that. Let me check on Rin." Kendall started going up the stairs.

"Hey, Kendall, why don't you have a key to the house instead of ringing the doorbell, that is aggravating as hell to answer the door for you. You are not a guest. You might want to work on that?" Blake said, winking her eye, while walking back to the den toward the laptop. Kendall slowly turned around halfway up the staircase listening to Blake. He heard her, but not actually listening to her. He continued up stairs.

"Rin, Rin, where you at?" Out of nowhere, Lauren ran up to Kendall, jumping into his arms, hugging him, "Where have you been and what took you so long?"

"Sweetie, you know Baltimore is not down the street…But, how are you?" He held Lauren around her waist pulling her back so he could look her in her eyes.

"I feel relieved now that you are here."

"Oh really, so what would you say if I picked you up and carried you into the bedroom?" Lauren started blushing when she heard the desire in Kendall's voice to sweep her off her feet.

"I wouldn't say anything at all because I have missed you so much." Looking into his eyes, she felt as if they were in sync with each other at that moment. She grabbed Kendall's head with her right hand pulling him toward her; she leaned in to kiss him passionately. Not holding back, Kendall picked her up and carried her into the master bedroom, placing her on the bed. He stood up straight, looking at her and slowly unbuttoning his shirt. Lauren not giving him time to do so, she grabbed him by his belt buckle, pulling him on top of her, "You love to do that huh?" Kendall whispered to Lauren in her ear.

"Shut up and kiss me".... "Is that all you want me to do?" Lauren began kissing Kendall harder, trying to stop him from saying anything. Kendall jumped up from Lauren, "Wait, we have to close the door first." Kendall walked over to the door closed it and turned the lights off. "Come here woman." Lauren loved when Kendall talked that way to her; it further let her know how much he wanted her.

In the midst of passion, Lauren whispered in Kendall's ear, "I want you here with me everyday, I don't want you to go back to New Jersey. Can you stay here with me?" knowing all the demands his job was placing on him at the time, Kendall wanted to please Lauren in every way he could, "Yes, babe, whatever you want." Lauren didn't know if that was him talking in the heat of the moment or if he really meant that, but was definitely something they would talk about later. Kendall began sucking her nipples slowly and softly while she yearned for more. The more she hollered, the slower he went to make sure he was savoring every moment.

"Put it in", she screamed as Kendall kissed her all over. She pulled Kendall up with both of her hands towards her face, causing his penis to slide right inside of her. Without even thinking of using protection, she wanted Kendall so bad, that it didn't matter to her anymore. She continued moaning louder and louder, "Shh, Blake is downstairs," Kendall uttered to her at a whisper in her hear. "You must really miss me".... "YES!" she screamed out to him. Kendall flipped Lauren over, placing her on top of him, she swirled her hair out of her face.

Kendall admiring his view, began rubbing her ass all over moving her body forward and back as she continued to moan for more, "I'm going to cum," she whispered to him. His response back to her, "That is what I want." She leaned in toward Kendall to kiss him, "So I guess you are going to turn this around," Kendall whispered to her. "Oh yeah," she continued to kiss him, moving down toward his chest. Lauren kissed his nipples licking him from one side to the next. She wanted to please him in every way she should. She could tell he was enjoying himself, "Ahh, gottdamn," were the words he uttered. He rubbed both of his hands through Lauren's hair insisting that she continued. While continuing to go down deeper, Kendall pulled Lauren up, kissing her passionately. "You make me so damn happy," he said to Lauren, which assured her that she was safe in his arms. After passionately, climaxing, they laid beside each other-- Lauren lying in Kendall's arms.

"There are some things I need to catch you up on since the last time I talked to you," she turned to look him in his eyes. "They decided to take the baby from Dalia, there was no way she could make if she continued with the pregnancy, and they couldn't save them both. She went into surgery earlier tonight about a couple of hours.

"Alright, so you ready to go?" Kendall anxiously trying to get out of the bed, wanting to take Lauren to the hospital, but Lauren stopped him.

"Wait, I have more to tell you."

"You can't tell me on the way to the hospital." Kendall already out of the bed and Lauren trying to keep his attention just a little while longer so she can inform in on the other news she had to tell him.

"A detective came to see me tonight here at the house, asking me a lot of questions about the crap that happened with Blake, but what is so damn funny is that this detective thinks that there is something up with Terrance." Kendall stopped putting clothes on and sat on the bed with a profound look.

"Terrance?   Is   that   Dalia's   ex   right?"

"Yea, that really threw me for loop, seriously.   The detective really thinks some dangerous shit went down with Terrance and what happened with Blake." Kendall started shaking his head and Lauren could tell that none of this was sitting well with him. Kendall starting taking really deep breaths that made Lauren feel uneasy about continuing this conversation.

"Damn Lauren, I just knew when I saw this on the news that there was going to be a lot of drama with this, but I didn't think you were going to be involved with it. I don't want you to have anything to do with this."

"What do you mean, Blake is my friend, and I am going to do what it takes to help her."

"What I mean is that I don't feel okay with leaving you here in this big ass house by yourself when I go back to New Jersey."

Kendall walked on the other side of the bed toward Lauren, "Do you know what I would do if something happened to you?"

Trying to calm Kendal down, she grabbed both of his ears, pulling him toward her without an ounce of clothes on, "There is nothing that is going to happen to me, no one is after me. The detective thinks Terrance was in cahoots' with Blake's sister. Don't talk loud Blake is downstairs."

"None of this makes sense to me. I think I should stick around for a little while, just to see what is really going on. I don't care to hear the details, but I care about you."

"Babe, I appreciate that, but what about work."

"Fuck it, I will get my assistant to send me some stuff to work on here and I will post my jobs on the job hunt websites. That will at least have me caught up for a couple of days."

Lauren hugged Kendall for making the sacrifice for her, "Alright, get dressed and let's go to the hospital."

"Where is my robe so I can go downstairs?" Being sarcastic, "Probably in the number two closet that you have," Lauren laughed while throwing her towel at Kendal, which was the closest thing she could get her hands on. She grabbed her robe and went downstairs to tell Blake that they were going to the hospital.

"Hey Rin, I am going to take a shower in your bathroom down here if that is okay?"

"Hey, that is cool; I have to take a shower too. Be ready in about 20 minutes."

"Cool, did Kendall tell you that I wanted to ride with you guys?"

"No, he didn't, but it's cool, I wouldn't leave you here. We can all ride together."

Kendall interceded in the conversation from in Lauren's bedroom, "We can't go no where if you all don't get dressed so we can go, chop, chop, gottdamn."

They all got dressed and left for the hospital.

Chapter 23: On the Prow

"Yes, how can I help you?

"My name is Detective Malik Williams, and I am looking for a Terrance Ross."

"Sir, this is the ICU unit, and only family are allowed back here. I'm sorry, but you will have to leave or try to get in touch with Mr. Ross at a later time."

"Are you trying to interfere with a police investigation?"

"Do you have a warrant for an arrest, if not, then you need to leave. We have very sick patients back here and we don't need anyone to agitate them now please leave."

"Oh, you better believe when I come back, I will have my warrant and there will be nothing you can do about it."

As Detective Williams leaves the ICU unit, his gets a call from his superior, "Yes, sir."

"Williams, give me an update as they on my ass up here."

"Sir, I just interviewed one of the friends and I think I have more reason to believe that Terrance was more than just a part of this."

"Have you interviewed the girlfriend?"

"Can't do that, she is in the hospital, unconscious right now, bad condition, sir, there is no way I can get to her right now."

"My next move is to get to Blake and question her, but I just got turned away from talking to Terrance because he is at the hospital with Dalia."

"Williams is a warrant stopping you from getting to him?"

"Yes, they won't let me near him at the hospital unless I have a warrant."

"Don't worry about it. I will have that to you first thing in the morning. I will get with the precinct down there so they can back you up. Find out all you can Williams, I want this shit wrapped up. You got it?"

"Yes sir."

He disconnects the call.

"It's getting late, I guess I will start fresh tomorrow morning." Detective Williams heads to his hotel room for the evening.

Arriving at the hospital together, Jayden, Brian, Blake, Lauren, and Kendall, they all met up in walking into the hospital. Jayden was the first to greet, since she spotted the others, "Hey, I didn't know you were in town Kendall. It's good to see you. Let me introduce you to Brian."

Brian shook hands with Kendall, "nice to meet you man, heard a lot about you. Good to put a face with the name now, same here." Kendall and Brian embraced each other warmly. The girls cleaved together, leaving the men to fend for themselves.

"Hey Brian, can I talk to you for a minute."

"Sure man, we can go over here next to the waiting room. Jay, I will catch up with you later." Kendall followed Brian's lead to the waiting area, "what's up?"

"Look man, I don't know what all Jayden has told you about what is going on, but I don't want my woman around all of this shit. Now, I am just talking to you man to man. I know that Blake is their best friend, but this shit here is ridiculous."

"Whoa, wait a minute. Man, I really don't know what you talkin' bout right now."

"I'm talking about this mess with Blake and this detective coming by thinking Terrance has something to do with Blake being shot."

"What the fuck! You sure you know what you are talking about?"

"Hell yeah, some detective came to see Lauren asking a bunch of questions about Terrance's involvement with this plot that cause Blake to be shot. The detective don't want her around him, which is the only reason why I am here in the first place. Other than that I would be in Jersey working. But since my woman needed me, I am here." Nodding his heading and listening to Kendall, Brian understood what he was saying and was in on the same page with him.

"Man, I feel you on that but, this is all news to me. You think my girl knew about this shit and didn't tell me."

"I don't even know. This just happened a couple of hours ago though. I just got into town. There is a possibility that she don't know. I just wanted you to be aware. Hell, I thought you knew since you were here with Jayden."

"Shit, I just didn't want her to be out here alone, in the middle of the night and having to drive by herself." Brian running his head trying to grasp everything that Kendall was telling him. "Damn, man you got me thinking cause I really don't know Terrance like that. I try not to get involved with these ladies and the stuff they have going on, you know, but if this is true, that is some bullshit."

"I can't leave here, if I don't think Lauren is going to be safe. I will be at work thinking about this shit."

"Right, right, I understand man. Let me holla at Jayden right quick before they go back there."

"I think they already back there."

"Shit, I don't even give a fuck right now."

While the men were having their conversation, the ladies held hands together going back to the ICU unit of the hospital. They were silent going back because they didn't know what to expect. It was late and they all were exhausted from what all transpired over the day. Lauren looked over at Jayden who was standing on the other side of Blake, "I have something to talk to you about," she whispered to her as they walked up to the nurse's station.

"What, Lauren I didn't hear you, what did you say?"

"Never mind, I will tell you later." Unable hear what Lauren was saying, she just responded back, "Okay."

"We are here to see Dalia Ross; we should be on the list of visitors." Blake was the one to ask. The nurse at the station informed them that Dalia can only have one visitor at a time and the rest of them would have to wait in the waiting area. Blake turned to both of the girls, "Whichever one of you wanted to go was fine with me. I can wait until you are finished."

Out of nowhere comes Brian, "Hey Jay, can I talk to you for a minute?"

"Babe, I am about to go in to see Dalia, what is it?' Lauren jumped in, "Its okay Jay, I will go and then you can go after me, go talk to Brian."

"Thanks Rin, I will be back in a minute."

"Brian, what is up?" Jayden had a no tolerance look on her face.

"I don even feel right with you being here right now. Come with me outside this ICU shit for a minute."

"Babe, why do you have a serious look on your face? What's wrong?"

"I just found out some shit and I don't know if you chose not to tell me of if you didn't know about it, but I need to know." Brian started hitting his chest hoping that he was getting through to Jayden. Knowing that Brian only hits his chest when he is close to getting mad, but trying to talk it out first.

"Okay, calm down, and tell me what you are talking about."

"I'm trying, but the more I think about this shit, I am getting pissed the fuck off." Brian took a deep breath. "I hear this nigga Terrance might have something to do with Blake getting shot and there are cops around questioning muthafuckas and shit about this nigga. What you know about dat?"

"Huh, who told you some shit like that?" Jayden placed her hands on her hips, "did Kendall tell you that?"

"Hell, it don't matter, what you know about that? Plus, the cops don't want people around this cat because he dangerous as shit. Jay, you know how I get down, why you put me in some shit like this babe?"

"Calm down, people are starting to hear you. I don't know nothing about that. Terrance! What the hell does Terrance have to do with anything. Wait, hold the hell up, Lauren was trying to tell me something just now, but she didn't get a chance to and I couldn't really hear her. I wonder if that was it. Anyways, babe, we are here, I need to see Dee, and I need to make sure she is okay...plus, you know I am not scared of the next nigga."

"This some other shit that you don't know nothing about babe, I'm telling you. I can't go back to jail. We got a fucking future I'm trying to build here." Jayden could see the rage in Brian's face.

"Okay, babe I'm just going to see how Dee is and we can go. But, I am going to find this shit." Jayden tries to calm Brian down by rubbing him on his chest, one of the many things he likes for Jayden to do.

'Hey, before you go back there, give me kiss." She kisses him on the cheek first and then he pulls her back for a kiss on the lips.

"Don't give me that half ass kiss on the cheek."

"I'll be right back." Jayden walks off from Brian into the ICU unit when Kendall walks up, "I wish they would tell us something, gottdamn."

"Man after the shit you just told me, I just want to get the fuck outta here and wrap my baby in my arms tonight, ya feel me?"

"Yeah, man I do."

On the inside of the ICU waiting room was Deborah, Dalia's mother, Terrance, and the girls. Deborah greeted the girls with hugs and kisses. The girls were a little hesitant to hug and embrace Terrance as they were now suspicious to the information they recently found out about. They tried their best to be cordial and supportive, blaming their awkwardness on their concern for Dalia.

"How did the surgery go?" Jayden asked Deborah and Terrance.

"The doctor said everything was smooth, but that just means, I lost a daughter." Terrance informed them.

"Aww, Dee had a little girl," Lauren said. Terrance I know this is hard for you.

"I just have so many regrets right now. I want her to wake up and be okay so I can tell her how much I love her. There is so much I need to tell her, but she can't hear me right now. Lauren, did you get a chance to see her?"

"Well, I didn't get a chance to physically go in because the doctor was in and they were changing her bedding and stuff, so I said I would come back." Lauren trying to change the subject because she was not in the mood to her Terrance excuses now wasn't the time. Blake seemed more interested in what he had to say out of them all.

The nurse entered the room, "Hi, you all are family of Mrs. Ross?"

"Yes, we are," Lauren answered.

"I'm sorry, but the doctor has requested that Mrs. Ross not have any more visitors tonight. Her blood pressure is starting to rise and they will be monitoring her all night."

They all rose to their feet, "but nurse, I am her husband, I need to be in there."

"I'm sorry, per the request of Dr. Cole, she can't have anymore visitors."

"Okay, thank you."

"Well, I guess we won't get to see her". Blake blurted out.

"Mrs. Deborah, where are you staying, did you get a chance to get that settled."

Deborah sat up in her chair, looking around, "no dear, I hadn't thought about it at all."

"You can stay with me. I am all alone in my house and I can bring you back here in the morning," Blake stated.

"Okay, thank you so much, that is so nice of you. You have been through so much lately; I didn't think you wanted to be bothered."

Lauren checking out Terrance's reaction, "Yes, ma'am I have, but Dalia needs me right now. I know she was right there when I was in the hospital and I am doing the same for her." Blake responded back to Deborah.

"Is everyone ready to go, because it is getting late?" Jayden said after looking at her watch.

"I appreciate you all for coming. Dalia loves y'all and I can see why," Terrance said while they were all preparing to leave.

"We will always be by Dalia's side," Jayden responded to Terrance while Blake and Lauren pretended as if they didn't hear.

Walking out of the ICU unit, the girls caught up with Brian and Kendall. Jayden and Lauren introduced Brian and Kendall to

Deborah, while Terrance went ahead outside of the hospital. After staying to the hospital majority of the day, he was exhausted and drained. Deborah looked over at Jayden, "How is your mother, I haven't seen her in a long time?"

"She is fine, just being Jackie that is all I can say. My brother is here, he just got in today. I think he is staying at my mothers."

"I will have to call her tomorrow; I know it is too late to call her tonight."

"And how is your father, I haven't seen him in a long time."

"He is good, him and his wife."

"Yeah, I did forget that he got married to uh….Karen."

"Yeah, that is her, they are doing great," Jayden being just a slight sarcastic.

"Mrs. Deborah, we all came here together, so we are going to my house first, that is where Blake's car is and then you all will leave from my house." Lauren instructed them.

"See you late, I'll call you tomorrow Jay, good to see you Brian," Blake said to them as they were getting in the car.

'Okay, drive safe, talk to you tomorrow." Jayden waved good bye to them as she got on the passenger side of Brian's car.

While in his car, Terrance makes a phone call. He leaves a message on a voice mail, "You need to call me. This shit is ridiculous. Dalia's friends are acting a little weird towards me and I know they have figured something out. I never wanted anything to do with this shit, so you better figure something the fuck out now!"

Chapter 24: The Grown Ups

Knock, knock, knock!!!

"Who in the world could it be this late?" Blake, barely seeing where she was walking, grabbed her robe running downstairs to answer the door. "Don't worry Mrs. Deborah, I got it, I don't know who it could be this late. Go back to bed."

"Okay, scream if need me." Deborah walked back to the guest suite, which was on the first floor.

Blake looked out the peep hole and she recognized the face, but she couldn't believe who it was at her door. She opened the door, "Boy, what are you doing here?"

"Man, I was out drinking on this side of town and I thought about, damn, Blake lives over here and I wanted to stop by and say hello."

"Jordan, it is two o'clock in the morning." Jordan leaned, falling on Blake.

"Boy, you are in no shape to drive. What are you doing? Are you trying to mess up your image?" Jordan starting eyeing Blake up from top to bottom, admiring the red lingerie she was wearing with the satin floral robe to match.

"Damn, you looking so gottdamn good right now."

"Boy, shut up and come inside before my neighbors see you."

"You ain't got no damn neighbors, this damn house is sitting on an acre, quit tripping."

"I should call your sister." Jordan grabbed her by the arm, "Naw, don't do that." He picks Blake up, closes the door with his foot, places her on the countertop of her kitchen and began kissing her all over her neck, before she was able to think twice.

"Jordan, what are you doing? I can't do this." Jordan not stopping to think about what Blake is saying, Blake grabbed the back of Jordan's head, "You should really stop before we do something that I can't deal with in the morning."

Jordan pushed Blake further back on the counter, kissing her passionately, "tell me you don't want it." He whispered in her hear. "When was the last time you had a man to give it to you like this."

Blake stopped and looked at Jordan in his eyes, "what!"

"Can we just have this night, fuck everything else?"

"Jordan, it's not that simple. I am too grown to make a mistake like this. You are my best friend's little brother."

"I am the same little brother that wanted you when you graduated from college and asked you out on a date."

"You were young back then." Jordan slid his shirt off over his head so that Blake could admire his athletically build. "Jordan, I can't…"

"You can't have me or you can't be with me, which one is it?"

"This is all crazy! You in my house at two in the morning and you are drunk. I think you should just stay in the guest room and in the morning, we can act like this didn't happen."

"Is that what you want?" For a minute, it appeared as if Jordan wasn't really drunk at all. He was focused, he stood up straight, and he seemed more determined than ever.

"Jordan, put me down, if you feel the same way in the morning, then we can talk."

"So, you turning me down," as he picked her up to take her off the counter.

"No, I am postponing you, there is a difference. I will show you to the guest room upstairs. You can sleep there until you wear off the liquor." With no comment, Jordan picked his shirt up and followed Blake upstairs. Still determined to win Blake over, he figured he would just follow her and give her what she wanted in the time being.

"Alright, it is one of the smaller rooms, but it will do. Do I need to lock this door so you won't get second thoughts?" Blake still couldn't get a word out of Jordan. Blake couldn't even get her thoughts together. Not for a moment, did she think of Jordan that way, but apparently, he did, wanting to get out of that room, so quick, Blake eased out of the room since Jordan stopped talking.

"Oh, my God, I can't believe this shit and he can kiss. Not Jayden's little brother. No, this is so wrong in so many ways. Jayden is going to hate me. She loves Jordan; I can't ever tell her this shit. Do you think this dude is serious? He can't be. Maybe when he wakes up tomorrow, he won't remember what happened". Blake kept telling herself these things over and over while back in her room. She slipped out of her robe, trying to return to sleep, under the circumstances.

"Damn, I wanted my life back, but not like this. Oh my goodness, he really got me wet. Has it been that long since I got some that Jayden's little brother got me like that? Oh, Lord, whew, tomorrow, it will be like this didn't happen."

Jordan, on the other hand, was in the guest room, knowing that he was in no shape to drive home, but he took the time to think. He thought about the conversation he had earlier that day with Brian and his friends and wondered what kind of woman would make you change your ways like that. He couldn't get the thought out of his head. Of course back at school, he only succumbed himself to very young, naive girls because they stroked his ego, but there was something about Blake that really caught his attention. He didn't know if it was the fact that he didn't conquer her a long time ago or that he really had feelings for her. Either way it went, he made a move on his sister's best friend, which really didn't mean anything to him because he felt that it wasn't like he was hurting her, he just happened to have feelings for her friend.

In his opinion, his sister shouldn't be mad, because if it is her friend, then she is good people, so there shouldn't be a problem. Of course, he knew that didn't work with women like it did with men, but it was worth a try. Not being able to go to sleep in the guest room, Jordan had the opportunity to think about what he was really trying to do instead of acting off his emotions, which was a first for him. "Man, I can't take this shit anymore....naw, I am going to chill and think about this shit, but damn, I am feeling her."

Part II

Lying in the bed together after making love, Brian began asking Jayden about the wedding plans. "Jay, have you made anymore plans on the wedding?" Groaning to turn over, "Since the mess with my parents, then with Dalia, I haven't done anything." Brian grabbed Jayden's naked body to kiss her, "Do you want to just do something small and then invite everyone to a reception since we have a lot going on?" Jayden wasn't expecting Brian to say that, but the thought never ran across her mind. "Well, I thought we wanted to have something where our family and friends could be a part and celebrate with us."

"You can't have all of your friends there when one of your best friends is lying in a hospital bed fighting for her life."

"Poor Dalia...she had been acting so fucking weird lately and she has popping off at all of us, I just didn't know who the fuck she as anymore." Brian listening attentively to Jayden, "What, is something wrong, why you looking at me like that?"

"Nothing, I am just admiring you, that's it."

"But, I am talking about something and your mind is elsewhere."

"Naw, its right here, I just want you to be my wife. I don't care about the bullshit, I just want you to be mine." Jayden starting blushing, it seemed the closer the got to walking down the aisle, Brian started to get more in touch with his feelings, which was something she was getting used to. Jayden just sat there for a minute, thinking, not knowing what to say at that moment, she knew she wanted her friends and family to be there most of all and she couldn't do it with Dalia being in the hospital.

"I have so much left to do though."

"You would have your mother to help you if you just talk to her."

"Oh, you wanna bring that conversation up again."

"Quit tripping, your parents are grown, babe. It don't matter what they do, neither one of them did something to outright hurt you. Now, you starting to act like those spoil rich people. Hell, is Blake rubbing off on you?"

"Shut, the hell up! First of all, you know how I feel about married people dipping. Second, my mother was the one who instilled it in me. Third, Jordan fucking knows and not me. What kind of shit is that?"

"It's fucking logic, gotdammit. Do you tell your parents everything we do? Alright, chill out about it. You not talking to them   is   crazy."

"I talk to them but it has to be very important, no small talk. I try not to talk to them so I won't be disrespectful. You know my mother isn't having that."

"I know she isn't. So what you gonna do, I love Ms. Jackie and I miss her from coming around, especially when she bake and shit. Oh yeah!!!"

"That is what this is all about; you just want some damn baked goods. Call her; she will make you whatever you want."

"Naw, I want you to call her and tell her to make me whatever I want," Brian trying to sound firm.

"You make me sick." Jayden frowned her face because she knew Brian won that fight, which wasn't too often that he did.

"Yeah, I may call her tomorrow," Jayden not sounding too sure about calling her mother.

"You know I am going to ask you tomorrow if you call her. You know good and damn well you miss your mother especially with planning the wedding. This is foolish. Why does it matter who your mother sleeps and when she does it....at least it's your father....actually it's kind of funny...old people getting' it in." Jayden became furious seeing how Brian was starting to take this for a joke.

"Have you forgotten that my father is married? Even though I can't stand that Karen, she is still married to my father." Before she was able to continue, Brian put his index finger on Jayden's lips to close her mouth.

"Shh, you being judgmental.....and plus you turning me on by getting upset." Brian started nibbling on Jayden's ears and neck until she couldn't help but to be drawn in by his soft, juicy lips. "I'm tired of talking. Lately, I haven't been able to spend time with you," as he continued to kiss on her.

"I know, I'm sorry babe," which was all she could say under the circumstances. She grabbed the back of his head and pulled him up, making his lips touch hers. From the softness of his lips, she couldn't resist spreading her legs. Brian was the only man that could take her to another high she never felt before each time and he knew it. He began licking her all over, sucking her nipples until she moaned louder and louder. She rubbed his back until her nails started digging deep into his skin. Of course, he loved every minute of it. He continued down to her thighs, sucking them individually and then licking her back up to her nipples.

He flipped her around, turning her on his stomach with her head leaning into the pillow as he throbbed inside of her until she yearned for more. He eased in slowly until he came to a rhythm and starting speeding up based on her moans. He grabbed each cheek and pulled them in as he reached deeper inside of her. Grabbing the headboard, Jayden was climaxing like never before. Brian took a moment to pull out, which gave Jayden an opportunity to take control of the situation. She turned over quickly, and she reached up to grab him, pulling by his ears so that she could kiss him passionately. She could feel his knees weaken from her kiss. Continuing to kiss him, she eased on top of him.

She raised her knees up to his chest, she felt every bit of his penis inside of her. She began to grind harder and harder, until she knew he was inside of her completely. She knew then he couldn't hold back. He started rubbing her breasts, in strokes and as gentle as possible. Trying to stay focused, Jayden couldn't help herself, but she wanted Brian to get all the pleasure. The harder she grind, the harder he rubbed her ass, then began pulling her backward and forward, trying to control the situation. Slowly, Jayden pulled his dick from out of her and he grasped for air. She moved slowly down past his navel reaching his pubic area. She placed her right hand on his dick and began stroking it slowly. She licked the tip of it until he couldn't talk anymore. She then began stroking his dick with her tongue slowly putting it fully in her mouth. At this point, he couldn't help himself, and she knew it.

She started going faster and faster, taking her left hand to stroke while she was deep throating it. Before she knew, he climaxed everywhere, but she thought she had him until he pulled her up and fucked the shit of her until she climaxed as well. She said in her head, *"fuck"*, but it was still good as hell to her. He rolled over so she could lay on top of him for the night and they fell asleep.

Chapter 25: Good Morning

Bang, Bang, Bang. There are knocks on the door, hard knocks.
"Who in the fuck is that at my door so early in the morning?"
"This is Detective Malik Williams; I am here to see a Terrance Ross."

Terrance who was on the inside trying to get his mind together opened the door and is ambushed. "Lie down on the floor, put your hands behind your back." Facing the ground, "Man, what the hell is this for, what did I do?"

"Oh, you will find out." Detective Williams read Terrance his Miranda rights as he agreed to them. They escorted him out of the apartment into the back of the patrol car. Along with Detective Williams were two other cops accompanying him just in case Terrance decided run.

At the station, they placed Terrance in a cold, dark room until someone came to question him. Entered Detective Williams, being backed by the local police there, with a file in his hand, thinking of how he was going to handle this situation with Terrance. His superiors are on his case about closing this case, and he wasn't going to let Terrance stand in the way of that. Even if Terrance wasn't to blame for this, he was the key to it all and he was determined to get it from him.

"Good morning Mr. Ross, do you know why you were arrested?" Terrance with the meanest mug ever, didn't even bother to look at the detective when he asked him the question. "Well, I am going to tell you anyway." Detective Williams placed the manila folder he had on the table and he took out the photos that he had of Terrance and Carmen in different places. Terrance turned his head at the first glance of the pictures. "I don't know where you got those pictures from."

305

"I bet you don't. My question is, are you responsible for Blake Lowry being shot in her family's business?"

"What! Man, are you serious? Is this why you have me down here? Naw, hell naw, I want my lawyer now!"

"Of course Mr. Ross, but this is not going to get you out of this." Detective Williams walked out of the room, leaving the pictures on the desk for Terrance to continue to see. When Detective Williams walked out in the station, he knew it was going to be hard, but the captain at this precinct was assisting him with everything he needed, "Malik, how is your suspect holding up?"

"Uh, he is playing innocent right now and he's hollering for his lawyer."

"Hey, Malik, me and your captain go way back so I want everything to go smoothly with this. If you can break this case, its going to do wonders for your career." The captain patted Malik on the back. "Your captain speaks great things about you, so make him happy."

"Hey, anyone got a phone this guy can use to call his lawyer?" Detective Williams took a phone to Terrance so he could get representation, but while in the room, Detective Williams tried to persuade Terrance that if he could tell wanted he wanted to know he could walk out the police station a free man.

"Man, I don't have nothing to say to you."

"You sure about that, we have evidence that proves you had the motive and opportunity to manipulate this situation to make it appear that you were the one who put Carmen up to this. You were sleeping with this woman in the house you shared with your girlfriend. That is not going in your favor, son."

While dialing the number, Terrance stopped and put the phone down. "What do you mean you have motive? That bitch set me up!"

"Oh, now we are getting somewhere. How did she set you up?"

"Man, you are going to turn this all around on me and I don't want to talk to you anymore."

306

"If you can convince me that you were manipulated in this situation, we can work something out, you have my word." Detective Williams appeared to be sincere to Terrance. He just wanted to solve this case, so he could have this under his belt.

"Wait, let me get a tape recorder to document your statement." Terrance hesitated wondering if he was making the right decision. He knew had to think about Dalia before he could do anything else. All he wanted right now was for her to recover and forget about everything that had happened so far. Detective Williams returned to the room and he could see the doubt on Terrance's face.

"Before we get started, I want to say this, there are too many brothers getting caught in stuff like this and I don't want you to go down for something you didn't have nothing to do with or caught up with, you see where I am going with this. If you tell me the truth, I will do my best to help you and your wife." Terrance looked Detective Williams in his eyes wondering if he could really trust him. Not really knowing what Terrance was going to tell him or confess to, he wanted to open the door to the possibility that he could tell him the truth so that he wouldn't make his job that much harder, because if he had to find out the truth, it wasn't going to be a pretty picture. Terrance stood up, rubbing his head, "Aww, you promise you can help me?" "I will try my best, are you ready to begin?"

"When I was a little boy, I always looked up to my father and he did some things that I learned about later in life." He was like my role model, but he made some bad choices and that caused him everything." Looking confused, Detective Williams didn't really know where this was going, but he continued to listen. "He had a friend, who he did everything with and when I say everything, I mean everything. They went to the same college and both aspired to be lawyers. Unfortunately, the friend couldn't pass the bar and my father was determined to help his friend so he took the test for him. Along with him taking the test for him he paid some people take some things off his friends' record. Apparently, my father knew the right people." "Keep going," Detective Williams added.

"Somehow, it came out that my father took the test for his friend, he got into a lot of trouble, plus they figured he used his connections to cover up some other things and instead of this friend telling the truth, he lied and blamed it all on my father, so the friend went on to open this big law firm and my father had to do hard time. He ended up taking the wrap for all the crimes his friend committed, do you see where I am going with this..." "It sounds to me like you are wasting my time." Detective Williams didn't see the connection between the story Terrance was telling and the case. Terrance continued with his story, "Let me finish first."

"When Carmen came to my doorstop last year, she knew about all of this and she offered me a deal to help her."

"Wait a damn minute; are you trying to say that your father's friend is Bernard Lowry?"

"Yes, and he let my father take the fall for it all and he never once tried to help him. So, when Carmen said that she had a way for me to get back at him, I just took her up on the offer. It was never a part of the plan to shoot Blake or hurt her mother. We had been meeting a couple of times, but we never discussed that."

"C'mon Mr. Ross, are you expecting me to believe that you knew nothing about this at all?"

"I knew that she was angry for being left out and tossed aside. I didn't know the bad blood between Blair and Blake, Dalia never talked about none of that. I didn't even know Carmen was married." Detective Williams rubbed his face in dismay. "We have to connect the dots here. When Dalia walked into the house and caught you guys in bed together..."

"She drugged me with something, next thing I knew, my baby was walking in the house catching me in bed with this woman.'

"Terrance, if you knew this woman was Blake's sister, why didn't you tell Dalia?"

"They would have blown my plan."

"And exactly, what was your plan? My plan was to help take over the company."

"Sounds like you were up to something illegal with Carmen from the start."

"I wanted to find evidence to get my father out of jail and make him hurt for what he did to my family."

"This man is dead; he died from a heart attack. Do you know what you got yourself into messing with this woman? First, you are saying that Bernard Lowry faked his licensure, committed crimes before becoming a lawyer, and then his outside child came to you because she knew all about it and you teamed up with her to get the company from him. Do you not realize that the only people to get hurt from this was his wife and daughters?" Terrance held his hands up to his face, rubbing his head.

"I didn't think about that at the time. I just wanted revenge. I wanted to be able to do something for my father, now he can't ever practice law. That man is not all he hyped his family and those people in New Jersey to believe."

Detective Williams turned off the recorder, "Do you know you gave this woman ammo to go after Blake?"

"Detective, if I knew all of this, do you think I would have let my wife go to Jersey or don't you think I would have been there? I was with Brian, Jayden's fiancé' the day all of this happened and prior to that I was at work."

"Just by saying that young man, you might have saved yourself. We have to makes sure that Brian can corroborate your story."

"Off the record, let me tell you something, I feel your pain, but you can't get revenge off of people like that. Your wife is in the hospital and you put her in harm's way and her girlfriends. You were out of your league with this one and you didn't even know it. In order to have you scot free, you would have to testify to this in court when the trial comes up for Carmen and her husband. I really hope you are telling me the truth, if not; I will be back for you."

"Wait, where are you going? I have to file charges on my real criminals."

"Detective, do you think once my wife wakes up that she is going to forgive me?" Detective Williams turned around facing Terrance and closed the door. "Well, she is your wife, but she is going to feel betrayed that you couldn't confide in her from the beginning, plus, you lied to her over and over about this. Once I turn all this evidence and your statement over, we have to make sure that you don't have any other charges to worry about." Terrance looked stunned for a minute.

"You told me that if I told you the truth I wouldn't have to worry   about   that."

"No, you wouldn't. That still doesn't mean the DA won't try to prosecute. You should be fine for now. Go to the hospital, see your wife, and be there for her. I will be in touch if I need you." Detective Williams left the station with a couple of other to charge Carmen and her husband, Michael for attempted murder of Blake and conspiracy charges. Even though the duo couple was previously arrested, they were able to get out on bail, but with the new profound evidence that Detective Williams had, there was no way there were getting out now. He also figured that Terrance would catch his own hell when the Blake and his wife found out his role in the plot. Since Blair was nowhere to be found and they were still searching for her, he knew he could somehow get the answers out of Carmen and her husband. There was no way she was going to take the wrap for all the charges alone when she knew Blair played a part in it too. It was like she dropped off the face of the earth after she left the hospital from visiting Blair once Barbara told her to leave. Since then, no one has seen or heard from her, which was not too shocking.

He also thought about what all Terrance was telling him and how it somehow made sense to him. He schemed out what Carmen could have been thinking trying to get Terrance on board with her and she turned around to double cross him in the end. Detective Williams was able to steal a minute to check out Terrance's alibi to make sure that he was at work when he said he was at the time of the shooting and that he actually was with Brian. So fortunate for Terrance, there were surveillance cameras at the gas station that he and Brian stopped to on the way to his house after getting off from work that showed him being there at the appointed times. There was always something in the back of Detective Williams head about Bernard Lowry. Everyone had nothing but good things to say about him, like he never did any wrong. He knew there was more to that story and Terrance sealed the deal where those suspicions were concerned.

But, there was still something not adding up with Michael. How could he come from such a good background right under his grandfather and turn to something like this, which still puzzled Detective Williams. Maybe he was the bad seed the family was trying to cover up or he fooled his family too. The only thing is that since the weapon was found and his prints along with Carmen's prints were on the gun, this case is air tight. Since Terrance profoundly had nothing to do with the incident at the law firm, he sure attributed to the whole plot taking place. Deep down, Detective Williams knew Terrance wasn't really the culprit he was looking for, but he led him to the answers he wanted and needed. He needed to have a solid case against Carmen and Michael. Since Terrance is testifying, he was guaranteed they would do time for it. All he had to prove was motive and the opportunity to strike and he found it all.

With a little more researching and investigating, Detective Williams was able to find out how Blake met Michael, how he persuaded her and that she talked to him when she found out her father died. He was being a gentleman to her, even inviting their companies to do business together. All along, Blake didn't know what danger she was putting herself in. He also found out that Blair and Blake went on the search together trying to find out who their long lost sister was. But, Blair didn't share with Blake that she ended up meeting with her and those two ended up sharing notes. He found out that Blair was very bitter about many things from her childhood up until now. She had been doing some underhanded dealings with the company where the father was tempted to throw her out of the firm before he died. Unfortunately, the rest of the family didn't know about it, because the old man died before he could put everything into play. Blair started taking in clients that her father would turn away as it would have been bad publicity for the high profile firm, but she had a point to prove and that as proving she was a better lawyer than her father. Little did she know, before Bernard died, he knew all about his daughters plan he wanted her out. For some odd reason, he died of a heart attack, even though he was a perfectly healthy man.

Blair only felt that her biggest problem now was Barbara, her mother, who had high expectations for Blake and Blair, but since Blake showed a different interest and worked for a different company, she didn't feel the wrath that Blair did. Even though Blair was far from the law profession, she was still held at high standards for what she did and how she conducted herself. Apparently, Carmen from a distance was very jealous at the attention these girls got and she wanted a part of the action. But, Carmen didn't seem that interested until Bernard died and I guess she really saw what her father was worth. The logic of it all is that it would be easy to take over when Barbara is not hands on with the company, Blake lives in another state where her job is very demanding and Blair being bitter.

When Detective Williams arrived at a house far outside of Baltimore to a small townhouse where Carmen and her husband had been staying until things cooled down, the bust him and arrest both of them. They were questioned, booked and charged with several crimes including attempted murder. As Detective Williams felt every accomplished to tell his partner and his superiors that he was able to solve a case and arrest the criminals, there was no thing lingering over his head, where is Blair? Since Barbara threw her out of the hospital the day Blake was shot, no one had heard or seen from her. There were rumors that she changed her identity, and had a face lift so that she was unrecognizable. Unfortunately, for her sister Blake, she didn't know if her sister would later come back to get her or if she would ever surfaced. This one simple piece of the puzzle lingered, how was she able to escape the cops at the scene and flee the country without any seeing, hearing, or noticing her anywhere. Detective Williams wrote these notes in the file and journal he kept on every case before taking it to records to be filed.

He did need a testimony from Blake once the trial began, but there was enough evidence to have a solid case between the two, plus he didn't want to bother Blake since she was trying to comfort her friend Dalia. It just seemed respectable, plus he didn't mind calling Barbara again and telling her the good news once he got back to town. There wasn't too much damage Detective Williams could do in that town since he didn't have jurisdiction there and he really didn't know how they operated. He was glad that he didn't have to release a snap from his holster at all. His captain would have been upset about that. He figured at this point, whatever else he needed to do with this case, he could finish up in New Jersey.

Chapter 26 Just Getting By

"Good Morning, did you sleep okay last night," Blake walked into her kitchen while Deborah walked out of her guest room approaching the kitchen. "Good Morning, I guess I slept as best as I could under the circumstance." Tumbling down the stairs came Jordan, pulling his shirt over his head, "Good Morning Mrs. Little, how you doing?" As shocked as Deborah was, she was still excited to see Jordan. She hadn't seen him since he was much younger and yet he still managed to look just like his father.

"I am doing good. I didn't know you were here." Blake chimed in explaining how Jordan got there, "yeah, he came by last night after you left, he had way too many drinks last night, didn't you." Jordan walked out of the kitchen on a search for his keys, "Yeah, I had a rough night last night and this was the closest place for me to crash" Deborah somehow believed the story. When Jordan found his keys on the counter near the door, he grabbed them quickly heading for the door. "Excuse me Mrs. Deborah," Blake ran toward the door trying to stop Jordan, she catches the door when he opened it. "So you are just going to leave without saying anything?" He turned around, "What do you want me to say?"

"I don't know, but I didn't expect you to leave like this. So, you don't have anything to say after last night."

"Last night! You wanna talk about fuckin' last night."

"Keep your voice down, Mrs. Deborah can hear you?" Blake pulled the door behind her so that their conversation couldn't be heard.

"Jordan, I think you were a little too drunk to know what you were doing last night."

"You think I don't know what I was doing? I know what I was doing. You're going to stand here and tell me that you don't have any feelings for me."

"Jordan, I see you like a little brother, and you are my best friend's little brother. I can't have any kind of relationship with you like that." Jordan took a step closer into Blake's personal space, "Look at me and tell me you didn't like me touching your ass or kissing your nipples." Blake was starting to feel uncomfortable, but very attractive to Jordan at the same time.

"I can't talk about this anymore. Its time for you to go," Blake took a step back. Jordan just walked off without saying anything back. Blake took a minute to regroup outside before she walked back into the house.

"So, do you want to go out for breakfast or do you want to have something here at the house." Without instantly responding back, Deborah took a look at Blake, "I didn't know the two of you are dating?" How does Jayden feel about that?" As shocked as she was, she outright denied the accusation. "Jordan and I are not dating, he only came by last night because he had too many drinks and he shouldn't have been driving."

"Is that what you young people call it nowadays?"

"No, its not, I don't have any feelings for him and we are not dating."

"Did you notice how that man looked at you this morning? A man doesn't look at a woman like that unless he loves her."

"Love, Jordan Miller doesn't know anything about love. He is a young, college football player that is about to enter the pros, his mind is far from looking for love."

"Now, you have told me everything about Jordan and his feelings, now tell me about yours." Blake looked at Deborah and just smirked, shaking her head.

"Mrs. Deborah, you are a mess. I don't feel anything for him. I looked at him like he is a little brother, that's all."

"He is Jayden's little brother, not yours. You are a woman and you have a right to have feelings for a man. Answer this for me, how long has it been since you have been involved with a man?" Blake took a deep breath and thought about her last time being with a man emotionally and physically.

"Wow, I can't even remember. I have been so wrapped up in other things that I didn't even think about it."

"Oh, you have thought about it, you just don't want to face reality. You are a young woman and you should find some time to open up to a nice young man that is worth your time."

"I guess you are right, but I can't focus on that right now. I have my best friend fighting for her life, me getting my life back, and my career." Deborah changed the subject as she learned from experience that it's best to let go of situations when they think they know what is best.

"I think I can whip up something here for us to eat for breakfast. We don't have to go out. Let me see what you have here..." Deborah went through the cabinets searching for ingredients.

"I'm going to call Jayden and Lauren to see when they are going to the hospital. I will be right back or just call when breakfast is ready." Deborah just shook her head, smiling at Blake of how she avoided the conversation they just had. Blake ran upstairs with her cell phone in her hand. When she got upstairs, she saw the note on her bed with her name addressed on it. She had a feeling that it was from Jordan, but she didn't want to confirm it by opening the letter. She pushed the letter aside and began to call Jayden and Lauren.

Two blocks over were Lauren and Kendall just waking up for the day. Kendall rolled over away from Lauren thinking about the ring he bought for Lauren and how he left it in New Jersey. He was beginning to beat himself up for leaving it. He wanted to be close to Lauren in every way, and he knew marrying her would seal the deal. Lauren was getting out of the bed, reaching for her robe, and getting started with her Sunday morning regime; most people thought Lauren's tight schedule was ridiculous, but Kendall thought just the opposite.

"Hey sweetheart, what time are you going to the hospital?

"Well, since I didn't get a chance to do my yoga this week, I have to do that first this morning. Then, I need to check my planner and make some phone calls." Kendall sat up in the bed while Lauren was talking.

"Sweetie, I thought we would go and get some breakfast, come back upstairs make love and then we would take a shower together, get dressed and then head to the hospital." Concentrating on finding her yoga clothes, Lauren barely paid attention to Kendall. "Ken, I am sorry, I need to get my yoga in and make some phone calls. It won't take me long, babe." Lauren walked over the Kendall and kissed him on the cheek to reassure him.

"Alright, if you say so, I guess I can go get my laptop from downstairs and post some jobs."

"Great, you do that." Lauren was happy Kendall wasn't pushing her to change her plans.

While Lauren was tying her hair up, she noticed her phone ringing it was Blake.

"Hey Blake, what's up?"

"Hey, I wanted to know when you were heading to the hospital today."

"Uh, first I have to do my yoga, and then make some phone calls and then I would be ready to head there."

"When are you going there?"

"Mrs. Deborah is making breakfast for us and after that, we are going to get dress and head there."

"Blake, you making this woman cook for you when her daughter is in the hospital fighting for her life."

"No, I am not. I asked her if she wanted to stay here or if she wanted to go out. It was her idea to stay here and cook."

"Lord Jesus, well anyway, did you talk to Jayden?"

"No, she was next on the list to call. I just ended up dialing you first."

"Hot damn, I almost feel special." Lauren still in the mirror fiddling with her hair..."You aren't special, heffa. Let me call Jayden and she what she is doing."

"Cool, I will call you when I am on the way there."

"Okay, tell Kendall I said hello."

"I will, take you later."

When Lauren hung up the phone, she left out of the bathroom running down stairs to her den area with her towel in her hand. She walked pass Kendall in her living room, who was on his laptop typing away.

"Any luck with finding some people?" Kendall didn't bother looking up, he just continued to type.

"I haven't checked it yet. I am trying to finish posting all the jobs first before I do that."

"Ken, don't you have an assistant for that?"

"Yeah, I do, but I need to make sure that the qualifications are listed right so it will screen out those who are applying, but don't qualify. Once we have the qualified applicants, I will give it to my assistant to schedule interviews."

"Seems like you have it all figured out, so I am going to head to the den for my workout."

"Can I get a workout when you are done?" Lauren laughed, while shaking her head, "We will just have to see."

On the other side of town at Brian's place, Jayden was in the kitchen cooking breakfast while Brian was in the shower. Jayden decided to call her mother just as Brian and she talked about the night before.

"Hello."

"Hey, ma, how are you doing?"

"I am good, how is Dalia? I have been wondering how everything has been with her?"

"Everything is…I don't even know where to begin. They couldn't save her and the baby so, they took the baby. It was a little girl and now we are just waiting to see how she recovers or if she ever will."

"Oh my goodness, I can only imagine how you guys feel and Deborah, by the way, where is she? I was just telling your brother yesterday that she could stay with me."

"Well, you don't have to do that. She got in yesterday afternoon and she is staying with Blake." Jayden heard noise in the background and she assumed it was her brother.

"Is that Jordan? Tell him I am sorry, I didn't get a chance to spend time with him, but I have been busy." There was a pause

318

on Jackie's end because the voice that Jayden was hearing was not Jordan's.

"Jordan isn't here right now, but I will give him the message."

"Well, if that isn't Jordan, who is that in the background?"

"It's your father?"

"Daddy? So, y'all still playing this game? Okay, then..? Jackie chimed in to explain to her daughter.

"Jayden Miller, listen to me young lady, you won't have this attitude with me. I am your mother and I will come over there and smack the taste out of your mouth. Do I ever say anything about what you do with Brian?"

"Ma, Brian is not legally married to another woman."

"That is not the point, I don't intrude with your business with him and I expect you to do the same with me."

"I don't get this at all. If Daddy wants you so bad, then why is he still married to Karen? He is playing both sides of the fence and you know it."

"Since you are so holier than thou, I would love to see you handle your situations with Brian."

"Why does something have to be wrong with Brian and me for you to see that it is wrong for you to be sleeping with a married man?"

"I am not going to tell you again to watch your tone.

"I know, that is why I would rather not talk to you or him about it. Tell my brother to call me and I will talk to you later."

"Jayden, just wait until you have your own children and then I want to see how well you deal with them judging your life."

"Okay, take care." Jayden disconnects the call with her mother, not even making amends like she and Brian talked about the night before. Brian overheard Jayden's voice in the shower and he wandered who she was talking to.

"Mmm, Mmm, it smells good in here." Brian didn't get any type of response out of Jayden.

"I said, Mmm, Mmm, it smells good in here." He still didn't get any response. "Jay, do you here me?"

"What, naw I didn't, what did you say?"

"I said it smells good in here."

"Oh, thank you." Jayden's mind was a million miles away. She couldn't get over her conversation with her mother. She didn't like disagreeing with her because they were always so close, but her mother did have her thinking; whether she was being judgmental or was it a personal thing she had with her mother and father hooking up.

"I heard you on the phone while I was in the shower. You sound like you were yelling, who were you talking to?"

"My mother," she responded as she picked the pancakes up with the spatula placing them on the serving plate.

"Okay, how did it go?" before he could get the question out, Jayden jumped down his throat as if she was blaming him for the conversation.

"I don't know why you wanted me to talk to her. I tried to get a nice conversation with her and then out of no where I hear good ole James Miller in the background." While taking a seat at the counter, sitting on the stool, he picked up a piece of bacon and put it in his mouth, "Oh, shit." Then, he laughed hysterically.

"What is so damn funny?"

"Your parents are acting like they are teenagers and its funny as shit to me, sorry, but it's funny."

"There is nothing funny about my mother sleeping with a married man and her thinking everything is okay."

The phone rings and it is Blake. With an attitude, Jayden answered the phone, "HELLO!"

"Hey, is this a bad time?"

"No, hey Blake, what's up?" Jayden was able to calm down.

"I was calling to see what time you were heading to the hospital."

"Well, we having breakfast right now, so I guess in about an hour we will be heading down there. When are you going?"

"Just as soon as eat, I am going to get dress and head down there."

"Okay, I guess we will be down there around the same time. Have you talked to Lauren already this morning? When is she going down there?"

"Yeah, I talked to her just before I called you and she has some things to do first and then she is coming?"

"Oh, goodness, you know what that means. She has to check that damn planner. What the hell will she do if she lost that thing? I would have thought once Kendall came along, she would have stop being so uptight with shit all the time."

"Jay, look at who you are talking abut, you know that is not about to happen."

"Alright chick, I don't want to burn these eggs, so I will holla at you when I get ready to leave the house." Jayden hung the phone up with Blake.

"What you got planned to do today?" Jayden asked Brian.

"I'm going to the race track for a little while, why what's up?"

"Are you going to the hospital with me today?"

"Naw, I didn't plan on it."

"Okay."

"Hey, hey, are you good babe?"

"Yes, I am fine." Brian got up from his seat toward Jayden, who is standing at the stove and he places his arm around her waist. "You gone lie to me?"

"I'm not lying, I am just thinking about some things." Brian starts kissing her on the neck, unable to deny his touch; Jayden dropped the dishrag that was in her hand. She grabbed the back of Brian's head with her left hand. Brian turned her around, facing him and he picked her up, placing her on the countertop, he opened her robe kissing her starting at the neck and moving his way down. Jayden began enjoying all the attention. She spread her legs welcoming him to continue making love to her, when there was a knock at the door.

"Ignore it," Brian continued to kiss her as if he didn't hear the knock at the door. There was another knock at the door, "let's go see who it is first." Jayden was able to say that in the midst of Brian taking control of her body.

"Damn Jay, my shit hard, c'mon ignore it." He continued to kiss on her pushing is dick on her. She moaned from the feeling she couldn't resist. The knocks continued to get harder. Jayden pushed Brian from off of her and she jumped down of the counter and headed to answer the door. She could tell that Brian was pissed off at her, so she didn't even look back. Jayden wrapped her robe back and tied it up just before opening the door.

"Hey sis, is Brian here?"

"Yeah, he is here….good to see you too, nigga."

"My bad, how you doing?" Jordan turned around to hug his sister.

"What's going on man? Its early as shit for you to be making house calls and shit." Brian tying his pants back together.

"Damn, did I catch you all at a bad time?" Brian was the first to respond, "Hell yeah, nigga, what you think?"

"No, little brother, I haven't had the chance to see how you doing and what's new with you?"

"Actually Jay, I need to talk to Brian about something."

"What the hell! Alright, I will go get dressed, but don't forget we have to talk about your living arrangements this summer. Jayden headed to her bedroom to get dress.

Jordan looked around the corner of the kitchen to make sure that his sister wasn't listening and that she closed the door.

"Eh, I couldn't get none this morning, so what the hell you had to talk about?"

"B, you know I couldn't stop thinking about the conversation I had with you and your homeboys the other day." Brian starting cleaning up the dishes in the kitchen, "Yeah…" "It's this chick that has been on my mind for a minute and I can't stop thinking about her man, this is some bull shit."

"Aight, nigga calm down. You must be feeling her ass."

"Man, I don't even know what it is. I made a move on her last night and I got rejected like a muthafucka, but it didn't even bother me and I still want her ass."

"Last night? You rolled up at this chick house last night and got all physical with her?"

"Man, I got drunk and she was all in my head so I went over there and she looked so damn good and at one point, I couldn't even control my damn self." Brian started shaking his head, "I can't even say nothing because I know I would have gone for mine regardless. But, if she rejecting you, it ain't a good sign."

"That is what I know, but she wasn't outright rejection. It was like she was feeling me at first and then all of sudden she had a conscious, you know how that shit goes." Brian wiped down the countertop, "Oh, she was feeling it, damn, you might have to feel her out. Hell, most chicks and athletes drop their drawers instantly. This must be a good-to-do chick."

"Oh, she got her shit together and she got bank, but none of that matters to me." Brian stopped cleaning and came to a standstill.

"Let me ask you this. Is this chick someone you just want to smash or you want to be with her for real?"

"I ain't never thought about no pussy like this so it got to be feelings, but I don't know, damn this is pissing me off."

"Calm down, man. You gonna be good. I like going for mine especially if I know there is a slight chance I can get in, fuck yeah. Wait, is she bad?"

"Hell yeah, she bad and her body is…"

"Whoa, not while your sister is here, you can tell me all of that when it's just us here." Brian looked over his shoulder just assuring that Jayden was no where in sight and that she didn't over hear anything. "You been home yet?"   "Naw, I will have to tell you that story later." Brian chuckled a bit, "hell naw, nigga. You starting trouble already and you ain't even been here a whole week, that is crazy." Jayden came out of the room dressed, "I hope y'all finished with whatever you were talking about." Neither one of the men responded. "Anyway, Jordan did you still want to stay at my place while you are here?"

"Hell yeah, when I can bring my stuff over?"

"I haven't been there in about two weeks, so I don't know what it looks like."

"I don't even care about none of that. I can't stay with your mother for a whole summer." Brian looked at Jordan giving him the okay to make his move on his lady friend he was just talking about.

"Babe, are you getting ready to go?" Brian asked Jayden.

"Yeah, I need to do one more thing before I leave and I will be out."

Jordan got up, "Alright, good people, I am out. I'ma get ready to move my stuff over to the house today."

"Jordan, where are you going to be at later today, I may need you to do something?"

"Shit, I don't know, just him me up later."

"Okay, lil brother, whatever you say." Jordan gave Brian dap and he left the house.

"Now, what do you have to do before you leave?" Brian turned and asked Jayden. "This," Jayden grabbed Brian by his pants and pulled him in toward her, kissing him passionately. Brian didn't expect it, ended up falling back on the couch massaging Jayden's ass gently. "Alright, you won't make it to the hospital." Jayden continued kissing Brian ignoring that his nature was starting to rise and she knew she couldn't do this to him twice in the same day. "Babe, I gotta go, "she uttered in between his tongue going down her throat. "Just give me five minutes," Brian began lifting Jayden's shirt, rubbing her body in an upward motion. There was no response, but her body said it all.

Chapter 27: Relax, Just A Little

"Hey, when did you all get here?"

"We just got here a few minutes ago."

"Have you heard anything from the doctor?"

"No, Mrs. Deborah was going to go see if we could get an update, but no one has been in here since we got here."

"Have you all seen Terrance?"

"No, he was here when we got here; you all didn't see him anywhere outside?" Lauren frowned her face, "I am pretty sure he is not going to be here when we are anyway."

"It doesn't matter. He is Dalia's husband regardless of what any detective thinks and regardless of how any of us feel." Jayden turned her head facing Lauren as she made her point. Deborah walked back into the room, "the doctor said he would be in to talk with us in a bit."

"I hate seeing her with all these machines hooked up to her like this."

"I know Blakie, that is how we felt when we had to see you in the hospital, "Lauren grabbed Blake and hugged her, "but, she is strong and she is going to make it, right?" They both looked at each other trying to put on a good front for everyone. Jayden stood over to the side just staring at Dalia, wanting her to just wake up and be okay, but that wasn't happening. The doctor entered the room with a displeasing look on his face,

"Good morning, how are you all doing this morning?"

"Great, doctor, I want to know how my daughter is doing."

"Her body didn't adjust well to taking the baby and we thought it would have been a temporary thing, but she hasn't come out of it yet. We are trying to keep her as comfortable as possible and with plenty of nutrients."

"Wait, why didn't anyone call us and let us know."

"I called and told her husband. I assumed you knew; I am so sorry."

"Doctor, its Doctor Cole right?"

"Yes, It is."

"How long is my friend going to stay like this, like a vegetable in this hospital room?"

"Well, miss…."

"Miss Miller…"

"Miss Miller, it is up to your friend now. You want to keep her in good spirits. Come visit and sit with her, laugh with her, and talk with her. She can hear you. We are going to move her to a regular room so she will be most comfortable and it will allow her time to recover."

"Oh my God, are you serious?" shocked as she could be, there was nothing that they could do for their friend right now. Jayden, with her hands on her hip, couldn't believe what the doctor was telling her.

"Look ladies, don't give up. This is the time where she needs your support the most." The doctor tried his best to encourage them, but they were still in shock.

"'Jay, Blake, we have to be strong and stick it out with her. She is not going to be in here long. I think we should come up with a plan or schedule to come see her." Lauren was trying to change the tone of the room.

"Rin, I hear what you are saying, but I can't deal with this right now. I will have to come back later." Jayden picked up her bag and left the room. Lauren and Blake ran behind her, "Jay, wait!"

"It's hard, it's damn hard, but we can't give up."

"That's right, my friend is gone and you two are acting like everything is okay."

"No, we are not acting like anything. Just think what would have happened if the three of you weren't at my hospital side when I got shot." Jayden wiped the tears from her eyes and decided to take a walk with Lauren and Blake. They started reminiscing about the good college days where everything was smooth. They laughed, cried, and enjoyed the time together. Then out of no where, Jayden asked them about the schedule to start with visiting Dalia.

"I think we should at least come by for an hour everyday so she will know we are here and we are turning our backs on her. That is the least I think we could do, since we don't know where her beloved husband is."

"I don't think we can worry about him, because in the end, we are all that she has," "Right, Rin." Blake added.

"We can't stay out here forever. Let's go back in the hospital and find out when they are going to move Dalia into a room." The other girls followed Lauren as she headed back into the hospital.

"Jay, have you had any luck looking for a job?"

"I really hadn't had the time between everything that has been going on," Blake asked just to see what position Jayden stood on finding employment since she was laid off a while back.

"I am going to go to the Marketing Firm tomorrow and see if I still have a job." Blake seemed excited about going back to work. "I know you all have your own opinions about what I should do, but I think I am going to be okay."

Jayden looked over at Lauren, "Chick, you have no idea what I was thinking," Jayden chuckled.

"I think it is great that you want to go back to work and start back with your career, good for you Blake."

"Lauren, you so damn animated that it's ridiculous."

"Now, you're not happy that Blake is wanting to go back to work to take her mind of off everything?" Lauren turned and asked Jayden.

"No, I am happy, gosh, y'all turn everything a sista say around. Blake knows I am happy and I want to hear all about her day tomorrow when she gets off, if that makes you happy Lauren Daniels."

"Oh, so I don't get invited to this?"

'Hell naw, you don't get invited for bringing me out like that."

"Oh, okay, heffa."

"You know I missed this when I was away." Blake drew Jayden close to her, Lauren on her left side and Jayden on her right side. The walked inside the hospital and they ran into Deborah, "What's wrong?" Lauren asked Deborah.

"They are getting ready to move her to a regular room and its going to take a while to do that, so there was no point in waiting in there."

Blake took Deborah by the hand, "do you want to leave?"

"Yes, please." Deborah became emotional with just the thought of Dalia being comatose, laying in the bed, unconscious unaware what was going on around her.

"C'mon lets get out of here. I'll take you back to the house." Blake put her arms around Deborah, to console her while walking to the car.

'I'll catch up with you all later." Blake made sure Deborah was in the car first, before getting in the car herself, Jayden and Lauren watched as they got into the car.

"Rin, do you believe spoiled little Blake is riding Dalia's mother around in a Range Rover and taking her back to her lavish house out of true concern. Wow, I am so shocked right now.'

"Stop Jay, you act like Blake was selfish."

"She had everything and she didn't know how to bring herself down, you know that."

"Yeah, she was a little deprived, but she wasn't selfish."

"She did have a heart, but she didn't know how to use it."

"Jay, she can't help it that she came from a well off family, who gave her everything, that didn't mean she was a bad person."

"Now, Blake isn't a bad person, she is genuinely sweet, but she has come a long way."

"Yes, she has."

"Let me ask you something, I noticed you brushed Blake off about the job thing, is everything straight with that?"

"Brian has been handling everything that I can't right now and there haven't been any jobs calling me, but I am trying to put myself out there in between the crisis."

"You know if you need my help, I am more than happy to help you. I have an idea. Kendall's is starting a new firm here and he is looking for a lot of staff."

"Rin, I don't want handouts."

"No, but you have a mortgage. You can't live off that severance for ever and plus you have a wedding to pay for."

"Let's go get a drink of something; I need one after all of this news today."

"Hell, I thought you would never ask."

"C'mon girl," Lauren invited Jayden into her house.

"Either it's me, or I haven't been here in a while."

"No, you haven't been here in a while." Lauren placed her pocketbook on the table, heading toward her wine cellar, "Alright, what kind of drink do you want?"

Yelling from the great room, "What kind of liquor do you have?"

"Liquor, what about a nice glass of red wine?" Jayden frowned her face as the thought of the glass of wine when actually she wanted something stronger so she could feel the affect.

"Brown liquor, I know you have some of that around this house somewhere. I know Kendall drinks some brown, or do you have him on this wine kick to? I think you have me mistaken for Dalia." Lauren thought about it for a moment, "Hell, maybe I did have you confused with Dalia. She does love wine." In a cabinet facing the wine cellar was some brown liquor, some of Jayden's favorite, Hennessey.

"I take it since you found that, you are going to drink that right?"

"You damn right, now go in that fridge and find me something to mix this with."

"What the hell do I look like? You went and got that Hen, you should have brought your ass to get you something to mix with it."

"You so damn feisty today," Lauren grabbed a nice large wine glass from her cabinet with a bottle of red wine.

'Aight, Jay, what's new?" she flopped down on the sofa in her great room.

"Man, I always thought this was the best spot in your house." Lauren took a sip of her glass like she was waiting for Jayden to say more.

"What are you going to do with your wedding plans?"

"Aww, hell, I haven't even thought about it since this stuff with Dalia."

"How long do you think Brian is going to hold off on making you his wife?"

"Girl, please. He will go with the flow."

"Don't underestimate a man that is ready to get married."

"I'll talk to him because he did ask me about it a couple of days ago."

"See what I'm saying...did your brother get here okay, I know this is about the time he comes down?"

"Yeah, he got here yesterday. He actually came by the house this morning, but he was acting funny."

"Acting funny how?" Lauren took a sip of her wine.

"First of all, he was at the house early this morning, looking like yesterday and he wanted to talk to Brian in private."

"Okay....he talks with Brian, what is wrong with that?"

"Hell, I am his sister and he didn't even want to talk to me, he wanted to talk to Brian."

"I don't think its nothing."

"That is what you say, I know my brother."

"If you say so, how is football going for him?"

"It's going great; he should be getting drafted this year."

"Wow! Tell him congratulations. The first professional football player I know."

"Yeah, but Mommie is a little concerned about his agent and how he isn't putting my brother first or some shit like that."

"Why does she think that?"

"The man hasn't made the best moves for my brother, but I haven't talked to Jordan about it yet, not really sure if I want to get involved, but you know how mothers can be and I don't think he gets that yet."

"Oh, hell yeah, I know all about that. I didn't call my mother last week, so she called and left me a voice mail, telling me off. That was crazy." Jayden just laughed while she took a gulp of her Hennessey and apple juice.

"Man, I haven't seen your mother in a long time, how is she?"

"Her crazy ass is good, just busy as ever and I thank God for that."

"So, are you saying you don't miss having your mother around?"

"Uh, hell no, my mother is too much and you know that. She has to change everything and she has to over plan everything."

"She sounds like someone I know." Lauren got up from the sofa to get another glass of wine.

"I hope the hell you aren't talking about me, because I am nothing like my mother Jay. If I am like my mother, you are like yours."

"The hell if I am. I just don't know what to say about that woman."

"What's going on with your mother?"

"For some reason, she and my father think it is a good idea to be sleeping together like he is not married or some shit."

"Shut up! Jay, I can't believe that."

"Hell yeah, apparently it's been going on for a minute, because Jordan knew all about it. I just happened to find out because he slipped up and said something, plus I caught their asses."

"Okay, I can't hear that about Miss Jackie. But, are you mad because you didn't know or because you think it is wrong?"

"I am mad because it is wrong."

"Okay, at the end of the day, you are going to risk the relationship with your mother and father because of a personal choice they made?"

"Rin, do you know Karen, my father's wife blames me and my mother for everything. She always made comments about me and my mother, but I thought she was being a bitch, now I don't blame her, she probably thought I knew all about this."

"Aww hell, you worrying about her feelings, that is crazy when you don't even care for her."

"Shit, I need another drink fucking with you." Jayden got off the sofa and went into the kitchen to fix another mix drink. I know this Hen isn't yours, so who does it belong to?"

"Who in the hell do you think?"

"I know you feeling that damn drink because you cussin' at me."

"Chill out, now you still ain't giving me a good reason why you aren't talking to your mother."

"Shit, I ain't talking to James Miller either, he is the one that is married, and he is definitely on my shit list!"

"Oh Lawd, let it go, life is too short. I understand you have "morals" that you are trying to live by, but you can't judge a book by its cover."

"Well, I will judge this shit." Jayden finished making her drink and sat back down on the sofa, while Lauren was on her fourth glass of wine.

"Damn, I am hungry"…."Shit, me too."

Jayden looked over at Lauren, who was laying her head back on the sofa, feeling the warm sensation of her wine, "Do you think we should invite the men?"

"I guess we can…you call yours and I will call mine."

"Hell, Brian was supposed to go to the track today, so I don't even know if he will hear the phone when I call. Aww, hell, I will just text him and see what he says."

Lauren called Kendall who picked up on the second ring, "What's up sweetie?

"Jay and I were hungry and we wanted to invite you guys to come join us for dinner."

"What time are you trying to go?"

"Maybe in an hour or so?"

"Okay, that is cool. I will have to meet you there though."

"Alright, I will shoot you the address."

"Alright love you."

'I love you too."

She hung up the phone and turned to Jayden, who was replying back to the text from Brian.

"Kendall is in, what about Brian?"

"Yes, he is coming. He told me to tell you to make sure that Ken boy don't do any politics talk at dinner."

"Tell your man to shut the hell up." They both laughed at the text from Brian.

"Hey, Rin, let me ask you this, since no one was said anything about it."

"Jesus, Jay, do I need a drink for this one?"

"Naw, I want to know where the hell Terrance ass is at and why he didn't feel the need to call any of us and say what was going on with Dalia."

"Damn, you know I forgot all about his ass when the doctor came in the room."

"Fuck no, I ain't forgetting shit. Now, he is starting to make me think his ass is guilty." Lauren pours another glass of wine.

"I didn't even think about it like that."

"All I want to know is where his ass at and why he wasn't at the hospital earlier. I don't like this shit."

"But, for real though, what are you going to do." Jayden gave Lauren the eye as if she knew what she was capable of. "Oh, c'mon Jay, we have grown from that and we don't do shit like that anymore."

"Naw, you don't do shit like that anymore. He seems a little shiesty to me."

"And me, may be, but you need to chill out on this one. I thought I would have seen that detective again, maybe something happened."

"I really don't care at this point about no damn detective; I want to know why Terrance happy ass wasn't at the hospital and didn't call us to tell us about Dalia."

"Please drink your drink, go home, and get ready to go out tonight."

"So, now you want to kick me out your damn house, its all good," Jayden was being sarcastic as she got off the sofa heading toward the kitchen. "What you wearing tonight?"

"Clothes, chick!" Lauren yelled back to her. "Why you gotta ask that every time we get ready to go somewhere? Just find something in your closet and be ready in 45, how bout that?"

"I think your ass has had too much to drink, cause you bugging. If you know I ask these damn questions, why not just answer me when I ask you."

"Me answering you is still not going to help you find out what you are going to wear in your closet."

"Shut up!" Jayden cleaned her glass and placed it in the sink. "Alright, I'm about to head out and get ready. When you figure out the restaurant, let me know."

"I know it is going to be somewhere downtown."

"Alright, shoot me a text with the name or address." Jayden slammed the door when she left.

Outside in the car, Jayden had a talk with herself, "whew! Too many drinks that time get yourself together so you can drive home. How in the hell does she expect me to be ready in 45 when it is going to take me about 15-20 to get home. Oh well, I am not going to rush."

Back in the house, Lauren goes in the internet looking for a new restaurant downtown that none of them had been to in a while. She knew Jayden liked seafood and Kendall liked Steaks, it didn't take long to find one, "Ha, we will go to McCormick's off of Pratt Street. That's done!" Lauren headed upstairs to find something to wear, like always she had to turn on her music while she was getting dressed.

Jayden arrives at Brian's house noticing a couple of cars in the yard. She pulled up and parked her SUV in the garage, which Brian hardly opened. Jayden wondered who could be in the house when Brian knew they had to meet Kendall and Lauren. Not wanting to have an attitude, she walked in the house and was embraced by some old friends of Brian's she met a while back. She politely walked through the house greeting all of them, "Brian, can I talk to you for a minute." He got up and followed Jayden to the bedroom.

"What's up babe?"

"Are you serious? You really gonna ask me that right now?"

"Okay, they are about to leave."

"It ain't just that Brian, you know we have to meet Lauren and Kendall in a bit, why would have them over here if we have to go somewhere."

"Damn, I forgot. I'm glad you didn't say anything in front of them."

"Hell, I guess you think I don't have any class. I know this is your house, and I won't disrespect that. Now, if you would have tripped out there, we would have had a problem."

"Shit, I know that." Brian kissed her on the cheek. Jayden went straight to her closet to find something to wear. Brian returned to his friends out in the den area.

"Nigga, you ain't gotta say nothing to us," coming from one of the guys drinking a beer. "I know your ole lady is home and its time for us to leave, but my nigga, you didn't tell us how fine Jayden has gotten."

Brian shook his head, "Now, I know you done had too many of dem damn beers for you to be talking like that in my house." His friends laughed it off, "I'm just saying though. You betta wife her up real quick."

"Just as soon as I can," Brian gave his friends dab and they left the house. He rushed to the bedroom to get dressed so they could join the others for dinner.

"Babe, you found me something to wear yet," Brian yelled from the bathroom. Jayden in the bedroom with a confused look on her face, "What the hell," she said to herself, but for some reason it came out of her mouth.

"What did you say babe?"

"Oh, nothing, I don't know what you wanna wear."

"Just get me some fresh ass jeans and a button down that you like."

"I just got a text from Lauren, we are eating at McCormick's downtown. I don't know what that is?"

"Hey, I heard of it. Some of the guys from the job have been talking about that place."

"I hope I like it."

"I think you will. Get your ass out that shower and put your clothes on." Before they knew it, they were dressed and headed downtown. Jayden texted Lauren on her way as they jumped in Brian's Ram 1500 heading downtown. Jayden ended up wearing her dark denim skinny leg jeans, a silky halter top and a short blazer to compliment her 4 inch sandals.

"You look nice, babe," Brian complimented Jayden as he reached over to kiss her on the cheek.

"You clean up nice yourself," as she returned the favor.

Chapter 28: Ain't No Telling

"Mrs. Deborah, it's just going to be the two of us tonight. What are we doing for dinner tonight?"

"I am not hungry; I can't get Dalia off my mind."

"Every time I think about her lying in that hospital bed aware of what is going on, I just get the chills."

"I just wish I could do something for her."

"Mrs. Deborah, I can take you back to the hospital if you want to spend the night with her."

"I don't want to put you through all of that. I know you have a tough time as it is just being near a hospital."

"Don't worry about it, Dalia is my best friend and she was right there for me when I was in the hospital. C'mon, get your things and I will take you down there and in the morning, I will pick you up and we will have breakfast somewhere."

She went back to her house and she noticed how empty it was. She didn't think about anyone else, all she wanted to do was block out everything. She knew tomorrow would be her first day back showing her face at work, or what she used to call her career. She didn't know how she would be accepted or what to expect from her superiors or co-workers. Even though she wished for the best, she had to prepare for the worst. She grabbed an old bottle of wine she remembered getting from the store when she was on vacation with her mother. She opened it and sat in front of her television downstairs in her den watching reruns of Law & Order. The more she drank of the wine, the more she daydreamed about what happened at the law firm. The images in her head became more and more vivid in her mind.

While Blake was at home drinking, Lauren and Jayden went to dinner. They arrived at the same time, greeting each other with hugs from the ladies and dab from the men.

"Jay, have you eaten hear before?"

"Look, who you talking to? Hell naw, I haven't been here before."

"Great, that means we will be trying a new spot. Maybe we could be bring Blake here and Dalia once she gets better."

"For just a couple of hours, can we not talk about Dalia?" Jayden became emotional at the thought of thinking about Dalia, especially because of the situation she was in. Brian grabbed Jayden by the shoulders to comfort her as they continued to walk in the restaurant. Lauren empathized with her friend, so she became silence about Dalia for Jayden's sake.

Lauren walked up to the hostess station, "hi, we have reservations for four under Daniels."

"Okay great, right this way." They all followed the hostess to their table.

"Man, how is work?" Kendall strikes a conversation with Brian.

"Shit, same old stuff, just taking it one day at a time, how bout you," Brian and Kendall seemed to start off right, so that gave Lauren and Jayden time to talk a little to themselves. Lauren leaned in to Jayden, "So how has the job hunt been going?"

Jayden looked around to make sure the men weren't listening. "I have been so busy with the wedding lately and all this other chaos that I have been applying here and there, but nothing has been potential, why you ask?"

"I was concerned that's all. I know you were doing good with the severance, but that can't last you forever."

"Yeah, you right and I think that since I had Brian's help, I just didn't think about it twice lately."

"How long do you think this man is going to pay for two mortgages?" Lauren whispered to Jayden.

"He hasn't brought it up and normally, I will pay that, he will handle some other things for me."

"How about you come by the house tomorrow evening or some time next week and I will see we can help you find something?"

"Hell, I am all about help if you got it. But, I can tell you right now, I am not about to work at the new firm Kendall is about to set up."

"I didn't even think about it until you said something, but that is not a bad idea."

"Yes, it is and keep your voice down because I don't anything about law and hell, half the time, I need the law to contain me."

"Girl, you so stupid," they laughed it off. After they finished their private conversation, the waitress walked up and they ordered drinks. The waiter gave them time to look over the menu while he went to get the drinks. At the other side of the table, the men were in an interesting conversation themselves, "Man, you a cool ass dude," Brian said to Kendall.

"Hell, I try sometimes," Kendall patted his chest, "I hear your big day is coming up soon."

"Yeah, I'm about ready to make her all mine."

"That's great, man. How long have you two been dating?"

"Oh, shit, we have been dating on and off for about two years and solidly for a year, so altogether three years."

"So, have you all talked about living arrangements, because I know she had her own spot."

"Well, we didn't make a big deal about it. I mean, she staying at my house now, I just assumed that we would be living at my house and then she would do whatever with her house, if money allows us to keep it." The waiter returned to the table to one bud light, a Heineken and two patron margaritas.

"Here you go. Are you all ready to order?" The ladies placed their orders while the men were still engaged in their conversation.

"Yes, I am ready and so am i?" the ladies gave the waiter their order while the men were still talking.

"Babe, what do you want to eat," Jayden asked Brian. "Just order me some steak will be cool." Brian asked for the same from Lauren. The ladies ordered their food while the men continued talking.

"So, you and Lauren seem to be pretty damn close to me."

"I will have to tell you about that later, but yeah we are. I don't know if Jayden told you, but my firm is starting a new office here and I am setting it up."

"That's what it is! What's that look about?" Brian could pick up from the vibe that Kendall was putting off like he wanted to talk about something in private.

"Maybe after dinner we can drop the ladies off and have a drink at the bar?"

"Aight, that's cool with me."

"I know I might be a little out of place for asking this, but have any of you talked to Terrance?" Kendall out of blue asked about Terrance.

"Naw, dude you must be asking them that because I barely even know dude like that", Brian eased his way out of the conversation.

"Funny you should ask," Jayden was ready to attack that subject. "This dude hasn't been back to the hospital yet. I know that damn detective was asking questions, but now he has me thinking he was guilty. He didn't even call to tell us that Dalia was in a coma." The men had an astonish look on their faces.

"Babe, what the hell you mean, in a coma?" Brian raised up in his chair.

"Yes, my best friend is in a coma. When we got there, the doctor thought we knew because her husband knew, because he was there before we got there." Kendall looked at Lauren with sincere remorse for her; he grabbed her hand under the table. He just knew that was heartbreaking for her to hear.

"I was trying to keep the girls positive about it, but it's so damn hard when she is lying in that bed like a vegetable." He squeezed Lauren hand tighter as she spoke. "It's going to be alright." The whole mood was beginning to change at the table.

"If you all want to go home, that is cool with me." Since the ladies became a little emotional at the table, Kendall suggested that maybe tonight wasn't a good night for them to go out to eat.

"No, we are here, we can stay and eat. I will go there in the morning while everyone else is at work." Jayden wiped her face with a napkin from the table.

"Eh, babe, I can take you the hospital in the morning on my way to work and you can finish making your wedding plans. Then, I will pick you for lunch, how bout dat?"

"Oh wow! Brian, you are going to do all of that?"

"Yeah, I would." With no argument or extra lip, Brian committed himself to taking Jayden to the hospital and taking her to lunch. Lauren kicked Jayden under the table and they winked at each other. The waiter came to the table with their meals.

"Thank you."

"Is there anything else I can get for you?" the waiter waited patiently until everyone was settled.

"No, we are good, thanks for asking."

"Shit, I guess we better handle these checks." Brian reached into his pocket getting his wallet. Kendall got up out of his chair, reaching into his wallet to pay for his bill. The men paid the bill while the ladies got themselves together.

"We should do this again Jay?" Lauren asked her friend as they were walking out the restaurant. She knew she was putting Jayden on the spot on purpose, but Jayden is always on top of her game, "you act like we leaving town or something, we will be here. Call us when you wanna have dinner, chick." Lauren laughed because she knew it was Jayden strange sense of humor that made her who she was.

"Rin, I will see you tomorrow at the hospital right?" Jayden yelled across the parking lot.

"Yeah, I will come after work."

"Cool, have a nice evening, bye Kendall."

While they took a nice ride back to their homes, Blake was still sitting on her couch watching television. Blake flopped back on the sofa in her den to continue watching Law & Order and then her phone rang, "Hello".

"Hey, you busy?"

"Uh, no, who is this?"

"You don't recognize my voice."

"Jordan, what can I do for you?"

"Damn, you are going to talk to me like I'm a client?"

"No, but you haven't said yet, what I can do for you?"

"I have a list of things I can say you can do for me."

"Jordan, is that why you call me?"

"I'm really feeling you and I can tell you feel something for me, but you don't want to admit it to yourself."

"Jordan, stop! I know there is someone else that you could be calling right now instead of me."

"There are plenty of females I could be chasing, but I want to get into you. When was the last time you had good conversation with a real man."

"Wow! You must have been talking to your sister."

"Why would my sister tell me something like that? A real man can tell when a woman desires the presence of a man."

"Oh really, I have had too many drinks to have a real conversation and with you."

"Blake, would you mind if I came over there just to talk."

"I doubt that you would be coming over here to talk one bit. Okay Jordan, I am hanging up the phone now."

"I am not giving up." Blake disconnects the phone. Blake grabbed a blanket nearby and wrapped herself up to watch television and fell asleep on the couch. To herself, she thought, "I don't know what is up with him, he needs to get over this crush he has." The phone rings again just as she was getting up off the couch to turn off the television to go upstairs. It was Barbara, Blake's mother.

Barbara was calling to check on Blake, she had no idea of all that transpired over the past couple of weeks and most importantly what was going on with Dalia. She knew her mother would be more than concerned because she opened her home to Dalia when she was planning on making some changes in her life. Blake knew it was going to be a long night once she answered the phone, so she took a deep breath and explained it all. Blake knew her what her mother's reaction would be and that she would be anxious to fly and she really didn't have the time for that when she desperately wanted to focus on her career and making sure that Dalia recovered okay.

It drew late and Blake was still on the phone with her mother sorting out details about Dalia and Terrance. She knew her mother was going to say that she was coming and Blake was waiting to her the words. She knew wasn't going to be successful in talking her out of it, so she just continued through the conversation until she said it. She also told her mother that Deborah, Dalia's mother was staying with her also. To some extent, her mother felt that Blake was doing her part and she was pleased. One of her concerns was whether Terrance was being completely honest or if he was just got mixed up with the wrong people. Under the circumstances of whom he was dealing it, she gave him the benefit of the doubt.

She didn't think it was strange that they hadn't seen him. She thought he felt embarrassed and ashamed of what he had done. She couldn't seem to convince Blake of that, but it was worth a shot. After two hours of conversing, Blake's mother allowed her to get off the phone so she could get up for work tomorrow. Just when the call was getting ready to end, Barbara invited herself down. Blake, not surprised at all, welcomed her mother and said she would be expecting her some time this week. They ended the conversation and Blake passed out for the night.

"What's good, man?"

"Ain't shit, just dropped Lauren off to the house."

"Nigga, you know Lauren ain't with you going out late." Kendall gave Brian this look like he was a grown man that doesn't answer to no woman.

'So, you wanna get on me? I know your woman don't play that."

"Don't get it twisted, she might get me a little, but she knows her limits."

"So, that is your excuse."

"Hell yeah!"

"Shit, me too." Brian and Kendall both laughed at each other.

"Do you want to ride together or separately?"

"Hell, it don't matter to me."

"I got you. We can ride in my car." So, the men jumped in Kendall's car to a nearby bar, something a little more to Brian's customs.

While sitting at the bar, the men shared a lot of common things like work, cars, drinks, music, and women. Come to find out, they shared more things than expected.

"Damn, I would not have thought I would have so much in common with a corporate nigga."

"Don't get it twisted. I chose my career, it didn't choose me. I have to act professional while at work, but I have another side that everyone can't see all the time. I have a law license I have to maintain. Bro, do you play basketball?"

"Do i? Me and some of the guys from work get together every Friday to play a game, if we all have time." While talking the guys lost track of time, drinking beer after beer and then raising the stakes to shots every so often.

"You will have to hit me up sometimes to play a game or two."

"That's what it is. I'll have to get your number before the night is over." The men started back drinking their beers and out of nowhere a young, gorgeous woman slid in between them at the bar, "Mm, who in the world would leave two handsome men alone in a bar, you must be single?"

Brian didn't even look her way, "excuse me, do I know you," he asked her.

"No, but I would like to get to know you." She leaned in with her breast touching his arm. Halfway drunk, Brian didn't notice all the contact she was giving him.

"Listen, I have a woman aight!" she took offense to how strong Brian came off so she turned the other way facing Kendall, "and what is your excuse for being in a bar alone?"

Kendall looked at her up and down, "Me and my homeboy just came out to have a drink, we don't want any trouble."

"But, you didn't answer my question."

The Upside Down of Things

Kendall turned his bottle of Heinken up, "Hell, I didn't think I had to answer you, what you about 20, are you even legal to be in this bar?"

"Man, you crazy as hell, how you gone ask her that?" Brian barely able to keep his composure laughed continuously at how Kendall was talking to the young lady. She seemed disgusted with Kendall words so she walked off, but they both took a good look as she walked off.

"Gottdamn, if I was single..."

"Don't even talk about it."

"Shit, she probably don't even know how to cook."

"Naw, she probably don't have a real job." Sloppy drunk as they were, they were able to make sense of the young woman coming on to them at the bar.

"Now, I try to be a good man, but that bitch almost made me slip up."

"Naw, I heard your woman is crazy as hell.."

"You got that right, she done pull a gun in my house before on a young chick."

"Damn, you been caught before and you still living?"

"Naw, a friend of mine had his little cousin stay at the house for one night until she could move in on campus and I didn't get a chance to tell Jayden. Man, she came in the house blazing....nigga, she was blazing with a gun that I helped her pick out. I don't even know why the hell she had the damn gun on her." Kendall was shaking his head in dismay.

"Hell, in that situation, you can expect a woman to do anything. So, what the hell did you do to get her to put the gun down."

"Shit, I had to stand in front of her. If she was really going to shoot, she would have had to shoot my ass first, gottdamn."

"That's some serious shit. Man, I guess that's love."

"Shit, if you say so. So, what's the deal with you and Lauren. Hell, it's been a long time since we've seen her with a man. Aw, shit, I guess I wasn't 'pose to say that. Don't pay me no mind, shit I feel good off dem shots."

"Naw, you good, I can't even describe it. I met her and she was like a dream or some shit. I just had to have her and I didn't want anyone else to have her either."

"You know what, I am glad you realized that early. Last year this time, I was taking Jayden for granted, big mistake. So, you gone move her or something?"

"I bought Lauren a ring and I left it in New Jersey. I didn't think it would be the right time to ask her to marry me so I left it." The bartender came back and brought Kendall and Brian another shot and a beer.

"Preciate it bartender,"Brian started rubbing his hands over his face, letting the alcohol to take its toll on him. "You betta get that damn ring."

"Now, I am regretting leaving the damn ring. But, yeah, I plan on moving here and I was thinking of asking Lauren can I move in with her, but I don't know how she will react to that."

"Shit, I couldn't tell you either. You know out of all of them, I know more about Dalia, but not that nigga Terrance, don't get them confused. I stayed out that shit, because I ain't want to know."

"I feel ya, one more for the road, man?" held the shot glass in the air next to Kendall's.

"To...the good women, good sex, and liquor." They clicked glasses and drank away. The bartender ended up calling them a cab because neither of them was in any shape to drive.

"Man, you really good peoples."

"Yeah, you aight too."

Chapter 29: Back to Work

"Damn, its six already?" Blake woke up not as anticipated as she expected to be on her first day back to work. She really didn't know what to expect once she got back, but she couldn't prolong this day from happening. She got out of bed and went into her bathroom and turned on her clock radio on the counter, "alright Blake get it together." She spent the next hour prepping herself in the mirror, getting dressed, doing her makeup, hair, and getting her mind together for another corporate day. Blake arrived promptly at work at eight o'clock. She parked in her normal parking space. She felt good to know that no one was replacing her yet.

"Good Morning Miss Lowry, welcome back." She was first greeted by her secretary.

"Good morning Tina, its good to be back." Just when Blake was getting ready to walk in her office, she noticed out of the corner of her eye some of her colleagues were staring at her, but she didn't pay that any mind, she pranced right into her office. She opened the door, and there was a bouquet of white roses on her desk.

"Oh, my goodness, I wonder who these are from." She opened the card attached to the roses and it read;

Blake,

I know this has been a rough time for you and your family. Due to unforeseen circumstances, I was unable to contact you. Hope your day back will be a prosperous one.

Take care,

Mr. Sellers

"Wow! I can't believe he gave me flowers." The intercom came on in Blake's office, "Miss Lowry, you have a call on line 1".

Blake hit the button, "Thanks Tina, this is Blake speaking how can I help you?"

"This is Jim, how are you?"

'I am excellent, what can I do for you?"

"I hear it's your first day back and I don't want you to feel overwhelmed, but I have a client that I desperately need your help with, but there is one catch, he wants us to complete and be prepared for a marketing presentation on Friday." Blake took a deep breath, "Jim, what kind of company is it?"

"It's an upcoming retailer here and they are willing to invest a lot of money with the company, but we have to have to right strategy for them. This is the third company they have tried."

"Wow Jim, and you said they want a presentation by Friday?"

"Blake, I need you on this one. I have made promises to this guy and I want to keep them. I will give you whatever you need to make this happen."

"Its not a problem Jim, shoot me an email with all the info you have on the company and I will let you know what I come up with by Tuesday afternoon, is that good?"

"Excellent, thanks Blake. I will let Sellers know you are working on something for me….and Blake, welcome back. We missed you." Blake felt back in her zone now. She had something to occupy her mind and she was busy doing what she loved to do. she hit the intercom to Tina's desk, "Hey, I know its my first day back, but I need you to work some overtime tonight, is that going to be a problem?"

"No ma'am, is there anything you need for me to get you?"

"Or course I do. There are some files for retail marketing that I need….matter of fact, get everything in the storage room for retail marketing, and it's going to be a long week, dear."

"Good Morning, Miss Daniels, I have a couple of message here for you," reaching for the messages from the receptionists,

Lauren placed her briefcase on the floor going through each of them one at a time.

"Thanks Joyce, you are the best," Lauren picked her briefcase up from the receptionist area making her way to her office. She opened the door, putting her scarf on the coat rack and her briefcase in the chair, "Okay, first I need to check my email, make notes, review accounts, return calls, get coffee, schedule appointments and finalize books. Damn, I have a lot to do."

There was a knock at the door, Lauren busy checking her email, "Yes!"

"Good Morning, one of your clients called while you were out one day last week and they were requesting some files. I didn't want to go through your things like that, but I did want to give you a heads up about it."

"Do you remember who the company was?"

"Not off the top of my head." To herself, Lauren was trying to figure out why he would even step to her office with it, *"was he trying to make me look or feel bad?"* Lauren brushed it off, "Okay, I have some phone calls to return today, maybe it is one of those clients, don't worry about it, I will handle it." She looked up over her reading glasses with a sarcastic smile on her face.

"Okay." He didn't know what else to say to Lauren, she addressed him and said she would handle it. Lauren continued going through her emails. She preferred that her clients contacted her through email; she really didn't have time to communicate with them over the phone especially when she was dealing with ledgers and spreadsheets all day. She sent out an email to Terry, John, and Jack who consistently worked on her team with her clients. They liked working with her and she liked working with them.

"Man, this is looking like its going to be a long Monday for me and I promised Jayden that I would go over some jobs with her, but I forgot that it is getting close to the end of the month so I have to get these numbers done." She said to herself. "We might as well order pizza tonight, we have a lot of work to do." it seemed as if Lauren couldn't get a break, just a soon as she sent the email to her team about working late on a project, her boss rang her phone, "Lauren, I need to see you in my office." Before she could even say hello, he was chiming in at her on the phone. "I'll be right there." Walking down the hall, Lauren had several things going through her head of why her manager wanted to meet with her at such urgency.

Lauren knocked on the door, "Lauren, come in" Gary said with a warm smile.

"Have a seat." Lauren cleared her throat in hesitation to take a seat. She knew this wasn't good news, but she was going to hear it if she wanted to or not.

"Connie, close my door please...thank you". Lauren, a couple of your clients have called and they have been highly impressed with your work."

"Thank you Mr. Lawson."

"Wait, I'm not finished. There have been some concerns with your team though." With a very confused look, Lauren couldn't imagine who or what he could have been referring to. "I think they have been to accessible to confidential files in this office."

"Mr. Lawson, with all due respect, I don't follow you."

"Let me explain it this way. We have to let Jack, John, and Terry go! Apparently, security has found them in appropriate areas, looking at inappropriate files."

"Mr. Lawson, are you saying that they were stealing on my accounts and mismanaging my files on purpose?"

"Lauren, I can't put in between this. Legal is already aware of the issue and we have to get these people out of here before we lose these clients. Legal had to contact them and let them know. We could face a lawsuit."

"Oh my goodness, I had no idea."

"We assumed so. I am sorry to tell you this, but you are going to have to handle your clients alone for a while. You have to be the only go to person in order to keep our clients happy." Lauren got up from her chair, pacing back and forth in Mr. Lawson's office.

"Now, it makes sense why Mark told me that one of my clients called me. I didn't see the point in him giving me that message directly."

"You are right. They have been instructed to give your clients' messages directly to you."

"Mr. Lawson, you know I love what I do and my clients, but there is no way I can meet my deadlines for all of them under these circumstances."

"Miss Daniels, you are more than capable of completing these tasks or you wouldn't be employed at this firm. Sit down for a minute."

"I know you aren't comfortable with these changes, but you didn't start out with a group of bookkeepers to prove that you could handle small business accounts. Do you remember when we hired you? You were energetic, bright, and intelligent plus you graduated top of your class. I expect the same then as I do now." Lauren took a deep breath, taking in all Mr. Lawson had to say, not actually agreeing with him, but she was listening.

"Yes sir, I will do my best to make sure my clients stay happy."

"That is what I like to hear, but I just sent them an email telling them we had to work late."

"Don't worry about it, just go on from here." Lauren got up from her chair, towards the door. "Yes, sir, have a good one." Walking down the hall, Lauren was trying to figure out in her head how she was going to manage this with all the other things going on in her personal life right now.

"Hell, I haven't even finish going through my email or my voicemails. This is some Monday already and its not even noon."

Back at her desk, Lauren continued going through her email. Majority of them were updates and information regarding her clients. This was stuff she had to do now since he wasn't going to have her team any longer. She knew she had to come up with a new strategy, but she was star struck at the moment. She was going to spend most of the day re-organizing her structure and work load. This would have to be done before she could jump right into her files. She definitely needed to contact her clients and have appointments with them because she hadn't touched base with them in a while. While writing her notes down, she thought for a minute, "I can do this at home. Maybe I will take a couple of days to work at home and I can come back in on Thursday. That sounds like a plan. I will have to let Mr. Lawson know. I hope he doesn't go against it." She dialed his extension and he picked up on the second buzz.

"Yes, Lauren...."

"Mr. Lawson, I am going to work from home in my office there for a couple of days to get my files sorted and communicate with my clients that way. I am going to make some personal visits this week and return back to the office on Thursday." There was a slight silence on the speaker.

"Lauren, you still there....?"

"Yes, I was wonder if you heard my proposal for the next couple of days."

"Yes, dear, that is fine. I knew you could do it. Meet with me on Thursday when you come back in and we can discuss where you are with everything...and don't forget the department meeting we are having Thursday afternoon."

"Yes, sir, I will send you an email when I am gone for the day."

"Great, talk to you later."

Part II

"Babe, can you just sleep in this morning."

"We already have, do you see what time it is?" Jayden rolled from under Brian, looking for the alarm clock to see the time.

"It's only nine; we can sleep in a few more hours."

"Babe, I wish I could, but I have to go to work." Brian rolled over to get out of the bed.

"You are just going to leave me here naked," she pulled the cover from over her body.

"Gottdamn, you make it hard for me to leave you!"

"Then, stay here...."

"Naw, I can't. If I don't go to work, who is going to pay the bills." He leaned in towards Jayden and placed a kiss on her cheek. Even though she didn't like the comment, it was the truth. Brian headed to the bathroom to take a shower.

"You still taking me to the hospital right?"

"Yeah, so hurry up and get dressed….Babe, will you iron my work clothes please….thank you!"

"*This negro ain't even gonna give me a chance to answer.*" She said off to herself. Jayden went and found Brian's work clothes in the closet next to his shirt he had on the night before. When she picked up the shirt, she noticed the scent of perfume on his shirt collar. She didn't want to assume anything, so she had to make sure she was smelling what she thought she did. She pulled the entire shirt close to her nose and the scent was even stronger, "*I know the hell not.*"

She thought she would save this argument for another time, but her anger was getting the best of her.

"What the fuck is this shit?" she ran into the bathroom, pulling back the curtain while Brian was washing.

"What the hell you talking bout?"

"Don't play stupid with me, why is there perfume on your shirt?"

"Oh, Lord, not this shit again…"

"What do you mean again?"

"The last time you started this shit, you pulled a gun on Dre's little cousin for no reason."

"I apologized for that."

"It don't matter. You keep accusing me of shit that I am not doing."

"Bring your ass out the damn shower and explain to me why there is perfume on your shirt, the one you had on last night."

"Hell, it ain't your perfume? I ain't been around no one."

"This is not my perfume Brian!"

"Then, I don't know where it came from." Brian jumped out of the shower, angrily, "Why you always assuming some shit. Why the hell can't you trust me?" The water was dripping off his naked body as Jayden just stared at him.

"I trust you, but can you explain the perfume."

"Some chick brushed up against me last night, but I brushed her off, that is it, damn!"

"Why couldn't you say that from the beginning and it could have all been squashed?"

"Because my fiancé shouldn't have to question me, didn't I come home last night and fucked the shit outta you? If I had been with someone else, I wouldn't have given it to you. Damn, you act like I still some jump off or something." Jayden walked passed him going into the bathroom, "I have to take shower."

"So, you just going to ignore what I said like it don't mean nothing. Jayden, don't walk away from me like that."

"Brian, what do you want me to say?"

"Hell, you can apologize or something….don't disrespect me in my house!"

"Oh, so that is what this is all about." She hesitated jumping into the shower.

"You don't listen to nothing I'm saying. You accusing me every time you think something ain't right."

"No, negro, I asked you that is it." She placed her hands on her hip.

"You gonna make me late for work, I ain't got time for this."

"Are you still taking me to the hospital?"

"Naw, you gonna have to drive." Brian put on his work clothes and walked into the other room. Jayden had a stunned look on her face like she was confused. Brian grabbed his work jacket and belt and left the house without saying anything.

"I can't believe he just left like that. He must really be mad." Jayden said to herself, just before heading back to the bathroom to get dressed.

"Hello, who dis?"

"Yes, may I speak with a Jordan Miller?"

"This is he, who dis?"

"This is Bart."

"Why the hell you sound like that?"

"Like what…anyways, you are going to jump out of your seat when I tell you the news I have for you."

"Bart, what is it?"

"I just got you a deal with the Baltimore Ravens. I think it's a fairly good deal. You don't have to do this last year of college; you can go right in and sign a four year deal with them for $2 million a year." Jordan jumped off the couch he was sitting on in amazement that the same agent that his mother didn't trust got him a nice deal to live out his dream.

"Bart, are you serious? It seems their guy got cut. I had the opportunity to show them you and this is what I got, so what do you say?"

"Wait a minute, I need to see this in writing and I need to meet with you before I verbally agree to anything and plus I have to talk to my family about this." In actuality, Jordan didn't expect any type of deal of this magnitude right now. He thought he had another year to show to his family that he was serious about finishing school and most importantly, he wanted to take his time pursuing Blake.

"Alright man, I will fly in tomorrow so we can look over paperwork and get lawyers involve, but you can't get a better deal than this."

"You let me decide that. I will see you tomorrow." On the inside, Jordan was elated something like this was happening to him. He wanted his father to be with him when he met with his agent, not his mother. He knew how her attitude would be towards Bart. He knew he didn't want to tell Jayden until he had all the good news and he didn't want Blake to know because she might think he had ulterior motives.

"Damn, if I wanna I gotta go hard and get her." Jordan said off to himself.

Chapter 30: I Got to Get Her

"Thank you for calling Johnson & Cole Marketing, how may I direct your call?"

"Blake Lowry, please."

"One moment." The operator was getting ready to transfer the call to Blake's assistant.

"Hey, Tina, I have a call for Blake, is she available?"

"Do you know who it is?"

"No, but it's a man."

"That could be anyone, transfer it over....Thank you for holding, this is Miss Lowry's assistant, how can I help you?"

"This is Jordan Miller, may I speak with Blake?"

"Hold please." Tina ran to Blake's office, "There is someone on the phone for you name Jordan."

"JORDAN! Transfer him over."

"Hello, Jordan, I am working."

"I wanted to know what were your plans for lunch."

"Uh, I don't know if I am taking a lunch, I have so much work to do."

"It would mean a lot to me if you would join me for lunch, your choice."

"Jordan, I know there is some other young chick you could be taking out for lunch."

"But, I want to take you out. I will be there around noon."

"Jordan, you just aren't going to take no for answer are you?" Blake was beginning to like how consistent Jordan was being. It was making her blush.

"No, I'm not. Don't work too hard and I will see you in a little bit."

"Okay." Just as soon as Blake hung the phone up, Tina was standing in the doorway, "Uh huh, now who is Jordan."

"Girl that is Jayden's little brother. He is on break from school. So, where are we with this presentation?"

"Doctor, I think my daughter moved her hand." Deborah went to the nurse's station in a frenzy because Dalia showed some motion in her right hand.

"Okay, I will come in and take a look." Dr. Cole went in the private hospital room where Daila laid helpless. He checked her vitals and motor skills.

"What doctor? Is there any change?"

"I'm sorry, there is no change, and she is still in the same state ma'am." Deborah wanted to break down, but she knew she had to keep her faith that Dalia would wake up. Spending the night at the hospital, it appeared that Deborah was restless and she wanted answers about her daughter, but the doctor couldn't provide that to her. She spent most of the night praying and watching television as nothing changed. She was just waiting for the opportunity for Terrance to show his face. He seemed to be mistreating Dalia from his absence from the hospital. She needed this alone time with her daughter without her friends and her husband. Most of the night, the nurses came in and out checking on Dalia, changing her linen and her feeding tube to make sure that she was eating; Deborah could hardly get any sleep or rest with all the commotion going on throughout the night.

Knock Knock!

"Come in."

"Hi!" Barbara enters the room with a beautiful bouquet of flowers and a grin that could brighten any room.

"Now, you look familiar to me, but I can' place the face." Deborah paused for a moment. "Barbara!"

"Yes ma'am, that is me in the flesh." Deborah walked over to Barbara and gave her a hug.

"It's so good to see you again."

"Its good to see you too, now how is my baby?"

"She's hanging on. I am trying to get these pillows on this bed comfortable for my baby."

"Oh, let me help you with that." Barbara rushed to her aide. "I know what is like watching your child lying in a hospital bed and you can't do anything for them, I have been there honey."

"My goodness, I forget you were in this same situation.

"Blake is fine, better than fine, she is blessed beyond belief. We have to make sure that we get Miss Dalia nursed back to health. Where are the girls?"

"I know your daughter had to go to work today and so did Lauren."

"Wait, where is Jayden because she isn't working?"

"Oh, I don't know, I haven't heard from her."

"Maybe she is coming later. I thought Terrance would have been here."

"I haven't seen him at all last night or this morning so far."

"He may show up. He loves her don't worry." Deborah wanted to change the subject about Terrance, because she didn't know any kind of way to feel about his absence at this point.

"When did you get into town?"

"I just got in so I came straight here." Barbara could tell by the pain on Deborah's face that she wanted to talk to someone.

"You know I have been running this through my mind over and over and it still doesn't make sense to me." Barbara pulled a chair up to sit closer to where Deborah was, which was in the chair next to the bed.

"What you mean Deborah?" she said with a slight lift in her voice.

"I don't understand. You know we teach these girls everything we know and they still do what they want to do, you know?"

"Oh yeah, I know what you mean. No matter how much you teach them, they still do the opposite of what you told them not to do."

"Oh, and they think they know everything, Lord, have mercy!"

"No, they act like we weren't young before, but we have been there and done all of that."

"Now, Barbara I don't know if you know or not, but I told this child of mine to leave that man alone and worry about herself and this child, but she wouldn't listen to me. I knew she was keeping some things from me, but I told her you can't make no man be where he don't want to....you can't make them even when you married to them."

"Amen to that! My child is the opposite. She thinks I don't know what she is doing, but she is living her life like she don't need a man. I want to see how long that is going to last. She better try and get one while she is young, because when she get ready to get one, he is going to be married...and she can't bring a married man to my house."

"I know that is right. All we can do is pray for them, maybe one day they will do the right thing and they can avoid so much heartbreak. You know, they think we tell them these things because we are trying to run their lives, but things could be so much smoother for them without all the hurdles we had to go through."

"Oh no, they are not going to see it that way. I told Blake, go to law school that way you will have a guaranteed job and you and your sister could run the company together. She could live at the house and not worry about nothing...girl, that was a mess trying to figure out all her stuff when she was in the hospital..paying her mortgage, house bills, car notes, insurance, and all this other mess she got. I was tired on both ends."

"No, no no. I called my child and she told me that she was moving to New Jersey. I had no words; I just threw my hands in the air. Then, she says she needs a new start and I knew that was a lie. She was trying to get away from Terrance and look what happened; she was busy running behind him when all of this happened." They both took deep breaths and lay back in their chairs.

"I guess I'll get comfortable and watch some TV and keep you company." Barbara said with a warm smile.

"Excuse me, are you ready to go?" Jordan clears his throat as he enters Blake's office.

"Whew wee, look at how you clean up?" she admired his attire for lunch.

"I can do a little something when I get ready. I have this for you." Jordan handed Blake a red rose that he had behind his back for her.

"Aww, thank you. That is too sweet. Who told you I liked roses, your sister?"

"Naw, a lucky guess."

"By, the way, did you tell your sister that we were going out for lunch today?"

"Let me tell you this, I'm a grown man. I don't know what my sister has said to you, but I am all man, but you will find out on your own." Blake took a deep breath.

"If you say so Mr. Miller."

"I like the sound of that. C'mon lets go." Jordan rented a car for the day so he could impress Blake. He definitely didn't want to take her out in his mother's car. With the money he would be making, he would never have to drive anyone else's car again. Deep down, he knew Blake was all he wanted, he just had to prove it to her. There was only one thing standing in the way of that and her name was Jayden. Jordan didn't know how she would react to him pursuing Blake so he would rather do it without her knowing for right now just in case she ruined everything.

He took Blake to a nice restaurant not far from the job. She didn't ask any questions about whose car he was driving. Of course she knew it wasn't his mother's or Jayden's so she was content with that. She followed his lead and let him be the gentleman. He opened the door for her and helped her out of the car. He held her hand while they walked into the restaurant. He had reservations so the host was anticipating them when they walked in. He pulled out her chair and assisted her sitting down. She thanked him and he took his seat. He let her order first and decide what wine they would have for lunch.

"I didn't know you could be so sweet."

"There is a lot you don't know about me." She grinned to herself. "You look beautiful as always."

"Thank you. The last time you saw me, I was in my bed clothes."

"Correction, you had on lingerie like you were waiting for someone."

"Boy, those are my night clothes. I don't wear them for anyone."

"Not yet."

"Excuse me, what did you say?" the waiter walked up just in time to take their order. Jordan knew he was saved with that one. There was a part of him that wanted Blake to hear how he really felt, but he knew he would have time for that, but he didn't want to take it too slow since there was a possibility he would be moving with his NFL career getting ready to take off.

"Thank you."

"It won't take long for your food to be out." The waiter collected the menus and headed to the kitchen.

"So, how has your return to work been for you?"

"A lot. I have a new project already. I don't know what these people are thinking."

"I'm surprised that you want to go back into corporate. Didn't your pops leave you with enough bread that you didn't have to work again?"

"Yeah, he did, but money doesn't give you a career and work ethic."

"You got a point, but most people choose a career so they can live comfortably and do things that take money to do."

"You are right, but my career means more to me than that."

"That says a lot about a person. So would you move to another job somewhere else if you had a better opportunity?"

"Right now, I probably would depending upon the opportunity faced. Now, enough about me, let's talk about you Mr. Miller. What have you been up to since you've been back." Jordan laughed her question off as he didn't want to mention anything about his contract or going into the league. He didn't know how she would react to that and plus he hadn't mentioned it to his family either.

"School is good, football is good. I am just chilling right now, trying to iron out some things."

"What things are you trying to iron out? You laughing again, that can't be a good thing."

"Naw, its cool. I am working on some business ventures that I would rather not talk about, but I am on a break remember, so I have a lot of free time to focus on someone special." Jordan looked directly in Blake's eyes from across the table, while reaching for her hand, massaging it slowly and carefully.

"Jordan, what are you doing?" she whispered across the table to him. "I already told you, we can't be like...."

"Be like what?"

"You know what I mean..." the waiter brought the food out.

"Wow, this looks good. Eat up Jordan." He smiled, pulled out his napkin and placed it on his lap to eat his lunch.

"How is your food?"

"It's good; don't think you can change the subject on me. Let me ask you something, are you nervous around me?"

"Why would I be nervous around you?"

"I don't know. I mean, you seem to be more comfortable when you can put me in this little box of being Jayden's little brother, but you get all uneasy when you see me as a grown man."

"I don't know what you are talking about. I act the same. There is no difference."

"Really! What would you do if I leaned in right now and kissed you?" Blake took a deep breath. She became warm on the inside. She wasn't expecting him to say that. She thought for a moment to herself, *"Oh my god, if he kissed me right now, I would melt....damn, he's coming close to me..."*

Jordan leaned in and kissed Blake on her lips softly and slowly, just how she liked it. He let his tongue glide in her mouth while lips softly pressed on hers. She closed her eyes and kissed him passionately back.

"Jordan, stop, what are you doing?"

"Shh, stop talking and kiss me." She kissed him back without hesitation. She was having a feeling on the inside like nothing before. She wanted him and she wanted him bad. He wanted to put his arms around her waist and feel every inch of her body, but he couldn't because they were still in the restaurant.

"Excuse me, can I get you two anything else?" They both stopped and looked at the waiter.

'Naw, we are good."

"She is a beautiful woman, if I may add."

"Thank you." Blake was blushing at the comment he the waiter made.

"You can bring us the check." The waiter turned away to get the bill.

"We're leaving already." Blake was beginning to become more and more comfortable with Jordan and she liked it.

"You have to go back to work, don't you?"

"Yeah, I do." she wasn't expecting Jordan to say that.

"Oh crap, I forgot I have to run to the house and get something that I need for work." Blake pulled out her cell phone.

"Wait, I can take you to your house." Blake looked at Jordan.

"I don't know if that is a good idea."

"Why do you say that? You are just going to get a file right? I can swing you by your house and then take you back to work. Plus, I need to catch up with Jayden, so its fine." The waiter brought the bill to the table. Jordan gave him his credit card to rush him away from the table. He loved having Blake's undivided attention and he definitely loved that he could be her savior right now.

"Alright because I really need this file from the house."

"Calm, down, we can go just as soon as he brings my card back. If I don't get a chance to tell you this later, thank you for coming to lunch with me." He leaned in, grabbing her arm, running his hand down her forearm. Blake once again was getting caught in the moment with Jordan, just one more thing she didn't want to do.

"Here you go sir and you two have a nice day."

'Thanks man." He turned to Blake, "You ready?" Blake grabbed her bag and got up from the table avoiding direct eye contact with Jordan on purpose. Jordan raced in front of her so he could open the door for her to exit.

"What's wrong?" Jordan asked Blake as they were walking to Jordan's car.

"Nothing, just thinking about work, that's all." Blake started going through her blackberry even though there we no new emails coming through. Jordan made sure that he was on his best behavior and not too abrupt with Blake. He opened the car door and he stayed there until she was well put in the car. He smiled to himself as he walked to the driver side. Blake was very quiet on the ride to her house; Jordan didn't know what to make of it. He didn't want to think too much into it so he just focused on getting her to her house and back to work.

"Stop it, stop it! You can't have feelings for him. He's Jayden's little brother. Get a grip of yourself. Are you this desperate that you want your best friend's brother? That is pretty pathetic..or maybe this is my chance like Mrs. Deborah said....No, No, No this is wrong, no matter what." All of these things were running through Blake's mind, but she just couldn't choose which way to go. Instead of deciding, she wouldn't say anything. Jordan pulled in the driveway of Blake's home and pulled down under the garage.

"Here we go."

"I'll be right back." Blake got out of the car, while taking her keys out of her bag to open the door.

"Do you need any help?"

"No, I got it. I'll be right back." Blake opened the door to her house hurriedly and turned the alarm off in the den area. She ran upstairs to her bedroom, *"Ughhhhhh, what is wrong with me? Damn, I feel warm, bothered, and horny...I need a shower, but I can't."* Blake was pacing in her bedroom trying to get her nerves together before going back downstairs in the car with Jordan. At that moment, she wanted Jordan, but she was going to keep it to herself. *"What is wrong with me?"*

"Nothing." When Blake heard the voice, she quickly turned around and saw Jordan standing in the doorway to her bedroom. "I want you too."

'What are you talking about? I thought I told you to wait in the car. I just knew this wasn't a good idea for you to bring me here." Jordan listened to Blake rant and rave about it wasn't a good idea. The only thing he could think about was Blake in his arms.

"Are you done?" Jordan walked closer to Blake and he noticed she was shaking, nervous as hell because she couldn't take Jordan kissing her again like he did at lunch. Jordan was so close that their bodies were touching. He was undressing her with his eyes.

"Jordan, I am not your jump off." Jordan placed his finger on her lip as he took his left arm, placing it around her waist, he leaned in to kiss her just like he did at the restaurant. She no longer could fight her feelings. She grabbed the back of his head, pushing him to kiss her more passionately. He unbuttoned the jacket to her suit as she moaned for more. She backed away, grabbing Jordan by the hand, pulling him to her bed. She took her heels off while Jordan stood there watching her. She pulled him closer to her by his belt buckle, kissing him as she fell back on the bed. Blake allowed Jordan to reach every intimate part of her body. Never had he felt the way he did about any woman, Blake seemed perfect in his eyes. While they were both naked under the satin sheets, Jordan looked Blake in her eyes, "Do you still think I am not serious?"

Just the thought of his words made Blake melt. She wanted him even more than before. She kissed him on his neck moving her tongue to his lips. He caressed her body gently, making sure he satisfied her in every way possible. She craved for a man to satisfy her and Jordan was doing just that. Not in a million years did she expect Jordan to fulfill her in this way, but he damn sure was doing the job. They made each other climax several times, enjoying and satisfying each other.

"Hi everyone!" Jayden entered the Dalia's hospital room and by surprise she saw Barbara and Mrs. Deborah.

"Hey, we were just talking about you. We were wondering where you were."

"Oh, goodness, I don't have to guess who said that," she was making eye contact with Barbara.

"And you know it...How you doing dear?" Barbara got up to hug Jayden.

"When did you get into town?"

"I got here a few hours ago and I came straight here and me and Deborah have been talking."

"That don't sound like a good thing. Mrs. Deborah, have the doctor's been here and said anything?" Deborah shook her head before responding.

"I thought she moved her hand earlier this morning, but Dr. Cole told me it was just a reaction and no change in her condition."

"There is nothing they can do?"

"No, baby. We just have to wait and pray. You brought your lap top?"

"Yeah, Lauren is supposed to come by later today after work and help me look for some jobs. So, I figured while I was here that I could search for some on the web." Barbara sat up in her chair.

"Now I thought that Lauren's new boyfriend was starting a new firm here..."

"Yeah, he is, but that is not in my field."

"O, you hear that Deborah?"

"Hmm....mmm."

"Is this supposed to be an inside joke or something?"

"No, search for your jobs on the internet." Barbara and Deborah laughed to each other at Jayden's expense. Jayden plugged her computer up in the wall and started typing away.

"Its almost lunch time why don't you all go get something to eat and Mrs. Deborah, I know you need a break from this room and you been here all night."

"Barbara, is this child trying to tell us what to do?"

"I think so..but, I don't mind going to get something to eat."

"Alright, let's go. Jayden, do you want anything?"

"No, I am fine. I ate before I left the house this morning. Y'all can bring me some desert back though." The ladies grabbed their bags and headed out.

"We won't be gone long."

"Alright."

Jayden sat in the room searching the internet for jobs. All she could hear were the sounds of the machines pumping into Dalia and her body pushing upward and downward. There was a feeding tube in her arm to make sure that she received her lipids and fats each day. Jayden didn't want to focus on it, because it would be too depressing, but she wanted to support her because she would have done the same for her if she were lying in the hospital bed.

Slowly the door creped open and when Jayden looked up it was Terrance. She just looked at him and he looked back at her.

"Uh hey, any change with her?"

"I don't know you tell me." By this time, Jayden had removed the reading glasses from her face and she was prepared for anything Terrance was getting ready to throw her way.

"Jayden, I know you mad and pissed off at me, but I can't do this…"

"What the hell you mean you can't do this, do what exactly?" Jayden wanted to clarification from Terrance before she said how she really felt.

'I can't come here and see her fighting for what is left of her life day in and day out. She can't hear me. I can't show her how I feel." Terrance broke down in front of Jayden, but she didn't have any sympathy.

"Is it that you can't do it because while she was trying to fight for whatever the two of you have, you were scheming with Carmen? I think its call a conscious muthafucker."

"I never said I was prefect Jayden. Shit, you don't know why I did what I did or what I was going through."

"Honestly, I don't give a fuck because when you married her that means you took vows to be there for each other and you missed that part."

"So now everything is my fault?"

"No, you not being here like a husband should is your fault and when she wakes up, I am going to tell her that you were lost for a while, but you decided to resurface to tell us that you couldn't do it anymore."

"Jayden, you wouldn't do that. That is some bullshit."

"It's what the fuck you are doing. If you want sympathy, I am not the one to give it to you. You must have thought Mrs. Deborah was here, but she is not. If you aren't here to be a good husband, then why are you here?"

"I came to say goodbye. I already lost my baby and now I could be losing Dalia, I can't deal with that too. I am leaving town and I am not coming back. Tell Dalia I love her." Jayden took two steps closer to Terrance.

"You son of a bitch, you would leave my friend when she needs you most." Jayden started swinging on Terrance, turning over the table and chairs in her pathway. Terrance couldn't even fight her off. One of the nurse's in the hallway heard the ruckus and came to break the two of them you.

"I will have to ask the two of you to leave if you can't control yourselves. This patient needs support, not all of this bickering. Work it out or I will have you removed."

"Don't worry about it nurse, he is leaving." Terrance had no words. There was no way he could respond to Jayden's attack on him. He turned around and left out of the room.

"I can't believe him. I hope he never comes back." Jayden said as she turned towards Dalia bedside rubbing her head. "Don't worry about him; I am right here for you. You can always count me, the girls and your mother to be here for you."

Chapter 31: Everyone Can't Do Love

"We have to get up; I have to go back to work." Jordan kissed Blake on her neck.

"Do you have to go back to work?" Blake became memorized with the affect Jordan's kisses had on her.

She slowly responded, "Yes, I do. I have some new projects that I have to work on with a strict deadline." Jordan didn't stop, he continued kissing hoping that Blake couldn't resist him and she couldn't. They lay back under the sheets, making love again.

"You can't keep doing this to me." Blake moaned in the heat of passion.

"Blake, your body is so soft and sweet that I don't want to stop kissing you." Every word this man said to her just swept her off her feet without him even knowing it. He had a touch that Blake couldn't deny. He touched her soul, mind, and body, that no one has been able to touch for a very long time. With everything she had been to over the past year, this man was taking her mind to new heights she never experienced. She no longer thought about him being Jayden's little brother, but this amazing man, who is changing her life.

Blake had no insecurities with Jordan. He was making her happy inside and out. As she enjoyed every kiss from Jordan, she felt that she was finally in a happy place. *"To hell with work for just a couple more minutes,"* Blake said to herself.

"You ready to go back to work?"

"Are you ready to take me back to work?"

"It's whatever you want babe. But, I don't want you to be in trouble with work."

"Damn! I know I need to get back." Jordan stopped kissing because he didn't want to put her in a bad position at work, just one thing led to another.

"C'mon, let's get dressed and I'll take you back. I'll see you later." Blake smiled, "Of course, you will."

All kind of thoughts were running through Jordan's head. It didn't matter to him that she came from a wealth or that her sister attempted to kill her, all that mattered to him was that he cared for her and he wanted her completely.

He wanted Blake to see the genuine side of him and fall for who he was not who he was to become. Even though from what he knew about Blake she was nothing like that, he didn't want her to get the wrong impression by sharing too much in the beginning.

As he got dressed in Blake's bedroom, he glanced at her sliding back into her suit and straightening her hair. He kept thinking to himself, *"Damn she is beautiful."* Apparently, she was reading his mind because she gave him the most beautiful smile back. In their own way, they were connecting like to lovers who have known each other for a lifetime. They enjoyed their moment and they had no regrets.

"Jordan, I am ready."

"Alright, let's go." Blake walked down her stairs like a new woman with a new attitude. Jordan followed behind her. Just as soon as she reached the bottom step, she turned around, "Can you believe what we just did?"

"What do you mean?"

"I just slept with my best friend's little brother. How am I going to tell her that?"

"What are you going to tell her? You fell for her little brother. You are making too much of it."

"You really think I am making too much of it?"

"I don't think you should say anything to her until we have talked and decided what we are doing."

"I didn't think there was anything to talk about. I can tell how you feel Jordan by the way your lips touched me and I feel the same way. I can't keep this from her."

"I don't think it's a good idea to do that right now. Everything is still fresh and new, give it some time, when it is right, then we can tell her together. But for now, let's just keep it between us."

"Jordan, I don't know how long I can do this." Blake made her comments walking out of the door to her house. He opened the door for her and he could tell she felt uncomfortable about the situation. He got in on the driver's side, "So, you are going to mess up a good afternoon over what you think my sister is going to think or feel about us." Blake took a deep breath.

"I guess you are right. Jordan, I just don't want anymore drama. I have had enough."

"I understand, but I don't think my sister is something to worry about right now." She took a deep breath again and lay back in the seat.

"Okay Jordan if you say so." On the ride back to the marketing firm, Blake couldn't really get past Jayden finding out about her and Jordan before she decided to tell her, but if she wanted a relationship with Jordan it would be something she would have to deal with and face later when the time was right. He could see the tension in her face; he took his hand and massaged her thigh.

"What are you doing," she asked softly.

"I am trying to make you feel better. It's gonna be alright, trust me."

"You have a word for everything, don't you?"

"Naw, just for you." No matter what this man was saying, he always knew what to say to make her feel better and it worked every time.

When they arrived back at the marketing firm, Blake jumped out of the car, not sure if she was supposed to kiss Jordan or not, she turned around to see if he was waiting on one anyway. But, just as soon as she turned around, he was prepared.

"I have somewhere to be right now, I will call you in about an hour, are you going to be free?" without even thinking clearly. "YES!" Jordan smiled back at her, "Alright, I will call you in a little while, beautiful." She was so elated on the inside, but she didn't want to show too much emotion too early on. She closed the door and walked back into the building. She pretended to keep her cool returning back to work an hour later than usual when she takes her lunch break.

"Hey, Blake, I am glad you are back. Jim has been calling for you like crazy the past 30 minutes." Tina ran up to Blake when she got off the elevator.

"What the heck did he want, did he say?"

"No, he just started asking for you and when you would be back."

"Okay, give me a minute, I will go in my office and call him." Blake closed her door as she was already prepared for a long evening ahead of her. She dialed Jim's line, "Hi Jim, this is Blake; I am returning your call."

"Hey, I have some new information that will help you prepare for the presentation on Friday that I know you are going to need. You know Sellers is quite happy that you are taking on his new assignment."

"He is…is he?"

"Oh yeah, he has a lot of faith in you and that is why I am trusting you with this project. I am going to shoot you an email with some files and you can send Tina by my office to pick up the charts I have. This should ease your burden a lot in preparing. Don't forget to check in with me on Wednesday for our meeting to determine where you are and what needs to be done. I have a meeting so I will talk to you on Wednesday."

"Ok, take care." She could barely get a word as he was going nonstop. She knew this assignment was huge so she had no time to play. She had to prove to everyone in the company that she didn't get the job off her money, but her hard work and dedication to the company.

Just as soon as she got a head start on her project, she received a phone call. "Hello"

"Hey, beautiful." She automatically knew who that was on the other end of the phone.

"Hi, there, what are you doing?"

"I just got finished with a meeting, what about you?"

"I am working on a project that I have to have completed by Friday."

"If I am disturbing you, I can call you back later."

"NO, you are fine." She was waiting for Jordan to jump in and say something.

"What are your plans for the evening?"

"Nothing at all, I was hoping that you would be in them."

"Hell yeah, I like it when you talk like that. Well, we could go out for dinner and maybe a movie, whatever you like."

"Its all good with me....oh shit, I forgot, I have to go to the hospital to see Dalia, I promised the girls."

"That's not a problem babe, we can do whatever when you leave the hospital. I'm not going anywhere." She could exhale for once. This man said all the right things and it didn't matter if he was just acting on his best behavior because it was just what she needed in her life right now.

"Okay, let me talk to you later, I have some work I need to finish up or I won't be able to leave on time."

"Call me when you get off."

"I will."

"Dang, I haven't taken a lunch yet."

The phone rings, "Hello, this is Miss Daniels."

"Hey, babe it's me. I thought you would have called me on your lunch break, but I didn't hear anything."

"Hell, I have been stuck at my desk all morning and I have so much work to do it is ridiculous."

"You sound frustrated babe. Have you eaten today?"

'No, Kendall I haven't eaten anything."

"Would you like for me to bring you something?" Lauren took her eyes off her computer screen for a moment and thought about having lunch in her office and having someone deliver it to her: that sounded so good.

"Oh, babe, you would do that? That would be great, bring me a salad and it doesn't matter what kind."

"Dang, were you waiting for me to ask you that?"

"Naw, not really, but since you did, bring me a salad."
She laughed at his comment.

"Alright, I will be there in a bit."

"K, gotta go, I have plenty of work to do before I leave today."

Lauren disconnected the phone before was able to say anything back to her. Her focus was now on satisfying her clients. She had a lot of numbers to crunch and a lot of phone calls to make. The last thing she needed was interruptions and distractions.

Lauren tried her best to stay focus and get as much accomplished as possible before she left for the day, but it was hard after hearing that her team was being let go because they were all stealing. She was glad she avoided that bullet. She had too much financial responsibility right now to even think about not having her job. She wanted to talk to them or try and save their jobs, but from the way her boss looked, she didn't want to keep pressing because he might get suspicious of her. Lauren spent the next half an hour trying to locate the files and ledgers that Terry prepared for her on all her clients and getting the files that John and Jack compiled for her. Once she had all of that, she could prepare their files for hand delivery when she made her visits this week. She was more hands on than any other accountant in the firm. She liked to meet with her clients and get a feel of how they like things, not to make them feel intimidated, because that was the way the employees looked at her when she did make visits, but it was far from her intentions.

There was a knock at the door and she knew it was Kendall with her lunch, after working all morning and skipping over her normal lunch time, it felt good for her to come out of the mode of crunching numbers and plus seeing Kendall was great too. She would be able to see how his day was going.

"Come in."

"Hey babe."

"Awe, you didn't have to do that." Not only did Kendall walk in with food and snacks Lauren liked, but with a bouquet of flowers to make her day better.

"You sounded like you needed a break, but you couldn't get away from your desk, so I thought this would put a smile on your face." Lauren rose from her chair with her arms opened wide to accept the flowers, she kissed Kendall on the cheek telling him thank.

"Oh hell no, I drove almost cross town to bring you lunch and flowers and you give me a kiss on the cheek. Woman, you better come back here and give me a real kiss." Lauren turned around and gave Kendall a nice, long kiss to his liking. "Now, that is more like it."

"Thanks for my lunch and the flowers; they are beautiful. They will go great here in my office. So, what have you been doing today?"

"Well, I brought in a couple of new attorneys fresh out of law school, which is good. I want some temps, but I know it won't take long to get them in and working. I just need to make sure that I get people that want to work. This is a lot of work, but its coming together." Lauren started eating her salad while she was listening to Kendall talk about his morning, because she was tired of going over hers.

"Babe, that is good you have gotten that much accomplished. Are you going to meet your deadline?"

"I am just so nervous about that too, because if we get walk-in cases right now, guess who will have to take them?"

"No, not you?"

"Yes, ma'am, so I need to make a move on it. What I really need right now is a office manager, who can handle hiring people so that by the time I see them, they are already screened and I am the final face they see before being hired......Mmm, but I don't know anyone." Lauren was thinking to herself, still while eating her lunch, *"Damn, I hope he doesn't call Jayden's name because she already said she didn't want to work for Kendall. She thought that was going to be a bad idea."*

"Babe!" Lauren almost jumped out of her chair.

"Why are you calling me like we are not in the same room?"

"My bad….do you think Jayden would come be my office manager for a little while?" Lauren was thinking to herself, *"damn"*.

"Uh, Ken, I don't know about that. I mean, Jayden doesn't know anything about law, politics, or that paralegal stuff."

"She don't need to know that," he said is if that was irrelevant to what he was asking.

"She has a wedding to plan…." She was about to run out of excuses.

"How is she going to pay for it?" he thought for sure she couldn't come back after that one.

"What do you mean….between her father and Brian."

"Damn!!!!!"

"Right, but if it means that much to you, I will ask her." Lauren got up from behind her desk and placed her containers in the trash can. "That salad was really good. Why didn't you bring yourself something to eat?"

"I already ate and I thought you did, if I would have known Miss Daniels, I would have had lunch with you in your office….so, what had you all ruffled up this morning?" Lauren put her glasses back on the tip of her nose, so she could go back to crunching numbers.

"You think you want to know?" she looked at Kendall out of the corner of her eye.

"Dang, is it that bad?"

"It's bad enough for me..." she leaned in closer to Kendall, "They let go of my team this morning."

"WHAT!!!"

"Yes, they said they were stealing monies, not directly, but making sure it was covered up in the books for my clients." Kendall's eyes grew bigger.

"How in the hell did you let that happen?" Lauren took offense to Kendall trying to blame her for it.

"What the hell you mean?"

"If they are working on your clients, you are the accountant, not them. They shouldn't be able to get to your books like that and if they do, they damn sure shouldn't be able to change some

376

of files with monies like that. I hope you all have a good legal team."

"Are you saying that I am wrong and this is my fault?" Lauren became very defensive.

"I wish you would stop getting all defensive...."

"No, you are saying this is my fault."

"Whose idea was it for you to have a team to assist with your books?"

"Mr. Lawson said that with the number of accounts that I have and the request that I was getting, I should have a team to handle the work and that I only need to step in when necessary."

"Are you serious? You can't do that when you are dealing with people's monies."

"Shut up before they throw you out of here for talking so loud."

"Quit this job and you can run the Accounting Department at my office."

"WHAT!!! So, now you just want to hire everyone and have them under your thumb."

"Do you know depending how this may fall out, those companies could turn around and sue you, the company and your team in civil suits?"

"I didn't think about that."

"I know you didn't, be thankful your man is a lawyer. I need to stop giving this advice away for free." Before Kendall knew it, Lauren was using hand motions.

"No, no, no, no...I worked hard to get this office and to have a team under me, to have private clients, and this flexibility. Do you know how hard I worked to get my home and the car I drive and you want to just leave this firm because some people decided to take some money that didn't belong to them. I don't think so."

"So money is the problem?" Kendall sat down with his hand over his mouth as this seems so simple to him.

"You don't get it. I have been here a long time and right now, I don't want to start at the bottom of no one's CPA firm." After her ranting for about ten minutes, Kendall stood up in her face and grabbed her by the waist.

"Hey, calm down," he said quietly to her while looking into her eyes. "No matter what, I got you, you don't have to worry about no house, car, or job." Lauren squeezed her eyes and titled her head back a little from him, "Whatcha mean?"

Kendall just smiled back at her and kissed her on the lips, "don't worry about it. You will find out in time."

She hugged him back, "what am I going to do with you?"

"Na, what are you going to do without me?"

"Dee, I know you can't hear me, but I have a problem. You know how I always jump off and you will tell me to chill out. I really need you to wake up and tell me that I need to chill out, please! I miss you and I need you to wake up. No one understands me like you. Do you remember how much fun we used to have when we were younger and all the mess we went through in college? Remember all the crazy stuff we did at my father's wedding....I need you to wake up so I know that you hear me and you do remember."

Tears ran down Jayden's face for more reasons that one. Of course, it was eating away at her that her best friend was fighting for her life in the hospital and there was nothing she could do. She felt helpless and the silence in the room just made everything worst. Along with her pain for Jayden, she knew she was killing her relationship with Brian by jumping to conclusions all the time. If anyone could get her straight about her attitude it was Dalia and she needed her now, especially since she never really made amends with her mother.

"Oh, Dee, I hope you can hear me." Jayden rubbed her hands through her hair. She stared at her helpless friend, thinking of good times and happy thoughts. She felt vulnerable and not many people get to see that side of her, but she showed weakness where Dalia was concerned.

"Barbara, look at that. You know dem kids ain't nothing but babies anyway." Barbara and Deborah returned from their lunch and walked in on Jayden lying in the hospital bed next to Dalia.

"Honey, did the doctor come in while we were gone, did they say anything about her condition?" Barbara was very concerned about Dalia's state and whether the doctor was doing all he could for her.

"Barbara, you know you don't see tears like this all the time for this one. Something else must be wrong."

"Hold up, I bet I know what it is...."

"Me too...." They chuckled at each other and in unison, "A MAN."

"Why do you women always have something to say?" Jayden hopped out of the bed wiping her eyes to remove any remnants of her crying. Deborah looked out of the corner of her eyes at Jayden, "tell me we are wrong?"

"I am not saying anything."

Knock, knock!!! The door opened and it was Jackie, Jayden's mother.

"Hi ladies, how are you all. You must be Barbara; your daughter looks so much like you."

"Well, yes I am, I don't know if I know you or not." Barbara looked with a puzzled look on her face.

"I am Jayden's mother, Jackie."

"Oh my goodness, nice to meet you."

"Same here," they shook hands with a smile.

"Deb, how is she doing?"

"Jackie it is so good to see you." Deborah hugged Jackie. All she could do was shake her head.

"It's going to be alright...." She turned her energy to Jayden who was looking out of the window, "hello, Jayden, you aren't going to speak to your mother."

"Hello," Jayden said without any emotion. Her mother didn't look too pleased with Jayden's attitude.

"Jayden, let me talk to you for a minute outside in the hallway." Jayden and her mother walked out into the hallway.

"I haven't heard anything from you at all. You didn't tell me anything about Dalia and what was going with her. I was worried about where Deborah was going to stay and I didn't hear anything from her. Plus your brother is in town and you still ain't call. I just don't know what is wrong with you. Hell, I didn't even know this child was in a coma. I didn't raise you to be disrespectful, but don't think you can live in this world alone Jayden Miller. You have a lot of growing up to do, now what do you have to say for yourself." By this time, Jayden was just listening to her mother fuss. It reminded her of when she was a teenager and she made bad choices with friends or missed curfew, either way, she wasn't feeling it.

"Ma, I have a lot going on and if you really wanted to know how Dalia was doing, you could have called me," she said with the most sympathetic look on her face. Then, did Jordan tell you that he was by the house the other day so I saw him, but he came to see Brian, he didn't come to see me and he has been staying in my house. I have been checking in on him and he has been in touch with me, everything is cool with that."

"So, you are just being disrespectful to me and your father?"

'Oh, Lord Jesus! I don't want to talk about this at the hospital."

"I'm just going to say this. GET OVER IT! You live your life how you want and I don't say anything. I can do the same. I wish you would grow up and see that." the nurse walked by and saw how intense the conversation was between Jayden and her mother, "Ladies, you will have to keep it down."

"Now you look like something is wrong, what is it?"

"I really don't feel like talking."

"Hell, I didn't ask you how you felt; I said what is wrong with you? Is it Brian?"

"Why does everyone say that?"

"Because it is the truth. It's hard isn't it?"

"What's hard?"

"Trying to play wife?" Jayden looked at her mother and she realized too that she was just like her mother.

"Ma, it's more than hard…it's trust, communication, love, companionship, togetherness, and staying all of that…man, I don't know." Jayden sat in the first chair out in the hallway.

"I know, I had the same problem with your father when I was younger."

"So, that is what kept you and Daddy a part."

"Oh yeah, that and some other things, we were fine together, but marriage, no! That wasn't going to work for us back them."

"We got into a big argument this morning. I accused him of something and he got mad like the world was over. He walked out the house…I've never seen him this angry over an argument."

"You know no one said you had to rush this engagement. You can always take your time and do it when you are ready, but don't wear a ring and not plan to get married. You might as well put it in a jewelry box for showcase." They laughed together, which hadn't happened since she found out her mother and father were still sleeping together.

"But that ain't it. Terrance came here earlier and I jumped all over him literally for not being here for Dalia. He was getting on my nerves. Everything he said just sounded stupid to me."

"What did he say?"

"Basically, that he was coming by to say goodbye because he couldn't take seeing her like that. He loved her, but he couldn't come see her helpless like that, literally his words ma."

"You have got to be kidding me. He is a grown man or at least I thought he was." Jackie's mouth was open listening to Jayden talk about her altercation with Terrance.

"I was trying to keep my cool for the longest with him and there was no one there to hold me back, I just went off and so did my punches."

"Have you told Deborah what happened?"

"She just got back with Mrs. Barbara from lunch."

"Well, where is Deborah staying, I want her to come stay with me?"

"She is staying at Blake's house."

"Oh, no, no, no…I'll bring her with me so she can let that young girl be young."

"Ma, what! You know what, if that is what works for you, then that is what it is."

"Come here and give me a hug. I haven't hugged you in a long time. You should go home and work out that problem that you and Brian have."

"Yeah, I am about to go. I thought I could wait on the girls, but I don't know about that."

"Oh, they are coming?"

"Just as soon as they get off, both Blake and Lauren, Jackie looked at her watch, "You don't have much longer to wait on them."

Chapter 32: Tuesday!

"Bart, my man, what you got for me." Bart pulled his briefcase out on the table to pull out contracts he had for Jordan to sign to be with Baltimore. For some reason, Jordan wasn't too sure about this deal that Bart had to tell him about, even though he only briefly discussed it with him. All night, Jordan tossed and turned all night about his career and Blake. He found himself falling for her harder than expected. He spent the evening with her, just getting to know the things she liked and what she didn't like. They had dinner and a movie, quiet at home. They didn't have to worry about Deborah being there because she decided to stay with his mother. He knew she was the one and he couldn't move to fast with her, but he has his reasons for wanting to. He knew once he made the decision to sign with a team, his life would be in the lime light and there would be no turning back.

Then, it was his family that played a role in this too. He was always close to Jayden and he really didn't know how she would react to him falling in love with her best friend. He couldn't expect her to just be in love with the idea, but he would expect her to respect his decision and deal with it. Now, there would be another story with Blake and Jayden. He didn't know how his sister would now treat her when their relationship goes public. It was all too much for him to think about.

The news he got from his meeting Monday afternoon after he dropped Blake off had him confused also. He didn't tell anyone about this meeting because he wanted to weigh out his options. Even though his mother didn't think he knew how to handle his business, it was far from the truth with that. Jordan wasn't the irresponsible college boy they knew and grew to love unconditionally over the past couple of years while he was in college. He had transformed himself to be more mature. He was ready to be the man, he was raised to be and he was ready to share that with someone special. Somehow that special someone happened to be Blake.

Depending upon what Bart really had to offer him at this meeting would determine a lot. This meeting would set what he would spend the next couple of years of his life.

"Well Jordan, I talked to the coach for Baltimore...."

"Man, you ain't saying nothing yet." Jordan couldn't quite read his face.

"Baltimore wants to offer you good money, but only a two year deal."

"Bart that was the best you could do."

"Hey, you can go to the Lions and get a five year deal and get about $5 million a year, but do you think you will get a ring there, think about it Jordan. This deal isn't bad. You could make a name for yourself." Jordan took a deep breath thinking about what decision he should make. He knew Bart knew how to pull strings, but now he was wondering if he was pulling the right ones for him or was he being too uneasy about his Bart.

"Well, I had my own meeting yesterday."

"OH...." Bart looked shocked as ever. He never thought Jordan would come out like that or go behind his back and handle his own dealings.

"Carolina wants me too."

"CAROLINA! No one said anything to me."

"I know I was talking to them. They seem to want me pretty bad. They are offering a good deal too, so what else you got?"

"Jordan, I don't get it. Do you not trust me or something; why else would you steal this deal away from me?"

"From you! This is my career, and no one said that I couldn't be involved and that I couldn't get my own deal."

"Alright Jordan, what kind of deal did you get?"

"They offered me a four year deal with $3 million a year and $1 sign on bonus."

"Wow! I don't know what to say. How did you manage to pull that off?"

"As long as my agent wasn't involved, they were ready to deal."

"You didn't sign anything did you?"

"Now, Bart, why would I do something like that? I brought my papers here, I wanted you to look over them and have my lawyer look at them too."

"Alright, let me take a look at them." Jordan pulled out his folder that he had been holding in his hand for the past hour sitting with Bart. He slid the papers over to Bart as if he were proud of himself. While Bart was browsing through the papers, Jordan decided to order some breakfast for himself. Jordan already knew this deal was solid because the new head coach at Carolina was the assistant coach at his school that he grew to have a good relationship. This was one minor detail he failed to share with Bart on purpose. He wanted to see what Bart could do on his own to test his loyalties to him. Jordan didn't know what to think when Bart really seemed hurt by the other offer he got when he found out it was done without him.

Bart pulled his glasses off and stacked the papers up in the folder looking at Jordan, "Wow! That seems to be a more solid deal than I had, I can't even argue with it. It's everything you said it was. I would be lying if I told you not to take this offer."

"You serious man or are you just pulling my leg?"

"I am very serious Mr. Miller; it looks like you are going to be a Panther."

"WHEW!!!!! Wait, wait, wait, I forgot about Blake."

"Blake, who is Blake?" For a minute Jordan was elated that he made his mind up about his career, but at the same time, he didn't know how he would tell his family.

"Jordan, I guess we will really see in the draft."

"Damn, I forgot about that."

"How could you forget about that? That really decides where you are going and the money you are getting. Are you going to attend or just sit home?"

"I'm not going. I got some other things to work out. As long as I know my money is coming and where I am going, I am good."

"At least you know you have Baltimore and Carolina as the highest bidders."

"I really think Carolina is going to be my home."

"That is going to be big difference from here. Take a look around you and see all the city here. You are not going to get that in the south like that."

"There is only one thing that I am worried about moving down south and it has nothing to do with being down south." In the back of his mind, Jordan kept thinking if Blake would come with him or if he would have to leave her. He was so sure that Carolina would pick him up that he knew it was time for him to talk to Blake, but he didn't want to pressure her. He wasn't too concern with the feelings of his family right now, because he was more concerned with his future, a family life of his own. He hoped that his parents and his sister would support his decisions with the move to Carolina and wanting to spend the rest of his life with Blake.

"Hey, Jordan, I have another appointment to get to. I will let you know if I hear any other good news for you and or anything about the draft." Bart shook Jordan's hand and pats him on the back. "If I didn't say it before, I am really happy for you."

Now that he knew he was guaranteed $4 million a year, Bart knew his portion was coming for all his hard work. The only thing Jordan wondered was how the draft really was going to turn out and when he should tell Blake about his plans. "Thanks Bart, thanks for everything, I will be in touch." They parted ways and Jordan went on with the rest of his day.

Part II

"Hey Girl, what you doing?"

"Hell, I am trying to get this presentation ready for Jim. He wants to see where I am at on this project by tomorrow. But, I am about to take a break to talk to my best friend Lauren."

"What the hell? You sound too excited to talk to me."

"No, I am great. What did you and Kendall get into when you left the hospital last night?"

"We didn't do too much of anything. We grabbed something to eat and headed back to the house. He had a lot of work to do with the office and I have to get my clients reports together."

"Dang, y'all busy over there."

"Hell yeah, I am telling you I am earning my damn money now. I told Mr. Lawson yesterday that I needed to take a couple of days off so I can get myself together."

"I hear that."

"So, what did you do when you left the hospital last night?" off in a daydream, Blake was thinking about her evening with Jordan. Of course, he was gentleman she was used to. They didn't go out, they stayed in. he bought a bottle of wine and brought take out. He knew Blake had a lot of work to do with this new project so he gave her back rub after they ate and drank some wine. He gave her time to do work and when he felt like distracting her, he knew exactly what to do.

He appeared at door to her office, which was on the other side of her kitchen with a pair of pajama pants and no shirt so she could admire his muscles. He took her glasses off her face and ran her a nice bubble bath that they shared together most of the evening. Ending their time in the bathtub, he grabbed a towel to dry her off and after that she definitely couldn't go back to work. She fell into his arms and they made love, but that wasn't something she wanted to share with Lauren. Hell, she didn't even know they were seeing each other, plus this was new for her too.

"Uh, I just got me something to eat, watched some Law & Order and called it a night." She was lying through her teeth, but she wasn't prepared to have a long drawn out conversation with Lauren about her love life at this moment.

"I think the best thing we did was have at home offices. I never thought I would use it this much."

"Hell, yeah, I use mine more than anything. But, when you think about the type of work we do, we have to have it. We can't really leave our work here. We have to take it home sometimes."

"You are right about that. Hey, you know tomorrow is Wednesday. Do you think we should do something or no?

"Rin, this may seem insensitive, but I really need this break and it would be nice for us to do something together. Do you know how long it has been since we have done something together? I wish Dalia could come and be with us, I miss her so much, but I know it can't be right now."

"I understand how you feel; do you think Jay would go for it?"

"Hey, I think she will."

"I want to call her first and see how she feels. You know she hasn't been taking this too well."

"Alright call her and call me back. I will work on something until I hear something from you.

Part III

"JAY, what you doing?"

"Lauren, why the hell you calling me sounding like a stalker?"

"Because I like to mess with you...well, anyways, I was just talking to Blake and I was telling her that tomorrow is Wednesday and I wanted to know if the two of you wanted to do anything with Dalia's situation and all?"

"Wait a damn minute, what did the princess say?"

Lauren could barely speak a word as she was laughing at how Jayden always found a humorous way to refer to Blake.

"She said that she would like for us to do something because she is stressed out with work."

"And what the hell did you tell her Rin?"

"Why the hell can't you just answer the question? You gotta know what everyone else says before you say anything...that don't make any sense."

"Alright hell, I want to do something. I've had a rough couple of days. I need a massage bad."

"Girl, you got Brian for that."

"Yeah, but I don't know for how much longer."

"Umph, see yeah we need girl talk. Okay, I will call you later with the details for tomorrow. I'll see you at the hospital this afternoon."

"Alright, I'll see you then."

Part IV

'Hey Jordan, are you busy?"

"Uh, naw, babe, what's up?"

"We need to talk now!"

"Right now babe?"

"Yes, we need to talk; can you come to my office right now?"

"Aight, I am on the way." Blake is frantic as she knows when she is with the ladies on tomorrow, she will feel that she needs to share her new love affair, but the problem this time around is that is Jayden is Jordan's problem. She really didn't know how long she would be able to keep that from her best friend, even though she and Jordan agreed to wait to tell her.

It was about fifteen minutes before Jordan arrived to Blake's building when he hurriedly jumped on the elevator, anxious to see what was so urgent that Blake needed him to come over ASAP. He knocked on her office door, "Come in."

"Babe, what's the matter?"

"Dilemma! Jayden, Lauren and I are going out tomorrow as we do on Wednesdays…"

"Okay, then what's the problem?"

"I'm going to tell your sister."

"WHAT! Bee, we talked about this. Now is definitely not the time for you to do this." Jordan sat in the chair right in front of Blake's desk, pleading with her that it wasn't a good time for her to tell that kind of news to her.

"Jordan, I feel really bad about this. She is my best friend. She needs to know I am fucking her little brother."

"Whoa! Wait a minute, is that how you see me?"

"No, that is not how I mean…you see what I am saying…my mind is all messed up because of this." Blake starting tapping the pen in her hand on the desk. Jordan took a deep breath and then he slowly got up and walked around to the other side of Blake's desk. He grabbed both of hands, raising her up out of her chair, "listen to me, everything is good. Don't mention this tomorrow; it won't be good for you to do that, alright."

"Are you saying that you would rather tell her?"

389

"We can tell her together."

"She is going to think I lied to her…and she is going to wonder why I waited so long to tell her…and…." Jordan cut Blake off with a kiss on the lips, soft and slow. "….don't do that to me.."

"Don't do what? Do you know what you mean to me? I love you Blake!" Blake was stunned to hear the words come out of his mouth. She was so stunned that she didn't hear Tina knocking at the door.

"Babe, answer the door."

"Uh, come on. Tina walked in slowly, peeping in the door as if she didn't want to intrude.

"Jim dropped off some files for you that could help you with the meeting tomorrow and he said that you can send him everything via email that you didn't have to have a formal meeting if you didn't need to."

"Great, okay thanks Tina." Tina left and closed the door behind her, not giving any attention to Jordan being there or his presence.

"Is your assistant always that rude or she don't know any better to speak to people?"

"No, no, no, she isn't. She doesn't like to appear nosey, so she will act like you aren't there out of respect to my privacy. I have worked with her a long time, I know how she thinks. I don't know what I would do without her." Still directly in her face, Jordan looked Blake in her eyes, "did you hear what I said earlier?"

'Uh-Uh, yeah I did."

"..and you don't have anything to say?"

"Jordan, can we talk about this later, please, not in my office. You know I don't like to do this kind of stuff at work." The expression on Jordan's face was un-readable at this point. Blake couldn't tell if her response affected him or not, but she knew she couldn't avoid talking about "love".

"So, you just want me to leave."

"I didn't say that…"

"Then what are you saying?" The tone in his voice was giving Blake the impression that he was a little bothered by her not saying she loved him back.

"I'm saying that I want you to sit here and have some conversation with me before you leave, that is all." Blake was trying to break the ice, the tension that was starting to swim around the room. Jordan sat in the chair, quietly waiting for Blake to say something to him.

"Jordan, what are we going to do when I get off?"

"What did you want to do?"

"I want to spend some time with you and I want you to hold me in your arms until I fall asleep."

"Okay, cool, that is fine." Jordan didn't seem as thrilled as she thought he would have been, or how he normally is about spending time with her. Either was really bothered by her reaction to him saying he loved her or something was on his mind. Blake started back working on her project moderately when she noticed Jordan wasn't saying anything at all.

"Jordan, I know you wanted me to say it back to you, but I would rather not talk about it here, that doesn't mean I don't love you too."

"Really!!!!"

"Yes, now can you get out of here so I can focus on my work. I know you have something to do today."

"Whoa, I need to ask you something. I don't know how you would feel about it or not, but I'll ask anyway...." Blake pulled her glasses off.

"What is it, it can't be that bad?"

"I want to go to your house early before you get there and have stuff planned out for you.....you know what, never mind, why don't you come by the house tonight?"

"Uh, you mean Jayden's house?"

"Yeah, you know that is where I am staying."

"Jordan, I don't know if that is a good idea, she might stop by or notice my car in the yard."

"My sister has not been over to the house since I have been back home, so please come over, if she does, I will handle it okay...or babe, you can just put your car in the garage so she doesn't see it."

"Oh, thank you Jordan, you are the best." She couldn't believe the words that were coming out her mouth. She said he was the best, apparently she meant it, since she said it.

"Then, I will see you in a couple of hours."

"Yeah, I am going to run to the hospital first and then after that I'll be over."

"Damn, I was supposed to go by there myself. I'll get there. See you in a minute." Jordan walked out of Blake's office. Left in the office, Blake had the biggest smile on her face, as she was happy as ever. She was starting to understand how happy her father made her mother for the first time in her life. Caught up in her daydream, she couldn't even hear her phone ringing.

"Blake you have a phone call on line 3."

"Thanks Tina!"

"Hello, this is Miss Lowry."

"Hey, it's me. Okay, this is the plan; we are going to meet at Starbucks in the morning. What time are you going to be free?"

"I am going to try and skip out of here by ten, is that good?"

"Shit, me and Jayden will be done talk down by the time you get there."

"Damn, what time are you trying to meet there?"

"Probably about nine or nine thirty."

"Aw, hell, you acting like you were going to be there at eight in the morning, k, I will be there."

"Okay, see you tomorrow. I am going to call Jayden and tell her.

"Alright, see you tomorrow." Blake continued wrapping up her objectives for the information she wanted to send Jim because she really wasn't in the mood to have a long drawn out meeting with him. Her plan was to come in early in the morning, do the last touches on the project and forward it to Jim in an email and she was going to be out for the remainder of the day or what she considered working from home.

Chapter 33: Keep Going

"There is no way I am going to be able to get all of this done. These people have lost their minds with firing my people like that." In a daydream, Lauren was thinking about what Kendall said to her about being responsible for her bookkeepers have too much access and that she should consider coming to work for him. All kinds of thoughts ran through her head, even though it would be a nice idea to change the scope of her career right now. For some reason, it was heavily on her mind to give this some great thought. It wasn't that she didn't like to work hard, but there was no need to limit herself to this if she had other career opportunities available.

Dealing with everything going on with Dalia and Blake over the last year, she knew that life was too short to set boundaries like that unless they were ethical and morally related. She knew she couldn't make it to the top without taking risk plus she didn't have any kids nor was she married, she decided that making a move might be a good idea. But, would the move be good to take with her man?

In her office working, Lauren heard the door opened to her house, she knew right off that it was Kendall. He must have forgotten something for me to be there in the middle of the day. She wanted to have a good reaction once he walked in her office,

"Hey babe, you busy?" Lauren's head was buried in her files.

"Hey, babe, what are you doing here, I wasn't expecting you until later this afternoon."

"I thought that I could bring us something to eat and I could come here to have lunch. Hell, I didn't just want to come here and eat knowing that you were working from the house today."

"Good job, boo. What did you get me?" Lauren was already going through the bags that Kendall placed on her desk to see what was in the bags.

"I bought you a grilled chicken salad, just how you like it." Lauren got of her seat to get the salad out of the bag and while doing so she kissed Kendall on his cheek not knowing that most of the morning he was horny, but he didn't want to bother her so he let her be. When her lips touched his face, Kendall felt his nature rise. He dropped everything that was in his hands, "Rin don't do that, I have to go back to work," he whispered softly to her.

"What if I don't want to stop?" she whispered back to him. He grabbed her by the waist pulling her closer to him and her lips to his. He looked her in her eyes and kissed her passionately until she couldn't keep her composure. She flung all her files on her desk onto the floor, not thinking about the damage she could do to them by slinging them across the room. He lifted her body up, placing in on top the desk knocking off what was remaining on the desk, kissing her neck as she moaned for more.

He lifted her dress slowly, touching every part of her legs moving his hands up towards her thigh, then to her stomach as she groaned for his touch even more. She unbuttoned his dress shirt and tie, ripping most of the buttons from his shirt in the moment of passion, as the scent of his cologne made her yearn for more of him. "Put it in," she cried out to him.

He unzipped his pants slowly as he continued to caress her body on top of her desk. His pants dropped to the floor as she placed both of her legs around his waste. She could feel the hardness touching her innermost the more she moved upwards and downwards on his body. His penis hardens from her soft touch, his perfect fit made him even happier. It assured him that she belonged to him and him only. As he went forcefully inside of her, pleasing her every fantasy, she grabbed the back of his head, pulling his body toward her as her body became warmer, the more she felt him inside of her.

The Upside Down of Things

"Oh, my god," As she whispered in his ear as she leaned in on top of his, moving the upward part of her chest on his; She continued to pull his head so that he could more of him could be inside of her. "Damn, Rin, you feel so good." He grabbed her hair pulling it from the root as his hands moved down to the tips of her hair. She was enjoying every minute of it. He picked her body up by the waist, easily turning her on the opposite side. He pushed her back in, with her chest leaning in closer to the desk. He pulled her thighs towards him, causing her ass to be directly on his penis. He eased himself inside of her, pleasuring her immensely. As she moaned for more, the more he came inside of her. They passionately steamed the room in the moment of ecstasy. Forgetting about the food Kendall bought for their lunch, they no longer craved food, but they craved each other. With both of them climaxes like none other, Lauren rolled over on her back, with Kendall lying on her chest, exhausted from all the energy exerted.

Part II

"Brian, can we talk before you go to work?"
"I really don't have nothing to talk about."
"Brian, this is serious, we need to talk."
"Now, you want to talk, if you wanted to talk, you would have come home last night instead of staying at the hospital. If I didn't know any better, I would have thought you were avoiding me." Jayden didn't make any comment.
"BRIAN, I DON'T WANT TO GET MARRIED ANYMORE." She blurted out to Brian while he was getting dressed for work.
"WHAT! ARE YOU FUCKING SERIOUS? HELL NO!"
"BRIAN, THIS IS TOO MUCH, I CAN'T DO IT. I THINK WE WOULD BE BETTER JUST DATING."
"I can't talk about this, I gotta go to work. You just go say it like that." Brian laughed it off as if the words didn't come out of Jayden's mouth.
"Brian, I still love you, I just don't think I'm marriage material."

"Man, who the fuck have you been talking to with this shit; all along you been cool with getting married, I have changed my life around you and you going to tell me you don't want to get married. That is some selfish ass shit."

"I'm being selfish?"

"Hell yeah you being selfish, think about all the shit we've put together and it's all worked out for us. Something is up with you."

"There is nothing up with me. I have been thinking and it's me."

"JAYDEN, that is some bullshit. I think you are trying to make us like Kendall and Lauren, but you know that ain't me."

"I haven't said anything about them; their relationship has nothing to do with us."

"Exactly my point, you have never talked against getting married or even being with me."

"Brian, just the other day, you basically told me that I can't keep accusing you of stuff and that something had to change."

"You damn right! That had to change, not our life time commitment we were making to each other."

"Brian, I don't know what you want me to do anymore."

"What! What you mean? Is this shit with Dalia getting to you?"

"Yes it has been getting to me, but that has nothing to do with the decision I have made about our relationship."

"You have some fucking nerve to make a decision about our relationship without talking to me first. I don't know if you think this is your friend's shit that you are always running, but you don't run this relationship like this."

"Brian, I think it is about time for you to go to work." Brian reached down on the table in the den and picked up his cell phone as if he were leaving for work.

"This conversation isn't over. Are you going to be here when I get off?"

"Why?"

"What kind of fucking question is that? You know what Jayden, do what you want. I will call you when I get off."

"That is fine with me too." By the time, Jayden was able to get her words out, Brian charged out of the house, slamming the door behind him.

"Oh my god, he gets on my last nerves with that." *The phone rings.*

"What!"

"Damn, what is your problem?"

"I am not have a good day, what's up?"

"Get that attitude together, and I'm going to pick you up. You are at Brian's house?"

"Yeah, I am. Rin, wait!"

"What's up chick?" Jayden stopped Lauren from hanging up the phone to talk to her more indebt, but she changed her mind.

"Never mind, what time are you going to get here?"

"Give me 45 minutes and I will be at your front door."

"Okay, that's cool." They ended the call and Jayden knew if Lauren said that she was going to be there in 45 minutes, she was going to be on time. She was nothing like Dee and her tardy ass.

Part III

Blake and Jordan lie in bed kissing each other as their way of waking up for the day. Blake normally worked from home on Wednesdays unless she had a mandatory meeting. Of course, this time she was able to get out of her meeting because she was caught up with her new project just given to her by Jim, a department manager. Today was supposed to be time with the girls. Lucky for her, that morning she spent it with the new love in her life, Jordan. This man had blown her off her feet in no time. She felt a new feeling that she never felt before and she was loving it. The only downside to it was that she fell in love with her best friend's brother, which was a feeling she'd been battling with for some time now. Of course Jordan didn't quite understand the relationship that she shared with Jayden, Lauren, and Dalia that didn't keep secrets like that from each other, but if she wanted to do right by her man, she would keep her mouth closed this time.

"Babe, I don't want you to get up."

"You know I have to meet the girls in a little while." Blake leaned in to kiss Jordan on the lips.

"I don't give a damn about none of that. Your man needs you."

"My man got me all last night and this morning, plus we haven't gone out in a while since Dalia has been in the hospital. We need this time to catch up."

"I know Bee, I was just messing with you, but I would like it if I could get some more time in before you leave today." It felt good to Blake to finally have someone in her life that truly cared for her besides her mother and friends. And even though she didn't take them for granted, it was nothing like the move from a man that chooses to love you back.

Blake got out of bed, slid on her robe, hoping that Jordan wouldn't stop her from trying to get dressed. As much as she loved to be with him, she wanted to spend some time with her friends too.

"You just gone leave me like this, dick all out."

"Jor-dan, you know I have to get dressed. I tell you want, you can join me in the shower."

"Fuck yeah." Jordan quickly jumped out of the bed to join Blake in the shower.

"Boy, you so stupid."

While Blake was at her home getting ready for the day, Lauren was heading to Jayden's house to pick her up.

Beep, beep

Lauren blew the horn waiting for Jayden to come out of the house. Lauren could tell from the look on Jayden's face that she probably didn't want to hear what was wrong this time.

"Hey girl, what is going on with you?"

"Shit, as always, where did you run your man off to today?"

"Hell, he got to work. Naw, I just gave him some of this chocolate chip cookie that he is back at the house trying to recuperate."

"Bitch please. You mean some of that vanilla ice cream." Lauren knew Jayden wasn't going to let her get away with that so they both laughed how Jayden made that comeback about her skin tone.

"Okay, since you want to rain on my parade, what is up with that ugly ass face you made coming out the house?"

"Aww hell, you know Brian gets on my last nerve."

"Uh, no, not since he put that ring on your finger, it seemed that everything changed. Hold a damn minute, did Brian change or was it your ass?"

"Here we go. Shut up! I just got a lot on my mind right now."

"Your ass just wait until I get Blake."

"Ain't nothing the baby millionaire can say or do to me right now."

"Blake is going to check you one day for cracking on her like that." All Lauren could do was laugh at how Jayden always had something to say about Blake even though she knew they were all jokes.

"Anyways, are we supposed to meet her or are we going to get her too?"

"Hell, I just thought that we were meeting up at Starbucks around lunch time. You know I asked that chick about meeting up early this morning, but for some reason her ass couldn't make it so I had to push the time back some."

"Shit, some…that was a whole different time of day Lauren."

"Wait, I am going to call and see if she wants me to pick her up." Lauren dialed Blake's number and the phone rang a couple of times before she answered. There was a lot of giggling in the background before she answered.

"HELLO!"

"Girl, if you don't stop yelling in my damn ear. Look, I wanted to know if you wanted me to pick you up? Jayden and I were riding along and we wanted to know if you wanted us to come get you."

Hysterical as Blake was, "Uh-uh, no, I will meet you guys there...its Starbucks right? Okay, I have to finish putting my clothes on and I will be there, okay." It appeared to Lauren that Blake was trying to rush her off the phone.

"Blake, what is that noise and why in the hell do you sound like that?" Jayden on the other end started to get concern because of Lauren's reaction on the phone.

"Ugh, it's nothing."

"Is that a man I hear in your background?"

"Why you so damn nosey?"

"Why you being so damn defensive? Anyways, we are on our way to Starbucks, bring yo ass?"

"Getting dressed now, see you in a bit." They ended the call, but Lauren still thinking something wasn't right about what Blake said.

"Rin, maybe the damn girl was finally trying to get her groove back and you asking all these damn questions."

"Shit, I didn't even think about that."

"Hell, too late now, you already did that damage."

"Shut the hell up. You do the same thing to Dalia all the time."

"Ooh, Dalia. I wish she could be with us."

"Have you talked to Ms. Deborah today to find out if there was any change?"

"No, I didn't. I figured we would go by there once we finished doing what we had to do."

"I think I may be going later. I have to finish up some work later on this evening. How is Jordan? I thought he was in town."

"I haven't talked to that fool since he came by the house wanting to talk to Brian about something."

"You gone call him?" Jayden pulled out her cell phone. "Let me see what this fool is up to in my damn house." Jayden put the phone up to her ear, waiting for it to ring; the phone rang a couple of times before Jordan answered. There was noise in the background.

"Sis, what's up?"

"Well, hello to you too. What is all that noise in the background?"

"Nothing man! Why you worrying? What you doing?"

"I hope that ain't no woman you entertaining in my house?"

"Is that why you called me?"

"I like how you tried to change the subject, but actually, I called because I haven't heard from you in a couple of days. What have you been doing? Normally, you bother me a little bit more than this when you come home."

"Maybe I have something else to do." On the other end of the phone, Jordan stared at Blake as his other thing to do nowadays. Blake eyeing Jordan not to say too much to tip Jayden off as she wasn't one you could put things pass too easily.

"I wanted to come over later and chill with you for a minute and talk about some things." Jordan hesitated before he responded back to her.

"What time were you thinking about coming over?"

"I don't know yet, I will call you later once I am done with the girls. Wait, that voice sounds familiar, who is that?"

"Jay, you don't know who that is…"

"Oh, so it is a woman."

"Got-damn, I will wait till you call me back this afternoon. Hit me up. I'm out." Jordan disconnected the call before Jayden could ask anything else.

"Well, I'll be damned. This boy hung up on me."

"Jay, maybe he was busy. That boy needs to get some too."

"Hey right, but that voice sounded familiar."

"Now I am going to tell you to stop being so damn nosey." Jayden laughed at how quick that came back on her.

"Damn, we ain't at Starbucks yet?"

Chapter 34: There's No Turning Back

"I think she is going to like this one. How soon can you have this one ready for me to take?"

"Mr. Brockington, if you give me about twenty minutes, I can have this all packaged for you." Kendall paced through the high-end jewelry store waiting for his merchandise by the sales woman. He made some phone calls to kill some time since he accomplished his goal for the day. Leaving the engagement ring he initially bought for Lauren in New Jersey, he decided to buy another one that he assumed would be more to her Lauren's liking and once he returned to New Jersey he would take that ring back to the store.

"Okay, Mr. Brockington, your package is all ready for you. I want to explain some things to you before you take this ring with you. Follow me over to this end of the store and I can explain in more details." Kendall followed the sales woman to a different counter.

Here comes Jordan walking in to the same jewelry store looking for an engagement ring for the special woman in his life.

"Hello sir, how may I help you today?"

"Yes, I am looking for an engagement ring for my lady. She is very special to me, so I want to find something that expresses my love and also suites her taste."

"Okay, I am sure I can help you with that. Tell me more of her taste."

"Man, I could be here all day telling you about her. She is a little shorter than me, beautiful skin, wonderful personality, and a smile to die for."

"Whoa, she sounds to be amazing."

"She is and I want to surprise her with the right ring. I can't get anything too small or too big. Even though she has money, I don't think she is into all of that." While Jordan is being assisted by the salesman to find the perfect ring for Blake, Kendall happens to hear his conversation as any guy in the jewelry store talking about the woman he wants to spend the rest of his life with, with such enthusiasm would bring attention to himself. Kendall just watched and listened for a while to the conversation as he could relate to how this guy was feeling about his woman.

"I want to make sure that her ring is really classy because she is a classy woman."

"Okay, what does she do?"

"She works at one of the Marketing Firms downtown. She's been there for a while, it's uh, Johnson & Toal Marketing Firm." As Kendall lost focus of his own situation and getting the ring for Lauren, he was listening to this guy across the store expressing his passion for finding the right ring. When he hears the guy mention the name of the company that his significant other works at, he became alarmed by the company name he mentioned. He kept pondering through his mind wondering where he heard that name before that made him even more curious to continue listening, even though by now he was ease dropping.

"Sir, it seems that your lady friend has an interesting career."

"Yeah, she does. She has been under a lot of stress lately about the new responsibilities at work, plus she just went back to work after dealing with some family issues and I think that this would be the right time to pop the question to her." The more this man talked, the more this situation was sounding so familiar to Kendall, but he couldn't quite put his hand on it. Many thoughts began to run through his mind, *"I don't know too many people that work at a Marketing Firm, but that sounds very familiar to me. I wonder who this guy is, he looks familiar too. Mmm, Mmm, family issues eh? I think I should listen some more to see if I can put this together."*

"Can I see that ring?"

"Sure, this one is very nice. Haven't sold too many of these, it's a new model, two carats?"

"Nice. She may like that, don't know. Let me see what else you have." By this time, Jordan's conversation slowed down with the salesman and he became more focused on finding the perfect ring. There were many people walking in the store who began staring at Jordan.

"Excuse me, are you Jordan Miller?"

"And who wants to know?"

"OH MY GOD, it's really you. I have followed your career since your freshman year in college. Do you know how the draft is going to turn out?"

"Well, thank you so much for following me, but I am trying to keep a low profile and I'm no star for you to think so much of me."

"Yes you are, with all the millions you are going to be making, I want your autograph now."

"Sure, here you go…please ma'am, keep this between the two of us." As Jordan was able to make this woman go away swiftly, it didn't stop others from over hearing.

"Muthafucker! That is Jayden's little brother, but I didn't think he was seeing anyone, if he was, she hasn't mentioned it and Lauren hasn't mentioned anything to me. Oh my God! It can't be, but I could just be assuming shit. Let me mind my own business." Kendall turned around facing the jewelry display in front of him looking at some nice pearl earrings for Lauren. "My baby would like this."

"Oh yeah, you can put this on my black card ma'am."

"Sure Mr. Brockington, I will be more than glad to handle that for you." Kendall handed his credit card to the sales woman to fnish her transaction.

"I will be right back with your receipt and information for you." All the while, Kendall couldn't help himself listening to Jordan in the background.

"Mr. Miller, I think you have picked a fine choice for your lady friend, but unfortunately in order to have it engraved, you will have to wait a couple of days."

"Damn! I was hoping I could get it sooner than that, well, I guess it will give me time to get the whole event set up for her then."

"Oh yes Mr. Miller, she is going to love the ring you picked out for her."

"I hope she does."

"Mr. Miller, please leave your contact information so that we can contact you once your ring is ready okay."

"Sure, if you happen to leave a voice mail, don't say where you are calling from, she may check my voice mail and I definitely don't want her to get suspicious."

"Yes sir, will do and if I am not the one to call you, I will leave a note for the next person."

"Thank you sooo much, my soon to be fiancé will thank you for it." Jordan left the jewelry store so sure of himself. All the while, Kendall was on the other end of the store, with every intension to figure out if Jordan was talking about what his suspicions were leading him to believe.

"Here you are Mr. Brockington, you can read over this information later, but I am sure that your lady friend will be well pleased with your choice."

"Thanks! You have a good one." Kendall not even thinking about the very expensive ring he just bought for Lauren, but about Jordan and this mystery woman in his life that he was planning to propose to.

Kendall returned to Lauren's home to prepare his evening for her, the girls' first stop was Starbucks. Lauren and Jayden arrived first, so they grabbed a table to wait for Blake to show up.

"Rin, what do you think is up with Blake, you know, when you called her in the car?"

"Hell if I know. But you think I won't find out when she gets here."

"I know you will."

"Your mood has changed since we got here, what's up chick?"

"It's everything now. I mean, I don't have a job, Dalia's in a coma, things with Brian and me aren't the best."

"Yeah, yeah, tell me what is going on with you and Brian."

Just before Jayden could answer Lauren's question, Blake walked through the door talking loud on her cell phone. Lauren and Jayden both looked at her with a slight frown on her face, "I miss you too. I know. I will see you in a bit, I have to meet the girls right now and once I leave here babe, we can watch the movie or whatever you want to do." Before Blake could turn around to see if anyone was listening, Jayden and Lauren were in her face, "Who the hell is that," Lauren asked. Jayden stood to the side waiting on an answer with her hand on her hip. "Okay, let me call you back." Blake quickly disconnected the call before Lauren or Jayden could hear who was on the other end of the phone.

"It's no one", Blake tried to portray that it was no one when they could clearly see and hear her talking to a man that she was trying to deny.

"Trick, we ain't heard you mention a man in a year and out of the blue you talking baby talk. Now you know we first heard a man in the background on the phone on our way here. Now you walk through the door with this big smile on your face with baby this and baby that, who the hell is he?" Jayden, being more blunt than, Lauren tried to get the news out of Blake.

"Why y'all being so nosey, damn!" Blake figured this approach would be the only way to get them to leave her alone, but she knew she had to do more than that to get them off her back, especially Jayden. "Can I get my coffee please before the two of you start jumping all over me?"

"Blake, why are you getting defensive, if you have a man, you have a man. If you do, I am happy for you. I just hope he is single this time and you know something about him." Lauren wanted to back off from it since Blake was forthcoming with information. Jayden on the other hand wanted details and she wasn't going to take no for an answer.

"Naw chick! Hurry up and get that drink because I have a lot of questions for you. I no longer trust you to pick and probe your own men, not since all this mess happened." Blake just rolled her eyes because she knew there was no way out of it. She thought to herself, "*Dammit, I have to think of something to tell her or she is going to figure it out. Aw hell, I could just tell her, it won't be the end of the world. Shit, I don't know what to do and I can't even call Jordan. Fuck it, I am grown, what can Jayden do to me. Yeah, but I am sleeping with her little brother. Think think think!!!! I can telll her that I met a guy at work. Hell no, that is going to make her ask more questions because I met Michael at work too. Then, she is going to think something is wrong with him too. Aw hell, what to do...*" Blake walked up to the counter, ordered her coffee drink and waited on the side instead of going to the table with the rest of the girls so she could think of something to say to Jayden. When her drink was ready, she picked it up and headed to the table with a smile on her face hoping to through Lauren and Jayden off.

"Blakie, do you really think you are going to come over here, sit down and act like nothing happened?" Lauren took a sip of her Frappuccino waiting for Blake's response.

"Are y'all still on that?"

"Uh, hell yeah. You walk in here on the phone talking seriously and lovey dovey with some man and you think we aren't going to ask any questions. You got us twisted." Jayden started twisting her finger in the air, with lots of expression.

"No, I just know that you two are nosey as hell!"

"Rin, did she just catch an attitude with us?" Jayden was astonished how Blake came off to her and Lauren.

"When you all get done talking about me, I want to know what is up with the two of you." Blake took a sip of her drink throwing the conversation off to Jayden and Lauren in which Lauren was the only one to take the bait.

"Well, I have been trying to deal with all my accounts without my deal. I told y'all that they got rid of my bookkeepers so I have to make all my contacts and ledgers by myself which I haven't done in forever."

"You were lucky to have that. We don't have that at Johnson & Pole at all". We have a few actual accountants in the building and everything that we throw at them, they handle on their own. We even give them crazy deadlines and they have a lot to do. I always wondered why they give you bookkeepers."

"Wait a minute. Are you all hating on how I got it going on at my job?" Lauren asked with much attitude and her neck rolling as much as she could roll it.

Jayden felt isolated out of the conversation since she was no longer working. For the first time, she missed the working environment. She knew that was a part of her life that needed fulfilling. For a moment at the table, she zoned out of the conversation thinking about every aspect of her life that was falling a part; her career, relationship, the relationship with her mother that she was trying to mend, Dalia, and her brother. She wondered what was going on with her brother that he hadn't reached out to her since he came to town. She had so many voids in her life right now that they all were beginning to take its toll.

"Rin, I want you to do something for me....shut the hell up, okay!" Blake burst out laughing because she knew by saying that it would make Jayden laugh, but she didn't get any reaction out of her. "Jay, did you hear what I said? What is up with you?" Blake snapped her fingers to know Jayden out of her daydream.

"Oh, you were talking to me?"

"Hell yeah, we were having a conversation and your ass zoned out of it. What the hell is on your mind?"

"I just have a lot going on right now." Jayden spoke softly as she wasn't completed back focused with them. Lauren looked at Blake with a sense of urgency as she knew it was serious for Jayden to be in this mood. Normally, she is the firecracker that they have to calm down. Lauren knew she had to say something to ease the silence.

"Hey, do you all remember the last time we were here?" Blake looked around not knowing what Lauren was getting at.

"Uh....no, I don't remember, Jay do you know what she is talking about?" Blake quickly threw the question off to Jayden to draw her into the conversation. Jayden quickly responded, "Hell if I know." Lauren was surprised that neither of them remembered the last time they were there.

"Damn, y'all make me think I am getting old. The last time we were all here we ran into Terrance and Dalia was acting funny, remember now?"

"Damn Rin, you are right! Has it been that long?" still no reaction out of Jayden. Blake and Lauren both took a deep breath as they were trying to take another approach to bring Jayden back into the conversation.

"Quit with the bullshit and tell us what is up with you." Blake became irritated that Jayden seemed to be so distant. "Look I could be doing some work right now, but I wanted to hang out with you all because we haven't done this in a long time and you acting like you don't want to be here right now, either you talk or I'm leaving."

"Hell, Blake if I am bothering you that much then maybe you should leave." Blake stood up from the table. "Wait a damn minute! This is not why we are here today. What's wrong with y'all?" Lauren interceded in the confrontation.

"Blake sit down and Jay, talk to us. We are your friends honey, we are here for you, right Blake." Lauren gave Blake a nudge in the arm, "Yes, Jayden knows that." There was complete silence before any one moved. Jayden took a deep breath and they knew it was something big.

"I'M GOING TO BREAK OFF THE ENGAGEMENT WITH BRIAN." Once she blurted it out, all she could get was the reactions from Blake and Lauren both at the same time. "Are you serious?" "You have got to be kidding me. What the hell happened, Jay?" Lauren and Blake were both waiting on an explanation that would cause Jayden to want to break off her engagement all of a sudden.

"You guys don't even know the hell we have been going through lately." Blake stopped her before she was able to go any further, "please don't tell me you are referring to the typical fights and arguments that you two have?"

"It's that and some." Lauren looked at Blake, "C'mon, Jay, are you serious? You are ready to throw it away, just like that. I can't even believe you right now. This man has put up with your mess for the past couple of years and now you are saying you don't want to get married anymore."

"Hell, I know it's me; I know I'm the problem. I don't want to get married that is why I keep picking arguments and that's why I am insecure about things in the house."

"Wait, what things?" Lauren asked.

"Do you remember the other night we went out to dinner?"

"Yeah."

"Remember Kendall and Brian both went out for drinks after they dropped us off…"

"Yeah, oh lord, what happened?" said Blake on the outside of the conversation looking in.

"Well the next day when I was picking his shirt off the floor that he wore the night before, I noticed something on his collar."

"Shut up"…."Girl, stop, are you serious," were the reactions from Blake and Lauren.

"What did you find, Jay," Lauren wanted to make sure before she starting jumping to conclusions.

"I smelled some woman's cheap perfume on his collar." Lauren looked at Blake before saying anything.

"What, don't do that to me, just say it, hell, I already know what you are thinking anyway." Jayden blurted out to them.

"First of all, you don't know what I was thinking," Blake started. "Perfume!" Anyone could have brushed against him at the bar or he could have saw someone he worked with, don't tell me you flew off the handle over that?"

"Wait, Blake, Jay may have a point with this one. I don't know how I would feel if I were going through Kendall's things and I smelled perfume on his clothing. That would make me think something right off hand."

"Hey, but you wouldn't react like this fool probably did." Blake looked at Jayden waiting for her response. Lauren thought about what Blake said and they both looked at Jayden.

"Y'all will not keep looking at me like that."

"What did you do?" They propped their arms on the table with their heads in the middle waiting for Jayden to explain what happened.

"All I did was ask him about it and he assumed I was accusing him of something and that I didn't trust him."

"Duh, how else did you expect him to react?" Blake was waiting for a response. Lauren just shook her head at her. "Okay, what else happened?"

"The argument got really bad. He felt that we should be at another point since we were engaged and that he wasn't going to take me accusing him every time he looked around."

"Wait," Lauren stopped Jayden. "Did he ever explain how the perfume got on his shirt?"

"He said some woman was trying to push up on him and Kendall, but he brushed her off and that was how the perfume got on his shirt." They both cleared their throats.

"What! You know what, y'all get on my nerves for real."

"Hold up, so why don't you believe him?" Blake just couldn't resist.

"Out of all the times Brian has gone out and gotten drink with his friends, not once has he ever come back with any perfume on his shirt."

"So, why in the hell don't you believe the man if he told you that is what happened? Before you say something…then, has this man ever cheated on you?" Lauren began using hand motions to stop Jayden from interrupting her.

"The both of you get on my nerves. Why aren't you ever on my side."

"Hell, we are on your side, we just have to make sure that we are on the right side..Hello, goodbye. I mean, c'mon, Brian is one of the best guys that I have ever met and I feel you are jumping to conclusions when you could have dropped it once he explained himself, but just like Blake, we know that is not the problem is it?" the only thing Jayden could do was hold her head in her hands at the table.

"I don't want to get married anymore and that's it. I shouldn't have to explain myself."

"The hell you do. This man has shaped his own world around you and now you have figured out you don't want to be married. I would just leave you alone and be done with you." As pissed off as Blake was, she left the table going back to the counter to get another drink. "Rin, do you want anything?"

"No, I am good. I want to talk to Jayden alone anyways." Blake walked off while Lauren reached across the table grabbing Jayden by the hand, "Jay, what is going on with you? You know Brian inside out, why are you jumping to conclusions? Is this really all because you don't want to get married." Lauren paused for a moment as she knew Jayden wasn't going to respond. "Look, maybe you should go home and talk to Brian about this."

"We have already talked about this and he is mad as hell for me not wanting to get married anymore." Lauren took a deep breath before she said anything.

"Then, maybe you should move back into your house until you are able to sort things out. I am sure your brother wouldn't mind you coming back." Blake returned to the table with her latte.

"Hey, what are you doing for the rest of the day?" Lauren asked Blake.

"Nothing I don't think, why what's up?"

"We are going to help Jayden move some of her things back into her house." As frantic as Blake was, she had to keep her composure or she was going to blow her cover.

"When did you all decide that?" In the back of her mind, Blake was hoping that she could reach Jordan and give him the news before his sister would really see that her brother had been occupied with her.

"It's obvious that Jayden has made her mind so why not move her back into her house."

"Rin, I think you are jumping the gun...let Jayden decide when she wants to move."

"Blake, why do you care if she moves back into her house or not?" Blake knew she was starting to be too obvious and suspicious so she had to pretend otherwise.

"Well, if this is what Jayden wants, then I'll help her move. So, when are we going to do this?"

"Since you aren't doing anything now we can get started now." Lauren hopped up from the table, grabbing Jayden's bag at the same time in a hurry to help Jayden move her things out of Brian's place; the only thing Blake could think about was Jayden not finding out about her and Jordan's relationship too soon.

"Okay, I have an errand to run first, so I will meet you guys over there."

"Blake, you just said you didn't have anything to do."

"Lauren, it's just a quick errand, I will meet you all there." Neither Lauren or Jayden thought to question Blake's motive.

Chapter 35: When it Rains, it Pours

The door slams.

JORDAN! JORDAN, Are you hear! Blake ran through the house hysterical, looking for Jordan, but he didn't answer as she repeatedly called his name. As she walked passed the kitchen, she noticed that there were candles lit, rose petals on ground, and soft jazz music playing, which was her favorite thing to relax to. Her steps grew slower and slower the more she noticed the mood was changing in the house. She whispered softer, "Jordan, where are you?" She didn't know if she should go upstairs since he was no where to be found downstairs or to keep searching through the lower level.

Blake put her pocketbook down on the sofa in the den area and slid her shoes off. From out of nowhere, Jordan appeared behind her. He startled her by kissing her on the neck, "when did you get here?" he asked. From out of shock, she hit him on the arm, "Are you trying to scare the hell out of me?"

"Babe, I want to you to come over here and sit for a minute."

"I can't; I came here because I have something to tell you." Jordan began pulling Blake by the arm as if she were to follow his lead upstairs.

"Whatever you have to tell me can wait."

"No, it can't...please, just listen to me."

The phone rings.

"Babe, let it ring."

"I can't it could be important." Blake picked up the phone, "Hello."

"Yes, is this Blake Lowry?"

"Yes, it is. Who is this?"

"This is Melissa from Memorial. I was told to call you and inform you that your friend Dalia took a turn for the worst. She didn't make it. I'm so sorry!" Blake began hysterically crying and screaming into the phone.

"Babe, what's the matter? Who was that on the phone?" Jordan picked up the phone, "Hello, who is this?"

"Sir, I am Melissa from Memorial Hospital."

"What did you tell my wife?" Jordan began yelling at the woman on the phone as Blake was still screaming in the background.

"Her friend....Dalia just passed away." Jordan dropped the phone and instantly grabbed Blake who was falling to the floor, leaving the phone, which fell to the floor. Jordan sat on the floor with Blake holding her, rocking back and forth. Hysterically crying, "I can't believe this is happening. I am the one that was supposed to die, not Dalia."

"Babe, don't say that." Jordan rubbed her head, kissing her forehead, comforting her to make her feel better the best way that he knew how to. Immediately Blake thought about Lauren and Jayden. "Oh my god, Rin and Jay, I wonder if they know."

"I'm pretty sure the hospital called them like they called you babe."

The door bell rang.

"Babe, sit here I will get it." Jordan went toward the door, opening it not thinking to ask who it was. When he opened the door, it was Lauren and Jayden as they had received the news also.

"Brother, you heard." Jayden went into the arms of her brother, crying, not thinking that he was at Blake's house; Lauren ran immediately over to Blake as they consoled her each other.

"Rin, what are we going to do without Dalia. It's always been the four of us." Blake stopped for a moment to ask Lauren if she had talked to Kendall, but she didn't have time to phone him.

When Jayden finally pulled herself together to even face Blake, the only thing they could do was cry together and hold each other.

"Jay, I know she was like a sister to you."

"No, Blakie, she was like a sister to all of us." Jordan stood off to the sidelines. "I'm going to get you all some hot tea." Jordan went off to the kitchen to start making the tea.

"I know. I just can't believe that she is gone."

"I can't believe it either. The doctor told us that we had to prepare ourselves for it, but I didn't want to believe it."

"Babe, where are your tea bags." Jordan yelled from the kitchen.

"Babe! Who are you calling babe?" Jayden quickly dried up her tears. Lauren couldn't wrap her head around it.

"Jay maybe you misheard what he said, just let it go." Lauren knew everything was about to get out of hand, so she wanted to ease everything down before it even started.

"No, don't stop me Rin, I know what I heard. Jordan Miller, who did you call babe?" Jordan made his way of the kitchen and Blake holding her head down wit her hand covering her face. Lauren looked at the expression on Blake's face and then she walked over to her. Quickly, she asked Blake, "Please tell me Jordan wasn't talking to you?"

Blake didn't want to answer, but from her not responding, Lauren had her answer, "Oh, my God, I can't believe it." Lauren backed up because she knew this was about to be a scene.

Jordan entered the room, "Jay, let me take you home and we can talk about this later." Jordan wanted to calm the situation before things got out of hand.

"Boy, I ain't going no where, just tell me who the hell were you talking to." She looked over in Blake's direction, "Blake, are you...and my brother...?"

Blake interrupted before Jayden was able to say anything, "Jayden, I wanted to tell you but we wanted to wait."

"WE!!! Who the fuck is we?" Jordan knew his sister was going to make a deal about it, but he didn't want her to take it out on Blake.

"Eh, Jayden, let me take you home and we can talk about it."

"Hell no, I want this bitch right here to tell me that she has been sleeping with my little brother behind my back and then smiling in my face."

"Jayden, I know you are upset, but you are not going to disrespect me in my house."

"Oh yeah. You sleeping with my brother, what the fuck else are you doing?" as the conversation got heated between Blake and Jayden, they began walking closer and closer towards each other as if they were enemies. The argument grew even more heated before Jordan and Lauren were able to diffuse the argument.

"Jay, why don't you let Jordan and Blake explain before you say things you don't mean. You already have enough on your plate, you don't need to add this on to it."

"Rin, you expect me to believe that there is some explanation for her to be sleeping with my little brother even though she knows he has a future."

"What the hell is that supposed to me?" Blake felt insulted by the comment.

"However you want to take it." By this time, Blake and Jayden were coming to blows at each other.

"Whoa, Jayden, I am not going to let you talk to her like that."

"Oh, so now you are coming to her defense, what the fuck is this all about?"

"Look Jayden, we might as well tell you the truth because like always you act like a damn fool, that is why you and Brian can't make it." Blake and Lauren backed up because that was even a low blow for Jordan to make.

"Why don't you sit down and I will tell you all you want to know and after I tell you, you better not have nothing to say to Blake, do you hear me?" Jordan had a very serious look in his eye that Jayden never saw before, but it frightened her because she knew it was serious since her brother stood up to her for the first time in his life. Jayden took a seat on the couch while Lauren and Blake went into the kitchen as the teapot on the stove started going off in the middle of Jordan talking to Jayden.

417

"C'mon Blake, let's go into the kitchen and let them talk." As they walked into the kitchen, they could hear the passion in Jordan voice talking to Jayden.

"Look, I am in love with Blake. I didn't plan it, it just happened." She tried to brush me off, I wouldn't accept it. I wanted her. For once, I found a woman that I could be with for the rest of my life, who didn't judge me, but loved me for who I was, I ain't never had that before. She makes me happy and I want to be with her."

"If she means that damn much to you, then why did you feel it was necessary to keep it a damn secret, and a secret from me, I am your sister."

"We didn't tell you because we knew you were going to act like this. You never know how to deal with shit, so I told Blake not to say anything to you," emphasizing the "I" so that Jayden wouldn't think it was Blake's fault.

"Hell, I bet she loved keeping that secret."

"Stop the bullshit Jayden, she wanted to tell you every time she saw you. I convinced her not to say anything. What the fuck is wrong with you? Man, I used to talk to you about anything, now you are being just as judgmental as Mommie."

"Don't turn this around on me Jordan Miller. You are sleeping with my ex-bestfriend. The both of you have been lying and sneaking around for who knows how long, now that your fucking cover was blown, you want to pour your heart out, I'm not buying it." Jordan became more furious with his sister as he knew this wasn't going to be an easy battle, but she was being more unreasonable than he'd ever imagine.

"Jayden, I am grown ass man. I can do what I want to. I am not your little brother who needs you for everything anymore. Blake and I are together as my sister, I need you to respect my decision and respect my woman." Jayden rose up in Jordan's face.

"Are you fucking serious? So, now you are grown man, but you are living in my house, running up my bill there and you want to talk about respect and being grown. Give me a break."

"Who the fuck you think you are talking to? I don't need your damn house. When I get drafted, you won't have to worry about me at all. I'm only staying at your house now, because I know how much it means to you for me to be around you and the fam, but I can handle my own." From the kitchen, Lauren and Blake could hear the arguing escalating. It was getting worst.

"Jordan, what is wrong with the two of you?"

"Jayden, this is your brother, what are you doing, you have lost your mind? Lauren couldn't believe the words she was hearing from Jayden, as Blake on the other hand, was trying to calm Jordan down. Blake grabbed Jordan face, pulling him directly to her, "What are you talking about a draft?" Jayden overheard the conversation, "oh, so you didn't tell her about the draft? I knew you didn't change; you are the same selfish, conniving little boy you have always been. You won't change as long as me, Daddy, and Momma are here to take care of you."

"Jayden that is enough, we should leave and let Blake and Jordan talk." Lauren grabbed their bags off the couch, "Blake, Jordan, I am so sorry about all of this." She looked to Blake, grabbed her hand, "Don't forget we just lost Dalia today and we have to be there for her family."

"I haven't forgotten. I will call you later." For a moment, Blake was lost in herself and she almost forgot that they all lost someone today.

"I want you to stay away from my family, bitch!" the last words that Jayden said to Blake.

"Jay, you are going to regret saying that and because I love your brother, I won't say anything. I respect him too much." She leaned in to give Jordan a kiss.

"You two make me sick."

"Jayden, let's go, you have said enough." Lauren grabbed Jayden by the arm forcing her to leave the house. The slamming of the door startled Blake.

"Babe, I am so sorry about all of this." Jordan grabbed Blake by the arm, soothing her to assure her that everything was okay.

"Jordan, have you been lying to me." Tears began to roll down her face.

"Lying to you about what? And why are you crying, babe? "You mean everything to me," Jordan grabbed her other hand, pulling her towards him.

"I heard you mention the draft...you've been drafted and you didn't say anything to me. What, what you were going to do, just sleep with me until it was time for you to go and then just up and leave, say something?"

"Woman, listen to me." Jordan placed his index finger on Blake's lips to stop her from talking, but he couldn't stop the tears from rolling down her cheek.

"Wait, right here, I will be right back," Jordan jetted off into the other room, leaving Blake for a split second.

"Jordan, I am not in the mood for games." The next breath she took, Jordan was back as if he never left.

"Blake Lowry, I have waited a long time to meet someone like you. You are everything I want in a woman. I want you to have my children, spend the rest of our lives together. I don't want to be without you." Jordan pulled a navy blue velvet box out of his pocket, opening it to show a 5 carat cut diamond ring that sparkled and gleamed off the lights in the room, "Blakie, will you marry me?" Her heart started to flutter, beating faster than normal as she couldn't believe that Jordan said marry and her name in the same sentence. She was thinking it was a dream.

"Jordan, do you know what you are saying to me? Oh my God, are you serious? I don't know what to say." Blake's hands were trembling, her face became flushed, her tears stood still.

"Are you just going to leave me without an answer?" Jordan didn't have any doubt in his mind that Blake would turn him down after the both had admitted the way they felt about each other.

"Wait a minute J. if you are getting drafted, where are you going?"

"I'm being drafted to the Carolina Panthers. I want you to come with me, we can start over, have our own family, a new life, just the two of us babe!"

"Jordan, this is too much. You want me to leave my life here, my house, career, friends, and everything I have worked hard for?" Jordan looked Blake in her eyes, "Babe, did you say the other day that I was your man and that I complete you, do you believe that I will make you happy?

"Jordan, we can be happy here."

"I can't take care of you here. I want my woman where I am in Carolina. I want you to be the mother of my kids. You can do whatever you want; you can open a marketing firm there or get a job if you want. You don't have to work babe, I just want you with me, just say yes babe." Blake took a deep breath. She looked down at the ring, then back up at Jordan. She took another deep breath and when she looked in Jordan's eyes, she saw something she never saw before in his eyes, "Yes, yes, yes, I will marry you." Jordan placed the ring on her finger. He picked her up, kissing her passionately.

"We're getting married."

"I'm moving to Carolina. I don't know anything about the south. What do they wear down there, what is the weather like, what do the houses look like. I don't think Marketing is a booming industry there. I wouldn't know what to do."

"Babe, you have time to do all of that. Don't panic. After all of this is over, we can focus on us and our future."

"I don't know what I will do with my house."

"You can keep it. We will come back here babe, my family is here and your friends are too. Calm down babe, we are going to work everything out. We have to deal with Dalia right now. I wanted the proposal to be special and I didn't want it to be like that, but I couldn't help myself by calling you "babe". Ain't that some shit, all the time, I have been telling you to be careful and I ended up being the one to slip up."

"Its out now, don't worry about it. You are right though, I have to think about Dalia. I just can't believe she is gone." Blake rubbed her hands through her hair, trying to absorb everything that happened in just a couple of hours.

"Come sit down for a minute and I will get you that tea."

"Thanks, I am shaking so bad right now and I don't know if it is because of the news about Dalia, your sister, or the fact that I have this big ass ring on my finger right now. I am such a mess, but I can't focus on me, I have to check on Mrs. Deborah and be there for the girls." Blake grabbed her pocketbook and keys, heading for the door.

"Babe, I will drive you…wait a minute."

"Do you think it's a good idea for you to come to the hospital with me since your sister is going to be there?"

"I'm not worried about my sister right now. She is being stupid for all I care."

"Jordan, you can't be like that. She is still your sister and you still have to talk to your parents."

"My parents aren't the problem…"

"That is what you say. You still have to tell them."

"I will. Hell, my mother will probably be at the hospital when we get there."

"Hey, she probably will, we need to get there." They both walked toward the door with Jordan following Blake.

"Whoa, Blake, are you alright?"

"Yeah, I don't know what happened." Blake felt light headed and landed right into Jordan's arms right when they were walking out of the door.

"Maybe it's not a good idea for you to do anything right now."

"J, I can't stay here when I just lost one of my closest friends."

"Blake, you just past out into my hands. If I weren't there, what would have happened to you?" She thought about what Jordan said to her, but regardless of how she was feeling, it was no comparison to the pain Dalia's family was going through. "Are you sick? Is there something you haven't told me?"

"Something like what..?"

"Do you have sicknesses in your family that causes you to do that? Or babe, have you taken your pill?" Before she could answer, there was a knock at the door. "I'll get it; you stay here, on the couch and get some rest.

"Who is it?"

"It's Barbara!" Jordan quickly opened the door.

"Hey, how are you doing?" Jordan instantly gave Barbara a hug.

"You look familiar to me, son, who are you?"

"I am Jordan, Jayden's brother. I don't think I have met you before. It's nice to meet you, Mrs. Mowry. I have heard a lot of good things about you."

"Oh, you have. It can't be too nice; you haven't invited me into my daughter's house yet. Now, where is she?"

"I'm sorry, come in please ma'am. Blake is lying on the couch in the den."

"Layin' down, what is her problem?" As Barbara began walking to the den, Jordan explained to her how Blake fainted in his arms as they were heading out to the hospital.

"Honey, what is wrong with you...why are you laying here?"

"Ma, I'm not feeling too well."

"You don't look too good; maybe you should just lay here and get some rest." She leaned in to whisper to Blake so that Jordan could not hear, "I see you have some help here, Jayden's brother, he is handsome and he has manners."

"I know that is why I fell in love with him."

"Blake Terrin Lowry, are you telling me that you are in love with your best friend's brother." Barbara chuckled a bit as if she was getting a kick out of her being in love with Jayden's brother. Without saying a word, Blake lifted her hand so her mother could see the ring on her finger.

"Blake, is this what you really want?" her mother asked looking her in her eyes."

"Ma, he has made me feel that love that you talked about that you and Daddy had. He makes me happy, even though I didn't want it in the beginning. I just fell for him." Barbara began massaging Blake's forehead out of concern for her.

"Honey, I know you don't want to hear this, but can he take care of you, provide for you and support a family?" Blake leaned up for a moment to whisper to her mother, "He's being drafted into the NFL. The only problem is that I have to move to Carolina, but I will visit and you can visit me."

"WOW! Blake, I am happy for you. After all you have been through, I just want you to be happy. Go, live your life, be happy and enjoy it...now, where is my son-in-law to be?" Barbara got up and looked around for Jordan who was in another room.

"Jordan, my mother wants you." Jordan swiftly came from around the corner, not knowing that Barbara was ready to embrace him.

"Son, I don't know much about you, but you have apparently made my daughter happy and that is how I want her to stay, do you hear me?" she said with a firm tone. "When I saw you open the door, I had a good feeling about you. I already know under the circumstances with you being Jayden's brother and Blake being her best friend is already going to be a challenge within itself, but whatever you need, I am here okay, now come give your mother-in-law a hug."

Blake really didn't know how her mother was going to react, but she did throw her for a surprise by embracing Jordan as she did. It was just too good to be true.

"Now, we just have to figure out what is wrong with you. How long have you been feeling fatigue or having these spells?"

"I just happened today for the first time."

"How about we get you some Tylenol just to be on the safe side to get you some relief now so we can still head to the hospital. Stay here and I will get you some water to take the Tylenol." Barbara headed to the kitchen to get the water while Jordan came to Blake's side, "Babe, I think you need to take a pregnancy test."

"Shut up, not in front my mother! She has ears in the back of her head." Jordan began to whisper, "I'm going to pick one up from the store."

"Why are you so quick to think I am pregnant, is that what you were trying to do all along?"

"WHAT! Is that what you think of me?"

"No, its not, but you are too anxious to want me pregnant."

"How many times do I have to tell you that I love you? I will marry you tonight if I could. I want you to have my babies and if you are pregnant now, that makes it all the better."

"I'm not ready to be anyone's mother right now, Jordan."

"Why not? I know you, the beautiful, caring, and loving woman that I spent has shown me things I know I could use to help me be a good father." Jordan rubbed his hands across her chin and on both of her hands, reassuring her how much faith he had in her to be a mother.

"Aw, Jordan, you know what to say all the time, but I still have my reservations about this. We will talk about this later, my mother is coming."

"Here you go babe. What were you too talking about? The both shouted the same time, "Nothing!"

"I know you are lying, but whatever you do in the dark comes to the light, uh huh." Blake looked at Jordan from the corner of her eye and mouthed to him, "didn't I tell you?"

Chapter 36: The Fall of Jayden

"Will you wait a minute, chick!"

"For what? This bitch has been sleeping with my brother and now she has him talking to me any kinda way."

"Wait a damn minute so I can talk to you..." Jayden and Lauren were taking a long walk across the parking lot at the hospital. Jayden still very upset about her brother and Blake's relationship and Lauren, chases behind her trying to talk to her, but she finds it hard since Jayden doesn't want to hear what anyone has to say.

She finally catches up with, by grabbing her hard to stop her, "Jayden! You are being the bitch in this situation. Gottdamn, do you really know why we lost our best friend today; it's because she was being hard headed too and now you are doing the same fucking thing. I tell you what, I can't watch all of you fuck up everything and end up in a grave."

"You wait one damn minute; don't turn this around on Dalia. We weren't friends to her like we should, that is why Dalia is gone."

"You really believe the bullshit you say. Dalia pushed us away and she made some bad choices. We were there for her. Do you want the same thing to happen to Blake?"

"I don't give a damn about her no more than she cared to tell me that she was fucking my brother."

"Oh my God, get over it. Your brother is a grown man. That is what he was trying to tell you, but you weren't listening. Just like you weren't listening to Dalia. I know she talked to you, she always trusted you with everything." Jayden got close into Lauren's face as if the rage in her was starting to come out. She

426

raised her hand up, "I wish you would!" Lauren grabbed her hand before she was able to strike.

"I know you are grieving, but if you ever raise your hand to me, I will whip your ass like a damn stranger. Get your shit together and stop being an ass whole. Dalia just died, do you not get that? You want to argue with Blake, who has been there for you just because she fell in love with your brother. Did you hear what I said, fell in love not fucking, there is a big difference."

"What the hell ever? I don't believe it."

"Why not, because you aren't happy in your relationship, well that is your problem. You have too much going on right now. You need to work on one thing at a time. I can't deal with this shit with you because you piss me off so damn bad until I don't want to even talk to you."

"You have your perfect little life that you think you can tell everyone else what to do. Well, it doesn't work like that." A car pulls up in the parking lot that looks familiar to Jayden and Lauren.

"Whoa! What the hell is wrong with y'all. We got the notes you left at the house." Brian and Kendall came to the hospital together as Lauren and Jayden left notes telling them what happened and to meet them at the hospital.

"Babe, why the hell are you fighting with Jayden?" Kendall looked very confused. "It's a long story, I will have to catch you up later, c'mon let's go into the hospital.

"Alright, I'm right behind you."

Jayden and Brian were still standing in the middle of the parking lot. Jayden not breaking her silence or responding to Brian's presence; Brian leaned on the car, waiting for Jayden to open up to him "why you out here acting like this…with your best friend and where the hell is Blake?"

"Please, don't say her name."

"Why not? Peep this. I really don't give a damn what you are mad about. The only thing that matters is the fact that Dalia is dead, do you hear me and you and Lauren standing out here like its an after school fight like y'all about to throw blows. That some bullshit."

"Brian, I don't need you judging me. They can all go to hell for all I care."

"Listen to yourself. I don't even know if I want to be around you myself right now."

"I didn't ask you to be here in the first place."

"What the fuck you talkin bout, you left me a damn note on the table. Jayden, I love the shit out of you, but I can't take your attitude or the shit you been pulling lately."

"Brian, please, for years we have been doing this back and forth thing and it worked for you. When your homeboys starting talking shit, then you want to be committed and shit. I know it all. I know who you been with, what you did, and how you did it. You ain't innocent. Then, all of a sudden you want to wife me up. You ain't shit, never been shit. You are just an entry level worker that doesn't know how to come out of the hood mentality."

The more Jayden talked, the more furious Brian became. Jayden let her rage get the best of her, but she just opened the window for more trouble to come her way.

"Real Talk! That's how you feel." Brian took a step closer to look Jayden in the eye, "is that what you really think of me? Fuck it. You wanna know what really went down....you remember Nicole, yeah, she was really feeling yo boy and I was feeling her too...since you were on your independent kick, Nicole was there for me, even when I got hurt at work and you were busy with your job. we got really close. She wanted to be with me and then she got pregnant. I asked her to get an abortion because I knew it would hurt you because deep down, I wanted to be committed to you, but you kept reminding me that you didn't want it and that I wasn't ready to commit, but the reality of it was, its you and always has been you."

"So, now you want to blame your mistakes on me now."

"Giving up my child wasn't a mistake, it was a choice I made, I regret the decision, but my intentions were to make you happy."

"That is bullshit. You always make excuses when you screw the hell up."

"Hell, you even ran off to take this trip with your father without telling me, saying you needed time to think. That was bullshit and you know it."

"You were asking too much of me."

"After two years, you were still contemplating if you wanted to be with me or not...that is crazy. But I can tell you what. I won't be one of those dudes who gives up everything for a woman who don't deserve it."

"So, what are you saying, since you seem to have the answer for everything? You know what, it doesn't matter because I you knew this before you jumped into it that I didn't want to get married."

"Bullshit!!! You have been trying to please your damn friends and create this image that you ain't. Since you lost this job, I have seen another side of you, but I can tell you now, unless you want to keep your house, you better find some kind of job to pay the mortgage."

"You wouldn't?"

"Naw, since I work a no good job and I ain't nobody. Then, you can pay your own bills and handle your own. I'm out."

"Fine!" Brian jumped into the car leaving Jayden standing in the parking lot alone. Determined to keep it all together, Jayden made her way to the hospital.

"Jayden, Jayden," Ms. Deborah went straight into Jayden's arm grieving her daughter. "I can't believe she is gone."

"I was sitting right beside her when she slid away. She is in a better place now. I just wish I knew where Terrance was so I can tell him. I don't want him to hear about it from somewhere else." Jayden's face grew stiff just hearing his name.

"I want you girls to help me handle everything with the service. Wait, where is Blake?"

"I thought she was on her way, I will call her." Lauren stepped outside of the hospital to call Blake to see what the hold up was. She didn't realize Blake wasn't there until Dalia's mother brought it to her attention.

"Blake, where are you?"

"Rin, I really don't feel well. Jordan and I were on our way there, until I fainted in his arms."

"WHAT! What's wrong? Are you going to a doctor?"

"I just want to lie down. I am so, so sorry I am not there right now. I just don't have the energy to move. I do want to talk to Mrs. Deborah."

"Blakie, you don't sound good. Maybe you should get some rest. We should all see her body together though; we are going to need that closure. Oh, I don't want to forget to tell you this; Mrs. Deborah wants us to help her with the funeral arrangements. I think she wants something quick, but nice.

"Okay, when I get my strength back, I will come down to the hospital....uh, Rin, how is Jayden? Mrs. Deborah?"

"After the way she acted at your house, you are still worried about how she is doing...Blakie, you are something else, but Jayden is lashing out at everyone, she is here, but not really. Mrs. Deborah is just going through the motions right now. I am watching her too."

"Blake I have to go, I'm not feeling too well. I'll talk to you later." Blake disconnected the phone.

"Blake!" Her mother called. "Are you okay?"

"No, I need to take a nap, I think, but ma, I want you to go to the hospital and make sure everything is okay. Jordan is going to stay here with me."

"Are you sure?"

"Yeah, the Millers need you more than me right now."

"Hey babe, you alright? You don't look well. C'mon, I'm going to carry you upstairs." As he began to pick her up from the couch, he kiss her forehead reminding her of the love he had for her besides what his sister thought.

"Babe, I am going to run to the drugstore, I will be right back."

"Jor-dan, are you going to get what I think you are going to get?"

"I'll be right back." He avoided the question even though that was his intention all along.

"Rin, maybe you should sit down and let me get you something." Lauren quickly responded to Kendall. "I don't want anything. I just want to make sure everyone else is okay."

"Come over here for a minute and let me talk to you." Lauren walked outside of the waiting room that all of them were occupying since they received the new about Dalia.

"You talked to Blake, why isn't she here?"

"Blake is sick and she doesn't sound good."

"Sick as in she has a cold kinda sick?"

"No, I don't know if the argument has her sick or the news about Dalia, but it's serious. She's sounded so weak over the phone...there is just too much going on for me to even wrap my head around it."

"Argument, who was arguing?"

"Oh God, that is another story. I can't get into it now, but when we got the news about Dalia, Jayden and I were riding together, we just left Starbucks.."

"Yeah, yeah, I remember when you left the house to meet them."

"We went to Blake's house to get her and grieve together, and that is when Jordan answered the door at Blake's house."

"What's wrong with that?"

"Blake and Jordan are together, Kendall. Like together in love, real relationship..."

"Okay, come here, let me hold you."

"Kendall, this is all too much going on. What happened to the good times we had in New Jersey, even before that, we used to go out every Wednesday. We would even lie to our bosses so we could get the time off and we would do all kinds of things together. Do you know how long we have been doing the "Wednesday get together?"

"No babe." Kendall sat next to Lauren rubbing her back, consoling her trying to make her feel better, "My mother asked me one time why we chose Wednesday instead of a day on the weekend, when we all were off. She didn't understand that Wednesdays were special to all of us. When we were in college, no matter how hard we tried to tweek our schedules, we couldn't get a Friday off for anything. It so happens that we could get Wednesdays off for the most part. For some reason, if we had classes on Wednesdays, they were at eight in the morning and by ten, we were all done, so we had time to do things together.

On the weekend, I know I was meeting with my group with some accounting classes that was given me trouble, then, Blake would be in a tutoring group just because there was a guy she liked in it and Jayden spent that time working at a department store so when she graduated she could move up in the company."

"Dang, I should've gone to school with y'all." Kendall laughed as Lauren kept talking. He knew it would therapeutic for Lauren to talk instead of keeping everything bottled in. "So, what was Dalia doing?"

"Man, Dalia had a lot of dreams and hopes that she wanted to fulfill. She originally went to school to become a nurse, boy did she love the medical field. She met Terrance early in our college days. He always seemed so nice and a good fit for Dalia, in my opinion. There were some issues we all went through in college some of us managed to bounce back and some of us didn't, so Dalia didn't get a chance to finish getting her RN license, but she found a way to stay in the field."

"Lauren, Mrs. Deborah is looking for us, she wants to talk about some things about the service." Lauren wiped her tears from her face and pulled her hair back.

"C'mon babe, we can talk later at home." Kendall walked behind Lauren as she walked about in the waiting room where everyone else was gathered. By the time they got back to the waiting room, other relatives of Dalia arrived.

"Well, Dalia's Will indicated that she wanted to be cremated, so we have to honor we wishes even though as her mother that is not something that I wanted for my daughter's funeral, but that is not important right now." Deborah's words just brought tears to everyone's eyes. Lauren made sure she was close to Jayden's side because at this point, she has pushed everyone away that has cared for her.

"I'm staying at the Miller's residence, so if everyone here that I have asked to help with the service will meet me there in the morning around ten, I would greatly appreciate it." For once in their lives, everyone agreed and no one went against Deborah's wishes for her Dalia's remains. Everyone said their goodbyes and gave their condolences to Deborah before leaving the hospital that evening.

"It feels like we have been here all day."

"We have been here all day, it's almost nine o'clock Rin."

"Oh, crap, I didn't make any phone calls today. I know I am not going to work the rest of the week."

"Well, I don't have a job so that wouldn't include me."

"Jay, I'm sorry, I wasn't trying to imply anything..."

"No, no, it's not your fault." Jayden's attitude appeared to have changed at that moment, just before they all were getting ready to leave the hospital.

"Jay, where are you going to stay?"

"I think I may go to my mother's, that way I can be by my mother and help Mrs. Deborah when she needs it, plus my mother has the room and would like the company."

"Okay if you say so...are you going to tell her what happened?"

"I'm really not in the mood to discuss anything. I just lost my best friend, Brian's gone, and I don't have my brother anymore. Today just keeps getting better for me."

"Jay....." while Lauren was getting ready to say something, Jayden walked off

"Babe, let's just go home and I can give you a massage."

"Yeah, you will, but I have some questions for you too."

Chapter 37

Jackie poured coffee into two mugs, carrying them over to the table, one for her and the other for Jayden. She sat in the chair across from Jayden as she was fiddling with a napkin in her hand that was on the table.

"Hmm, you wanna tell me why you are here?" Jackie took a sip from her cup."

"I can't just be here for my best friend's mother while she is grieving." Jackie looked at Jayden as if she didn't believe anything she was saying. Jayden knew that wasn't going to be the end of the conversation.

"Ma, you really want to get into this right now!"

"No, we don't have to, I just thought I would bring it up since you looking so pitiful at the table....well, anyway, you talk to your father?"

"Yeah, I probably will call him and then I can tell him the news about Dalia. So, what about you and Daddy?"

"Girl, stay out of grown people's business. Your father and I are too far past that point to play house."

"You are never too old for love."

"Love huh, where is your love, Brian?"

"I don't want to talk about him right now!"

"You maybe upset, but remember you are in my house and raising your voice is still a sin, and in this house, sin leads to death lil girl, remember that."

"Ma, you haven't changed. Have you talked to your son?"

"No, I haven't, why I should? I thought he was enjoying his freedom staying at your house. Something has changed about him, but I think it is for his good." Jackie walked back into the kitchen refilling her cup.

"Ma, I really don't want to talk about him either."

"OKAY! Well, tell me where Blake was, she wasn't at the hospital. I know Lauren was there with her new man, he is very attractive. I really hope they work out. You girls need good men in your life, you know."

"Ma, you keep asking me about people that I really don't care to talk about right now."

"Jayden Miller, what is your problem? You don't want to talk about Brian, then you don't want to talk about your brother, and hell, you don't want to talk about Blake...maybe there is something wrong with you. Now, I was going to let it go, but you are just being stupid for no reason, so you know what, you are going to talk and you are going to tell it all. I don't care what it is young lady; you are going to talk to me before you do something stupid."

Jayden knew she could never win an argument with her mother. After raising up out of the chair out of frustration, she knew once her mother spoke there was no way out of the conversation.

"Okay, ma, where do you want to start?" She said in a sarcastic tone.

"What is going on with Brian?"

"We broke up, next?"

"Wait a minute, tell me what happened. Is this the reason why your mood has changed? Jayden, listen to me" Jackie leaned over towards Jayden grabbing her hands, "honey, I haven't seen you like this before, what is wrong?"

"I know Brian and I can't make it." Jayden broke down in tears, catching herself before she lost control. "I know I can't do marriage and I ended up hurting him in the process. I didn't mean to, but it just happened. We had a bad argument and I don't think I can trust anyone enough to commit a lifetime to. You're not saying anything...I thought you were going to stop me at some point."

"No, I knew marriage wasn't want you wanted. I think you thought it was the next necessary step, but there is nothing wrong with being in love until you figure out you want to spend the rest of your life with them."

"But, I thought I knew that. Something change, something happened. When I lost my job, I felt closer to Brian and I couldn't see myself with anyone else. I just don't know…"

"If you said something or did something wrong, you have to make it right, you have to correct it. Brian was a good guy and he was good to you, but you should have been honest with him from the beginning. I hope you haven't damaged him, Jayden."

"I hope not either. I have just been messing up everything lately."

"What do you mean? What else did you do?"

"I know I should let Jordan tell you, but I did talk to him."

"Jayden what is it, is their something wrong with Jordan? You taking too long to talk…." Before she knew, Jayden just blurted the words out, "Jordan's in love."

"WHAT! To who and when did this happen?" Jackie became enraged the more Jayden's words sunk into her mind.

"Let me tell you what happened. When Lauren and I got the news, we went straight over to Blake's house to get her to come to the hospital with us. When we got there Jordan answered the door, I didn't think about then, I was just happy to see him, because I hadn't seen him in a while. But, it all clicked to me when he called her "babe"."

"Oh my God, say they aren't….."

"So, when I heard it, I wasn't sure that I heard it correctly so I asked him who he was talking to. I didn't even give them a chance before I started going off on Blake."

"Jayden, what did you do?" Jackie started shaking her head, as she knew it was just about to get worst.

"Ma, she was messing with my brother behind my back. They have been sneaking around since he has been back in town. I don't know what he sees in her. Jordan knows nothing about being in love."

"Wait, wait…he said he loved her."

"Ma that is not even the half of it; he defended her. He took her side and not mine. He told me that I either needed to accept it or else...like he didn't care that he is messing with my best friend."

"Shut up for a minute girl. You never know when to keep your mouth close, now wait a minute, let me think about this....your brother, my son, Jordan, is involved with Blake, your friend and your brother, my son says that they are in love...how in love are they?

"What do you mean how in love are they?"

"You aren't even listening to yourself...you said your brother defended her against you right?"

"Yeah."

"...and did you say the words came out of his mouth that he loved her?"

"Yeah, what point are you trying to make?" Jackie went walked in her kitchen, leaning over the kitchen sink, with her arms placed on the counter.

"Lord have mercy, your brother is in love for real. I just can't believe it is Blake. I wonder if that was the reason he came back here in the first place."

"Ma, you don't know what you are talking about."

"Oh, I don't. See, you too caught up in your own mess that you don't pay attention to anything. See, what I know is that when your brother came back to town, his mind was different, he was different. He also went to see Blake his first night in town."

"What! You knew and you didn't say anything?"

"No, it was when Deb got into town, because she stayed at Blake's house. She told me that he came over, she put it together and she told me."

"But yet no one thought it would be a good idea to mention it to me."

"No one tells you anything because you can't be there for anyone else but yourself. Think about it, your brother would have come to you, but you reacted just the way he thought you would, an ass....SO, you have turned on one of the best friends that you ever had because she fell in love with your brother..hmm, after everything that she has been through this past year, you would have thought you would have different feelings about it. I wonder if you are jealous that they have found love and yours was falling a part. So what next, you are going to fall out with Lauren because she has a man? Jayden, you need to get it together before you don't have anyone."

"I'm not going to forgive her for sleeping with my brother."

"Girl please! No one gets up to live for you, where did you get that from? Why do you think they owe you anything?"

"Just because….everything I have done for Jordan. Plus, I wouldn't expect Blake to be like this, but I should have known, her spoiled ass wants everything she sets her eyes on."

"Shut up! I don't want to hear this mess. You sound real ignorant. The things you did for your brother shouldn't be because you expected something back. You know if he knew you felt that way, he would have never taken anything from you."

"Jordan is spoiled and he is will always be spoiled especially when he has everyone doing things for him."

"So, that is how you feel about me." Jordan slammed the door to the house.

"Son, don't listen to your sister, we were just talking." Jordan walked towards his mother, giving her a kiss on his cheek.

"I hear you call yourself a taken man nowadays." Jordan looked over at Jayden as if she couldn't keep her mouth closed.

"Well ma, I came over here to give you the good news."

"You know what…I can't take anymore of your good news." Jayden walked passed Jordan to show that was not interested in anything he had to say.

"Ma, I'm getting married to Blake. I know it's late, but I wanted to give you the news in person. I asked her a couple of hours ago and she said yes. Tell me someone is happy for me, damn!" Jackie hesitated before she said anything.

"Son, come sit down and talk to me." Jackie grabbed her son by putting her hands on both side of his face, "son, watch your mouth in my house, now come sit down."

"Why are you even talking to him?" Jayden walked back in the room hoping she could get some reaction from her mother or Jordan.

The Upside Down of Things

"Jayden Miller, you don't run this house now if you can't give your brother some respect, then you can leave and come back after he is gone." Without saying another word, Jayden left the room only distancing herself enough where she could hear the conversation.

"Jordan, are you sure you are ready for this, I mean, it wasn't too long ago, you couldn't even manage college by yourself. Now before you say anything, I want you to think about what I am saying son. You are getting ready to make a lot of money, more than most people your age; you haven't worked a day in your life, plus you don't really know what it takes to support a family."

"What! So, you are on Jayden's side? I really didn't come here for your approval." Jordan stood up from the table.

"Sit down! I didn't say I was taking Jayden's side. I am your mother and I am going to tell you the truth even if you don't like it. There was nothing I said that wasn't the truth. Now I really don't know what the hell you and your sister have been thinking lately, but you will not raise your voice in my house. You came over here because apparently you wanted my approval and you wanted my opinion, so gottdamit you are going to get it. Now sit down and shut up!" Jordan humbled himself to listen to what Jackie had to say.

"Now son the draft is next week. Don't you think all of this is moving really fast?"

"Ma, I've had feelings for Blake a long time and when I came back this time, I was trying to wait. I felt like I had something to offer."

"Boy, what do you know about having something to offer."

"Never mind what my sister thinks, I do know how to be a man and honestly I think you and Jayden have underestimated me a lot when it comes to women because right now Blake is as happy as I am right now. I've thought about all you have said and I've already made plans. You wanna hear about them?" Jackie couldn't believe that for the first time her son was sounding like the man she was hoping he would be one day.

"Son, I would be glad to hear what you have to say....continue, please."

"Ma, you are going to be proud. I was able to get my own deal without Bart's help. I know you didn't like him, so I kind of handled my own business. The Carolina Panthers offered me a better deal and I am going to take it. I don't wanna talk about money and those details..."

"Son, you don't have to tell me that. I just want to hear your plans."

"Okay, you know things are guaranteed in the NFL so the draft will tell it all. I'm not going, I would rather be at home with Blakie."

"Jordan, you are really in love aren't you?"

"Ma, that is what I have been trying to tell you...but, anyway, I am trying to convince Blake that she can have a life in Carolina, but she is thinking it is too slow..."

"Wait, this sounds to me like you are moving away from me for good...oh my God, Jordan, I am not ready to lose you yet. I thought I would have more time before you went off and did the married thing."

"Ma, don't do that."

"What about the wedding and all...oh, I forgot, you are marrying a trust fund."

"Don't say that. I don't want Blake to pay for the wedding. She is going to be my wife and I will be her husband, which means I am going to take care of that. I want her to have everything she wants."

"Honey, I know how you feel, but her father set everything up for her before he died."

"Ma, this just feels so right. I have a beautiful woman that I love; my career is going where I want it. I just wish my sister, the one person that had the most faith in me, is against me and my wife to be and ma...I can't forgive her for the way she treated Blake at the house."

"Before we even get to your sister, I want to finish talking about you and Blake. Has Blake talked to her mother?"

"Yeah, she came to the house and after all that Blake has been through her mother just wanted to make sure she was happy. When her mother saw that, she was happy for us."

The Upside Down of Things

"Wow! I can't believe Barbara was that happy for the two of you. If Barbara could be happy for you, then son, I am happy for you. Come give me a hug. I want to call Blake and tell her congratulations." Jordan hugged his mother and she went towards the phone.

"Wait ma, you can't call her right now. Blake isn't feeling well. I went out to get her some meds. Hopefully, she will be over here in the morning to help with the funeral arrangements."

"Okay, I will wait and talk to her, but I want to talk to you about your sister."

"Ma, talk to your daughter about acting stupid. She came at me like I was a little boy. I am grown man and I deserve some respect. She needs to apologize, not to me, but to Blake."

"Jordan, this is your sister, did you forget that?"

"Ma, you didn't hear all the BS she said to me and to Blake. Stop, stop defending her, we have been putting up with her attitude for a long time and no one says anything to her. I don't want her around my fiancé."

"Jordan, let me ask you something. How would you feel if you found out your sister was sleeping with your friend that you grew up, shared secrets with, someone you trusted around your family and trusted with you life....think about it son...that wouldn't go so well with you." Jordan started pacing back and forth in Jackie's living room.

"Uhhhhhh, man, I don't like it when you do that. Naw, I wouldn't like it, but I wouldn't disrespect my sister. Me and homeboy would have a few words though, but if I knew that they had something serious, then that would be something else. But, ma, you can't compare that because with men, as long as you aren't taking their sister as a hoe and you really into her, then it's good.

"HEY! I don't care about none of that. I care about my children getting along."

"Ma, I love you and I want you to be a part of my wedding. Blake loves you and she wants you a part of it too, I just can't deal with Jayden anymore!"

"Jordan! The door slams after Jordan left. Jackie was unable to get through to him this time.

"I can't control him anymore. Jordan has finally grown up. James and I did something right."

Chapter 38

"It feels so good to be home. I just want to take off these clothes and shoes and just relax. Between losing Dalia and the mess with Jayden and Blake, I don't know if I can take anything else."

"Yeah, you have had a rough day today. How about I run you a nice bubble bath and I give you a nice massage."

"Oh my goodness, that sounds nice. I'm going upstairs to change my clothes."

"Alright, I will be up in a minute. I need to make a phone call."

"Ken, you are going to make a call this late?"

"Yeah, I didn't get a chance to check my voice mail and email yet this evening."

"Okay, don't take long. I'm ready to take my bath." Lauren went upstairs while Kendall took his phone out of pocket checking his voice mail.

"*Damn, I knew I should have listened to my first mind. Buying this ring was all wrong. Ain't no damn way she is going to say yes when her damn best friend just died and her other friends are falling the fuck out. Shit! Think Ken, think, what to do.*"

"Ken! I'm ready for my massage." Lauren yelled from upstairs.

"Rin, I'm coming, I'm almost done. I'll be up in a minute."

Knock, knock.

"Babe, there is someone at the door."

Kendall opens the door.

"I'm here to see Lauren Daniels, is she here?" There was a tall, handsome, expensive suit wearing guy at the door looking back at Kendall in the doorway.

"Who the hell are you?" Lauren walked down the stairs in her silk champagne color robe, bouncing off the wall, "Ken, who is at the door?"

443

Before she knew it, she was seeing a ghost, "what the hell?"

"My man, you didn't say who you are and why you are standing in my doorway. Rin, do you know who this is?"

Jason looked at Lauren and she stared back at him.

"Is anyone going fuckin' answer me?"

"Um, babe, this is Jason…"

"Thee Jason…..Jason, why the hell are you here, did you get an invite?"

"If I remember correctly, I think this was Lauren's house, at least it was the last time I was here in her bed." Kendall revved up at Jason, just as soon as he was getting ready to take a swing at him, Lauren jumped in between the two of them.

"Kendall Stop! Please…let me talk to him alone."

"Talk to him alone. He just disrespected me and you want to talk to him alone, get the fuck out of here."

"Kendall, babe, please let me talk to him alone. Let me find out why he is here.

"Lauren, if I leave here, I'm not coming back."

"Kendall, don't do this, not now, please babe."

"Then tell his ass to leave. Why the fuck is that so gottdamn hard, huh? Or are you still sleeping with this dude?"

"What, Kendall don't do this in front of Jason. Please, I've had a long day, you know that, damn."

"Are you telling me please? Its late as hell and you ex appears at your door, and you telling me to let you talk to him." Pounding his hands in his fist, trying to get his point across to Lauren, he became even more enraged when Lauren was still insisting that Kendall give them privacy.

"Yes, please, I want to know why he is here."

"Fine." Without another word, Kendall left the room, heading toward the stairs. By this time, Lauren eyes were flustered with tears, her heart was racing all out of order. She wanted to get her thoughts together before she faced Jason at the door. She turned around, took a deep breath, "Jason, do you know what time it is?"

"Can I come in?"

"Well, you've caused all of this ruckus, you might as well. Now what do you want and don't hesitate!"

"I don't even have to stay long to say what I have to stay."

"Alright, well go ahead and put it out there so I can get back to my man." Jason smiled, "I wanted to let you know personally that I am going to be moving to Baltimore just as soon as a find a place." Lauren almost lost her balance and she was most definitely not expecting that. Even though, it was a while since she and Jason had been together or even spoke to each other, he still had to the power to get a reaction out of her and he knew it.

Lauren took another deep breath, "What is bringing you to Baltimore? You never liked it here?"

"My job is transferring me here."

"Stop, stop, the damn madness Jason! Why did you feel the need to come to my house late at night to tell me that your job is transferring you here? You got my email, house phone number, cell phone number, and work email....and you didn't see the need to relay the message in any of those methods?"

"No, I thought I would tell you in person."

"Why!"

"I don't want to talk about that right now. I want to know how you are doing."

"Really, you serious?" Lauren laughed to herself, hysterically.

"Why are you finding that so funny?"

"You really have some balls coming here, playing the good guy, stopping by my house late at night, seeing the trouble it is causing with me and my man, but you want to know how I am doing....if there isn't anything else, you can have a good night." Lauren opened the door for Jason to leave.

Without refuting Lauren, Jason left with his head bowed. "I'll be back when you have time to think."

"You have some nerve coming back here and then talking like I give a damn."

"Lauren, you don't care...you wanna look me in my eyes and tell me after all this time that you don't care or think about me at all." Lauren became speechless, even though she and Kendall shared something special, there still a part of her that reminisced about Jason every once in a while.

"Jason, you still here?" She slammed the door once he took two steps outside. She paused for a moment, trying to wrap her head around Jason showing up at her door, then she thought about the argument that she and Kendall had in front of Jason.

"Oh shit, Kendall! She ran upstairs looking for Kendall in her bedroom, "KENDALL! KENDALL! She went in the closet, bathroom, and all around upstairs, but there was no sign of Kendall. Then it finally it, "Damn, he's not here, he left." The only thing she could do was sit on her bed with her head in her hands, thinking of what went wrong in just a couple of hours.

"Where did he go? I have to find him....no, maybe I should think for a minute. I really don't want to make the same mistakes my girls' have been making over the past couple of years. How in the world did I get myself into this situation, now I am starting to understand how torn Dalia was when she was going through everything with Terrance. No, no, no, he will come back," she kept telling herself over and over as she kept overanalyzing everything.

"Bruh, open the door, I need to talk." Kendall kept banging on the door, half drunk, but still in his right mind.

"My man, what's good with you?" Brian opened the door for Kendall to come in.

Kendall took a deep sigh before sitting down on the couch. Brian had never seen him in this condition before.

"What the hell happened to you?"

"Lauren is what happened to me."

"Gottdamn, you wanna beer?"

"What the hell not, bring me one."

Brian went to fridge getting a beer for Kendall and for himself. He took a seat across from Kendall on the sofa.

"Now, whatever it is, it can't be that bad..."

"Sh-it. Man, her ex came by out of the blew and instead of her blowing his ass off to show me a little respect, she wanted me to go upstairs so she could talk to him." with a look of amazement on his face, "wow, did she?" Brian took a sip of his beer.

"Hell yeah, instantly, I was thinking she done lost her mind if she think I am about to sit in this house while she took to the next dude who used to tap." Kendall started chuckling.

"What you gotta think about it like that?"

"Because it is the truth and you know it. If that happened to you that would be the first thing you would be thinking especially late at night and this dude had the balls to knock on your door."

"Yeah, you gotta point, but....you left now what?"

"I ain't even thought that far out yet."

"You know Lauren's a good one, why you tripping?"

"Its respect man and you know it. Why give this dude the time of day? That shit makes me think maybe she have been talking to him or maybe she still got feelings for him."

"Finish that damn beer, man. Why in thee hell would she be interested in this dude again."

"...unless y you know something I don't."

"Naw bruh, you know I ain't messy like that. You know I am not the one to give you the answers, but you know you got a good one."

"Just because she is good don't mean I have to take her bullshit."

"Wait, wait, wait a minute....this sounds like more than just some ex coming over to the house..." the room went silent. Kendall went back to gulping down the beer without responding. "Hold up, you came over here with it, so it got to be something else bothering you about Lauren." Kendall reached into his pocket and pulled out a box.

"Nigga, what the hell is that?" When Kendall placed the box on the table, he instantly realized what it was. Brian leaned back on the couch, "Aww, damn..is it that serious that you thinking about not doing that?"

"Man, I don't even know."

"For real dogg? Naw, don't let this other dude come around and make you change your mind about the woman you want to spend the rest of your life with. Now if this was some issue that you and her had had for a while and thought it was something that couldn't be fixed then that would be something different. Up until now, y'all have been gravy. That is all this dude want…for you to kick Lauren to the curb so he can easily slide back into the picture. Now, wait let me ask you this. Is Lauren at home by herself right now?"

Kendall lay back on the couch, feeling the alcohol he consumed already that night, "Yeah."

"No, know the hell you didn't?"

"Did what?"

"So you left your woman home alone after her ex came there with the intentions to get back with her….hell, you might as well handed her over before you left and save yourself all the upset."

"I don't even know if that was the reason he came over. The fact is that she asked me to leave so she can talk to this dude."

"Did she ask you to leave the house or the room?"

"She asked me to leave the room."

"Hell, its still a little fucked up that she asked you to leave period, but you left the damn house, so now if Jason wanted to make a move, you gave him the opportunity if he didn't have it before. Don't create a habit of running every time something ain't fairy tale."

"So is that what happened between you and Jayden? My bad, I guess that is a sensitive subject."

"Naw, you good….naw, we had deeper issues than that. But, you are the first person to ask my thoughts about her though."

"I can tell she is still on your mind, hard!"

"Nigga, did you come over here to talk about my relationship issues or did you come to talk about your woman, I'm just asking?"

"Alright, alright, you right. Damn, I guess I done messed up, huh?"

"Naw, if you don't go home tonight then you would be messing up. I suggest you go over there while it's still dark and make it right with her….but, not without her knowing she was wrong for telling you to leave. Hell, if she is anything like Jayden, she is going to be waiting up for you so as you open the door, you are going to see her face, mad as hell."

"Shit, I might as well stay here and have another beer."

"Sho-u-right."

"Uh, I know you don't want to talk about it, but you may want to call Jayden, she got a lot on her plate right now."

"Yeah, I know she is probably taking Dalia's death hard..."

"She is taking that pretty rough, plus with everything with her brother and Blake."

"Her brother and Blake?"

"Shit, never mind man, I'm running my mouth when I shouldn't."

"Naw, you might as well tell it."

"Ugh, shit....they all found out tonight that Blake and Jordan got something going on and it's serious."

"Wait a damn minute..." Brian took a moment to think about the past couple of conversations that he had with Jordan concerning women and relationships. *"You mean to tell me that Blake was the woman he kept talking about."* Brian kept thinking to himself that he was the one that was encouraging Jordan to make a move on the woman he was interested in, never in a million years did he think that woman was Blake.

"Man, you ain't saying nothing."

"Nah, it's just that Jordan has come to me before about advice with this woman he was interested in, I just never thought it was Blake and you say Jayden went off on the both of them?"

"That is what Lauren told me...apparently it got really heated where she had to break it up or something like that."

"Look bruh, I don't want nothing to do with all of that. Jayden is a strong person, she can hold it down."

"Damn, you had a lot of emotion when it came to me and Lauren, but that shit goes out the window when you talk about Jayden...did she really hurt you that bad?"

Brian looked at his watch, "it's getting late my man if you want to make it back in the house and be able to get on her good side."

"Aww hell, you are right. Man, I appreciate you listening to me. You know I am drunk as hell."

"You good though. I needed the company…"

"I know the hell you do…yo woman gone." Kendall grabbed his keys and cell phone from the coffee table heading toward the door.

"Hell no, I got to go to work in the morning so I'm shutting all of this down when you leave."

"Call that damn woman Bee, you hear me."

"Yeah, yeah, yeah…." Brian was trying to push Kendall out of the door while he was still trying to convince him to call Jayden

While walking up the stairs in the house, he started unbuttoning his shirt and opening his belt. He reached the top of the stairs and noticed Lauren's bedroom door was closed. He thought about knocking, but if he did that, then he would be expecting her to not be alone, and that was the farthest thing from his mind. Her room smelled like a fragrance from Bath & Body Works, scents Lauren loved. He knows she had already taken her bath because of the scent in her room. He couldn't see her face as she covered her face with the silk sheets on her bed. He took his shirt off in anticipation to kiss her and make the evening go away. Before taking his pants off, he pulled the covers back to find Lauren fast asleep. He admired her beauty while she was sleeping and all he could think about was how much he loved her and how he wanted to make her happy.

He leaned in to kiss her neck as it was propped up. She moaned in her sleep from the touch of his lips. He whispered in her ear, "Babe, I'm home." Lauren turned over and opened her eyes.

"Where have you been all this time? I called you." she said in her sleep. Kendall thought about just making up something, but he couldn't help himself from being honest with her.

"I had a couple of drinks and then I went to Brian's house."

"Brian's house! What!"

"Shh! Be quiet. I got some making up to do." he whispered back to her. He slid into bed with her slowly, continuously kissing her. She reached for him and pulled him closer to her. In between his kisses, she whispered to him, "I don't love him Ken, I want you, I just needed to tell him that, but not in front of you."

"Shh! You don't have to explain it to me, I know." He placed his body on top of her easing inside of her as she moaned for more. while she put her arms around his head pulling his body closer to her as she enjoyed every minute of it.

"Wait, babe, I need to strap up." he whispered in her ear. She continued to pull his body closer to hers. Ignoring what he said.

"Don't stop!" she screamed back to him.

"Babe, we ain't ready for that."

"Ready for what?"

"I can't cum inside of you, not now, it will mess shit up, let me put this rubber on."

"Mess what up? Oh, my God you feel so good." Kendall wanted to take her mind off of what he just said, even though it slipped out.

"Let me make love to you." He whispered in her hear. She rubbed her fingers up and down his back as he motioned up and down against her body, feeding her every need. The slower he went, the louder she moaned for more.

"Ken, you feel so good. I want you cum babe."

"Is it mine?" he pushed himself harder inside of her as she begged for more as her vagina yearned for more on his penis.

"YES BABE YES" was all she could say before she climaxed and he did the same. He stopped abruptly, "Lauren," looking into her eyes as she wiped her hair back out of her face.

"Yes," she answered breathing hard in amazement of how good she felt. Kendal became hesitant so she knew it was something serious that he was preparing himself to say but the words just wouldn't come out.

"Ken, what is wrong?" she rubbed his forehead. Still looking her in her eyes, "Lauren, there is something I have been wanting to talk to you about for a long time now, but every time I get ready to do it, something comes up."

"Aww, Ken are you talking about moving in here and us doing this together. You think you got one over on me, but I knew you were waiting to ask me that, no sweat. I would love for you to live with me. I didn't like you commuting back and forth on the plane from here to New Jersey all the time anyway. I think it is all for the best anyway. I don't even know why you were taking so long to bring it up. You just procrastinate about everything. We have to work on that."

Babe, Babe, stop! That is not what I wanted to talk to you about. You are really making this hard." Lauren had a confused look on her face as if she was lost.

"Lauren, sweetheart, I want you to marry me....before you say anything. I bought this ring when I was in New Jersey and since everything was going on with Dalia, I decided to leave it at home, but when I got here, I changed my mind. I realized that I didn't want to go another minute with claiming you, wanting you to have my last name, and wanting to start a life together with you. Lauren Daniels, will you marry me?"

Lauren's heart fluttered. She was at a lost for words, she was not expecting a proposal, maybe an invite for them to live together, but not marriage. All type of thoughts ran through her head.

"Are you going to say anything?" She exhaled, "YES! YES! Wait, where is my ring? Hell, it don't matter, we can get it later." She hugged and kissed Kendall without letting him say a word.

"Babe, are you really happy?"

"Yeah, why wouldn't I be happy?" Kendall rolled over to the side of the bed with his feet hitting the floor.

"With all the bull that went on tonight, I thought you still had feelings for this dude."

"Kendall, there is no need to worry about Jason. He is a part of my past, that is it. I don't love him, I am in love with you that makes the difference. Do you understand that? Really?" She waited for Kendall to give her the confirmation she was looking for.

"I don't care about him. I care about you, does that answer your question?"

"I need to know that this is not going to be an issue that we have to deal with every time someone from my past comes around." Lauren got out of the bed, grabbing her robe from the end of the bed, making her way in front of Kendall to face him.

"Listen woman, I don't want to talk about him or any of dem' other dudes in this house again. I'm making you my wife they didn't. It's not going to be an issue unless you make it one." He pulled Lauren close to him, wrapping his arms around her waist, kissing her to make her understand how he felt.

"Its late, we should go back to bed." She said with the passion in her voice. Never had any man in her life demanded her love that way Kendall did and she was able to give it to him without a second thought. "I'm going to really need you this week. I have to bury one of my best friends and I don't know how I am going to get through it, especially with Blake and Jayden at each other's throats, I need someone I can lean on".

"Babe, I got you, don't worry." Kendall kissed Lauren on her neck securing her that he was by her side. The laid in the bed peacefully and went to sleep.

Chapter 39

"Good morning to you too," Jackie fixed Jayden a cup of coffee. "Was Deborah up when you came down the hall?"

"I think she has been pacing all night, but don't say anything." Jayden placed creamer and sugar in her coffee.

"Have you talked to Blake this morning, you know she is going to be over here in a little while to talk about Dalia?"

"Don't remind me." Jayden rolled her eyes with spite.

"How long are you going to play this game? Haven't you learned your lesson yet that life is too short, live while you have a chance.."

"I am living, just without thinking about her in my life."

"Is that what you are doing with Brian too?"

"Good morning, how is everyone?"

"Good morning, Deb, how did you sleep?"

"Well, I don't think I can ever sleep the same after you lose your only child, but I am making it...mind if I have a cup of coffee. It smelled so good from the hallway."

"Sure, coming right up." Jackie got up from the table and fixed Deborah a cup of coffee.

"Mrs. Deborah, is there anything you needed me to do for you this morning?"

"Actually I do...I want you to make up with Blake for Dalia's sake." She grabbed Jayden's hand as she was speaking with her.

"Mrs. Deborah, I love you to death and you know how much Dalia meant to me, but even she would understand how I feel about this." Trying to avoid anymore conversation about the situation, Jayden excused herself from the table. "I'm getting ready to head out in a little while."

"Jay, what about the meeting we are having this morning?" Her mother asked her from the kitchen.

"I know you all are going to do whatever Dalia likes. You all can fill me in later, I don't want to be in the same room with some people." Jayden went down the hall.

"I thought this thing was supposed to get easier when they get grown, but I see it doesn't."

"Jack, look at me, I have to bury my child...excuse me, I'm having to cremate her so it doesn't get easier, it gets harder."

"Oh Deb, I am so sorry," she reached over and hugged Deborah.

"Its okay, I am dealing with it. I'm actually doing better than I thought. It's just so good to be around friends and family in times like this. When her father died, I thought a part of me died, but I learned to move on and I will have to do the same with my child."

"As long as you know, you are not alone in this. I am here and you can stay with me as long as you want to."

"Oh, I can't stay here long, you have a life too that you think I don't know about."

"Deb, what are you talking about?"

"I'm talking about you and James...don't try and deny it. I remember all those years you and him always had that connection with each other"

"I think it's too late for all of that now, too much time has past and I'm getting too old to try and get married now..."

"Now who you think you talking to? I know you better than that now. You were always his first choice, Diane was his second choice and you know it."

"That is besides the point."

"Well, let me ask you this...do you still love the man?"

"Of course I love him, he is the father of my kids."

"No, do you lo-ve him?" trying to avoid the question altogether, "I think everyone is starting to arrive," Jackie moved towards the window admiring a car as it pulled into her driveway.

"Okay, I'm out. Hit me up if you need me." Jayden came from out back, walking fast with her glasses on her face, heading out the door.

"You're seriously not going to stay....sometimes I just wonder if I raised you or not." Jayden slammed the door leaving the house.

"Jack, she is upset, don't pay her any mind. She lost her man, you know how that is...then, she lost her best friend, then she found out that the other person in her life that she trusted, behind her back was sleeping with her best friend."

"Deb, I don't give a damn what is on her mind, she don't disrespect me in my house. She might as well go back to her own house and do what she wants."

Part II

"So, what's wrong babe?"

"Nothing."

"You're standing in the bathroom, shaking half to death and you are saying nothing is wrong, that's how our relationship is going to be?"

"Huh!"

"Babe, stop panicking, just take the test. You held this off last night when I got back. You can't do it this time, just take it and get it over with."

"Yeah, if I take it then I will know the truth if I am or not."

"Isn't that the point of all pregnancy tests?"

"The timing is just wrong. I am supposed to be meeting with everyone to discuss what we are going to do about the ceremony for my best friend." Blake gazed in the mirror in her bathroom with Jordan standing beside her in his silk pajama pants.

After the heated argument with his sister and talking to his mother the night before, Jordan was exhausted by the time he got back to the house. Blake was sound asleep on the couch where he left her. Her mother was there, staying in the guest room downstairs. Not sure what caused her to pass out the day before or what had her so weak, she seemed to feel better this morning but not 100% herself.

"Babe, the timing will never be right if you are waiting on one."

"Why do I have this gut feeling that you are smiling on the inside?"

"You don't have to wonder, I am smiling. I have the woman to be my wife, why wouldn't I be happy about a baby?"

"Jordan I can't be happy about this right now. I have to bury my friend."

"It can just be our secret for the time being. Now, gimme a kiss."

"Only a kiss, because I have to get ready to go over to your mother's house."

"I don't know if I want you to go over there alone, I want to come with you."

"Do you think that is a good idea? I don't want all this commotion going on over there because of me."

"That won't happen." Blake was still dangling the pregnancy test in her hand, still procrastinating to take it because of her reservations about being pregnant.

"Blakie, if you want to be on time, you better hurry up darling." Barbara yelled upstairs from the foyer downstairs.

"Okay, Mommie, I will be ready in a minute." Blake sped her process up getting dressed, still trying to continue her conversation with Jordan.

"J, I am going to be fine. Your sister will not act a fool with all of our mothers there."

"To say you two were best friends, you don't know her at all. My sister don't give a damn about people being there. She will show her ass no matter what."

"Yeah, you are right about that, but I can handle my own, trust me."

"Alright, if you say so, but we need to talk when you get back."

"Talk? About what J?" Jordan walked out of the bathroom without giving Blake another word.

"Blake honey, come on, we are going to be late."

"Coming…" She looked at Jordan while making her way down the stairs. "I don't know what you are up to, but I will find out when I get back."

"I'm not up to anything," then he whispered to her, "But, you still have to take this pregnancy test."

"Ma, I'm ready, let's go." Blake didn't want to listen to Jordan ramble on about the possibility of her being pregnant. Blake and her mother left the house, leaving Jordan standing at the top of stairs, "Damn, my sister…I know she is going to cause trouble, Blake doesn't know her like I do. Ugh, I gotta protect Blake, but she is going to be mad as hell if I come there and she already told me that she doesn't want me there."

Phone rings

"Hello."

"Son, it's your father, do you have a minute, and I wanna talk to you?"

"Hey Dad, man, do I need to talk to you. I am at Blake's, you can come over here."

"Alright, I think I remember how to get over there, I'm on my way. I will see you when I get there."

"One." They disconnected the phone.

"Dear, you don't look good at all. Is everything okay with you and Jordan?"

"Yeah, everything is good with us, why do you ask?"

"You look a little pale and you look tired in the face. Are you sure, is there something you want to talk about?"

"Ma, I am fine. Stop worrying about me, my friend is dead and I can't do anything to bring her back so I am trying to keep it all together.."

"Aww, dear I know how you feel, but everything has it purpose and you know that. Just think last year this time, you were fighting for your life and now look at you. You have a wonderful man who loves you and wants to take care of you. You have great job, a beautiful house, and I will add, a magnificent mother and friends."

"No, I don't...my best friend isn't even talking to me right now because out of all the people in the world, I fell in love with her brother.."

"Wait a minute, are you regretting your relationship with Jordan?"

"No, I am just saying...look at how things have worked out for me, look at how it has worked out for Dalia and Jayden..." Barbara took a deep breath, listening to her daughter vent while riding in the car to Deborah's house.

"What about Lauren? Things are going good for her right now, she's has a lot of positivity going on right now, talk to her."

"I have talked to Lauren. She is good, she's going through something right now, but it's nothing that won't get squashed, so I am not worried about that."

"Then what is the problem? You are just not used to strife in your life, that is all. Ever since you were small, you had everything given and handed to you. When you met those girls, I knew they were going to teach you things that I and your father couldn't. I was so happy about that. Now, you don't have the shoulder any more to lean on because you are grown, you have to make your own decisions and figure out what is right for Blake and not for anyone else. At the end of the day, who you spend the rest of your life with, where you live, and how you do it, is all up to you. Now you think I haven't been listening to some things that Jordan says, but let me tell you something, he might have been whatever they thought he was before, but he is not like that anymore. He is love honey and he is in love with you so don't play with that."

"Ma, really? You can tell that from listening to him?"

"Yes, you think I was born yesterday. Why do you think this man is going to battle with his sister? Just don't make him choose or make the situation worst. They will work it out."

"I don't know ma. I have never seen them go at it like this."

"Don't worry about it. Plan your wedding and do what you have to."

"Oh crap, that is right. We have to set a date, but I don't know how we could do that when we have to move to relocate and I haven't even decided on my job, where my things are going to go…"

"Why are you worrying about those things? That is minor."

"Here we are. There aren't a lot of cars here though."

"Well, all that needed to be here were Jayden, you and Lauren, really, unless there were some other people that Deborah didn't mention." Blake and her mother got out of the car after parking in the driveway. The knocked on the door,

"Hi, sweetie, how are you doing?" Jackie hugged Blake and her mother as they entered the house. "C'mon in and have a seat, Deborah went to the back but she will be out in a minute."

"Jackie, you have a nice house." Barbara said as she entered the living room.

"Thank you so much, now you all can come in and make yourself at home till Deborah comes out. Blake, your fiancé came by here last night and he told me the good news, Congratulations and I mean it okay, now come give your mother in law to be a hug." Jackie initiated the hug with Blake in which it made her feel that much special.

"Barbara, aren't you happy for the kids?"

"Yes, we didn't know how the atmosphere was going to be since Jayden wasn't taking the news too well."

"Oh my goodness, you just don't even know. I don't think she knows all about the engagement though, but honey, if you need any help just let me know."

"Yes ma'am, I am going to need all the help I can get. Wait, excuse me." Blake ran out of the room holding her mouth.

"I told her when we got in the car that she didn't look good, she looked really pale in the face." Jackie had a look on her face.

"Is she pregnant?" She whispered over to Barbara.

The Upside Down of Things

"You know what, it hadn't even crossed my mind, but she could be. How long had she been dating Jordan, it came out of nowhere to me."

"Well, between the two of us, it's been a while, I do know that. I just didn't think they would be taking this step so soon, but I guess it doesn't take long to know when that person is the right one for you."

"They just seem so happy. Blake doesn't need a baby right now. She needs to enjoy the relationship first and then see when it's the right time to bring children into the picture. You know I am going to ask her when she gets back about this baby thing."

"Hell, I don't blame you. If she is, I wouldn't be surprised if my son was the one who was trying to have a baby...you know how those men are sometimes..."

"Honey do I, my late husband decided that he wanted another girl and before I knew it...I was knocked up, but when I told him, he looked like he was just waiting for me to tell him. Yes, they are a mess."

"She will see when she gets married how it is going to be."

"Are y'all talking about me?" Blake walked back out in the living room.

"And if we are, then what?" Barbara blurted out.

"Nothing mother, just asking." Deborah enters the room.

"Good Morning, how is everyone?"

"Hi, Hi" can from everyone in the room.

"I am glad you all came today, I made a decision to have a private ceremony for my daughter tomorrow morning. It took me a long time to come out because I was making calls and preparations with a minister to say a few words and I wanted to let her co-workers from the hospital aware. They wanted to help as well. I didn't want anything big since she wanted to be cremated. I know everyone has busy schedules, so I scheduled her service tomorrow at noon at St. Luke Bapist Church. If I remember correctly, that was the church you girls attended in college.."

"Yeah that is the one." Blake interceded. We went there many a Sundays."

"Well, I wanted to schedule another time to spread her ashes, but I know some people want to pay their respects to her so that is the reason for doing the memorial service separate from spreading her ashes. I want to thank each of you for being patient with me. This has been rough for me and I know it has for all of those who cared and loved her just like I did. She was my only child, my only daughter and now I have to say good bye to her and a grandbaby that I never met. I thought I gained a son in law, but I lost one at the same time." The room flooded with tears after Deborah's speech.

"I don't want anything fancy for tomorrow. I already have a collage put together for everyone to receive for the services. I don't want anything drawn out, that would be too dreadful. I want to thank you all for coming at such a short notice and I will see you all tomorrow."

"Before everyone leaves. I have some snacks in the kitchen to have. You all can stay and have a few words if you would like...and thank you for coming." Jackie made sure that everyone felt at home, just to take their minds off the lost of Dalia, which was hard to do since there were nothing but memories surrounding them.

"Ms. Jackie, where is Jayden?" Lauren asked.

With a smirk on her face, "She had something that she had to do that permitted her from being here." Lauren had a puzzled look on her face, "I can't believe she didn't show up for this."

"Rin, you know how she has been lately with everyone, I can't believe that she would be like this for Dalia, out of all the people...this is some bullshit." Blake became more and more angry at Jayden's actions.

"Blakie, you watch your language in front of these adults, you hear me?"

"Yes ma'am, I just can't believe out of everything we all went through together that she would act a fool like this...but, you know what, it's my fault. Maybe if I weren't here, none of this would have happened. Maybe we should have stayed away after I got shot then I would not have fallen in love with Jordan, and I would have my best friends here with me right now."

"Hush up Blake! No one is blaming you for anything. My daughter chose not to be here for her own selfish reasons. She will have to make a count for that herself. When she comes to her senses, she will realize she missed out, not you all. Dalia was a special friend to all three of you, no one greater or less…all of you. If you didn't come back, my son wouldn't be as happy as he is and you wouldn't be as happy as you are right now. We have all lost love ones in the past couple of years, and it's none of our faults. I hope all of you are listening to me. We have to be strong and cope with it, because this is how it was meant to be. We are going to miss Dalia every day, but we cannot blame each other, because if we do where does that lead us."

"Jack, you are right. I want you girls to stay strong and be like sisters even though you came from different mothers, you girls have always treated each other like sisters. I lost my blood daughter, but I don't want to loose you girls too."

As they all got emotional, they felt some type of bond in the room that would keep them close together. Listening to the words of Jackie and Deborah, made Lauren and Blake feel even more united even more; though the one needing to hear it was Jayden, she was no where to be found.

Chapter 40

"Hello, Ken. Are you here?" she started sniffing because there was an aroma in the air that smelt so familiar to her.

"Hey babe. How was the meeting?" Out of no where Kendall came from behind the door with an apron on as if he were cooking.

"It was a little emotional, nothing I didn't expect. I just can't get over the fact that I am going to say goodbye for good to my best friend tomorrow." Kendall took her in his arms and hugged her.

"It's going to be okay. I planned a little something for you. I want you to follow me in the kitchen.." Kendall pulled Lauren by the arm, leading her toward the kitchen.

"Ken, I am really not in the mood for anything right now. I just want to go upstairs and take a bath."

"I cooked you lunch."

"COOKED! I didn't know you could cook."

"I have a couple of hidden talents. I don't like to cook often, but every once in a little, I like to do it. I figured since you have been going through a rough time, I should do something nice."

"Alright, what do you want me to do." Lauren caved in considering the fact that Kendall went out of his way to do something special for her.

"I want you to take a seat here at the counter and I will bring you a glass of wine."

"Babe, isn't it too early for wine?"

"Would you like something else sweetheart?"

"Hell no, bring me the whole bottle of wine. So, what have you been doing all morning?" Lauren snatched the bottle of wine from

Kendall's hand, pouring a heavy glass for herself. She began drinking the wine as Kendall starting telling her about his day.

"Well, after you left this morning, I thought about last night and everything was just running through my mind and...." In the middle of Kendall talking, Lauren looked at her hands and for a moment she thought something was wrong. She was listening to Kendall in and out. The more he talked about last night, the more she remembered. *"He proposed."* She thought to herself. *"Where is my ring?"*

"I realized that it wasn't worth it. I have the woman that I want to be with and she wants to be with me, there was no need to be upset about nothing...babe, you listening to me?" Kendall realized that Lauren's attention was diverted somewhere else.

"Uh, what did you say, I'm sorry?"

"I was telling you about my day like you asked."

"I know babe, I'm sorry. I need to go upstairs right quick. I will be right back." Lauren said the quickest thing that came to her mind to be able to get out of the room without Kendall noticing anything, but with the way she left, there was no way he couldn't have suspected something.

"Shit, where is that ring." She kept saying to herself as she ran up the stairs. She headed first towards the bedroom, rambling through her drawers, tracing back her steps. The last thing she wanted Kendall to find out was that she lost her engagement ring, especially since he just gave it to her last night. That would not have been a good look for her.

"That damn ring has to be somewhere." She moved from the drawers to looking under the bed. There was no sign of the ring in sight. She was running out of options. There weren't many places for her to look because she had only been a few places in the house since she got the ring. Trying not to destroy the room, she headed toward the bathroom since that was the second place she was, but she was hoping the ring didn't go down the drain or the toilet.

"Babe, the food is ready. Come downstairs and eat. Whatever you doing can't be that important." Lauren didn't want to panic, but her pressure was starting to rise. She had no clue where the ring was.

"Okay, I will be done in a minute." Lauren headed toward the staircase trying to come up with a way to hide her hand so that Kendall wouldn't notice the ring missing. Kendall starting preparing the plates and fixing Lauren another glass of wine.

"Come, sit here, I want us to share some time together." Lauren's heart was racing. She didn't know how Kendall would react if he found out that she lost the engagement he gave her less than 24 hours ago. She was out of breath, panicking while she sat on the stool at the counter in her kitchen, sitting directly in front of Kendall.

"What the hell were you doing up there? You were making a lot of noise."

"Nothing, I was uh…looking for something, but it's okay now I found it."

"Are you sure?"

"Yeah, I am positive, everything is good." Lauren was lying through her teeth. She was determined to find the ring no matter what and she definitely not going to tell Kendall that she lost it.

"How is the food?"

"Ken, did you really cook this?"

"Woman, didn't you see me slaving in this kitchen, hell yeah, I made it, how is it?" Lauren was so busy stuffing her face that she couldn't catch her breath to answer Kendall. "I take it, you must like it."

"OMG! Babe, this is really good. Where did you learn to cook like that?"

"Well, when I was an undergrad, I took some cooking classes. I thought it would be helpful somewhere down the line."

"Babe, will you promise me that once we are married, you will cook for me at least three times a week."

"I can do better than that, I will cook for you four times a week."

"Ooo, I like how you think Mr. Brockington." Lauren finally pulled her face up from her plate to kiss Kendall on his lips. "Are you just going to let me eat alone? Fix your plate and come eat with me."

"Wait a minute woman, there is something I want to ask you. Give me your hand." Lauren was a little hesitant because she knew that Kendall would see the ring missing from her finger.

"Babe, I am a little exhausted...do you have to do this right now." Lauren started stretching and yawning to show Kendall how tired she was.

"Are you really going to play me like that....right now, serious?" Kendall was beginning to frown his face knowing that Lauren was trying to avoid having a serious conversation with him. "Just let me say what I have to say and I promise I will let you be..."

"Ken, there is something I need to tell you first..." She tried to stop him before he noticed the missing ring.

"Babe...I wanted to ask you to marry me the proper way." Kendall reached into his pocket, got down on one knee, pulled out a navy blue velvet box, opened it and it was her ring. "Lauren Daniels, whew, this is hard to do...will you marry me?" Lauren took a deep breath, watching how serious Kendall was and how he was gazing into her eyes. She felt as if she was at the alter at that moment and the preacher was standing in front of her and everyone was waiting on her to say I do. She gazed into his eyes, as the connection between the two of them was elevating to another level.

"Yes, Kendall, I will marry you." she hugged and kissed him as he placed the ring on her finger.

"I got it engraved for you. I was drunk last night and I asked you impulsively. I wanted it to be special, more romantic than that, so I took it while you were getting dressed this morning. Is that what you were looking for earlier?"

"Uh yeah. You had me running around here like a chicken with my head cutoff when you had it the whole time."

"You didn't say what you were looking for either so don't blame me for that. You were trying to hide it from me."

"No, I wasn't. I just didn't feel like it was time to tell you, especially if I just misplaced it. I had to look first." Kendall grabbed Lauren around her waist, "Babe, I don't want there to be secrets between us, regardless if it is big or small, I want to know. I should be your best friend from here on out. You should count on me, depend on me, trust me, love me, commit to me and the rest of this shit is irrelevant."

"I've never heard you talk like that before." She grazed the side of his face with her hand.

"I love you and I want to spend the rest of my life with you, but we have to be on the same page in order for that to happen."

"You're right babe…that is why we should go to pre-marital counseling and we should start now so that we can be in sync with each other. I know this place a co-worker of mine went with her husband that would be great for us. I can get the number and we can start going this week if you want to…"

"Whoa, whoa, slow down babe. Is this what I have to put up with for the rest of my life…just kidding. Look babe, I don't need a counselor or a psychologist to tell me how to be connected with my woman. That is something we gotta work on together babe. You feel me? Like, we should have a connection where nobody can come between that."

"Ken, I hear what you are saying and all, but there are so many marriages that don't work out because they didn't take the necessary precautions, and I don't want to be a statistic."

"Rin, are you even listening to me?" Kendall felt as if his point didn't even resonate with Lauren. He didn't know if she was serious or just wasn't taking him seriously.

"I'm listening to you, but you haven't heard the stories that I have heard about failing marriages. I work with too many people who get married and then they have all these issues…and finally they lead to divorce. I don't want to follow that same path."

"Hell, I never knew you talked to your co-workers like that."

"I don't, but they tell all of their business at work for some reason."

"Anyways, these people don't have anything to do with us. I want us to spend time together to create a connection. But, I can't do it alone. You have to be on the same page with me. Ain't nobody talking about going to no damn shrink, it starts with us."

"Babe, I got you."

"I really hope you do."

"What is that supposed to me?"

"Just what I said...I hope you get it and mean it."

Part II

"Well, I guess I got my answer." Blake stood at the counter in her bathroom looking into her lavish vanity mirror. She looked at the pregnancy test in her hand, with the positive results staring her in the face. Still amazed at the test results, Blake sat on the toilet staring at the test in her hand, thinking about her future. *"OMG! Am I really ready to be a mother. I guess I have to, I am pregnant now. Jordan is going to be so happy. He wants this more than me. I just wish we could be a happy married couple first before a baby comes in the picture, but I guess we can't get everything that we want."*

"Babe, are you here?"

"Yeah, I am upstairs in the bathroom." Jordan ran up the stairs heading toward the bathroom to talk to Blake. He bust the door open, "Oh, babe, you alright?" by this time, Blake was beginning to shed tears over being pregnant.

"It's true, I have the confirmation now. You can look at the test yourself."

"Oh Blakie!" Jordan was so happy that he picked Blake up from the toilet, hugging her as her feet were swinging in the air. He began kissing her all over her face, squeezing her waist at tight as he could. "I'm so happy. You look more beautiful to me now than when I first made love to you."

"Jordan, you are going to make me cry." Tears were starting to form in Blake's eyes. She knew this baby made Jordan happy and making Jordan happy was the number thing on her list.

"Babe, I don't want to make you cry. I just love you." He rubbed his hands through her hair, soothing her and comforting her. "Uh, I have something else to tell you that you may not like...."

"What is it?"

"The draft is next week...so you know that is going to change our lives. I want you to be prepared for it. I know you got a lot going on, but I may have to head to Carolina for a while and leave you here to get things sorted."

"Wait, I tell you I am pregnant and you tell me that you have to leave me for a while."

"Damn, you making me feel bad. I won't be gone long, but once I get drafted I have to head down there to make some final decisions...please tell me you understand?"

"Keep talking...."

"Okay, I figured while I was gone, you could handle things with your job, pack up some things, plans some things with your mother...yeah your mother, while she is here, why don't you ask her to stay with you a little while to help you."

Blake took a deep sigh, "I guess I could, but Jordan, I don't want to be a part from you...we have wedding plans to make, a baby to get ready for, a life to build together...."

"Babe, I know, I know...I'm not leaving you all alone, but I have to go do this. You won't even know I'm gone long. I won't be gone over two weeks, I promise."

"You promise?"

"Yes, plus I am going to be here the rest of the week and the first part of next week..."

"Okay, I think my hormones have me going crazy, but I will be fine. But, I don't want to tell anyone about the baby yet...it's early and I remember my mother saying something about waiting. I have to finish up some projects at work and think about what I want to do with my house."

"I thought we talked about that already..."

"No, you were the one who said that maybe I should keep it so that when we come back to visit, we will have a place to stay, but I don't know about that."

"Why not?"

"Well, since your sister stopped speaking with me, the only person here for me to really communicate with is Lauren, and once Kendall actually moves here, things are going to change with her too."

"Stop panicking about everything...there is nothing wrong with keeping your house, but I know it's your house and you get the last say with it, but I think you should keep it."

"I figured that when we decided to come back and visit, it would be in New Jersey where my mother is."

"Well, babe, what about my family...they are here in Baltimore. My moms and pops are here...and I know you don't want to hear it, but my sister too."

"Why would you say that? your sister is upset with me, beyond upset. I know she is your sister and she is going to get over it one day"...*deep sighs* "and when she does get over it, y'all are going to be close like you always were."

"With the way she has been acting, I don't know if we will be close like that again. She has to realize that I a grown and I don't need her to make my decisions. If my mother can see it, then she damn sure should."

"Okay, I didn't mean to make you upset about it. We just have some things we need to work out and discuss. Like, my house, the wedding, the baby, where we are going to live, money, and all the other stuff."

"Alright, alright, tomorrow...when you are done with Dalia's ceremony, we will sit down here and talk about our plans. Is that cool?"

"Can we talk tonight about some things and then tomorrow we talk about the rest of it?"

"Uh, there was something I had to do, but yes, babe, over dinner tonight we can talk about whatever you want to."

"Good, would you mind if I invited Lauren and Kendall over tonight?"

"I thought you just said you wanted to talk about some things tonight and now you want to invite Lauren and Kendall over...I'm confused as hell."

"Well, I am going to need Lauren's help while you are gone for and I can't invite her and not Kendall, plus you are going to be here to talk with Kendall."

"Whatever, you want babe...just make sure you cook something I like." Jordan kissed Blake on the cheek before heading upstairs.

"You are too much Jordan Miller," Blake yelled to Jordan going up the stairs. Blake headed to the fridge trying to decide what she was going to cook for dinner then she thought, she hadn't called Lauren yet to invite her. Blake picked up the phone to call Lauren and invite her to dinner.

"Hey, Blakie, what you doing?"

"Hey Rin, nothing trying to find something in this kitchen for dinner tonight and I wanted to invite you and Kendall over for dinner with me and Jordan."

"Tonight Blake? You know we have Dalia's thing in the morning."

"I know we do, but I can't keep thinking about it because I get sick every time I think about losing her."

"Well, I take it you haven't invited Jayden."

"No, I didn't. I need to talk you about some things as well and Jayden doesn't need to be a part of that. Jordan and I are doing some things and I need your help."

"Oh, heffa, you didn't say all of that. Kendall and I will be there then. I will let him know, he is doing some work in the other room right now. Text me what time and I will be there....Wait, Blake when did you start cooking?"

"Shut up! My mother taught me a few things while I was recuperating on the beach. It was six months, I had to do something out there all by myself."

"WOW, so chick, you never felt the need to share that with us, huh?"

"I didn't even think about it. We got a lot of mother daughter time though."

"I bet you did, but that is good because you are about to be a misses and you have to know a lil' something about the kitchen."

"Yeah, I know...my mother came in right on time with that one..."

"You so stupid. Alright hit me up with what time you want us to come over."

"Wait..Wait, I can tell you now. Come around 7. Is that going to be too later for you?"

"No, that should be good. I can get my yoga in before I come over. Okay, see you later. I have to do some work in my office."

"Oh yell, you ain't doing nothing put planning out your week...Lord, when are you ever going to take a break from yourself....alright, see you tonight."

After hanging up the phone with Lauren, Blake headed back to the kitchen looking for something to cook for dinner. Her mind started wandering about where her life was heading. The past year and a half were extremely hard and she never thought her life would have been making a turn like this. Now, she was getting married, having a baby, and moving to another state. All of it happened in a blink of an eye...and just to think she was getting ready to pass all of it up because the man of her dreams happened to be her best friend's brother.

Then, she thought about what if she was having a boy, what she would name it...or what if it was a girl, would the baby look like her. All of these thoughts ran through her mind with a big smile on her face. *"Last year this time, I was getting out of the hospital, on a plane trying to get away from Baltimore, now I am getting ready to have a baby with my husband to be. Only if Daddy was here to see me now. I wonder if he would be proud."* Blake was standing in the doorway of the refrigerator.

"He would definitely be proud of you." Jordan startled Blake while she was daydreaming in the kitchen. "I didn't mean to scare you, but I overheard you mentioning your father." Blake wiped the tears that were falling from her face. Jordan walked over to her, caressing her stomach from behind with his chest touching her back, showing her comfort.

"I knew this time was going to be touchy for you with the wedding since you Dad isn't here. It's going to be okay...babe." Blake started sniffing.

"I don't get why he had to die and leave me alone."

"Babe, you aren't alone. I know I can't replace your father, but I am here and I will protect you and be there for you, no matter what." She could tell the passion in his eyes as she saw the words coming out of his mouth. She grabbed his face with both of her hands, "I love you."

"I love you too."

Chapter 41

"Pops, how you doing?"

"I'm good son, how are you doing?" Jordan greeted his father entering the house.

"Come have a seat in the den..."

"Alright, where is your bride to be?"

"She is upstairs taking a nap. She had a long morning with that meeting at mom's this morning.

"Yeah, I do remember your mother telling me about that. Dang, I hate to see everybody go through that...I still can't believe Dalia is gone."

"Me either. I am just trying to be there for Blake."

"What about your sister?"

"You don't even want to know how she has been acting lately. You should have seen how she has been talking to Blake. I can't even be around her right now."

"Son, that is still your sister, regardless..."

"Yeah, but Blake is going to be my wife and I can't have my sister being disrespectful to her like that. Blake is going to be the mother of my kids one day and I can't have my sister just saying anything to her."

"Don't you think you owe to your sister to have told her beforehand instead of her finding out some other way."

"You might have a point there..."

"Might, man let me tell you something about women...they are unique in their own, trust me when I say that. If you want to make your wife happy, do want she wants in the house, so she can satisfy you in the bedroom, you know. When it comes to handling business, don't involve her and she won't have to feel no type of way. Whatever you do in streets, don't bring it home. Always show your main chick, your woman, the uttermost respect. When you let the outside chick feel like she is important, she will step out of pocket and try to raise up at your wife, then that brings on another step of problems that you don't want and then you run the risk of losing your family, don't do that."

"Pops, you spilling a lot on me."

"I'm just trying to school you on some things. Are you sure this is the one?"

"I knew this woman was for me when I first met her. I was a little boy, but I wanted her then, I just never told her. When she first came in the house with Jay, I could remember how pretty she was and her smile, they image never left my mind. Then, something hit me last year that I needed to go after that one....and when I came back this time, I knew my life was about to go in a different direction and I needed to have that one person to go with me."

"Uh huh. Son, I am happy for you, I am just sad that everyone else in the family doesn't feel the same way, but I can tell you this...your sister is going to come around. I am pretty sure that Blake misses her, they are best friends....you know that?"

"Yeah, I know she does, but I am so mad with Jay that I don't want to talk to her so I can't expect Blake to do something else."

"Aw, son you have a lot to learn about women. Your sister is just mad because you didn't tell her first...she is so much like her damn mother that it is a shame."

"Yeah, I'm starting to see that, but I thought ma was going to be upset not Jay...she threw me with that one."

"Oh trust me, you threw your mother too. She saw the changes coming, you're her son, she saw it...she was just waiting to see what the change was."

"Eh Pop, there is something else I need to talk to you about...." Jordan appeared nervous at this point as he felt like he needed his father's permission. "I think Blake may be pregnant, but don't say anything to anybody, especially ma."

"Say what! Boy, you sure?"

"I'm not positive, but I think she is. I bought a test last night and she has been holding off taking it. I am waiting for her to take it."

"Son, you young. You sure you ready for a baby?"

Jordan took a deep breath and plopped down on the seat next to James. "Dad, I didn't think about it like that? I love Blake and we are getting married..."

"Son, I am not trying to discourage you, but you need to think about these things. I wouldn't be behind you if you didn't man up and do what's right by this girl. You know she lost her father, she's recovering from the incident with her family and being brutally shot, and now she is having a baby and getting married to a young man that she is barely going to see once the football season gets going. You hear what I am saying son?"

"Yeah, we got a lot to talk about, I didn't think about it like that."

"Son, you got to talk about the football season with your wife, especially if she doesn't know what she is about to get into."

"She already knows. She is supposed to ask her mother about coming to stay with her for a little while and the rest of it we haven't discussed yet."

"Whoa! Your mother in law in your house...." James started laughing.

"Man, why you laughing?" James shook his head.

"I'm just going to say this....if she stays in your house, keep her out your marriage, alright?"

"Mrs. Barbara isn't like that..."

"She isn't like that yet. Keep your feet on the ground in your house. When you pull your feet off the ground too long, you might slip and fall."

"Huh?" Jordan was confused as ever.

"Be the damn man in your house. Take care of home. Be the head of your household and not just in money...got that?

"Oh, okay."

"Material shit don't matter, if she want it and it doesn't hurt the household, give it to her, don't create something you can't finish. If you are going to start doing something, you gotta keep it up or she is going to through it up in your face."

"I, uh, have to go to Carolina for a little while to handle some things before the draft and I told Blake, but I don't think she is too happy about that…"

"Hmm…"

"What, I know you got something to say."

"Son, why not take her with you?"

"I thought about it at first, but then I know I won't be able to spend time with her like she is going to want me to, so I figured she could just stay here, pack, and get things together with her job and the house."

"Did you decide this all by yourself, because that is what it sounds like to me?"

"Uhhh, yeah I did. I didn't think it was something…"

"Let me stop you right there….don't ever think or assume anything when it comes to women, just talk to her about it…trust me on that."

"Uhhh, I'm messing up already."

"Naw, you are learning…you need to talk to her about it though, but if you go down there and she feels abandoned then that is going to be another problem for you, my man, so talk to her and feel it out to see how she really feels about it. One thing you will have to learn…and that is your woman. Once you know her inside out, then you know how to address her, what you take to her, and when to take it to her…"

"For some reason, I'm getting those feelings already. I can't even describe it.."

"My boy, its sounds like you in love." James began chuckling at Jordan.

The door opens, "Hey." Barbara entered the house. James and Jordan stood up when she walked through the door. He walked over to the door to kissed Barbara on the cheek. "Mrs. Barbara, I want you to meet my father, James Miller…Dad, this is Blake's mother Barbara Lowry.

"Nice to meet you James, you have a lovely son."

"Thank you ma'am, I try to do something with my only boy. Nice to meet you as well.

"Thank you Mr. Miller, it's good to see you. Jordan didn't tell me you were stopping by, I would have cleaned up."

"Naw, mama you didn't have to do that. You are already doing enough."

"Where is my daughter? I know she didn't feel well at the meeting this morning and I had to run out and get some things."

"Yeah, yeah, yeah...she is upstairs taking a nap. She just laid down about 30 minutes ago."

"Okay, I will go upstairs and check on her, so I give you too some privacy." Barbara headed upstairs so that Jordan and James could continue their conversation.

"Son, so has Mrs. Barbara been dating because I can see where Blake gets her beauty from."

"Well, no one has said anything to me about her dating anyone, why?"

"Hell, I was just asking..."

"Yeah, right...don't make my mother go stupid. I can't deal with anymore of these women going off..." they both laughed.

"Son, I am about to head off. Call me later, alright."

"Cool pops." James headed out of the door.

Chapter 42

"KENDALL! KENDALL!!" Lauren went through the house looking for Kendall. He was upstairs in the spare bedroom on his laptop, making phone calls.

"I'm upstairs." He responded back to her. Lauren headed upstairs. Lauren stormed in the room, "Ken, you aren't going to believe the conversations I just had."

"What's wrong?" Kendall closed his laptop giving Lauren his undivided attention.

Lauren placed her hands on her hips out of frustration. "First, I talked to Blake, she wants us to come over this evening for dinner, but I didn't know what you had planned."

"Naw, that is cool because I hadn't thought about it...so that is straight..that means we having dinner with just Blake or Blake and Jordan?"

"It's going to be with Blake and Jordan."

"Okay, so what is wrong with that?" Lauren took a deep breath before continuing.

"Well, she mentioned that she wanted us to come over because she had to talk to me about some things. I am afraid of what those things are first off...and for her to invite us over for dinner to talk, it has to be serious."

"I think you are making a big deal over nothing. Right now, you are the only real friend that she has so of course it is going to appear that way." Kendall stood up, kissing Lauren on the cheek. "So, you said first, so I assume there is more." Kendall placed his laptop in the case.

"Then, I call Jayden....boy, that girl is worst than I thought, seriously."

"Wait now...what did you expect. She lost her best friend, and within the same day she found out that her other close friend was sleeping with her brother and not just sleeping with him, engaged to be married. That is a lot for someone to swallow, well, for women."

"What is that supposed to mean?" she responded with a lot of attitude.

"Just what the hell I said, now help me find something to wear tonight to dinner." Kendall walked passed Lauren heading to the master bedroom to find something to wear.

"You are such a man..."

"And, I am glad to be that. Listen, you all are going back and forth for nothing. I wish that y'all just let Blake and Jayden just duke it out and get it over with. Stop putting you in the middle of it because it ain't doing nothing but stressing you out. Plus, y'all just lost Dalia, that ain't nothing for y'all to chill out then I don't know what."

"Damn, you right, but how can I make my friends see that."

"Stop catering to them.."

"I don't think I am catering to them, plus, me and these girls have been tight since college, I can't just turn away from them like that...and with Dalia gone, I don't want to be distant with them."

"Alright, so let me get this straight. Tell me this..Are we going to be talking about this Blake and Dalia thing tonight at dinner because I can just stay here and heat some in the fridge."

"No,no, no...I don't it will be about her. Hell, Blake didn't even invite Jayden, even though I told her when I was on the phone with her just now."

"You did what! You have got to be fuckin kidding me!"

"Yeah we were talking and I mentioned it...why what is wrong with that? At the end of the day, we are still friends."

"I don't think you know how mad Jayden is right now. I can't believe you were running your mouth like that. See that is what I am talking about with women. If Blake didn't invite Jayden it was for a reason, you just adding fuel to the fire."

"I don't think it's that big of a deal..but anyways, the second thing I wanted to tell you about was Jayden. She is acting so damn stupid. I don't know what is up with her. She thinks Blake and Jordan owe her something. She was at her house right...do you know she hasn't been there since Jordan came home and she was getting even madder as she was going through the house."

"What was she getting madder about?" Kendall was being sarcastic.

"Because, he isn't staying at her house anymore...so, I am assuming she is going to move back into her house...but that is another story."

"Aww hell, that just sounds like more drama. She should be concern with her relationship with Brian."

"What you talking about?"

"I haven't heard nothing about those two getting back together."

"..And why would you?"

"Hell, I don't know."

"Hmm mm, don't try and play me Kendall. You know something."

"I don't know shit...all I know is that you are looking real sexy, looking all mad and shit." Lauren couldn't help herself from blushing.

"You just make me sick, you know that..." Kendall stopped looking through his clothes, walking toward Lauren with a sneaky look on his face. He grabbed her by the waist and starting kissing her on the neck.

"You know if we start that now, we are going to be late going to Blake's house."

"Blake wouldn't mind" he whispered in her hear. He pulled her in the doorway of the closet, continuously kissing her neck as she moaned for more. She grabbed the back of his head, caressing his head so that he wouldn't stop. Her panties became wet has he rubbed his hands all over her body. His lips moved upward from her neck to her ear, slowing coming toward her mouth. She grabbed both of his ears with her hands, pushing his lips on hers. He motioned her body towards the bed, him moving forward as she began moving backward in the direction of the bed.

He pushed her down on the bed while he unbuttoned his shirt. She couldn't wait any longer, popped the buttons off his shirt, ripping it off his body. "Ken, I love you." she whispered to him as he glided inside of her, touching all four walls. She pulled on the sheets, pulling them towards her as she was being pleased in every way.

"Is that how you like it babe?" he whispered in her ear as he glided in and out of her. He leaned in, licking and sucking on her nipples. The more he sucked, the louder her moans became. He tossed her over on top of him, leaving her body moist from his kisses.

"Yes baby!" as she pleasured him, motioning slowly, pushing her body completely inside of him, she knew she was pleasing him. He squeezed her tighter and tighter as she grinded harder and harder on top of him. "Yes baby, I'm gonna nut."

"Come baby, come!" before she knew it, Kendall released himself inside of her, grabbing her ass as tight as he could. She bent over bringing her body on top of his. He rubbed her back as they laid there content and pleased. They stayed there laying for a couple of minutes before Kendall broke the silence.

"Rin, we haven't picked a date yet and I was thinking that we could get married sooner than later." Lauren raised her head, "How soon were you thinking?"

"Uh, maybe in the next couple of months, I don't know. Have you thought of any time?"

"Not with everything going on, I hadn't thought about a date yet...I tell you what, let me talk with my mother and I will get back to you."

"Why do you have to talk to your mother first?"

"I know my mother is always out of town and I want her to be there for my big day. Plus, I am going to need all the help I can get if I am going to be planning a wedding in the next couple of months." Lauren raised up to kiss Kendall.

"What was that for?"

"I can't just kiss you."

"The only time that you do that is when I have done something good or you want me to do something for you."

"Maybe you said the right thing, how about that?"

"Hmm, that is a new one, haven't heard you say that one before." Lauren smiled.

"You think you are going to figure me out that easy, no sir, ain't gonna happen." Lauren got out of the bed, putting her silk robe on.

"You just go to leave me here alone." Lauren walked back towards Kendall.

"You know we have to get ready and get our clothes out. It is going to take you forever to iron and you know it."

"Shit, I guess I better get up too. Wait, why are we getting all dressed up to go to Blake's house."

"Did you hear whose name you just called. You think I am bourgy, then you don't know Blake."

"C'mon now. I never called you bourgy."

"You didn't have to say it, it's how you look when I do things."

"Aww, you making shit up now..."

"No, I am not...I see you when you think I am not looking.." Kendall started laughing at Lauren.

"You are going to make us late. Excuse me miss, I have to iron my clothes in the other room."

"Oh, you wanna leave now, getting too hot in here for you."

"You just better bring your clothes if you want them ironed."

"Stop it, you are going to iron my clothes for me? I ask you to iron my clothes everyday and you tell me no...."

"Dammit, maybe today I feel like ironing them. You know you are going to be my wife...maybe I didn't want to spoil you in the beginning. I have to sprinkle some of my goodness on you bit by bit. I can't do it all at one time."

"Oh please."

Chapter 43

Knock, knock knock.

"Wait a minute, I am coming. You don't have to keep knocking on my door."

"Hi ma'am, I am looking for a Miss Jayden Miller."

"This is she, but who are you?" The carrier placed papers in Jayden's hands without saying a word and walked off. "Wait a damn minute, aren't you going to tell me at least what these papers are for." The car pulled off. Jayden hurriedly started opening the envelope. It was a certified letter from the mortgage company that financed her home. "Aww, you have got to be kidding me....shit!" Jayden's house was being listed on the foreclosure listing unless she could come up with the money to pay the mortgage.

She knew that she was behind on the house, but not to the point where she would be faced with foreclosure. Even though she was receiving a severance package from her job that money was running out. The monies coming in didn't compensate for the bills that she had. Without Brian's help she could barely make ends meet. Immediately, she started checking her accounts to see if she had something to tie her over until she was able to get back on her feet. Of course her pride wouldn't let her go to anyone for help so she was going to come up with it the best way she knew how. The one thing she didn't want to lose was her home.

"Just one more thing I needed today." Jayden pulled up her accounts and she saw that she had enough in her savings to last her two more months, but what was she going to do after that. Then she saw all the outstanding bills that were due to come out of her accounts.

"Damn, I have health insurance, dental, vision, life insurance, car insurance, Chase Auto, homeowner's insurance, MasterCard..wow...I didn't realize I had all these damn bills. I gotta do something. Hmm, I wonder what I could do for some quick money." Jayden started searching on the internet looking for possible jobs, but she wasn't coming up with anything. While searching on the internet her phone rings. She picks up, "Hello."

"Jayden, this is your father."

"Hey Dad, what's up?"

"I was hoping you could tell me that."

"Oh, goodness, who have you been talking to now..."

"Everyone but you I see. I am not far from your house, you mind if I stopped by?"

"How did you even know I was over here?"

"You ask too many questions."

"Alright, I will be here."

"Good, I will be there in five minutes." After hanging up the phone James, Jayden was thinking of ways to hide the fact that she was hitting rock bottom, with no money, no friends and no man. She had turned everyone away and those that were still around, she had too much pride to turn to them for anything. Waiting for her father to there, she opened up her resume, updating it and brushing off some things so she could send it out to different employers, but at this point Jayden really didn't know what she wanted to do anymore. After working for one of the top retailers in the country, it never appeared to her that one day she would be back on the job market. Yeah, she thought about it, but not this soon in her life. She wanted to make a name for herself and she assumed that the job offers would start coming in, but it didn't work out that way.

Immediately logging in, she saw her brother's page and there was nothing but pictures of him and Blake. This made her furious all over again.

"See I knew it, they planned this...they didn't just fall in love and everyone thought I was crazy. I am not crazy, they are the ones that is crazy." Just to give herself more reasons to be upset, she started checking out Jordan's status and more of his pictures. There were pictures of him and Blake out eating, at the park, and random pictures of them around the house. She wondered if he updated his status, "engaged". "Hmm" she thought. I bet he was quick to change that. Then , she started reading the comments on his page in which there were comments about her on there, which made her more inquisitive.

"Jordan, you knew your sister was going to act like that about you getting engaged. She wanted you to be her husband...lol"

"J-dogg, good luck, you snagged you a dime that time. Tell your sister to chill out, she need to get a man anyway..."

"Damn dude! Why is she hating so bad. Even when we were in school, she was jealous of you, you should really cut her off this time."

"Jor-dan, what's up! Congrats on the engagement dude. I knew you were going to settle down some time or another....sometimes you have to have to cut some people off regardless who they are...lol

"Cut that Hayden off....lmao!!!!"

As Jayden kept reading the comments posted on Jordan's page, she became heated, more than what she was before, but there was really nothing she could do.

"I almost have the nerve to go over there and see if I am invited to dinner since they asked Lauren and not me. Why couldn't they invite me anyway? No, if I go over there then I am going to look desperate. They all just get on my nerves." Even though the comments made her very upset, Jayden was curious to know what else she could find out about her brother and Blake's Facebook page.

She began searching under Blake's page, which was mostly full of wedding plans including colors, reception choices, and all of her friends' comments and suggestions. The more she read, the more she became disgusted with everything related to the wedding. "You have got to be kidding me." As Jayden searched under Blake's wedding party under her photos, she noticed that everyone was listed except her name. "This bitch really doesn't want me to be a part of this...I just knew it." Now her anger was beginning to get out of control. She started seeing pictures of people that she knew weren't really good friends with Blake and she got the impression that Blake was trying to replace her from the wedding. "I wonder if Jordan really knows what she is up to. Maybe I should go over there and let him know in person. I could really show her up for what she really is in front of everyone."

Part II
Doorbell rang.

"Hey, come in. how are you Kendall?"

"Hell, I guess you don't give a damn how I am doing huh? I don't care, I will talk to Jordan, Jordan how are you doing?"

"I'm good, how are you Lauren?"

"I'm good...ooh, in here smells good and I'm hungry." Lauren hugged Jordan as Kendall greeted Blake by giving her his jacket.

"Blakie, I know you have some wine I can drink before we eat dinner."

"Of course I do. Come in the kitchen with me while the men go into the den." Blake and Lauren went into the kitchen while Kendall followed Jordan into the den to watch TV. The ladies pulled a bottle of wine from Blake's cellar, "So, what has been up with you...and why you only pulled out one glass like you are going to let me drink alone."

"Oh, nothing has been up," Blake responded with a sneaky look on her face.

"So, you called me over here to tell me nothing, I don't believe it. Now, what's up."

"I will tell you that in a minute, but first, I need your help with making my wedding plans."

"Wait, before you tell me that. I have some news of my own that I need to tell you."

"Well, why is it taking you so long to say something." Blake's face lit up.

"Kendall proposed to me last night. We are getting married!" Lauren flashed her ring so that Blake could get a good view of it.

"Oh my GOD, look at that rock. Kendall did good. Rin, I am so happy for you." Blake gave Lauren a hug as she was so excited that she and her best friend could be happy together. "Have you guys set a date yet?"

"Naw, we haven't done that yet. With everything going on with Dalia and the funeral, we just put that off until everything else was done...which I think is for the best under the circumstances."

"Yeah, you might be right about that, but there is no need to put your life on hold. Dalia would have wanted you to be happy."

"I know. Don't you just miss her?" they both stopped and thought about Dalia.

"I am definitely going to miss her and her wedding planning ideas. Just imagine if she were here right now she would have been trying to plan both of our weddings and would have gotten mad if we asked anyone else to do it."

"Yeah, you know how she was...damn, that doesn't even sound right."

"I know, but she gotta deal with it somehow..."

"Okay, stop it, you are going to make me cry. I have been doing that every night since she died....what did you want to talk about?"

Blake started smiling from hear to hear. "My hubby to be has to leave and go to Carolina for a couple of weeks so he is leaving me to handle everything here, and I need your help."

"Hell, that don't sound like a lot...what you need help with?"

"I have to pack and get everything ready to move to South Carolina and I am going to need your help planning my baby shower." Blake waited to see Lauren's reaction to what she just said.

"Oh okay that is not a problem, I will make a list right now. You got a pad I can write this stuff down at?...okay, moving supplies...baby shower...BABY SHOWER! Bitch, you pregnant." Without even responding back to her, Blake just chuckled under her breath. Lauren started screaming loudly where the men could hear her in the other room. "OH MY GOD! I am so happy for you. Come here, give me a hug."

"I know you are tired of hugging me."

"No, girl, not for good news. The last couple of times that I hugged you were all bad times. We need to start having some good memories, you know?"

"Yeah, you are right. Don't remind me because I was the cause of some of those bad memories."

"Blake, please. You are not to blame for your crazy sister and half sister….SO, tell me…are you excited about the baby?"

"I wasn't at first because I am not married." She whispered over to Lauren.

"Now that sounds like some shit your mother would say…" Lauren took a sip of the wine she poured for herself.

"No, I'm serious. I wanted to be married. It's not right having children before you are married. You know that?"

"UH, I guess you do how you do Blake." Lauren shrugged her shoulders.

"Isn't that why you are waiting to have kids…until you get married?"

"Blake, I haven't had kids because I don't want them. Girl, you better start living for yourself and not for your mother. You seem to be happy with Jordan, enjoy it. How does he feel about being a daddy?"

"Would you believe that he is more excited than I am?"

"Yeah, I do believe it. What did I tell you? You better save your energy for the serious stuff and stop worrying about simple things."

"What are they in there talking about? They have snickering in there for a long time." Jordan just smiled at Kendall without responding. "So you do know."

"Yeah, I do know. Don't tell anyone, but Blake is having a baby. She doesn't want anyone to know, but man, that is hard you know?"

"Aww man, congratulations. I'm happy for you." The two of them gave each other a cordial handshake acknowledging Jordan becoming a father. "Eh, man, I know I'm not close to you or anything, but for all its worth, you should be proud of yourself. You got a lot going for you and you have a beautiful woman by your side. Don't worry about what no one has to say as long as she is happy and you are happy, because at the end of the day that is all that matters."

"Damn, nigga, you sound like my damn daddy."

"My bad, I wasn't trying to sound like your ol' man."

"Naw, you good, but I'm saying...that was the same exact thing he said."

"Eh, the older you get the more you know how to handle these situations..."

"So, when are you and Blake going to jump the broom."

"Hell, I don't know if she already told Blake or not, but we got engaged last night."

"For real! You serious! Well hell then, we got a lot to celebrate then. Congratulations."

"Man, let me tell you something. That woman in the other room makes me the happiest man in the world."

"I've known Lauren a long time and she seems so happy right now. They have all been through a lot."

"Now, I just have to ask you this, because I never had the chance to experience this in my life...what was it like banging your sister's best friend...I mean, I just asking. I couldn't only imagine being a youngster and I saw this fine older chick and then when I became a man, she actually gave me a chance...please tell me." they both laughed in dismay.

"To be honest with you, at first, I thought she was the finest chick around, now that is just how I felt. You know I had to build up some manhood to even step to her. She had it all and I felt that I had to bring something to even get her to notice me like that...and you know she threw me this line about being Jay's little brother. Hell, I had to let her know this was a grown man and that I could make her happy better than any other nigga that was out there."

"So, you had to bring it hard!"

"Did I? Man, you don't even know the half of it. But, once she actually let me take her out, I fell so damn hard it was ridiculous. Then, when we finally took each other serious, that was something else."

491

"Hell, I can tell that...she pregnant."

"Man, you crazy as hell. Wanna drink?"

"Yea, yeah, fix me something."

"You know she wasn't too happy at first, but I think I have convinced her to be."

"What you mean? She didn't want a kid?"

"Naw, I don't think so. She didn't think she was ready." Kendall took a sip of his drink.

"She seems happy to me, maybe she is just nervous. It's her first child. In a few months, she is not going to even remember having those feelings....on another note, how is everything with your sister?"

"Eh man, if you don't mind, I would rather not even talk it tonight. I don't wanna get my wife to be upset about that. I have to make sure that she and baby stay calm...."

"Already talking like a true husband...family first! Damn right. I know you were supposed to be going pro right?"

"Yeah, I have to leave in a couple of days to head down to Carolina. That is why Blake invited Lauren over here...she wanted to ask her to help with moving and planning her baby shower."

"Oh okay, now it makes sense. I guess I will be watching on the big screen coming up this year."

"Yeah more and likely I will." Jordan lay back in the chair with a sense of confidence. "So, I know you used to know Blake's father, is that right?"

"Yeah, he was my mentor for years. I did my internship at his law firm. He was a good man."

"I don't even think I ever met him to be honest. He didn't come down this way and after a while I wasn't even around like that..."

"He was something else. He thought the world of Blake and Blair. I only saw pictures of Blair and Blake, but I knew of them. I didn't meet her until they all came up to visit New Jersey over a year ago. It was a White Party, I believe and they came there because normally all the lawyers in the city come...and that is when I ran into Lauren."

"So you met all of them back then? So you remember when Blake got shot?"

"Yeah! I was at the hospital. By that time, Lauren and I were getting really serious. Once we knew Blake was going to be okay, we started taking vacations together and I started coming to Baltimore more often. Then, my boss said that he wanted me to open a firm here and I jumped on it because I knew that my baby was here."

"Either I was just out the loop or just focused on doing my own thing, because I didn't know nothing about that. So, have you seen Mrs. Barbara since she has been here?"

"Naw, I haven't seen her at all. I was hoping to run into her while I was here. I don't know where she is, but you can't keep up with her."

"Yeah, it would be good to see her again. I haven't seen her in a long time."

"I know these ladies finis talking by now, I am getting hungry."

"Yeah me too."

"You know I have to ask this question..." Lauren poured another glass of wine.

"If you don't quit drinking all of that wine, you are going to be too drunk to eat dinner.

"Uh-huh, have you guys talked about a pre-nuptial agreement?"

"Can we talk about that later?"

"We can, but I am still going to have this same question. I already know what you have and I know what kind of money he may be getting, but that is no guarantee there, now, I am just being honest, so you tell me....have you at least brought it up?"

"Yes! For God's sake Rin. We talked about it. We got it all under control...have you talked to Kendall about a pre-nuptial? Alright then don't come over here asking all of these questions. I need your help with other stuff and you are worrying about money."

"Yes, I am worrying about money. I don't want to see you out of everything. I just want you to make wise decisions. You know I care about you."

"Yes, I know you do....go get the men so we can eat dinner." Lauren got up from the counter where she was sitting to get the men from the other room so they could eat dinner.

For one moment in a long time, Lauren and Blake shared a good time together with their significant others. Without all the mess and drama that had been going on in their lives over the past year, it felt good to them. They laughed with each other and talked, no one crossing the line or being disrespectful to the other.

"Alright, I will take the dishes."

"Blakie, I will help you." Lauren and Blake took the dishes to the kitchen.

"Hey man you wanna beer?"

"C'mon, you gotta ask that question?"

"I'll grab it while I am here." Lauren headed to the fridge to get the guys' their beer. All of a sudden the doorbell rang.

Chapter 44

"Who in the world could it be at the door? Are you expecting someone?"

"No, I don't know who this is...my mother is out for the night." Blake walked over to the door. She opened the door only to see the one person she didn't want to face for the evening.

"Well aren't you going to invite me in?" Blake's face was speechless. She didn't know what to say.

"Blake, who is it at the door?" Lauren walked over to the door since Blake didn't respond to her.

"Jayden, not tonight. If you came to start something, do it another night, seriously."

"Oh, so now you are Blake's bodyguard. If Blake doesn't want me here, she can tell me that...won't you Blake." Jayden had the most evil look in her eyes that they had ever seen. She was being loud and obnoxious, something they hadn't noticed before. Blake not saying a word, Jayden walked passed her, walking into the kitchen.

"Jay, I think you should leave. You know this is not the time or the place for it."

"Rin, please. Where is my brother?" Blake's eye drew bigger when she heard Jayden ask about Jordan.

"He is in the other room."

"Oh, so now you can talk, you haven't said anything since I walked into your house. I guess I hit a nerve."

"Jayden, leave him alone, your problem is with me, not with Jordan."

"Naw, my problem is with the both of you. The both of you disgust me." Lauren saw that the conversation was going to get out of control so she interceded.

"Jayden, why are you here. Go home and I will call you later tonight."

"Lauren, I wish you would get out of my face."

"Jayden, do you really wanna make a scene here of all places. This is Blake's home and dammit, Kendall is here. Don't air all our dirty laundry in front of him, damn!"

"I don't give a damn about Kendall being here." Jayden looked down at Lauren's hand and noticed her ring. She grabbed Lauren's hand to look closer at the ring, "Mph, I see you are getting married too, so I guess all of that is going around now, but you couldn't tell me that either."

"NO, its not like that Jay. No one knew, I just told Blake, that is it."

"But, I just talked to you and didn't mention anything about getting married Rin. So now you are turning on me because of how I feel about my so called best friend sleeping with my brother!"

"What the hell is all this noise in here?" Jordan overheard the yelling coming from the kitchen. He walked up grabbing Blake out of harm's way. Jayden looked shocked that Jordan came around the corner to confront her.

"Babe, its nothing, it's just your sister. She is just letting out some steam, don't worry about it."

"Hell naw. Jayden why are you here?"

"I came to confront the both of you…"

"Man, ain't nobody trying to hear that. Look, you need to leave or I will make you leave, you hear me?"

"Jordan, don't do that, she is your sister." Blake saw the rage building from Jordan.

"Babe, let me handle this."

"No, Jordan just let her say what she has to say first."

"Yes Jordan, why don't you listen to her…" Jayden began marking Blake.

"Alright, Jayden say what you have to say and leave."

"NO, what I have to say to Blake, I don't want to say in front of any of you."

"Jayden is it really that serious, c'mon now." Lauren was getting irritated by the way Jayden was acting. "I think you are being picky now." By this time, Kendall had walked into the kitchen standing off to the side.

"Hell if it's going to make her happy, why don't you all let her and Blake be alone to discuss whatever it is they need to talk about." Jordan hesitated wondering if it would be a good idea to leave the two of them alone.

"Ken, maybe we should stay out of it and let Jordan settle this with Blake and Jayden." Lauren walked towards Kendall pulling him in the other room.

"Why is he even talking to me right now? Rin, you might wanna take your man outta this one." Without making a comment, Kendall and Lauren exited the room leaving the rest of them in the kitchen area.

"Jayden, I don't even want to talk to you right now. My fiancé has prepared dinner for us and I want to sit down at my damn dinner table without having to think about your selfish ass for a change." Jordan walked away.

"Jayden, what is it that you have to say to me?" Blake folded her arms out of frustration.

"Y'all are not going to gang up on me. I think you owe me an explanation about something and I don't need a crowd to talk about it."

"Alright, damn! We can talk in my office, you do remember where that is?" Blake walked off heading toward the staircase with Jayden behind her. Kendall and Lauren notice the both of them walking up the stairs, with a stunned look on their face, Lauren tries to keep her composure sitting on the sofa in the den.

"Oh goodness, that isn't going to be good. Where did Jordan go?" Lauren whispered over to Kendall.

"Babe, you go find Jordan, I will go check on the food in the kitchen. I hear the pots bubbling over."

"Good idea babe." Lauren kissed Kendall on the cheek before heading to another area in the house.

"Okay, Jayden what is it?"

497

"Well, I was just on Facebook and I noticed all the nasty little comments that your friends had to make about me."

"Is that what you wanted to talk to me about? Are you serious? You couldn't send me a text?"

"I see you have your wedding party altogether and I wasn't even asked to be a part of the wedding."

"Why in the hell would I ask you to be a part of my wedding when you have said over and over how I am the bitch that seduced your brother and that I am not good enough for him."

"Even though all of that is true, I am still his sister."

"I don't give a damn about that and neither does Jordan anymore."

"You are not going to force me out of my brother's life Blake Lowry." Jayden walked up in Blake's face.

Not backing down to Jayden, "I don't have to, you already did that. Now, if that is all, you can leave now."

"I am not done yet." Blake began to walk off, with Jayden grabbing her by the arm, "but I am done."

Blake pulled away from Jayden, opening the door to her office.

"Blake, I am not finished with you! Come back here!" Blake headed down the hallway, furious with Jayden and fed up with her.

"You can see your way out of my house!" Blake said as she began heading down the stairs. Without noticing how furious she was, Blake rushed down the stairs, with her foot slipping from under her. Before she knew it, she lost her balance, leaving her to glide down the 30 steps on her staircase, her head hitting the rail as she came down. Her head hitting the rail after she tumbled down each step, unable to gain her balance or to stop her fall, she felt every hit, every step. The pain hit in every way imaginable. Finally, hitting the bottom step, she fell with bruises on her face, arms, back and leaving her barely conscious.

"BLAKE!" Lauren yelled after hearing the thumb, running towards the den, JORDAN, COME HELP!" Jordan came, hurriedly through the house, not knowing what to expect when he came in the den, he looked down, noticing Blake in Lauren's arms on the floor, not responding and in pain. The only thought running through his head was his sister. He envisioned her being the reason for Blake's fall since she was the last person speaking with Blake and they were arguing.

"CALL 911 dammit. My friend is not breathing!" Lauren yelled to Jordan. He reached for the phone on the end table, dialing 911 as quick as he could. Kendall ran into the den from the kitchen noticing the scene, unable to grasp what was going on, he saw Jordan on the phone, Blake in Lauren's arms and Jayden was no where to be found.